# WHAT HAPPENS

# IN *Paris*

## ALLY WILLIAMS

# CONTENT WARNING

This story contains explicit sexual content and foul language.

# *Playlist*

**Alanis Morissette** - Ironic
**Phoebe Ryan x Quinn XCII** - Middle Finger
**Taylor Swift** - The Smallest Man Who Ever Lived
**Gunnar** - One Night
**Alanis Morissette** - Head Over Feet
**Jake Scott** - Like This
**Alanis Morissette** - You Learn
**Weathers** - ALL CAPS (feat. John the Ghost)
**Taylor Swift** - Paris
**Anna of the North** - Dandelion
**The Strike** - Just Friends
**Hunter Hayes** - I Want Crazy
**John Travolta and Olivia Newton John** - You're The One
That I Want
**The Airborne Toxic Event** - Sometime Around Midnight
**Ludvigsson** - Globetrotter (feat. Jobe)
**REMZEE** - Ironic

*For those who love too freely and forgive too easily.*
*Never change.*

# FEBRUARY

# 1

## STEPHANIE

The wrapper from Oliver's straw hits me square on the nose, and I jump so far out of my skin I nearly fall out of my chair.

I had been paying attention to the loudspeaker overhead–a flight that's thankfully not mine is delayed. The announcement dies with a crackle, the only sounds around us that of a bustling terminal and the restaurant's best attempt at making this tiny corner of the airport feel like it's not, in fact, in an airport.

I glare as I turn to him, watching him lower the straw from his mouth and stick it into his drink, swirling the ice around. He's relaxed, his limbs splayed out underneath the table and one elbow resting on top.

I showed up in leggings and an oversized sweatshirt–dressing for maximum comfort–whereas he's in jeans and a T-shirt that fits *just right*, the edge of his sleeve teasing at the compass tattoo on his unnecessarily large bicep. His luggage is neat and tidy, a black laptop bag that fits snugly on top of a rolling one. Mine is falling apart, a Walmart special from a good ten years ago with my high school backpack thrown haphazardly on top.

He laughs, and it spreads across his whole face, his green eyes narrowing with delight. "Man, that's gotta be a ten-pointer at least. I don't think I've ever actually hit someone *directly* on the nose when blowing straw wrappers."

I huff, grabbing my wineglass from the table and taking a long sip. I'm not a great flyer, and I know the only way to get myself to Costa Rica in one piece is to guzzle wine and hold my breath on the flight. For all eight hours. And no, I'm not going to accept that that's unrealistic. "Ollie, how often are you going around blowing straw wrappers at people?"

He pauses, taking a quick sip of the gin and soda in front of him. "I don't know. Once a week, at least. My sister usually gives me the same face you're giving me right now when I do it to her. Though to be fair, the best I've gotten her has been in the eye."

"It sounds like Eliza has a lot of patience," I say.

He shrugs, and my eyes wander back to my gate. I can just barely make it out through a sea of people in the walkway, and although I know boarding hasn't started yet, there's a small group crowding the door.

Another brush of paper across my cheek has me turning back to him.

"I'm trying to distract you," he says flatly, his eyebrows raised. He holds my gaze, his smile easygoing but genuine enough to crinkle the corners of his eyes. His long fingers tap a pattern along the table, and for just a second, I get lost in the steady rhythm of it, in the soft way he's looking at me.

"I don't want to miss my flight."

He holds up one hand, grabbing his phone with the other. The lock screen, featuring a picture of the cutest cat in the world–Bunghole, who one day I vow will love me more–gives way to the alarm app. "I'm going to put a timer on here for when boarding starts. You won't miss your flight, okay? You're torturing yourself, watching your gate like that. Try to relax for a few minutes."

I make a show of taking a deep breath and another sip of wine. "Do you have one for your flight, too?"

He shakes his head. "No. I've still got two hours before I even have to think about mine."

Ollie and I happened to have flights on the same day. Him, for a work trip that'll have him in Paris for the next two weeks, though he's actually taking some vacation time for about half of that.

And me, for love.

I'm going to meet my ex–a man I've danced around for the better part of the last decade–and see if this thing that has us coming back to each other time and time again can thrive when we're both in the same place at the same time. The marketing company I work for went fully remote this year, so as long as I can still interface with designers and craft our strategy docs, I can work from anywhere.

I can work from wherever *he* is, and give *Us* the chance we deserve.

But to make that happen, I first have to deal with the airport. With a metal death trap soaring through the air while taunting us with turbulence like it'd be *funny* if we all plummeted to our deaths in tropical waters, as if granting us a little reprieve–*well, at least the water's warm.*

Ollie fixes me with his gaze, green eyes so strong I find it difficult to look away.

"You don't have to do this, you know."

I let out a long breath and take another sip of wine. "I know I don't *have* to do this. I *want* to do this."

He shrugs. "I mean, all by yourself. It's nice, what you're doing, but isn't there a part of you that would rather wait until someone can be there with you? In the airport? On the flight? I know you're more than capable of doing it on your own. It just makes me nervous."

"It's just eight measly hours on a plane. I'll be okay. And Rod will be there tomorrow."

He nods, pressing his lips together as he takes another sip of his drink. "Yeah, that doesn't exactly ease my mind."

"I think my sister is getting to you. Might I remind you that you've never met him. And she's only met him a handful of times."

He nods. "Don't you think that's cause for concern? You've been hanging around the same guy for almost ten years and your sister hasn't spent enough quality time with him to actually *like* him? Not even *like* him. *Know* him. *Trust* him enough that she's not begging you to dump him once and for all every chance she gets?"

I sigh. "He's a good person. He's just on his own path. I'm meeting him where he is. If there's one thing I've learned in all of my therapy over the past three months, it's that everyone needs to get where they're going in their own time, in their own way."

Ollie's eyebrows shoot up quickly, but not quickly enough that I miss the expression on his face altogether.

He's no stranger to my experience in therapy. In fact, he's part of the reason I decided to start going in the first place.

About six months ago, he suggested I get screened for ADHD. He had it as a kid–and technically *still* has it, though he can manage without medication–and recognized the signs. His suggestion was so nonchalant–a passing idea during a night out with our friends–that it took me a moment to realize he wasn't suggesting the drunken noodles or pad thai, but a doctor's appointment.

By the time his words registered in my brain, he was already involved in another conversation. His eyes slid back to mine, his eyebrows raising almost imperceptibly, as if to check whether he overstepped a boundary.

It turned out to be one of the best things anyone has ever said to me. I've learned how to work with myself better. I started therapy when my first medication didn't work as expected, and continued it when I saw the benefits in *other* areas of my life.

I spent a lot of my life wanting the kind of perfect relationship that probably only exists in books and movies. And I'm not looking for that anymore.

I'm going to be the patience that my relationship with Rod needs to flourish. I'm going to be the one who meets him where he is, so he trusts that I'm not going to try to change him, but grow with him.

It would be different if my work situation hadn't changed. If this was a detriment to my life.

But as it is, the only thing I really lost are my plants. Which aren't really *lost*, but distributed out into foster care to every single one of my friends with detailed directions to ensure they're still thriving when I eventually return.

I'm not sure when that'll be, but I look forward to hugging each one of them individually when I do. I already miss them.

Ollie bites his lip before he speaks, as if considering his next words carefully. "Didn't Rod once tell you ADHD was a myth proliferated by psychiatrists to keep the population medicated?"

*The kill shot.*

Ollie's been fuming about it since I told him. And I told

him in a *ha, ha, funny* sort of way. Like, "hey, look how dumb my ex is."

This was before the therapy made me into a better person, of course.

"Yes, but he was easily convinced otherwise. And you know that," I remind him.

He lets out a long breath, his eyes flicking to mine as he rests his drink on the table. I take another sip of mine, my wine disappearing far quicker than I'd like.

His jaw ticks as he levels me with his gaze. "Didn't he stand you up on your birthday?"

And with that one little sentence, it's like all the air has been sucked out of the entire airport. It's the one thing we *don't* talk about.

Three months ago, Rod was in Philadelphia and promised he'd meet me and the girls to celebrate another year of Stephanie.

Long story short, he never showed.

Rod and I weren't together–he was just visiting for a few weeks, a rare break from his travels–but he promised me a fun night. One that I had gotten myself *excited* for.

And I wasn't about to let my birthday go to waste. So when Rod ditched me, I made a split second decision to take someone else up on their offer. Someone who had made it clear to me time and time again that he thought I was hot. That he's not interested in a relationship but would be happy to throw me around a little, if that was ever what I wanted.

Someone I knew I could trust.

Ollie was happy to oblige.

Our group ended up at the apartment my best friend slash work wife shares with Ollie's best friend slash college drinking buddy, and he showed up only an hour or so later, nonchalant as he poured himself a drink and melded into our conversation. We talked and laughed and drank, until people slowly started heading home.

And then he threw an arm around my shoulders, tugged me closer, and spoke low enough into my ear that only I could hear.

"You ready to get out of here?"

I nodded, swallowing down the knot of anticipation that jumped into my throat when he reminded me why I invited him.

Our walk to my apartment was nothing out of the ordinary—just two friends chatting and meandering down city streets.

And I almost forgot what we were walking back to.

Until I poured him a glass of whiskey and his hand landed tentatively on my hip, as if confirming that this was what I intended. Until I leaned into him, resting my wine on the counter behind him, and he took the opportunity to wind his arm around my waist, holding me close. Until I tipped my face up to meet his and his lips brushed over mine softly, once, and then punishingly after an accidental moan slipped from my throat.

Our drinks were abandoned in the kitchen, our clothes along the floor as we stumbled our way into my bedroom. He threw me onto my bed like I was weightless and anchored himself between my thighs, urging me to soak his face, to take him just a little deeper, to ride him harder and scream his name louder until it was early morning and we fell asleep naked, spent, and content.

At some point when the sky was lightening, we woke up and found each other again, his body settling easily between my legs and coaxing yet another orgasm out of me as his lips trailed along my neck, whispers jumping from them about how good I felt. How long he'd waited for this. How well I took him.

For a moment, I thought it could be more than one night. That maybe this connection Oliver and I had could be something more than a friendship.

But he left in the morning with a kiss on my cheek while I was still sleepy. Ordered me breakfast that was delivered half an hour later with a text that said he'd had fun. That he hoped he gave me what I wanted for my birthday. That he's around, if I'm ever looking for another one-nighter.

Pushing my mixed emotions to the back of my mind, I sent him something similar back. *Thanks for breakfast and multiple orgasms,* yada yada.

The next time I saw him was at some crowded party or another, and the first thing he asked me was how my new medication was going.

No heat in his eyes. No reference to that night.

We still haven't talked about it, but the memory of it has a little fire burning in my abdomen.

I swallow, unsure how to answer that question. Silence hangs heavy between us.

Ollie moves on easily, as if the silence is answer enough.

"How do you know he's the one?"

The question catches me off guard, and for a second I think this is the voice of God coming from the crackling airport speakers around us, asking how I know *Ollie* is the one.

Until I click back into my head and realize it's *Ollie* asking how I know *Rod* is the one.

This whole airplane thing has my mind in *shambles.*

"It's not that I *know* he's the one," I start. "But if you've been dancing around the same person for the better part of a decade, wouldn't you want to see if they could be? We've always wanted different things–he wanted to travel, and I guess I wanted to have a job and be with my friends and family. Not that I *don't* want to travel, but I'm not sure I want to travel every day for the rest of my life and clean toilets to get by. Now that I'm remote, this might be my opportunity to make that happen. The best of both worlds. I have my job and as long as we're living cheap, I can fly home whenever I want but ultimately be with him in the way that he wants." I let out a long breath as I down the rest of my wine. "And if we can't make it work compromising to the best of our ability, then I'll know."

"You'll know?"

"I'll know that he's not the one."

He nods, twisting his drink in small circles on the table.

"I hope you find the clarity you're looking for."

I snort. "Very diplomatic way to say you hope I tell Rod to get fucked."

He shrugs, throwing his hands out in front of him. "If you can find happiness with him, I promise I'll be happy for you. I just don't want you to put it all on the line for someone and end up with nothing but hurt in the end."

"If I end up hurt, I end up hurt. Where better to be hurt than Costa Rica?"

He nods. "Valid point."

The timer dings on Oliver's phone and I jump, thinking I'm going to miss my flight.

He holds up one hand in an attempt to stop my panic. "Five minutes until boarding *starts*, Steph. There's plenty of time to hit the bathroom and pick up a snack if you need one for your flight."

I nod, taking a deep breath.

He takes a long sip of his drink and then holds it out for me to take a guzzle. We paid the check when we ordered our drinks, so all we have to do is gather our things and head back to my gate.

"You don't have to wait with me," I tell him, as we start down the wide concourse.

He gives me a look. "Steph, I literally came to the airport six hours before my flight so I could wait with you. I'm not about to call it quits in the final quarter."

I give him a small smile. "Well, thanks."

He watches my stuff as I duck into the bathroom, and as I speed through peeing and washing my hands, I can't help but think how nice it is that he's here with me. That he knows I'm afraid of planes and went out of his way to accompany me. That he knew he was the only person who *could*, since he happened to have a flight the same night, and didn't hesitate to come early and hang out in a place that can only be described as a fluorescent torture chamber.

He grins at me as I come out of the bathroom, but I can't help my eyes flicking over toward my gate.

"Don't worry. They haven't even started first class yet."

I let out a sigh of relief. "Oh good."

He throws my backpack over my shoulder, and I grab my rolling bag as we turn toward my gate.

"Text me when you land, okay?"

I nod. "I will."

"And I want pictures of sloths and monkeys. As soon as possible."

I laugh. "I'll do my best."

We stop walking as we come upon the crowd of people waiting to board my flight. He wraps an arm around my shoulders, pulling me in for a hug, and I get a whiff of that fresh cedar scent of his that throws me right back to the night of my birthday. I don't know whether to inhale it like the last breath I'll take before touching down in Costa Rica, or to just go ahead and stop breathing now in the hopes it might stop all the images flying through my mind of Ollie's head between my thighs. The way his body arched over me. His hands touching me *everywhere* I ached to feel them.

An announcement asks for the next group to board. "Remember, people fly every day, and if it wasn't so safe, nobody would be sitting here calmly wondering what they're going to eat for breakfast."

"I know," I say into the fabric of his T-shirt. I don't want to let go.

I know this clinginess is a direct result of my fear to get on the airplane. Ollie has been a safe space for me since that day he suggested I get screened for ADHD. We had one night together that sticks in my head, but beyond that, he's been a great friend to me. He's there when I need someone to talk to, and he's always patient and supportive.

*That's* why these images are running through my mind right now.

Not because I have lingering feelings.

And that's why I don't want to let go of him right now.

Because fear does weird things to your head.

When he pulls away from me, his hands drop slowly from my shoulders, to my elbows, to my hands, and I want nothing more than to collapse back into his chest and request that he please buy a ticket to Costa Rica so I can just stay right here in the safety of his arms for the next eight hours.

The next group begins boarding.

He twists my arm so my palm faces him, my new tattoo stretched out along my forearm.

A bouquet of wildflowers Ollie drew for me when I dragged him and my sister to the tattoo convention and couldn't find a flower in the book of examples that suited me.

"Let me know how it heals," he says, his fingers grazing the skin there and sending a shockwave down my spine.

I nod to the tattoo peeking out from under the sleeve of his T-shirt. "You let me know how yours heals too."

"Deal," he says with a grin.

They call for my group to board.

Ollie raises his eyebrows and then pulls me in for another hug, his torso all warm and hard as he crushes me tight in his arms.

"Have a good time, Wildflower."

# 2

# OLIVER

Stephanie waves over her shoulder at me as she disappears into the long walkway.

My chest tightens, knowing she's going on that plane alone and the next eight hours are going to be torturous for her, but I'm also kind of proud of her for feeling the fear and doing it anyway.

That's just the kind of person she is.

I wait at her gate while the rest of the passengers on her flight board, just in case she panics and gets off. I don't think she's *that* scared, but on the off chance she is, I want to be there for her.

Over the past six months, Steph and I have become good friends. Dare I say, best friends.

We bonded first over our shared experience being diagnosed with ADHD, but our friendship has grown slow and strong over nights out with friends. Over nights spent with her sister, who's dating my best friend from college.

Over that one night we spent together three months ago that sticks in my head like glue.

I'm not someone who gets hung up on sex, but sometimes when I look at her, my brain breaks and I can taste her skin on my tongue like it was only moments ago that I kissed my way down her stomach and buried my face between her thighs.

If I had room in my life for a person, it would be someone like her. She loves so easily, freely and without judgment, and I love that about her.

In a friend way, of course.

I wander over to the window, staring out at Stephanie's plane. I can't see anything from here, but as I rest my hand on the glass, I hope she can see me. I hope I can give her a smidge of comfort before she embarks on her quest for love.

I stay there until the plane slowly backs out and taxies away, and it feels like a little piece of my heart is being pinched off and torn away.

Over the past six months, I've gotten closer to Stephanie than I have to anyone else in my life.

As much as I don't want to believe that this moment is a turning point in our relationship–she's traveling until further notice, to be with a guy who treats her like absolute shit–I know that things won't be the same in the future. Even when she does come back, her time will be filled with him.

As it should be, if they're truly able to find love with each other.

I realize, as her plane disappears around the corner of the airport, that I miss her.

I rub my hand over my chest, wondering where this stupid feeling is coming from.

Stephanie is a great person. She's fun and she's caring, and she lights up every room she walks into.

As much as I want to believe that's all this is, there's a

niggling feeling in my gut that says I like her a little more than I should.

I have a crush, I guess.

But that crush should, under no circumstances, be acted upon.

My life is carefully curated. I'm on a good track. I'm leveling up, instead of just getting through it.

So while the night of her birthday runs on repeat in my mind the second my thoughts get away from me, I know things can't go further than that.

I have my goals.

I glance down at the fresh compass tattoo on my arm.

I have my direction.

# 3

## STEPHANIE

*Have a good time, Wildflower.*

I know he only said it because of the tattoo, but something about it makes me feel like I finally get to be the ethereal one, the jet-setter off to her next magical destination.

It rings in my head while I board. While I gobble down a plastic cup of wine to quell the nerves from stupid turbulence, which "wasn't that bad," according to the jerk next to me. When I get off the plane and find my way onto a bus to take me to the car rental place. When I finally sit inside a car—*thank god for cars*—and orient myself to this new country.

Between the two of us, Rod always got to be the jet-setter. The free one. Until now, I was always the one stuck at home. When he graduated and went on a months-long Euro trip, I still had a year of classes left that kept me in Philadelphia. Once I graduated, I hoped he would take me on one of his big excursions as a celebration, but that year was one of the few he spent in one place. We dated for most of it, spending our time together going on little excursions around the US: Yellowstone, Vegas, Sedona.

That was my favorite of the time we've spent together. It was unpretentious, fueled by a mutual desire to explore the world around us, and I've never felt closer to someone than I did to him that year. I thought maybe that's what our lives together would become, traveling when we had the chance but ultimately revolving around one central destination: each other.

But as my savings dwindled and the reality of life crept up on me, I decided it was time to find a job in my field and start working.

And he decided it was time to travel again. Hence the years of breaking up and getting back together when he's actually in one place for long enough for us to reconnect.

But now things are different. As long as I can keep up with my work, I'm as free as Rod is. We have years of history together—years of falling in and out of love over and over again.

*Have a good time, Wildflower.*

It rings in my head again as I pull into the lodge.

From the grassy parking area, I step up to a wide, wrap-around deck with Adirondack chairs and hammocks scattered about. Off to one side are a few rolled yoga mats and sliding doors that lead into the lodge. From my spot on the deck, I see our host gathering her things from the kitchen counter.

I walk over to the railing, my eyes drawn to the expansive greenery around me.

This is paradise, for a plant-y person like me. The lodge is on the edge of a mountain, the tops of tropical trees presenting flowers of all colors to the edges of the deck. Off in the distance, there are pinpricks of other lodges nestled into the mountainside, far enough away that we all still have our privacy.

I reach out and rub one of the tropical flowers between my fingers, resisting the urge to march down in front of the deck and cut off a little piece to bring home and grow on my own.

The sliding door opens behind me, and I'm joined by the property host, who gives me a quick tour of the lodge and a rundown of activities nearby. She asks where my companion is, and I begrudgingly tell her he'll be joining me later.

She nods before she hands over the keys. "Enjoy your stay, Stephanie."

*Have a good time, Wildflower.*

~

ROD

Stephanie!

STEPH

Hey, are you almost here?

ROD

We took a little detour. We're going to be in Manuel Antonio for a few nights.

Can you come?

STEPH

A detour? It's five hours away.

ROD

I'm sorry, I'm at the whim of my friends here.

A bus to Arenal would take me 12+ hours.

Can you come?

I miss you.

STEPH

How long will you be in Manuel Antonio?

ROD

At least a few days. Maybe a week.

So here's my issue: I never actually told Rod why I was coming.

I thought it would be romantic to just show up, and I didn't want to put any pressure on either of us to *make* this work. I just wanted to create the opportunity for *Us*, because if our feelings for each other are true, everything else should happen naturally.

Regardless of whether I show up with grand declarations of love.

So I only told him I'd be traveling and asked if he wanted to meet up. I'm thinking of this like he's standing me up, but he's just trying to do what he loves. Traveling full-time isn't cheap, and moving in a group and splitting expenses keeps costs low.

I intentionally picked an area that's out of the way because I wanted to experience the beauty of Costa Rica in a place that's well-traveled but not overrun by tourists. I didn't even consider how difficult it would be for him to get here without a car.

I chew on my lip as I consider my options. I could drive to Manuel Antonio for a night and come back with Rod tomorrow. That would probably be my best option if I wanted to spend some quiet time with him.

Or I can stay here by myself and soak up this experience for the few days I have it. Rod has a tendency to attract friends wherever he goes, which is awesome when you're looking for a party, but it's not the vibe here.

I drum my fingers along the cloth of the hammock, debating. I *love* this lodge, and I'd be upset if I didn't use the remainder of my days here.

STEPH

I'll meet you there on Saturday.

ROD

Yes!! Can't wait to see you!!

I sigh and trade my phone for my laptop on the hammock next to me. While I won't be staying for the full length of my reservation, I'm at least staying for most of it. Knowing the way I usually work–no, the way I *used* to work– I would rush off to Rod's side just to be disappointed with whatever cheap place he's rented and annoyed that he wants to talk to everyone instead of just me, when I gave up so much for him.

I know how Rod thinks, and part of love is accepting someone as they are and working with them. He needs that freedom of not knowing what's coming next, and his financial constraints put him in a position where he needs to follow his group. Once we're back together, things will be easier. I can take care of lodging and a rental car for the time being, and then there will be no reason we can't go off and do whatever we want. No reason we can't truly reconnect and see if we can make this work, once and for all.

Off in the distance, a troop of monkeys whoop, and my heart thrums in my chest. I decide that if I can get an hour of work done and they're still nearby, I'll take myself for a quick hike and see if I can sneak a peek at them. I still haven't seen any wildlife, though I hear it constantly.

So I push thoughts of Rod to the back of my mind and refocus on my work.

And a few hours later, when I'm finally able to close my laptop, I grin.

It's time for that hike.

# 4

## OLIVER

After a night of little to no sleep thanks to a cranky baby on my flight, a day of corporate smiles and French greetings, and a dinner with my traveling companions that lasted far too long for my jet-lagged American brain, I finally pick up a bottle of wine and head back to my hotel room, a little boutique I schmoozed corporate into paying for instead of whatever deal the company got at some boring airport hotel.

I check my phone, pleased to see an array of pictures of my cat, Bung, in various places around my apartment. Carrie–Steph's ex-coworker and one of her many best friends–lives two blocks away from me and jumps at the chance to babysit Bung whenever I'm away. She sends *the best* cat pictures, and I make sure to Venmo her a little more than I would anyone else because it's so clear that she loves little Bunghole as much as I do.

I spend a moment scrolling through them, my heart aching to hug the little psycho. Bung curled up on the back of the couch, Bung hanging over Carrie's shoulder, Bung sniffing at his peasant dry food and even Bung taking a nice dump in his litter box, his eyes wide and bright with the flash from Carrie's phone.

I text her an overly exuberant thank you as I pour myself a glass of wine and flip on the kitchen light just long enough to take a picture of my tattoo and send it to Steph.

OLLIE

How is yours healing?

She sends a picture, her arm extended in front of her and in the background, a valley of green trees that leads up to a deck that looks like it must be hanging off the edge of the world. Flowering shrubs butt up against the cavities in the wood like they're ready to burst out and reclaim the deck as their own.

STEPH

Still looks new but healing well!

OLLIE

Still liking it?

STEPH

I LOVE IT!

Her text sends a surge of warmth through me. I drew her tattoo minutes before she sat down in the chair, not even considering that I would be on her body for the rest of her life.

And she loves it.

She *loves* it.

OLLIE

Where are you?

A second later she FaceTimes me, and I come to the

uncomfortable realization that this might be the first time I meet Rod. I clear my throat before answering.

Her mermaid hair is smushed up around her face, the blue and purple and blonde meshing with the multicolor cloth behind her head. It takes me a second to realize she must be in a hammock. She grins as the call connects, but her smile quickly fades. "Why are you sitting in the dark?"

"Because I'm exhausted but wired. Hoping the dark helps me get to sleep a little easier."

"Oh. What time is it there?"

"Ten. And I had a long day, but the jet lag is strong right now."

She sits up, smoothing her hair down as she does so, and I get a glimpse of the lodge behind her. The background of the picture she sent was so beautiful I thought for sure she was on a hike or at a fancy restaurant, but nope—I recognize the sliding doors of that lodge as the same ones she showed me when she was planning her trip.

"Don't worry, I'm sure a couple minutes talking to me will put you right to sleep," she says.

"It might help, but only because I need a distraction. Today was"–I consider going into it with her, complaining about my terrible flight and day of work on top of no sleep, but I think I'd rather just talk to her–"a lot."

"Traveling will do that to you," she sighs, and then shoots me a grin. We both know that I'm a little more experienced than she is. When it comes to traveling.

Not in any other way.

The night of her birthday pops into my head again. My name spilling from her throat. The constellation of moles across her hip. Her body, warm and taut and clinging to mine.

I push the thought away. We're *friends*.

"Have you thought about adding a European leg to your travels?"

And now it sounds like I want her to come join me here. Which to be honest, wouldn't be the worst thing in the world. But I'm not about to suggest she ditch her whole plan just for me.

She shrugs. "I don't even know where I'd start. But sure, I'd be open to it."

I think about this for a second. "My first thought would be the Netherlands, the tulips and all, but I think Switzerland could fit you too. Edelweiss and everything. Though that's also Austria." I shake my head, stopping myself from going on. My middle school obsession with World War II is showing.

I don't know why I feel this need to compare Stephanie to flowers.

Probably because I think of Steph singing her way through the Costa Rican forest like Julie Andrews on the mountain in the opening to *The Sound of Music*. She's probably having the time of her life finding all her tropical plants in their natural habitat.

Her smile stretches wider, and she bites her lip. "I love that."

I smile stupidly back at her, and blink at the small amount of wine left in the bottle on the counter. *How much did I drink tonight?*

I'm suddenly very thankful I took this call in darkness.

I take another sip. "So is Rod there with you?"

She sighs, her smile waning, and I immediately regret asking. "He's not coming to Arenal. He's beholden to the people he's traveling with, and if he wants to split off from them it'll be more than twelve hours of traveling for him to get here. So in a couple days, I'm going to drive out to him. It'll only be a few hours, for me."

I don't know if it's the wine in my brain or the vestiges of logic I used to have before drinking it, but something about that seems fishy. He knew she was coming. He should have planned for this.

"So first he couldn't meet you at the airport, then he couldn't show up on time, and now he won't even show up at all?" I bite my lip so I won't go further. *Why would you try so hard for someone who obviously doesn't care about you?* I'm mad at him, but I'm also a little mad at her for playing his game.

She shrugs, looking down, and my breath catches, wondering if I've gone too far.

"I didn't tell him why I was coming. He thinks I'm just traveling and we happened to land in the same country for a bit." She runs a hand through her hair, pulling it over her shoulder. "I was casual about it because I thought it might be romantic, you know? We could spend some time together and just rediscover our connection without the pressure of me coming here *for him*. I just didn't think it would be so hard to get us both in the same place at the same time. It's not his fault. My plan backfired."

*Oh Stephanie, you sweet thing.*

But this new knowledge doesn't change how I feel about Rod.

There's no doubt in my mind that anyone with a modicum of decency would have taken the twelve-hour bus ride or figured out a way to get to the airport to meet her, especially considering how scared she is of flying. She shouldn't have to ask for someone to show up for her.

There's a tug in my chest when I think of her getting off

that plane alone and navigating an unfamiliar airport without me by her side–

Without *Rod* by her side. *Rod* is who should have been there. Not me.

"Steph, I'm sorry. I didn't mean to be judgy about it. I'm happy you told me. You're probably right–if he knew why you were there, things would be different."

She looks back at the phone. "You think?"

I nod. "I know." *I don't.*

She takes a deep breath. "Yeah. I should have told him, but we'll figure it out."

"I have no doubt." *I have a lot of doubts.*

I know it's what Stephanie needs to hear, but my stomach churns as I say the words aloud. She should feel good that she's putting her heart on the line for someone. That she's so willing to forgive and march forward.

But I also wish she would recognize how little respect he has for her. He's shown her how much he values her, and after so many years of this, it's time for her to find someone who appreciates her.

An odd feeling passes through me as I imagine her walking out of the airport, eyes scanning a line of cars until they lock on mine, a smile blooming across her face.

"And if you don't figure it out, you can always meet me in Paris."

# 5

## STEPHANIE

I spend three days exploring the nature of Mount Arenal in absolute bliss. I go canoeing in the lake, listening to the water as it parts around me. I go hiking every day, and each time I pick a different path to travel down, exploring the nature just steps outside my lodge. I eat dinner at the barbecue joint at the end of the road and play dice with a group of locals each night, practicing my Spanish with them while they practice their English with me.

When I begrudgingly pack my things into my car, I find the nearest tree and give it a long hug because I don't think I've ever felt quite so home while not *at home* as I did in Mount Arenal.

And five hours later, when I finally arrive in Manuel Antonio, it's busier than Mount Arenal by a long shot.

I feel like I left a yoga retreat only to enter South Philly after the Phillies make it to the playoffs.

The streets are narrow and packed with cars, and street vendors shout into my window as I drive by in search of the hostel Rod and his group of traveling buddies are staying at.

He said he has space for me in his room, and I assume he means in his bed, but I'm guessing he doesn't want to be presumptuous by telling me that right away.

After this long drive, I'm ready for a drink and some thoughtless laughs. I pull into a parking space just big enough for my car and get out eagerly to stretch my legs. I unload my bags and trudge across the gravel of the parking lot to the entrance, heaving them up the two stairs to the colorful deck bar, where I search the crowd for Rod.

"Stephanie!" I hear him before I see him, his arms wrapping around me from the side. He crushes me into him, his cologne filling my nostrils as I drop my bags on the ground next to me and fold myself into him. He lowers his voice so only I can hear him. "I missed you."

I pull away only enough to look up into his big brown eyes, as he runs his thumbs along my cheeks. His dark hair is longer than the last time I saw him, with a light smattering of stubble across his jaw that tells me he hasn't shaved in a few days. He's the epitome of tall, dark, and handsome, and when he starts speaking Spanish in that low voice that's reserved just for me, sometimes I think I've left my body and gone straight into heaven.

"I missed you too," I say, anxious to press my lips into his.

He looks down at me with a big grin on his face, his arms still tight around me, and I think for a moment that he might actually use this opportunity to kiss me, sweep me off my feet in some grand romantic way because upon seeing me he's realized just how much he wants me in his life.

But he kisses me on the cheek instead and, after a second, releases me.

"Let's get your bag upstairs and then I'll introduce you to the group. Sound good?"

I nod. "Yeah, sounds great."

He takes my suitcase by the handle and throws my backpack over his shoulder, gesturing to a door that leads from the deck bar to the inside of the hostel. He waves at the front desk attendant as we pass by and takes a set of stairs toward the back of the small lobby up to the second floor. We walk down a narrow hallway to the last door on the right, and he uses a keycard to swipe inside.

He rolls my suitcase to an open wall, leaving my backpack balanced on top of it.

And I can't help but notice just how many bags there are in this room.

I bite my lip before speaking. "How many people are staying here?"

He shrugs. "All of us. We usually try to fit in one room," he says, holding the door open for me to walk back out. He seems to sense my confusion and continues, "There are five of us. But don't worry, the couch pulls out."

I try to make that math work out in my head as we head back downstairs. One queen bed plus one pull-out couch does not equal enough room for six people.

"Is there a trundle bed?"

His eyebrows crinkle together. "They're both queens—three people will fit easily."

"The bed and the pull-out?"

He nods. "Yeah, it's more comfortable than you think."

My bed at home is a queen and much too small to fit me and my two best friends, Kay and Leilani.

But I guess being pressed up against Rod all night isn't the *worst* idea. I've been craving that—the heat of a man behind me, strong arms around my waist.

I hate the lack of privacy. *But one night won't kill me, right?*

I shrug. "I trust you," I say, and let him lead me down to the bar, his fingers interwoven with mine.

His friends are set up at a picnic table near the back of the bar area where a large, industrial fan blows over the tops of their heads. He holds my hand while he introduces me, and a sense of relief washes over me when I see how willing he is to show these people that I mean something to him.

Rod can be a little flaky, but ultimately, he cares.

I recognize a few of his friends from college or post-college hangouts, and they're quick to regale me with tales of their recent travels. The hot springs outside La Fortuna where Vera slipped, and they thought she broke her elbow but it turned out to be just a nasty funny bone hit. The rain-forest hike with sky bridges two hundred feet above the river where they realized they were eerily alone for two hours—but Natalie swore she heard hikers behind them for at least half that time. Skinny-dipping at the base of a water-fall just because they could and a fish slithering between Andre's legs, prompting him to scream like a "little banshee," according to Celeste.

I feel like I've already missed so much.

"I saw online there's a hidden beach at the other end of the national forest," I say, thinking maybe this can be *my* contribution. We can take a hike through the forest and splash around in the alcove there. Maybe see some monkeys swinging between trees or spy a sloth slinking around.

"Oh, there is, but it's not worth going to. It's not really different from the free beaches. It's just a tourist trap to trick you into paying for something that no one else does," Vera explains quickly, waving off my idea with a gentle flick of her hand.

"Oh."

"But we'll definitely hit one of the free beaches over the next few days. As long as Celeste remembers to put on her sunscreen," she says, a wicked smile spreading across her face as her eyes land on Celeste.

The group laughs. "It was one time!" Celeste says.

"And you looked like a little red lobster!" Andre adds.

Natalie makes claw motions with her hands, reaching over to pinch the skin of Celeste's shoulder. "All you needed were some cheddar biscuits!"

And with that, the group is howling. Ordering more drinks. Getting small plates of food to split.

Somewhere between drinks two and three, I cross my legs and accidentally kick Rod under the table. He wastes no time wrapping a warm hand around my ankle, his fingers rubbing mildly along my skin. It's an unspoken conversation between the two of us where he lets me know he's glad that I'm here–glad that I'm finally a part of this.

Just the touch makes my heart thrum. And it reminds me *why* I'm here.

As nice as it is to sit and listen to their adventuring, I don't want to wait too late to talk to Rod. To let it be known that he's the one I love and that I want to make something of us during this trip.

I excuse myself to the bathroom as the buzz from my second drink descends upon me, and nod to Rod as I step into the dark bar. He raises his eyebrows and then says something to the rest of the table, following in my footsteps only a short while later.

"Stephanie," he says, following me into the small alcove where the bathrooms are hidden.

"Hey."

He winds an arm around my waist, pulling me close. He kisses my cheek and then looks me in the eyes as if asking if he can kiss me for real. I stand on my toes to kiss him first, and his hands trail down my arm to my hip, holding me against him.

"I missed you," I say, as he pulls away from me.

"Steph, I missed you so much," he says, winding his fingers through my hair in a way that sends little shivers down my spine. "*So much*," he whispers in my ear as he leaves little kisses along my jaw, my ear.

I put a hand on his chest, pulling his attention back to my face instead of my body, and he leaves one last kiss on my forehead. "Are you alright?" he asks.

I nod, words failing me now that I've made space to say them. "Have you ever thought about doing this... with us?" I ask, gesturing vaguely around us.

"Traveling, you mean?" he asks, his fingers running down my arm and leaving a trail of goosebumps in their wake. "You and me?"

"I feel like we've always been in two different places. You've wanted to travel, to be free and go wherever. And I've"–a lump builds in my throat that I swallow over. "I've always wanted you."

"Stephanie," he says, his arms winding together around me.

"Now that I work remotely, I think we can have the best of both worlds. We can travel together, go wherever we want. We can finally be together in a way that makes sense for what we both want out of the world."

He's quiet for a moment. "That sounds amazing."

All of my breath leaves my body. "Really?"

He sighs, his hand cupping my chin. "I wasn't kidding when I said I missed you. I would love to do nothing more than this, with you, forever."

"Wow," I say, momentarily rendered speechless by his

words. I melt into him and he peppers kisses all along my face, my hands.

There was a part of me that thought this would be so much harder. That he would be apprehensive of the idea or need convincing.

But Rod is in. My person wants me, too.

I WAKE up to Celeste's face only inches from mine. She's tucked into Rod's other arm, snoring lightly into his skin, and the jolt of jealousy that runs through me is more invigorating than any cup of coffee.

Sleeping three to a bed is not my style, mostly because in order to fit three people into a queen-sized bed, *somebody* has to be cuddling, and if it's not me, it's one of the other girls. Apparently last night it was me *and* one of the other girls.

I'm not careful about the noise I make getting up. I spent most of the night tossing and turning, trying to find a comfortable position without waking Rod. And after all of *that*, I wake up to *this*.

But I'm not allowed to be mad because "this is just what they do."

I slip on my sandals, grab my purse, and march down to reception.

The desk attendant smiles easily at me as I approach, his frizzy hair extending in all directions. "Good morning," he says easily.

"Good morning," I say, gritting my teeth underneath my smile. "Do you have any rooms available? I'm staying with friends but I think we need more space."

He smiles, holding up one finger. "Let me check." He

presses a few buttons on the computer, and makes a humming noise. "So, we don't have any shared rooms available but we do have a private on the third floor."

I let out a long breath, my shoulders relaxing as I nod. "Oh, that would be great. Thank you."

He nods, and requests my passport and car rental agreement, which he makes quick copies of.

"I'll just charge your card," he motions to the card reader in front of me, and my eyes nearly bug out of my head at the price. I could have stayed another four nights in Mount Arenal for the same amount.

I swallow. "Thank you," I say thickly.

"Sure thing! Here's your keycard." He presses it into my hand. "Enjoy your stay!"

I wave half-heartedly at him as I make my way back upstairs, only now realizing that I'm wearing my skimpy sleep set without a bra.

*God, I can't wait to be alone in my room.*

The five of them are still asleep when I sneak back in to grab my things. I take another annoyed look at Rod and Celeste and drag my bags out into the hall and up another flight of stairs.

When I push into my room, I blast the air conditioning and run a hot shower, thankful I don't have to use the communal one on the floor below.

I text Rod my room number and tell him to come find me when he wakes up.

And then I sign into my computer, the prospect of work ahead of me this morning a comfort after a night of tossing and turning. It's something familiar I can dig my teeth into when I'm otherwise plain *uncomfortable*.

And three hours later, when I'm deep in focus mode, there's a knock at the door. I jump, having forgotten I'm even in a different country, and reorient myself to the space around me.

*Rod. It must be Rod.*

I jump up from my chair and swing the door open.

Only to see Vera standing in front of me with a smile on her face, her hair in two long braids. She's wearing loose shorts with an army green tank top that somehow looks both chic but worldly at the same time.

"Good morning," she says, her voice bright, as she brushes into the room. "Wow, this is so spacious!" She hands me a cup of coffee and then clocks the identical one on the dresser. "Oh, I guess you already got your morning fix, but hey, here's an extra if you need it."

"Oh, thank you," I say, doing my best not to let my disappointment show.

She sits comfortably on my bed, throwing her bag down next to her. "So, Rod sent me up to get you–it's his turn to drive so he's just pulling the car around. We're heading off to a coffee farm this morning. Can you be ready in ten?"

I look down at the jammies I never changed out of. At my half-finished work on my computer.

"Uh, I didn't realize we were going somewhere this morning. I have to work for probably another hour or so."

She raises her eyebrows. "Oh, okay. Well, that's totally fine. Sorry, didn't realize you were that kind of traveler."

Something in her words feels mildly derisive.

"That kind of traveler?"

She shrugs. "Oh you know, the digital nomad thing. We usually just pick up odd jobs for cash so we're not beholden to a schedule. Just gives us a little more freedom. You should try it. You might really like it."

I blink at her. "Yeah, I'll consider it."

She stands from her spot on the bed. "Well, we'll see you

later then! We probably won't be gone more than a couple hours. Maybe we can do something this afternoon."

I nod. "Yeah, that sounds great."

She's gone as quickly as she came, and I'm stuck with double coffees and zero plans for the day.

THE NEXT DAY, I set an early alarm so I won't miss out on any activities. The group left around ten for the coffee farm, and if I can work straight through until then, I'll finish in time to join whatever adventure they have planned for today.

Rod is still asleep in bed, his arm thrown haphazardly above his head. He stumbled in late last night smelling of rum and sweat and fell asleep with a chaste kiss on my cheek.

That's probably a good thing, anyway, because I was about ready to give him a piece of my mind if he had ideas about doing anything else after sending *Vera* to come get me yesterday morning.

I sneak out of the room with my laptop and set up at one of the empty tables downstairs. I order a coffee and a light breakfast, and dig into my work, the light breeze from the fan lifting my hair, the sounds of early morning Costa Rica becoming the background music to my work.

I'm pleasantly surprised at how easy it is to work like this, the sounds of a small tourist town just waking up surrounding me, Costa Rican coffee in my cup, and a small, healthy breakfast to wake me up.

As time marches toward ten, I keep a lookout for Rod and the rest of the group.

I finish up a proposal that's due this week–with plenty of time, I might add–and head back upstairs to get a shower.

Only to find the room empty, Rod nowhere in sight.

I blink, wondering where he could have gone.

Then I notice the bags he dragged in late last night are gone, too.

A sinking feeling in my chest, I take out my phone and see an array of texts from him starting at eight this morning. I must have been so involved in my work that I didn't even notice them coming in.

The group has gone out in search of hot springs, and since they'll have to go most of the way to Mount Arenal, they took all of their stuff in case they have to stay over.

I shake my head as I lock my phone and throw it onto the bed.

I can't even really be that upset. He tried to text me. He let me know what was going on.

But I was so involved with my work that I didn't think of him at all.

Vera's poorly concealed disdain for my work flashes in my mind. Her suggestion that picking up odd jobs along the way allows for more freedom than being beholden to a work schedule.

I can only imagine Rod agrees with her assessment.

My job is the one thing I want to hold on to. I've given up my whole life for this. My apartment. My proximity to friends and family. For the sake of making *Us* work.

And it's still not enough.

I'm starting to wonder if Rod won't be happy until I give up everything that makes me, *me*.

With a huff and a head shake, I change into my spandex and head to the national park at the end of the street that Rod's group didn't want to go to. It's a short hike through the forest—and yes, it's littered with tourists, but it ends with a gorgeous hidden beach with warm, mild water and white sand. I wade in, my things held in a waterproof lanyard my sister gave me before I left, and watch the beach.

I let the easygoing waves push me around, the water like a blanket surrounding me. Fellow tourists shout a variety of languages around me: English, Spanish, German, and a few others I don't recognize. I people watch, and animal watch, and enjoy the noises of Costa Rica I never would have gotten to hear had I blindly followed Rod's group.

When my fingers get wrinkly, I find a spot underneath the shade of an almond tree to read.

I've nearly forgotten I'm in paradise when a monkey flies down from a tree nearby, causing a string of surprised gasps and laughs from people nearby.

My heart skips a beat.

*Finally! A monkey!*

I want to tell someone, to share this moment of excitement with someone, but I remember with a slow, sinking feeling that I'm alone.

I take my phone out and snap a blurry picture of the monkey, sending it off to Ollie with a couple exclamation points. As I do, the monkey jumps to a tourist's towel and steals something from their beach bag. While they roar in laughter, the monkey hoists himself back into his tree, hoarding his stolen treasure.

A park ranger walks over, his hands on his hips. "You gotta watch out for the monkeys!" he tells the crowd. "They have very sticky fingers!" More laughter.

STEPHANIE

That's his mugshot by the way–he just stole something straight out of somebody's bag.

OLLIE

What?! That's hilarious. Good for the monkey.

STEPHANIE

He deserves it, dealing with all these tourists.

OLLIE

Lol! Power to the monkeys.

It's a few seconds before he texts me again.

OLLIE

Glad you're having fun, Steph.

*Am I?*

Costa Rica is beautiful in every sense of the word, but I'm not sure Manuel Antonio is my place. I crave the nature of Mount Arenal–the greenery, the flowers, the sounds of monkeys living in their natural habitat rather than stealing from humans. I felt like I could take off my theoretical shoes there and settle in.

OLLIE

Still waiting on a sloth pic btw.

I hang out under the tree for a while longer, taking in the beach and the tourists and a few other monkeys that swing by.

And when I make my way out, I scan the trees for small, slow-moving bunches of white fur, but see none.

# 6

## OLIVER

I'm only vaguely aware that my phone is vibrating somewhere in the depths of my sheets.

My tired brain has trouble comprehending that Stephanie is calling me at four in the morning. I swipe to answer, putting it on speaker and dropping it down on my stomach.

I close my eyes. "Hello?"

"I can't find a fucking sloth!"

I open my eyes. "What?"

"Are you asleep?" she asks incredulously.

"Yeah." She's silent. "I mean no, but I was."

There's noise around her, like she's at a bar. "I can't find a fucking sloth," she repeats.

"I thought they were everywhere there."

She scoffs. "Yeah, me too!"

I can't help the snorting laugh that escapes me.

"Oh my God, Ollie, it's not funny!"

"Aw Steph, it's a little funny. Maybe you can find a T-shirt that says 'I went all the way to Costa Rica and didn't see a fucking sloth.'"

She laughs, slurping a drink close enough to the phone that I can hear it. "Ollie, I don't know what I'm doing."

I sit up, reaching over and turning on the lamp next to me that bathes the room in a warm yellow light. I run my hands over my face, struggling to wake up so I can follow this conversation. "What do you mean?"

She sighs. "I came all the way here for Rod, told him I want to be with him and travel the way he wants to travel. And then he just went off with his friends. Like, I don't want to be an asshole and take him away from them, but I feel like his half of this deal is putting me before his friends. He should have stayed behind instead of leaving with them."

"I totally agree."

She's quiet for a second, as if she's waiting for me to continue, but I don't need to add any context to that for her. We both know Rod's the problem here.

"And I feel like I should be more upset."

*That's interesting.* "Why?"

"Because I came here for love, right? I'm in a part of the country I wasn't excited to come to, I'm spending more money than I wanted to, and after all that, he doesn't care enough to hang back with me when his friends go off exploring." She pauses. "But I guess I just don't care as much as I feel like I *should* care. There's this beautiful hidden beach that they didn't want to pay for. It's fucking gorgeous, and so worth the couple dollars to get in. If I did things the way he wanted to–the way *they* wanted to–I never would have seen it. And that feels scarier to me than Rod telling me he doesn't love me anymore."

"It sounds like you've outgrown him."

"Yeah, but my whole idea was to grow *with* him, you know? You're never going to be the perfect fit for another person, but you can choose to *grow* with them." Her voice is muffled when she speaks, and I realize she's ordering another drink, probably with her phone buried in her shirt. "But you know what? I didn't tell him that, you know? I told him I wanted to *do this* with him. Maybe I should be telling him that I want something more serious than the flaky relationship we had before."

*You should tell him to pound sand.*

"Steph, why do you want to grow with him if you're not even upset he ditched you?"

She says a muffled 'thank you' to the bartender. "Because I came all the way here, and if I don't put it all on the line now, I'll always wonder. I want to find my person, and I want to know whether that person is him, once and for all."

Her resolve is impressive, I'll give her that.

"Well, that's really cool of you, Steph. You're more forgiving than most." I want to tell her to cut her losses early, but she seems set on this plan of attack. I respect her willingness to be so open with her heart, but there's another little part of me that wants to shield her from this. She says she doesn't care, but you don't fly internationally to confess your love to someone without feeling it at least a little. "I can't say I understand it, but I definitely respect it."

"Yeah, well, let's see if you still respect it when I call you angrily tomorrow about still not finding a sloth and Rod ditching me again."

"I would never lose respect for you over that. Forgiveness is a virtue."

"Is it forgiveness, though? Or is it blatant stupidity?"

I laugh. "Steph, come on. You're one of the smartest people I know."

"Really? You still think that after this conversation?"

"Always."

"Okay, did I catch you drunk or something? Why are you being so nice?"

I'm silent for a beat. "Steph, you realize it's four in the morning here, right?"

She inhales sharply. "Oh my god, I totally fucked up my time math. I thought it was four in the afternoon. That's why I was so confused when you sounded groggy. I'm sorry, go back to sleep! Oh man, I'm going nutty, I really need to get out of this place."

My words jump from my mouth before I can second guess them. "Come to Paris."

She pauses. "Was that a serious offer?"

"Sure. After tomorrow I'm on vacation. I can show you around, give you the full travel experience that Rod never did." *Why do I sound like a jealous boyfriend?* "If you think you'd like Paris, that is."

She scoffs. "If I think I'd like Paris. Um, yeah, I think I'd like Paris!" She laughs. "That's nice of you, Ollie. If tomorrow goes to shit, I might actually take you up on that."

"Then I sincerely hope you have a terrible day tomorrow."

She snorts. "Is that going to be the new phrase?"

I'm not sure what she's referring to. My brain feels like molasses, thanks to the time and the bottle of wine I took down last night. "The new phrase?"

"Oh, never mind."

"What's the old phrase?"

She hums. "You know, when I left for Costa Rica. You said, 'Have a good time, Wildflower,' and I guess it just got stuck in my head. Every time somebody says 'Good luck, Steph,' or 'Have a good day,' in my head it gets translated to 'Have a good time, Wildflower.' It's dumb, just one of those things that runs on a loop."

"Ah, okay. I forgot I said that."

"It was silly. I guess I just liked being the wildflower for once. I feel like that's always Rod, and I'm just some stickler who works on a specific schedule and doesn't like sleeping three to a queen bed."

"Three to a queen?"

"Yeah, it was completely terrible. Zero out of ten. Would not recommend."

"For what it's worth, you're not the weird one for disliking that."

"Thank you!" She slurps her drink again. "Okay, I'm going to get drunk by myself for a bit. You should go back to sleep. Sorry for bothering you!"

"Not a bother at all."

"Okay, goodnight Ollie."

"Goodnight, Wildflower."

She squeaks in approval as she hangs up the phone.

# 7

# STEPHANIE

ROD

The group wants to go canoeing on the lake today so we'll likely be back tomorrow. See you then Stephanie! I miss you.

I *want* to be angry with Rod. In fact, I'd say there's a large part of me that's annoyed with the way he's treating me right now, like I'm some superfluous hanger-on who's not a real part of the group.

But I'm also getting all of my work done and exploring this gorgeous country at the same time.

I like the comfort of having my own room. I don't have rent to pay at home, and I'm still working full-time, so I don't think it's that insane to live comfortably. I don't know why Vera had such disdain for the digital nomad thing. It's working pretty well for me, so far.

I've been working five to ten, signing on a little early to power through my individual work, and then joining meetings as they come up. The staff has gotten to know me over the past few days, and I'm greeted with smiles every morning when I go downstairs and take up one of the tables near the back of the restaurant while I work.

I get a FaceTime from my best friends Kay and Leilani when I'm just about done for the day.

"Hey, World Traveler!" Kay shouts as soon as the call connects. She's at her office, dressed up in a blazer with her golden brown hair perfectly coiffed. Leilani's at home still in bed, brown hair fanned out around her head; she usually has the dinner shift at the bar.

"Hey guys," I say, closing my laptop.

"How's the trip? How's Rod?" Leilani asks. She's one of the few people who have always liked Rod, but I'm pretty sure it's only because she's usually in the same position—in love with some guy who inspires copious amounts of side-eye among her friends.

"He's out with his traveling buddies," I say. "I had to work."

"Oh, that's a bummer," Kay says. "But are you guys, like, reconnecting?"

I nod. "Yeah, I mean, we're back together. Kind of."

My brain breaks as I try to unravel what we technically *are* now. I think after our conversation the other night, we're definitely more than friends. But there's a part of me that thinks a committed person wouldn't leave the person they *just* committed to, to go adventuring with other people.

*But that doesn't mean we're not something, right?*

"You're kind of back together?" Leilani asks.

I huff. I don't want to say we're back together, because that would mean leaving me here is kind of a dick move. But if we're not back together, I'm just a crazy ex-girlfriend who can't let go and follows him wherever he goes. "I guess we're somewhere in between."

"That sounds an awful lot like what you were before you left," Kay says.

I shake my head. "I don't know what to make of this. We had a conversation about, like, doing this together. Traveling and being with each other. But he went off to travel with his buddies again instead."

Kay cocks her head to the side. "How long is he gone for?"

"He left yesterday for the hot springs, and they're staying there again today to go canoeing."

Kay clicks her tongue. "Steph, I don't think he understood the conversation. That doesn't sound like a man who's trying to do life with you."

"No, it doesn't," I agree. "But honestly I'm not–"

"In love with him?" I detect a hopeful note in Kay's voice. She's never said it, but I know she sides with my sister on her feelings about Rod.

"I'm just not all that disappointed," I say. "I'm starting to wonder if it's Rod I want, or love, because honestly I've been having a great time by myself. I want my person, but it kind of feels harder when he's around."

Kay cocks her head to the side. "Well, I think that's your answer."

"It would be different if he put in the effort, but we've hardly had time to even talk, just the two of us, let alone make a plan for the future. He left before we could. I guess it doesn't matter to him."

Leilani burrows down in bed, her face twisted in concern. "You should come home, Stephy."

I sigh. "I probably should," I agree, then glance around the bar, at the forest that butts up against the other side of the road out front. "But I'm not sure I'm done traveling yet. For me. Not Rod."

Kay nods. "Do you, honey. Just don't stay somewhere you're sad and alone. At least come home if you're going to be sad, okay?"

"I promise," I say. "But I'm really not that sad. More like, apathetic."

Leilani sighs. "Steph, just come home. Apathy isn't a good place to be."

I hold up a hand. "Okay, okay. Apathetic about Rod, not life."

"Are you sure? Because I will come down there and *Taken* your ass."

"I'm sure, Lei. Thank you for being the most forceful mental health advocate I know."

"You're welcome. Also, I miss you, and I selfishly want you to come home because I'm dying to go dancing and if I can convince you, you can convince Kay, but without you, Kay's like an immovable rock."

"Yeah, because when you go out, you want to dance until four in the morning. Steph can at least accept a two A.M. cutoff."

I snort. "That, and I get you drunk so you stop caring."

She rolls her eyes. "Okay, I have to get back to work. We just wanted to call and check in. Have a wonderful time and please give Rod a kick in the balls for me," Kay says.

"And another from me if he doesn't shape up real quick," Leilani says.

I shake my head. "Bye, guys."

I bite my lip as I write out a text to him.

STEPH

Can we talk tomorrow?

ROD

Absolutely, looking forward to seeing you.

I huff. He says things like that so easily–that he misses me, or that he can't wait to see me–yet runs off at the drop of a hat to do whatever his friends want to do.

I'm starting to wonder if he means it.

## 8

## OLIVER

The three of us sit at a table too small to reasonably accommodate three people, my coworkers Jack and Emma on one side, squished against the wall. We came straight from the office, anxious to celebrate our last night of work.

Jack and Emma are both also taking vacation this week. And just happen to be on the same flight back home.

They explained that away quickly–*oh, well it was the cheapest flight, you know.*

I know. I booked my own flights too. But if the company is paying for it, I don't really care. I picked the flight that would get me home at night, so I can drag myself home and crawl right into bed with a shot of Nyquil.

The more obvious answer is that Jack and Emma are sleeping together and wanted the same flight home. It's been clear for the past few months; either things are getting more serious or they're getting tired of hiding it.

I don't particularly care either way, but I wish they didn't feel like they have to hide it. At least in front of me.

But I'm not going to blow up their spot. That's their business.

But in my head at least, I think of them as a unit. I ask what *they're* doing and how *their* night was and if *they're* enjoying the business hotel they're staying at.

I'm betting they are.

Emma twirls her wineglass in a spot of water on the table, letting out a long breath. "So have either of you heard anything else about what's next for the team?"

I look at Jack for his reaction. He only shakes his head.

"I haven't heard anything beyond that feeler conversation I had with Gail," I say.

"Same," he says.

A few weeks ago, our boss took each of us aside to get a read on where we want to go in our careers. Our team has had better ratings than any of the other training teams, but we're bordering on tapping out our travel allocation for the year. I don't think any of us have turned down a trip in months, and soon, accounting is going to start denying us trip expenses as per company policy to make sure employees aren't being *over*-traveled.

So the company is trying to figure out how to restructure the team in a way where people can be subbed out. They're looking for a director of training to lead a slightly larger team with a little less horsepower.

And that new position is going to be *one of us.* Emma isn't interested; she wants to move back to accounting where she can make a bigger impact. She knows the most obscure rules from seemingly every country, and although she's great for translating accounting questions, she could do a lot more.

Meanwhile, I have the software engineering background to match, a skill that is really only useful when explaining the logic behind the system or writing feature request tickets for the engineering team in a way that doesn't involve weeks of back-and-forth to get an understanding of the *problem*, let alone finding a solution.

And Jack... well, he's the darling of the group. Speaks four languages fluently, has a smile plastered to his face constantly, and never gets frustrated with someone who's having trouble with the training program.

The optimistic side of me wants to believe I'm going to be tapped for the new position.

The realistic side of me knows Jack will.

And it's part of the reason I'm taking vacation this week. I need a break from the corporate politics. From this confirmation that I'm *less than* despite giving *everything*.

Emma and I were transplants from other departments, filling in for other people until suddenly *we* were the people who would need to be filled in for. Jack was always right where he was meant to be.

Emma shakes her head. "They're really not making this easy, are they?"

"You know this company moves slower than molasses," Jack says, patting her hand lightly.

I don't mean for my eyes to catch on the movement, but it's like a collective realization passes over our table. Them, realizing their feelings are showing through. And me, realizing that this is supposed to surprise me.

Even though it really doesn't.

Emma clears her throat, tugging her hand off the table and resting it in her lap. She glances away, taking a breath and avoiding eye contact. Jack's eyes dip to his drink as he takes a long sip.

I wasn't going to say anything, but they seem like they're *torturing* themselves.

"Guys, I know," I say.

Emma's eyes dart back to mine. "You know?"

I gesture to them, referring to the hand touching incident that just happened. "It's hard not to, being with you guys twenty-four-seven."

They glance at each other, Jack leaning slightly forward in his chair.

"You could have told me, you know. I wouldn't have said anything."

Jack shrugs, and when Emma hesitantly rests her hand on the table again, he takes it in his, glancing at her with raised eyebrows as if to ask if it's okay.

"We didn't want to keep it a secret from you," Jack says, and then shrugs. "It was just too important."

I raise my eyebrows. *So this is a little more than just sleeping together.*

"Oh," I say, my heart swelling a little bit for them.

"In fact, we were planning on telling you really soon," he says. "But with this restructure or whatever it is they're doing, we wanted to wait. There's a possibility that if I get this director of training position, Emma would technically be my direct report."

I nod, the significance of their position dawning on me. "Oh, I see."

"Emma's put in a request to move to accounting, but neither of us have heard of any movement either way so we're just in this really annoying limbo where we don't know what's happening and we can't even be excited about what could come because if it happens in the wrong way, we're a little bit screwed."

"I didn't think of it in that way. And I, uh, didn't realize it was that serious, either."

Jack shrugs, glancing at Emma. "We want to get married."

"You do?" I can't believe I thought they were only *sleeping* together. They've been spinning up a whole life together right under my nose. "That's great. I'm so happy for you."

Emma grins, squeezing Jack's fingers between her own. "Thank you. We're happy too. We're just starting to get a little sick of the waiting. We want to know a plan. Any plan. You know?"

I nod. "I imagine it's stressful for you guys."

Jack shrugs, catching my eye. "I imagine it's stressful for you, too."

There it is. The acknowledgement that the good news they're hoping for would be bad news on my end. Jack and I have a playful competition going on—not all that different from what I have with my siblings, but in this particular circumstance, one of us winning means the other losing. Because one of us getting that director job means the other becomes a direct report.

I can only hope the company has something else up their sleeve.

"Worse things can happen in life than seeing a friend succeed," I say.

Jack smiles, reaching forward to tap his glass to mine. "I don't know what the future holds, but I'm looking forward to seeing all three of us succeed. In some capacity or another."

I PICK up another bottle of wine on my way back to my room, sure I'll need some liquid assistance in getting my body to sleep tonight, and pop it open at the kitchen table. I pour a glass, keeping the lights dim in the hopes my brain will understand it's time to sleep soon, but I find myself just getting more buzzed.

And in my slightly inebriated state, I scratch my arm without thinking and realize as pain lances through my skin that I hit my new tattoo. I shake my arm out, even more awake now.

I need to get my mind off this stupid promotion.

I open my laptop and do some lazy research for something to do tomorrow. As I click through page after page, not really digesting what I'm reading, one of the travel suggestions at the bottom of the page catches my eye.

A tour of Parisian secret gardens.

It's not really my thing, but I bet Steph would love it.

Our conversation from last night comes roaring back. I fell asleep right after and totally forgot about it until now.

She likes it when I call her Wildflower.

And I think I like that she likes when I call her Wildflower.

My fingers freeze above the keyboard. This feels like *something*.

Steph and I spent one wild night together three months ago and never spoke of it again. We were friends before, nothing more, nothing less. But since then, we've become closer in baby steps, from only speaking during parties, to trading the occasional meme, to hanging out intentionally, to confiding in each other.

I thought we were both clear on that night. It was her birthday, and I was available.

But now she likes it when I call her Wildflower.

And I kind of want to keep calling her that.

I drum my fingers along my laptop. I've been so focused on work, constantly striving for the next big thing, that I've neglected personal relationships outside of my family and my close circle of friends who don't care if I need to disappear for a while for work.

But if my fate is sealed with this job, what does it hurt to explore a bit? It's not like Stephanie is going to hop on a plane and come to Paris. But maybe she'll be looking for a bit of a rebound. A palate cleanser before starting fresh on her quest for love.

It hits me suddenly, that this might be what my sister has been pestering me about all along. Even when I felt like I was prioritizing my mental health, she would tell me I need to create space for other people in my life. I thought she was referring to her, our family, or even my friends.

Now I'm wondering if she saw something else. Maybe a certain loneliness that has me vacationing in Paris alone.

## 9

## STEPHANIE

I'm slightly hungover, thanks to one or two too many vodka sodas last night. The bartender, Devan, who is now wiping down the breakfast bar, smiles at me as I set up my laptop along the far side.

"Good morning, Stephanie," he says, his grin telling me he knows just how hungover I am.

"Good morning, Devan," I echo.

"Water? Coffee?"

"All of the above, please."

A few minutes later, he brings over both. "Have you heard from Rod?"

After my call with Ollie, I spilled the entire sordid story to Devan, who thankfully was having a slow enough night that he didn't mind listening to me going on and on about my boy problems.

I nod. "He texted me this morning saying they're on their way back."

"Good," he says, returning to the bar.

I chug my water and take a few cautious sips of the hot coffee before turning my attention to the proposal I'm hoping to crank out today. My boss forwarded me an outline of the client's request last night, and at first glance it seems simple enough that I might be able to start and finish it today.

Rod already left Arenal, but he still has a few hours until he'll be back in Manuel Antonio, assuming traffic isn't too bad.

So I request another water, which I chug immediately, throw down the rest of the coffee, and put my nose into my work. It's difficult to concentrate today even with my medicine, so I need to power through this morning because by the time Rod gets back, there will be way too many distractions to truly focus.

When I'm done, I order some lunch and check my phone. I worked a little later than I planned, and although Rod isn't technically *late* for anything, I did kind of expect him to be here by now.

I sigh, taking a bite of my sandwich and checking my text messages again.

OLLIE

Have a terrible time, Tulip.

I nearly spit out my food.

STEPH

Your texts should come with a choking warning.

OLLIE

We both know that's not a problem for you.

*Am I hallucinating?* I read the text again. This is the first time either of us has even hinted at the night we spent together.

OLLIE

Oops, did I say that out loud?

I put my sandwich down and pick up the phone. *What is he playing at?*

STEPH

I didn't hear anything.

OLLIE

Oh good. That would have been embarrassing.

STEPH

But I can't blame you for obsessing.

OLLIE

That's an understatement, Wildflower.

My jaw drops.

"I take it you've made up?" Devan asks, pulling my attention from my phone. He stacks pint glasses on the bar between us.

"Uh," I say, dumbly.

He raises his eyebrows, nodding to my phone as he wipes down a beer glass.

"I haven't talked to Rod yet."

He nods and then moves on to the glasses further down the bar. I turn my attention back to my phone.

"Where's he staying when he gets back?" Devan asks, taking me away again.

"Uh, I assumed here," I say, my mind running with Ollie's words.

He shakes his head. "We're all booked here," he says. "Most of Manuel Antonio is actually, unless you want to get into the real high-end stuff. Doesn't seem like their style, though."

I drop my phone on the bar and look at him. "So are you telling me that if they come back here, they have no place to stay?"

He shrugs. "Not in town, at least."

"Do they know that?"

He gives me a look. "I don't know."

I give Ollie's text another longing look before exiting out and calling Rod. I just hope he's not cooped up with the other four of them in the car, all of them judging me for being *that kind* of traveler while I ask him, as nicely as I can, where the fuck he is.

He answers on the second ring.

"Stephanie," he says, his voice light. There are voices in the background, but they sound far away–definitely not like they're all squished into a car together.

"Rod, where are you?"

"We stopped at Monteverde on our way back and ran into some friends we met in Nicaragua. You should come! You would love this place. There are something like five hundred species of orchids in the forest here."

I'm about to tell him off when I catch what he says. "Native orchids?"

"Yes!" he says, his voice so lively for a second that I think he might be genuinely excited to share this with me.

But if this trip has taught me anything, he's only excited about seeing me until the next shiny thing comes along. I consider the drive–consider the *orchids*–but at this point, I'm not even sure I trust Rod to be there if I make the trip.

*How far am I going to chase him across this country before realizing he'll never care enough to chase me back?*

"Rod, I thought we were going to do this together."

Gravel crunches under his footsteps as the voices around him fade.

"I know, Steph. That's why I invited you to come here. I want to do this with you."

I sigh. "But you left without me yesterday. You've made all these moves without me, when I came here *for you*. You're inviting me along like I'm just some friend you met in Nicaragua."

"Hey, I'm sorry," he says, his voice lowering. "I don't want you to feel that way. But you were working, and they wanted to continue on to the next place. I didn't want to make waves."

"Why are they coming first, though? You said you wanted to do this together, too, so why are their decisions coming before ours?"

He's quiet for a second. "Look, Steph, this is just the way we've always done things. I didn't mean to make you feel secondary. And honestly, I kind of wanted to see Arenal after you talked it up so much. You have your car and your room. You're self-sufficient here, but our group isn't. We rely on each other."

Devan sets a drink on the bar in front of me that looks suspiciously like a vodka soda.

"So how do you see us doing this? Like, traveling in a group, sleeping three to a queen bed until we're old and gray?"

"Well, what's so bad about that? This works for us. You want to work and live in luxury and that's fine, but I want the freedom that comes with this lifestyle."

I take a sip of the drink. "So because I work and want a private room, I don't fit in with the group?"

"No no no no no," he says. "Steph, you will always fit in here. It's whether you want to."

"Whether I want to?"

"It's your choice. I would love to be with you, to do life with you, but I've finally hit my stride here. I'm finally living the way I want to live." He lets out a deep breath that blows into the phone. "Stephanie, there will always be a part of me that loves you, but it's not easy to build a traveling group like this. This is what I've always wanted. This is truly fulfilling to me. I'm not ready to give this up."

None of this is new information to me, but it hits a little differently today.

In the same way I've been so protective of my schedule–of my job and my peace–he's been protecting his travel experience. We might have different reasons–me, for my ADHD; and him, for fulfilling a life dream–but does that mean either one of us should give that up?

I'm not sure I'll ever understand what he sees in traveling this way, but I suppose it was a little disrespectful of me to expect him to give up everything to fit into the way I want to travel.

I just thought it would be better. I thought having space and the ability to rent a private room would be a no-brainer.

But to him, the routine necessary for that isn't worth it.

And I know, now, that for me, routine is non-negotiable.

"I understand," I say. "Maybe in another life."

"I'm sorry, Steph."

I swallow over the lump building in my throat. "Me too."

As I end the call, I take a quivering breath and a long sip of the drink in front of me. Devan has one eyebrow raised, leaning against the bar across from me, and I do my best not to let the emotion show on my face. I don't need to add an instance of crying into my drink to my Costa Rica trip.

Our relationship has never not been messy. And now that I've tried to clean it up a little, I've learned that it was messy by design, Rod's preferred way of living life. I think there was a part of me that knew this wouldn't work out, but there was a stronger part of me that really wanted to be proven wrong.

"Are you okay?" Devan asks.

I nod, biting my lip to keep the tears in.

He keeps an eye on me as he pours two shots on the counter in front of us and hands one to me. I throw mine back as he does his, and the burn in my throat cancels out the lump growing there.

"So what's next?" he asks, clearing the shot glasses from the bar.

I take a deep breath and suck in another mouthful of vodka soda.

"I'm going to Paris."

I LEAVE the rest of my drink on the bar, along with a hefty tip and heartfelt hug for Devan, and head upstairs to book a flight to Paris. I throw my stuff haphazardly into my suitcase and backpack, and load them into the back of the car. My flight leaves late tonight, but I don't want to take chances with traffic.

I plug my music into the rental car and lean into the drive, embracing the start of my European adventure.

And I try my hardest to ignore the eighteen hours of travel I have ahead of me, thanks to a layover in Madrid.

About twenty minutes out from the rental car drop off point and *hours* early for my flight, I spot a sign along the side of the road boasting sloth tours. I slam on my brakes and turn in.

I'm not leaving Costa Rica without seeing a fucking sloth.

I wait in line with a German family, a group of American high schoolers, and two girls about my age who speak fluent Spanish to each other. Our tour guide, a guy who introduced himself exuberantly as Brandon, scans the trees as we follow him along the path.

He stops for a moment, lounging casually against a tree stump.

"As you can see, a sloth's natural habitat includes plenty of trees and green things, so they're generally vegetarian, though you might see them indulging in the occasional insect—ants or termites." He turns to what looks like a hive behind him and reaches inside.

"This is a termite nest," he says, pulling his hand out covered in small brown insects. "And they are great sources of protein." He puts his finger in his mouth, sucking off the bugs, and gives a dramatic *ahh*, before wiping off the rest of the termites on a nearby tree trunk.

His attention turns to the trees, and I catch the eye of one of the Spanish-speaking girls in my group. She gives me a look and mouths, "What the fuck?"

Apparently that's universal.

"And here's a sloth," he says casually, motioning behind us.

I whip around, searching the trees, and for a second I wonder if these things must be invisible, because I can't even see them when one is right in front of me.

And then I spot the little ball of white fur. He's moving slowly, his little claws reaching out and slowly, slowly, slowly, pulling him up the tree trunk.

"Oh my god," I mutter, pulling out my phone to take a picture. The others in my group are doing the same.

"Would anyone like a picture with Maria here?" he asks.

"Me!" I shout, unashamedly, and hand my phone over to him. I throw on my best smile as he lines up the camera and takes a picture of me with Maria. Before he hands it back to me, he quickly turns it around and snaps a picture of all three of us, throwing a peace sign with a few lingering termites crawling up his fingers.

I laugh as he hands the phone back to me with a grin.

That picture's getting framed.

He does the same for the rest of the people on the tour, and a giddy feeling takes root in my gut that I *finally* saw a sloth.

Before the end of the tour, I get pictures with Jose, Ana, Jimena, Daniel, and Carlos. When we're done, I fire off pictures to everyone I can think of, including Ollie because I don't really know how to answer his texts yet and sloth pictures seem like a reasonable way out of trying to.

STEPH

Here's your fucking sloth!

And then I realize I should probably also tell him I'm coming to Paris. This morning was such a whirlwind it didn't really occur to me to.

STEPH

Also, see you in Paris!

I take a screenshot of my ticket and send it off to him. Just in case.

I return my car and take a bus back to the airport, using the couple of hours before my flight leaves to get a head start on tomorrow's work.

And once on board, I do my best to think about anything other than this stupid flight. It's a necessity to get to the places I want to go, but I can't help thinking planes were invented by a sadist who wanted to stick too many people in a flying death trap and just see what happens.

And after another short flight from Madrid to Paris, I've finally arrived.

The flights were long, but somehow the journey just to get out of the airport feels even longer. I pause before the doors to pull my jacket on and restart my phone yet another time–it's telling me I have service but no texts are coming through–because I sent *a lot* of sloth pictures before leaving.

And a small part of me hopes that Ollie texted. That maybe he's sent me the address of where he's staying or a bar to meet him at.

I start to wonder if he meant it when he said I should come to Paris.

As I stare at the bars at the top of my phone, I feel a deep discomfort in my gut. I went to Costa Rica almost flippantly and had no issues confessing my feelings to Rod. Yet now that I'm in Paris after one dirty text from Ollie, something about this feels like so much more.

But maybe I'm just tired. I've been traveling for eighteen hours and in Costa Rica, it's morning.

Maybe I should just find a place to stay and get settled–I can follow up with Ollie in the morning.

I'm about to restart my phone one more time when I hear someone call my name.

"Stephanie!"

When I turn, a gust of a breath leaves my body, and I smile at the familiar face. He grins back at me, big green eyes as welcoming as ever and the dimples showing in his cheeks. Dark jeans and a dark shirt, with a thick jacket over top.

"Ollie." I drop my bags on the ground next to me and go

in for a hug, his arms wrapping easily around my neck and pulling me close. He smells like soap and something woody like cedar, and I can't help pressing my face into his chest, breathing him in. "You met me at the airport."

"Of course I did."

# 10

## OLIVER

She looks good in jeans, with a little sun on her face. A hair tie is woven loosely into her hair that looks like it's about to fall out, and I grab it before it does, the blue and purple and blonde strands between my fingers inspiring thoughts of her birthday night.

"Oh," she says, taking it from me. "Wow, I thought my hair felt funny."

"Flights," I explain, as I pull away from her.

She pulls the hair tie onto her wrist and runs her fingers through her hair, and I'm hit with whatever shampoo she uses that always smells so nice. Like some combination of mango and banana.

I reach down and pick up the suitcase that clattered to the floor when she hugged me, and she winds the backpack over her shoulder. "Thank you," she says, and I don't think she's referring to the bag.

"No problem." I lead her outside to where my cab is impatiently waiting.

I try to get a read on her while loading the suitcase in the trunk and joining her in the backseat. Our texts yesterday were flirty–thanks to a little too much wine on my part–and then totally stopped.

And now she's in Paris.

She doesn't seem upset, but I can only imagine something happened with Rod if she chose to abandon her big trip in favor of coming here.

Almost like she's choosing me over him.

But I push that thought from my mind. That feels like dangerous territory.

"How was your flight?" I ask as we fall into the backseat and the driver pulls away from the curb.

She sighs, leaning back into the seat. "It was tiring." Her eyes are a little dark.

"How long was your travel time? I saw you had a layover."

She raises her eyebrows. "You checked my flight?"

I shrug. "Well, yeah. I had to check it if I wanted to know when to pick you up."

A hint of a smile flutters across her face. "That was really nice of you."

"Just human decency."

She rolls her eyes. "I didn't give you much notice. It would have been totally understandable if you couldn't make it work." She glances down at her phone as it buzzes in her lap. "Oh thank god," she mutters, checking her messages. "I thought my phone wasn't working. I guess it just needed some time."

She grins at the texts as they come in. "Okay, so the sloth pictures were a big hit."

"Of course they were. They were adorable." More because of her than the sloths, but I won't say that out loud. I don't know what mental space she's in right now, and I don't want to overwhelm her.

"They are so fucking cute," she says. She slides closer to me, her thigh rubbing up against mine, and turns her phone toward me. I throw my arm over the back of the seat to give her more room, and she nestles into me, swiping through picture after picture of her sloth friends.

"I can't believe you saw so many," I say, hardly paying attention to the pictures because the heat of her body against mine reminds me so viscerally of her bare skin. In the darkness of the backseat, I can close my eyes and it's like no time has passed at all, like we're right back in her bed, bare skin to bare skin. "How did you find them all?"

She flips to another picture, this one with a very tan guy with a mass of curly hair on his head.

I'm paying attention again.

"I went on a sloth tour where you're guaranteed at least three sightings," she says. "And this is Brandon, the tour guide, who will live forever in my mind because"–she zooms in to a few black spots on his hand–"see those spots? Those are termites."

"Ew."

She turns to me. "He straight up stuck his hand in a termite nest and *ate* them."

"Just when I thought it couldn't get worse."

She grins. "Naturally, I asked him to marry me, so after my trip to Paris I'll be returning to Costa Rica to shack up with the love of my life and eat termites for dinner every night."

The words pop out of my mouth before I can think through them. "At least I know what I'm up against."

I swallow quickly, taking a second to gauge her reaction.

Her brow raises almost imperceptibly, and then she smiles. "There's no competition," she says, leaning back into me. A beat of silence passes. "Sorry, Ollie, you just can't beat a man who eats termites for dinner."

I snicker. "You seem like the kind of girl who's into bug-eating."

"Only as it pertains to carnivorous plants."

"Nothing sexier than the snap of a Venus Flytrap," I say, suddenly wondering who out of her friends is babysitting her carnivorous plants.

"So you get it." She leans her head back into my shoulder, sighing as she looks up at me. I *like* having her tucked into me like this. "Thanks for inviting me to Paris."

"Thanks for making the trip."

I know she didn't technically come here *for me*, but there's a part of me that's flattered that she totally rearranged her plans to make this part of her trip work. I'm sure that if shit didn't hit the fan with Rod, she would have gotten here eventually, probably with him in tow, and they would have had a delightful little Euro trip.

Not because of him, of course, but because she carries a certain lightness with her wherever she goes.

She looks so perfect right now that for a second I think this is the right time to kiss her, her body pressed up against mine and the glow of Parisian street lights filtering through the windows.

And then we hit a pothole, jarring us from our little trance.

"*Désolé, désolé!*"

"*C'est bon,*" I say, glancing back down at Steph. Her attention has strayed to the windows, watching as the highway melts into city streets.

When we get to the hotel, I grab her suitcase from the trunk and show her into the courtyard and along the brick walkway to my room. I leave it between the bed and the pullout couch, unsure what to expect from the night. I'm apprehensively planning on taking the couch myself, but ideally, we'll just sleep in bed together.

Nothing has to come from it, after all, if she doesn't want it to. But as thin as the mattress is on that couch, it should probably be avoided at all costs.

She falls into a kitchen chair, pulling that mermaid hair over her shoulder and tying it into a ponytail. "My God, I'm exhausted." I take the seat next to her.

"You should probably push through if you can," I say. "We can get some dinner, if you're hungry. Spend a few hours out and then come back and crash."

She nods. "Even if I try to go to sleep right now I don't think my medicine will let me, but I am *so* tired." She rubs her eyes, a motion that's somehow both endearing and erotic at the same time.

"Come on," I say, helping her up by the elbow. She follows me to the door. "There's a little place down the street I've had my eye on. Besides, I think you owe me a story."

I slide the second room key into her hand, and her head cocks to the side as she looks at me. "A story?" She pulls her wallet out of her backpack and loops it over her wrist.

"Yeah. The one about how you drunk dialed me in the middle of the night and a day later showed up half a world away to hang out with me."

She grins. "You're just trying to come between me and my termite-eating lover."

I lock the door behind us as we step outside, getting a whiff of warm mango and banana again as she passes me. "I think that's for your own good."

## 11

## STEPHANIE

I always knew Oliver was attractive, but seeing him in Paris is totally different. He's so relaxed, and even though he says his French is terrible, it sounds like silk. He translates the menu for me and orders for us, and only a minute or so later our server leaves two small glasses of champagne on our table.

He leans back in his chair, his body too big for this small cafe, and checks over his shoulder to make sure he's not infringing on the next table's space.

When he turns back to me, he's grinning. "So tell me, Steph, what happened between the drunk dial and your arrival in Paris?"

I take a thirsty sip of my drink, and run him through the whole sordid story, a well of unresolved emotions bubbling up as I get to The Break Up Phone Call.

"I just wish that for once, I got to be the one in control of this relationship. We've been on-again-off-again for so many years now, and almost every single time it's been because of something he's decided without me. Like I'm just along for the ride for however long it takes him to get sick of me." I shake my head, taking a hasty sip of my drink to stamp down the tears threatening to make an appearance. "For once, I want to be the one to make the decision. Not the person who holds on too long but the one who tells him, face to face with no distractions or travel buddies in the periphery that I'm done with him. Once and for all." I take a breath, eyeing Ollie. "You probably think I'm nuts."

He sits pensively, looking out over the small crowd in the cafe, nodding but not providing any feedback.

"You want closure," he says simply. "I don't think that's so nutty."

I shrug, taking another long sip of my drink. "I guess you could call it that. It just feels immature, like I have to stick it to him for the sake of—I don't know—coming out on top."

Ollie grins. "Steph, there is no doubt in my mind that you won that breakup."

I snort. "That feels immature, too."

He shakes his head. "It's not immature. Sometimes you need to assign a winner or loser to big emotions to make them feel a little more manageable."

I eye Ollie. Sometimes I forget about the somewhat subdued, introspective man hidden underneath the layer of grins and jokes.

"You don't think less of me?" I ask.

His face is unreadable for a moment, and then he smiles. "I think you're remarkable," he says, but the stoic expression on his face makes me wonder whether this is a compliment or not. "I think it takes a special person to love in the way you do, freely and without requirements." He shakes his head. "It makes me worry for you, sometimes, like one day you're going to get hurt and it's going to take that away from you."

I shrug, heat creeping up my neck. "That's life, isn't it?"

I'm painfully aware of the conversation we still haven't had about my birthday. It hangs between us as we delicately poke at it, allude to it, dance around it, as if saying it aloud suddenly makes it real and until that moment it's only a fantasy.

But all of this talk about love and relationships has me wondering what he's thinking. There's *something* here–he invited me, and I hopped on a plane–but I don't know what it is. *Mutual attraction? Definitely.* And I'm not opposed to falling into bed with him and making the most of this vacation together.

*But he worries for me? Because I love too freely?*

It gives me a warm feeling in my chest, and if anything, I become more dedicated to loving so freely, if that's what we're calling it.

"It's nice that you worry about me," I say, smiling sweetly at him. "But it's going to take a lot more than Rod to take that away from me."

He nods. "Good. He's not worth another second of your time."

*And you are?*

I shrug. "We just want different things. He's not a bad person because of it. I'm glad he laid it out for me."

Ollie shakes his head. "He didn't need to have you running around a foreign country by yourself before telling you that. That was"–he seems to have trouble finding the right words, gesturing in front of his face as if he can sift them from the air. "I mean, God, Steph, that was downright dangerous."

A laugh bursts from my chest. "Downright dangerous?"

"Yeah. I mean, you're traveling alone in a country you don't know"–I raise my eyebrows–"driving for hours on treacherous roads. The scams alone are enough to cause concern, not to mention the pickpockets."

"This, coming from a fellow traveler," I say. "You do it just fine."

He shakes his head. "It's different for me. Most of my travel is in Europe, a smidge in Japan. At this point, I've been to a lot of these places already. But you, hopping on a plane to an undeveloped country you've never been to before, renting a car and a place to stay alone? I am simultaneously in awe and having serious regret about ever letting it happen."

I pause before taking a sip of my champagne. "Letting it happen?"

He reconsiders his words and then doubles down. "I took you to the airport. I could have turned around and put an end to that whole trip."

"I would have gotten another flight. And then billed you for the one I missed."

He shrugs. "Would have been worth every penny."

I watch his face as I speak. "But I wouldn't be here now, if you did."

He nods. "That would have been an issue."

A beat of silence passes. "An issue?"

Our server arrives with our first course: two very small salmon crostinis and two glasses of red wine.

When I look back at Ollie, he smiles at me, our spell broken. "Well yeah, I can't eat all this food by myself."

I laugh as I reach forward and pick up one of the miniature crostinis, and he takes the other.

"Oh man, I think I'm full already," I say, taking a bite.

He snorts, taking the entirety of his in one bite. "I think if I eat anything more, I'll pop."

"You better be careful eating like that or you're going to make yourself sick."

He shakes his head. "I'm going to have to hit the gym extra hard when I get back from this vacation." He makes a show of patting his stomach.

"Yeah, wouldn't want to lose those abs of yours," I say, my mouth going dry as I speak. The memory of my birthday night thaws the February chill that's settled in my bones since I stepped out of the airport.

He cocks his head to the side, a slow smile spreading across his face, and heat runs up into my cheeks. I take a hasty sip of wine, abandoning the rest of the crostini on the plate in front of me.

"I definitely wouldn't. Especially now that I know you're checking me out."

I put my wine back on the table. "I mean, I have eyes."

"That you use to check me out," he says.

"Well, when you're naked there's not much else to look at!"

He rears back, trying unsuccessfully to tamp down the grin on his face. "So we're talking about that night now?"

"How else would I know you have abs?"

He shrugs, glancing down at himself. "I don't know. Thought maybe you could see them through my shirt?"

"What are they, cartoon abs? You can't see abs through shirts." I shake my head. "At least we know how highly you think of yourself now, that apparently your abs are so big they defy human biology."

"Well, maybe not my *abs*," he quips.

"Oh my god," I mutter, hiding my face in my hands.

He reaches across the table, pulling my hands into his. "Steph, why the embarrassment?"

The feel of his hands on mine soothes me. I take a

breath, urging my face to cool. "Because we haven't talked about it."

"We're talking about it now."

My leg jiggles under the table, but his hands still surround mine so I can't nervously down more wine.

"I'm not embarrassed," I start. "It's just, you know, three months ago, *that* happened."

"We had sex," he fills in the blank for me and the heat rushes to my face again.

"Yes, we had sex," I repeat, and just saying it out loud makes my blood pump faster. "And it was like nothing ever happened. Which is totally fine with me. I think that's what we were both after, that night. But now, us being here together–it feels different."

"Different from how we were that night? Or different from how we've been since?"

I struggle to find the right words. "Both? I mean, we're here, in Paris, together. Like, our actions are saying something different than the lack of words between us over the past three months."

He nods, taking a sip of his wine with one hand, his other still wrapped around mine. "They are, aren't they?"

I wait. "Do you have anything to add?"

He shrugs, and for a second, I think he's going to leave it at that. "Look, why don't we just take things as they go?" he suggests. "We don't have to label anything. We're on vacation in Paris together, you know?"

I nod, digesting his words.

"Steph, your shoulders are up at your ears. Relax," he says, reaching over and placing his hands on them. "It's simultaneously too early and too late to have the what-are-we conversation, don't you think?"

"I guess so. It was just weird, going so long pretending it

didn't happen to, you know, meeting you in Paris. Although in my defense, you started it."

"I started it?"

"Yeah, with that text you sent me."

His eyebrows crinkle. "Uh, no, you started it the night before when you drunk dialed me."

"How did that start anything? That was like, the least sexual drunk dial I've ever made."

"Wildflower?"

I forgot about that part. My cheeks turn red again.

"Oh, don't get shy on me now," he says. "Not to mention, if we're talking about who started things, I think your birthday makes you the pursuer here."

"Only because you made it very clear before that night that you'd be willing to fulfill that need for me."

"I'd say there's a big difference between me telling you you're hot and you getting on the phone and demanding sexual favors."

I swallow. "Jesus Christ, I'm going to burn up," I say, holding my cold hands on my face.

"Am I getting you all hot and bothered?"

"Oh my god, Ollie, stop!"

The server brings over our main course, and I quickly gobble down the rest of my crostini while I have the chance. I take a big gulp of wine as the plate is cleared, and Ollie eyes me, a devilish little grin on his face.

He keeps his eyes on me as the server refills my drink, and then leans in closer just as I'm about to take a bite of my food. "I think it was more along the lines of"–his voice goes higher, mocking me—"Oh my god, Ollie, don't stop! Right there!'"

I let my fork fall to my plate, shooting him a look, and he snorts into his food.

"You're cute when you're embarrassed," he says, taking a bite.

"Yeah, well, you're–"

"I'm what?"

My words fail me, and I take a bite of my chicken instead, shaking my head.

"Handsome when I smile?" He throws me a put-on grin. "Sexy when I smolder?" He gives me joking bedroom eyes.

"Funny when you're horny," I say.

He scrunches up his face, thinking about this. "I can't decide whether to take that as a compliment that you think I'm funny *in general*, including when I'm naked, or prepare myself to be laughed at when I'm naked."

"Awfully presumptuous of you." I take a bite of the veggies on my plate, feeling like I finally have a handle on this conversation.

He presses his lips together. "Whoops. I'm going to stop talking now." He focuses on the food in front of him, skewering a baby potato with his fork. "Although I can't help but notice you didn't deny any of my suggestions, so I can only assume that in addition to being funny when I'm horny, I'm also handsome when I smile and sexy when I smolder."

I narrow my eyes. "I decline to comment." I cut off a piece of chicken and pop it in my mouth.

He grins. "Stephy thinks I'm handsome," he says in a singsong voice.

*Yup, he is definitely handsome when he smiles.* I point my fork at him. "You thought I was hot first."

He nods. "Still do."

Those two simple words send a rush of fire into my abdomen.

The server comes over to clear our plates and refill our wine, and we order a crème brûlée to split. I'm a little buzzed, and as Ollie clinks his glass to mine, I can't help but notice the way my cheeks hurt from the silly grin I've been wearing all night.

It feels so good to laugh like this.

"So now that we've established we're both attractive," he starts, with a quick grin that I mirror without thinking, "tell me about Costa Rica." He leaves his utensils on his plate and pushes it away. "Other than the Rod business." He adds a quick eye roll.

I take a sip of my wine and let out a long breath. "I would happily die in Arenal. Everyone was so nice and welcoming, and the wildlife was incredible. Didn't see many animals, but I'm okay with that. They were just off living their lives and I decided to drop in for a bit. It was peaceful."

"So you'd go back?"

I nod vigorously. "Oh, absolutely. Maybe not to Manuel Antonio–that was very lively and touristy, great to visit once–but definitely to Arenal. I was bummed because right before I left, Rod called me"–Ollie gives me a look—"He's relevant to the story," I explain. "So Rod called me telling me to come to Monteverde, which is pretty close to Arenal, because in the forest there are five hundred different species of orchids. Five hundred! And I didn't get to see them."

Ollie cocks his head to the side. "I thought you weren't a fan of orchids."

I was considering getting an orchid tattoo first, and then Ollie suggested wildflowers instead.

"I like orchids. I just kill them."

The server slides our dessert onto the table, freshly torched, and we thank him quickly.

"Something about that is very metal."

"Metal?" I ask, grabbing a spoon and taking a bite of crème brûlée so delicious I might melt in my seat.

He takes from the other side of the ramekin. "Yeah, like, 'everything I like dies,'" he says.

I snort. "Plant parenting is pretty metal honestly. Making pretty things appear from dirt. And it all happens so slowly too. I've had days where I've literally watched my plants grow, you know? And you *can't* see it happening. But you do get the occasional leaf unfurling if you pay close enough attention; that's super rewarding. But yeah, the only change you can really notice is when you leave and come back and suddenly things are *there* where there were none before. It's spooky, really."

His smile is softer this time, his playful grin transforming to something lighter as he listens.

"You didn't need to know all that," I say.

He shrugs. "No, but now I feel a greater sense of duty to the plants you gave me. It's obvious how important they are to you." He pushes the last of the crème brûlée toward me. "All yours."

I fight a quick battle in my brain over how quickly I should shovel down the last of this dessert. On one hand, I'm not kidding when I say I *need it inside of me*, and on the other, I don't want to take away whatever it is about myself that Ollie thinks is hot.

I throw caution to the wind and gobble it down, briefly considering licking the ramekin but deciding against it.

"That was incredible," I say.

"Good. I've had my eye on this place. I'm happy it worked out."

"Me too," I say, and then continue without thinking. "It's nice to eat with someone."

His eyebrows crinkle together, a hint of pity crossing over his face, but he has the courtesy to ignore it. "I'm glad I could be that someone."

We have another drink at the table, and by the time the server drops off our bill, I'm bordering on drunk.

Ollie smiles. "Dinner for the weary traveler on me," he says, and I think I might fall over.

"You don't have to do that."

"I'd like to," he says.

"You're just trying to get in my plants."

He raises his eyebrows.

"My pants," I correct, my tongue heavy. I shake my head. "I think I had too much wine."

He grins. "*Bienvenue à Paris,*" he says. The server comes over with the card machine and he swipes.

"Thank you," I say.

"My pleasure."

His hand rests on the small of my back as we weave through tables to the sidewalk out front. I zip my jacket against the cold, and his arm falls easily over my shoulders, tucking me into his side as we walk.

*And, god, I could fall asleep walking like this.*

His warmth and my tiredness make a lethal combination, my eyes begging for sleep.

When we get back to the room, I'm tempted to beeline for the bed, but I need a shower first. Not to mention, that might make me the presumptuous one. There was plenty of flirting tonight, but that doesn't magically mean I'm welcome to his bed.

"I desperately need to shower," I say as we get inside.

He nods. "Go, be clean."

I dig through my bags for my shower stuff and something clean to wear to bed, and hop in. His body wash sits on one of the shelves, and I take a moment to smell it. I'm immediately transported back to my birthday night, the cedar scent of his skin as my lips brushed against his chest, the way he gripped my hips so roughly.

I put the body wash back on the shelf. The faster I finish this shower, the faster we can reenact the naughty things we did that night.

When I step back into the room, my hair woven up into a towel, he's shirtless, and my mouth nearly goes dry at the sight.

"I'm just going to hop in real quick too," he says, one hand on my hip as he leaves a kiss on my forehead. My fingers trail over the bare skin of his torso, the abs that he expected to show through his shirt.

"Yeah," I say, my brain struggling to find any other words.

He disappears into the bathroom, and I hear the water turn on again.

And now I don't know what to do. His body wash inspired fantasies of desperate undressing and frenzied kisses, and now I just have to wait patiently for him to come back.

I pull the towel out of my hair, hanging it on the back of the kitchen chair to dry, and plop down on the edge of the pull-out.

And a metallic screech rings in the air as the bed folds up around me, sandwiching me like a piece of meat between the two halves.

"Steph!"

The bed shakes and creaks as strong hands pull me out by my legs, wrapping around my knees and my hips and my back as he slowly extricates me from the woman-eating couch.

"Are you alright?" he asks, smoothing down my hair. He has one arm around my back, holding me close to him, as his eyes travel up and down my body, searching for injuries.

"Uh, I think so," I say, taking stock of each limb. I glance down, looking for cuts or the beginnings of bruises, and quickly realize he's naked.

"Oh my god," I say, the words slipping out, and I avert my eyes.

"Nothing you haven't seen before," he says, a hint of a smile playing across his face. His fingers dance along my back, sending warm tingles down my spine.

"It was still unexpected," I say.

He nods, clearing his throat. "Yeah, I'm going to go shower now while I'm still able to." His arm tightens around my waist, and he presses his lips against my temple. I close my eyes as his breath rushes over my skin.

He steps away from me, turning toward the shower. "And get in the bed, you silly girl." With one palm on my hip, he pushes me, my knees connecting with the bed and sending me tumbling.

He disappears into the bathroom again and I stare at the ceiling, wondering how just a week ago I flew to Costa Rica to profess my love to Rod, only to end up in Paris about to sleep with Ollie.

I run my hands over my face, the mental image of Ollie's words and his naked body fresh in my mind when I close my eyes.

*Get in the bed, you silly girl.*

## 12

## OLIVER

I shower at a record pace, eager to join Steph in bed. Only a few hours ago I was apprehensive about her joining me, but sometime during dinner, things took a turn. The pink in her cheeks when we finally talked about our night together told me everything I needed to know.

And the way she bit her lip when I pulled her out of the couch. She averted her gaze quickly, but I caught the way she looked at me, her eyes wide and her breathing shallow.

I've been waiting to repeat that night for months. I didn't want to push her. Steph is looking for her big love, and that's something that I just can't be for her. But if she's looking for a rebound...

We're both here and obviously still attracted to each other. My muscles are nearly spasming with anticipation.

I dry off at warp speed and wrap the towel around myself before stepping back into the bedroom, imagining some swift undressing. I can already feel the silk of the sleep shorts she put on, the warmth of her skin through them.

She wasn't wearing a bra, and I can nearly taste the little pointed tip of her nipple.

But when I step into the bedroom, I'm met with the sound of mild snoring.

She's splayed out across the bed, her arms above her head and one knee open toward my side. Her mouth is slightly agape, her face relaxed and her nose twitching adorably.

She's fast asleep.

And I'm wrapped in a flimsy towel rocking a semi that I was really hoping she'd take care of.

I sigh, kicking myself for deciding a shower was more important than taking her when she was in my arms ten minutes ago. I wanted to be the best I could be for her, and that meant at least starting clean.

Instead of burying myself inside her like I'd really like to do, I pull on a pair of underwear and flick the lights off. I climb in next to her, nudging her knee so I have some room, too, and she tips easily onto her side, her breathing steady. I pull the blankets up and over us and wind my arms around her waist.

Tomorrow.

I WAKE to the sound of furious typing.

Steph is at the kitchen table on her laptop, her hair pulled into a messy bun on her head. Her face is pinched, like she's concentrating too hard on something.

She notices I'm awake when I reach over to grab my phone from the nightstand.

"Sorry," she says. "I was trying to be quiet."

I shake my head. "All good."

It's almost eight, so I actually slept in for once. I guess I really am on vacation.

I lean back in bed, throw my arm over my face, and lie there for a few minutes. I'm sure she wants to finish what she's working on before doing anything today, so I probably have plenty of time this morning to be lazy, maybe run out and pick up some espresso and croissants.

I don't think I've vacationed like this for a long time. Normally I stick to my schedule.

But I think I might actually do... whatever the hell I want.

It's freeing, to think that I can spend this day just how I'd like.

When I finally sit up, I run my hands over my face. Steph eyes me, her typing coming to a halt.

"What?" I ask.

"Nothing."

I grab a pair of sweatpants from my suitcase on the floor and pull them on, and transition immediately to the pillow on the floor by the large armoire. I narrowly avoid the folded up pull-out couch that looks to have a broken metal piece sticking out from the bottom. Thank god that didn't hit Steph.

I push the thought from my mind, sitting down on the pillow and doing my best to focus my mind. I start my fifteen-minute timer and clear my head.

I start my days with my mindfulness minutes, a term my mom coined more than a decade ago to make it sound like a *fun* exercise. It was one of her many attempts at giving me tools to work through my ADHD, and although I hated it at the time, it's the only coping strategy that's followed me into adulthood.

Taking fifteen minutes to center my mind every morning has made enough of a difference in my life that I can manage without medicine. I still have rough days sometimes, and if I'm under a lot of stress I'll go back on meds until I'm in a better place, but it's rewarding to know that I can mostly manage independently.

I always struggled with the whole taking-medicine-on-time thing, too. Stephanie seems to manage it well. She said something about being able to concentrate during work hours being as important as not having babies before she's ready for it, so she just put her birth control and ADHD meds on the same schedule and–*bam*–each pill encourages the other.

My mindfulness minutes are my coping mechanism. Her routine is hers.

She's done so well managing a later-in-life diagnosis.

Just as the thought of her inspires a smile spreading across my face, I smell mango.

I do this every morning–maybe not the thinking about Stephanie part, but the mindfulness part, at least. But I've never conjured a smell from thought.

"Steph," I warn, sure she must be directly in front of me.

"Yes?" She is.

"What are you doing?"

"I want to participate."

I open my eyes.

She's sitting cross-legged on the wood floor in front of me, mimicking my posture. Her hands rest loosely on her knees, her hair in a wild blue and purple and blonde pile on her head. She smiles at me and quirks her brow, like she's waiting for direction.

I don't know how she got over here so quietly, but I clock thick socks on her feet that probably aided her stealthy movement. She's still wearing her silky little sleep set from last night, and it makes me want to abandon the whole mindfulness thing and pull her straight down into bed. *Who needs to concentrate on vacation anyway?*

"Okay. Close your eyes."

She closes them, and I take a daring second to look at her, her chest rising and falling with each breath, her silk shorts barely covering her tanned thighs. Those ridiculous socks she has on.

"Just focus on what you hear. You don't have to name it. Just listen."

She nods, and I wonder if she knows that I'm looking at her or if it's just a reflex.

I force my eyes closed and do as I instructed.

We sit for a few minutes like that, and I can't help but search for the sounds of her moving. I don't hear her breathing or fidgeting. No growling stomach or little sniffs.

I open my eyes again when I'm about to transition into the second part of my mindfulness minutes, and I'm almost surprised to see she's still sitting in front of me, her eyes closed and perfectly still, a pensive but calm look on her face.

She jumps when I speak but keeps her eyes closed. "I usually finish up with a mind-body exercise. Something future-based to set an intention for the day. Like the feeling of my feet and how they'll ground me or move me, metaphorically or literally. So like today, my feet will move me through Paris and allow me a full vacation experience. My knees will bend to do the same, but maybe also bend to your preferences since you're joining me on my vacation. Stuff like that, whatever makes sense for you."

She grins, her eyes still closed. "I'm focusing on the feeling of Ollie's willpower as it bends to my every whim."

"Perfect," I say, stifling my laugh. I wonder what part of me, physically, corresponds to my willpower, because there's a lot of me that would be delighted to bend to her every whim.

Her smile softens as she focuses, and out of the corner of my eye, I see her toes wiggling.

*God, she's adorable.*

I don't want to close my eyes, but I know if I don't, I'll feel scattered all day. So I force them shut and do my best to focus on the exercise and not on the girl sitting in front of me. If anything, a strong distraction probably makes this all the more effective.

When my timer goes off, I open my eyes. Hers are still closed.

"Is it over?" she asks.

"Yeah, that was it."

She opens her eyes and nods. "That was fun."

"Worthwhile?"

"I think so. I don't think I'm very good at it, though. My mind kept wandering back to my work."

"That's why I usually do it first thing in the morning. Your mind was already set on work this morning, so that's what you keep coming back to. If it's something you want to keep doing I can wake up earlier for the next few days. We can do it together. It gets easier over time."

She cocks her head to the side. "You would wake up early on vacation for me?"

"Sure. I usually wake up a lot earlier anyway. When do you get up?"

"Five."

*She has to be joking.* "Five?"

"Well, yeah. In Costa Rica I woke up early so I could spend time with Rod in the afternoon, but once he ditched me I realized how well that works for traveling. You know, get work out of the way in the morning and the rest of the day I could do what I wanted, aside from the occasional meeting. But I think that's just the cost of being a digital nomad."

I snort. "Are you a digital nomad now?" I ask. I *have* to poke some fun at that. "Traveling for all of a week and you've got it all figured out, don't you?"

She gives me a look. "You of all people espouse routine. You should be flattered. I took your suggestions to heart."

"You did, didn't you?" I hold her gaze for a moment. "I don't know about waking up at five, though. I'm honestly surprised you were able to, after the time change and traveling yesterday."

She shrugs. "I woke up to pee and just stayed up. Benefits of a small bladder. It's okay, maybe I'll try it without you."

*That* sounds even worse than getting up at five.

"You know what? I can get up at five just fine. We'll do it together tomorrow."

She bites her lip, her eyebrows crinkled.

"Do you *want* to do it alone?"

She groans. "No, I don't. But I also don't want you getting up early for no reason and then just hanging out for hours. Part of the reason I'm getting up so early is so I'm not interrupting our day, you know? But if you're getting up at five, then you're just waiting around for me for hours."

"I don't mind."

She raises her eyebrows as if she's expecting me to keep talking.

"I don't. I'm on vacation."

"Right. *You're* on vacation. I technically still have to work, which directly impedes your vacation."

Her expression is pinched, and I can only assume this is some vestige of Rod's attitude toward her working rearing its ugly head.

"Stephanie." I reach out, placing my hand on hers. "Paris will wait for *us*."

"I don't want to ruin your vacation."

"You couldn't if you tried." She still doesn't look convinced. "It works out perfectly for division of labor, right? You work in the morning, and I take that time to work out, find us breakfast, and figure out what we're doing for the rest of the day. Honestly, I might need you to work a little longer so I have time to get through all of my tasks in the morning."

She narrows her eyes. "I will tentatively trust that you're not blowing smoke up my ass."

I hold my hands up. "No smoke."

She takes a breath. "Okay. Well in that case, I'd better get back to work."

She scrambles up from the floor, her overkill socks masking all sound.

"What's with the socks?" I ask, as she takes a seat at the kitchen table.

She motions to the sleep set she's wearing. "I packed for Central America." She holds one foot up so I get a better look. "These are what I wore to the airport and they're just about the only thing that keeps me warm."

"Don't you have a sweater or anything?"

She pauses as if waiting for me to catch up. "I packed for Costa Rica," she repeats. "The only warm thing I have is my jacket, which I wore over my one and only long sleeve, which is, well, super dirty at this point. And I just can't wear a puffy jacket over jammies." She makes a face and then shivers. "The texture of a coat on bare skin just gives me the heebie-jeebies."

I pull my bag over toward me and grab one of my long

sleeves, tossing it to her. She grabs it before it falls on her computer.

"Until we can get you to a store for some winter clothing, put that on."

A hint of a smile passes over her lips as she pulls it over her head. It's big, as expected, but it also looks *so fucking good* on her.

"Thank you," she says, pulling the sleeves over her hands and diving back into her work.

"You're welcome."

I grab my phone and scroll through some missed text messages, my parents asking how my trip is and my brother asking whether I've heard any news about the director of training position. As if on cue, I get a group text from Jack and Emma asking if I'm free for dinner tomorrow. I confirm that I am, but I tell them to make the reservation for four.

# 13

# STEPHANIE

Ollie runs out in the morning while I'm still working, and just as I'm finishing up my last email of the day, he returns, sending a flood of cool air through the small hotel room. I shiver as I turn to him, wrapping his sweater tighter around me.

"Brought you coffee," he says, resting it on the table next to me. "And"–he reaches into the small brown bag in his hands–"some fresh socks."

"You got me socks?"

He nods, grinning as he rips them from their cardboard backing. "I would have gotten you some winter clothes, but that sounded like a disaster waiting to happen. You can borrow my sweaters until we go shopping for you." He hands the socks to me, and I stare somewhat dumbly at him. "What, do you want me to put them on you, too?"

I laugh. "No. I guess I was just surprised. Thank you." I take the socks from him gently. They're made of thick wool and I'm sure they'll barely fit in my boots, but they feel *so* warm. I slip out of the old ones I'm wearing and pull the new ones over my feet, wiggling my toes into the ends.

He shrugs. "I wanted to treat myself to a little something, too, and the store next door happened to have socks. Felt a little bit like fate."

I close my laptop, turning to him and pulling the sleeves of his sweater down over my hands. "What did you get?"

"Just some stuff for drawing," he says.

I raise my eyebrows. Ollie is an incredible artist. Since college, he's hung out with the same group of guys who have game nights every other week or so, and we girls usually make a point to end our night with them. Every single time, I'm floored by whatever game board Ollie has put together. So much so that I asked him to draw the wildflowers that are now tattooed on my forearm.

"What are you going to draw?"

He lets out a long breath. "I don't know. I didn't really think that much about it. Just wanted to have something to do while you're working, you know? If it was just me, I might wander around a bit. Maybe watch TV in my down-time, but I don't want to disturb you."

"You can still do those things if you want," I say. "I don't want to throw a wrench into your vacation. I don't have to stay here, even. I can find another room."

"Stephanie," he warns.

"I know. You said. I guess I'm just a little out of my element."

He takes the seat next to me, dumping out his brown bag of materials onto the table next to my laptop. "Why is that?"

I bite my lip, watching as he flips to the first page in his brand new sketchpad and slowly lines up all of his new materials. Pencils, pens, charcoals. "I feel like I'm Rod but with more requirements."

His attention turns to me, his eyebrows raising. "What does that mean?"

"I'm a freeloader who shows up when I want to, disrupts everything you were planning on doing, and then comes up with their own ideas of how travel should be done and *you* have to fit in with what *I* want."

He laughs as he uncaps the pen and draws a quick line across the sketchpad. "I probably shouldn't be so thrilled that you came to that conclusion on your own about Rod."

I huff. "That was so not the point."

He shrugs, throwing me a grin as he drags a pencil across his sketchpad. "Stephy, you're easy. So you need to sit in front of your little laptop for a portion of the day. You realize I was vacationing by myself, right?" He turns the page in his sketchpad and leans back, balancing it on the edge of the table.

"Yes, I realize that," I say, a hint of snark slipping into my words.

He gives me a look and I bite my lip, pulling one leg up onto my chair and resting my chin on my knee.

"You made big moves for somebody who doesn't care for you in the same way you care for him. That's a little fucked. But now we're both here by happenstance, with no obligations except you to your job. I don't mind working around your schedule if that means you'll join me for dinner at night."

I can't help the smile that comes to my lips. "Yeah?"

His eyes flash. "Wait, keep that smile on your face."

I raise my eyebrows. "What?"

"No, not the surprise face. The smile."

"Ollie, are you drawing me?"

He doesn't answer, but he presses his lips together as his eyes dart rapidly from my face down to his sketchpad.

"Ollie," I say.

His eyes flick back to mine. "Yeah, that smile right there."

"Ollie."

"The bashful one is cute too, but save that for the next drawing."

The heat rushes to my cheeks every time he glances at me.

And a few minutes later, when he's done, he flips the sketchpad over and slides it across the table to me.

I can't help but grin at his version of me. I want to cringe at the wild hair, the oversized sweater and the chunky socks, but there's something about the entire sketch that comes together so flawlessly that it all seems like a necessary part of the whole.

I run my fingers along the side of the page. "You made me so pretty."

He shrugs. "I just drew what I saw."

## 14

## OLIVER

"Where are we going?" she asks, for about the hundredth time since leaving the hotel room.

"You'll see."

I take her hand as we wind through the park and guide her to the first glass building I see, hoping I can get her inside before she realizes where we are.

The botanical gardens have stuck in my mind since the first day I saw the ad and thought of how much Stephanie would love it. The two images went together, like the gardens didn't really exist unless Stephanie was there to see them.

She's switched into a pair of jeans but she's still wearing my sweater, and she uses her free hand to pull the neck up to her chin, boxing in her heat. She eyes me, and in that one quick look I already know what she's saying: wherever I'm taking her, it better be worth the freezing trek.

It will be. I know it.

I had her throw some snacks and drinks into her bag so we can sit for a while, and I convinced her to let me slip my sketchpad in there, too. The greenhouses are supposed to be warm, so hopefully it'll be comfortable enough that she can watch some plants grow.

And I can watch her. Draw her.

I haven't really drawn people in years. I've drawn cartoon characters for game nights, and I've drawn our game boards and doodled quick little things during meetings because it helps keep me focused sometimes. But not real people. It feels a little bit like muscle memory, like I'm relearning something I used to be good at but haven't done in ages.

And Steph is so fun to draw. Her hair is always a little wild, and she's got that cute little pointed nose and warm brown eyes that always seem to have a hint of a smile to them. My only regret is skipping out on the colored pens I was eyeing in the art shop. My logical brain told me it wasn't worth the money or the carry-on space to buy them, but my creative brain is telling me I missed a golden opportunity to draw that freaking mermaid hair.

I might have to run out and buy them later.

Steph isn't paying attention when we reach the first greenhouse, but her eyebrows knit together as I tug her toward the door and open it for her. Her eyes are glued to the sign, but I don't think she can make sense of it. Her gaze flicks inside as a rush of warm air envelops us, and her jaw drops.

"Ollie!" she squeaks, immediately rushing forward to the artificial stream along one side of the greenhouse. She points to the plants lining one edge. "Ollie, calatheas!"

*So that's how you say that word.*

I nod. I did some research this morning while she was still working and directed us toward the tropicals first. "You like?"

She turns to me, eyes wide as she nods. "My god, this place is gorgeous. Monsteras, calatheas, aglaonemas!" She turns to a climbing plant next to her with leaves bigger than her face. "I don't even know what this is, but I'm going to identify it and buy one!"

I can't help the grin that passes over my face. "Oh no, am I feeding the beast?"

She gives me a mock-serious face. "The beast will eat whether you feed it or not."

I laugh. "Okay, so you've been really stamping down the crazy plant lady inside of you."

She pulls her phone out of her bag and snaps a picture of one of the big leaves. "And she'll go right back into hiding once she knows what this plant is."

"Why?"

"Because it's pretty! And look how big the leaves are!"

I shake my head. "I mean, why make her go back into hiding? I brought my sketchpad for a reason. Go full plant lady."

Her attention flicks from her phone up to me. "Really?"

I shrug, taking her purse from her. There's a small concrete ledge that runs along the length of one edge of the greenhouse that I've been eyeing since we came in that seems like the perfect place to make myself comfortable. I nod to it. "I'll be over there when you get bored. If you get bored. More likely you'll get hungry before you get bored, but that's why I brought snacks."

She snickers. "You thought this through, didn't you?"

"I learned from that time I lost you at the pop-up plant shop."

She bites her lip. "That one was bad, wasn't it?"

It took me an hour to track her down because she'd made friends with one of the shop owners and they were discussing importing some exotic plant for her from Thailand.

"I was just happy I didn't have to file a missing person's report. And now I know to keep you just a little bit hungry so you eventually find your way back to me."

She snorts, her eyes finding mine for a second as I realize what I just said.

*Is that what we're doing? One night to stoke the hunger and now, all these months later, we're snapping back together like magnets?*

"Don't lose your planties," I joke.

She rolls her eyes and with that, turns her attention back to her phone.

I leave her be, getting myself as comfortable as is possible on what amounts to a thin, concrete ledge. And I open up my sketchpad and dig my pen out of a purse of–I don't know what to call it other than random *stuff*: greeting cards, receipts, a mixture of dollars and Euros.

And I put pen to paper and recreate what I see.

Calatheas. Aglaonemas–*that's what she said they were, right?* Monsteras.

And Stephanie, in her element.

CONCRETE BENCHES DO NOT MAKE good beds.

But I was getting uncomfortable perching on the edge, my neck snapping up to the plants around me and back down to the sketchpad in my lap.

So I'm splayed out, my head resting on Steph's monster purse and one leg propped up on the concrete to support the sketchpad. I have a clear view of most of the greenhouse, including Stephanie winding her way between plants, taking pictures and doing research whenever she comes to one she can't identify on sight.

She bites her lip, her fingers tapping across her chin as she scrolls through her plant ID app. And then she looks up, smiling slightly at the climbing plant and running her fingers gently along one leaf.

I try to freeze that expression on her face in my head. The one that looks so content staring at a big leaf. I let out a small huff of laughter. *This woman.*

I go back to her face, drawing a vague outline of that contentedness while it's still fresh.

And a moment later, she's in front of me, taking a seat at my feet on the concrete ledge and looking out over all the plants.

"You're not done already, are you?" I ask, tidying up the lines of her face.

She grins at me. "We've been here almost an hour. Aren't *you* done?"

I shrug and nod to the sketchpad. "I brought entertainment. We can stay as long as you want."

She turns to me, wrapping her arms around my knee and resting her chin on top of it.

And that is both helpful and erotic at the same time. I swallow as I will the boner away, my eyes darting around the corners of her face as I copy it down while she's staying in one place. She smiles at me, her eyes fixed on mine.

I can't help but hold her gaze for a moment, my fingers coming to a stop above my drawing.

She notices my lack of movement. "Are you finished?" she asks, leaning away from me again and brushing her hair over her shoulder. I immediately miss her warmth.

"I don't know if I'm ever really finished," I grumble, wishing she'd take that position again. Maybe run her hand along my thigh like she did the night of her birthday, her nails digging into my skin. I realize that just like I memorized her face to copy down a moment ago, I memorized her body the night of her birthday, too.

I could probably recreate the pattern of moles along her hip with my eyes closed.

"An artist's work is never done," she mocks. She crosses her legs, resting her elbow on top of her knee and her chin in her palm.

That same contented look falls across her face. Steph can be so wild sometimes–the brightest and loudest person in any room–but there's something so peaceful about her here.

"I don't think I would have been able to look at the orchids like this," she laments.

I sit up, dropping my legs to either side of the concrete ledge. The area between here and the glass greenhouse wall is free of plants, or I'm sure Stephanie would scold me for potentially disrupting their habitat. My eyebrows crinkle together. "The orchids?"

She turns to me. "In Costa Rica? Remember Rod wanted me to go to Monteverde because they have five hundred different species of orchids?"

I nod. *Fucker*.

"I mean, you never know how the future is going to go, I guess. But I can't help feeling like if I had gone, I wouldn't have been satisfied. I wouldn't have been able to hike enough or get to a really in-depth tour. Or who knows, maybe Rod wouldn't have even been there anymore by the time I made it."

"But you feel satisfied now?"

She snorts. "Yes, Ollie. You know how to satisfy a woman."

*Damn straight I do.* "How forward, Stephanie."

She rolls her eyes. "My mistake. Must have confused you for someone else."

I narrow my eyes, and she presses her lips together in response, biting back a grin. She's baiting me.

"I don't think you'll ever confuse me with someone else after screaming my name the way you did."

She bites her lip, and I wish I could save the exact shade of pink that rushes across her cheeks. She turns away from me, hiding behind her knee. "I'm a naturally expressive person."

I brush her hair over her shoulder so I can see her face, and she nestles further into her knee.

"Oh, I know. You expressed a lot to me that night."

She groans, shaking her head so her hair falls across the side of her face again.

I shake my head. "Stop getting embarrassed over it. It was hot. And I left kinda feeling like a god after the noises you were making."

"Jesus," she mutters.

"You can call me Oliver Long, Professional Orgasm Giver. I'm available for birthdays and Parisian vacations."

I realize as I say it that I just kind of *assumed* we'd fall into bed together during this vacation. I have the urge to eat my words. To say something else to cover up the blatant offer I just threw in her lap. She just broke up with someone. It's not like she followed me halfway around the world because I made her come *that* good.

Although, I wasn't kidding about those noises she made. It certainly sounded like I made her come that good.

Last night is screwing with my head. We were so close to *something* that I can't shake the thought of her. I would understand if she wasn't ready to hop into bed with me right after all of her Rod drama, but I can't help wondering what would have happened if she hadn't fallen asleep last night.

She turns toward me, quirking an eyebrow over her knee. "Available, you say?"

"Interested?"

She sits up straighter, throwing her hair over her shoulder and sticking her nose in the air. "I will get back to you on that."

I raise my eyebrows. "What, in five to seven business days? This is a limited time offer, Wildflower."

Her eyes flash when I say her nickname. "What, does it turn into a pumpkin at midnight?"

"I don't know if it'll get *that* thick, but if anyone could do it, you could."

She presses her lips together to hide her smile, but it only lasts a second before she bursts out in laughter. "Ollie, you're so naughty."

I shrug, the laughter a welcome relief from the blood surging into my dick. I shake my head. "Sorry. I think I spent too much time staring at you today."

She leans forward, one hand resting on my leg as her eyes drift down toward the sketchpad that I still have angled away from her. "Can I see?" she asks, her eyes light as they flick up to mine.

I take a glance down at what I've drawn so far and suddenly feel self-conscious. I wasn't thinking about the end result as I drew, just the act of drawing. And I guess Stephanie, a little, too.

It's arguably done, though I could spend a little more time with the curves of her face. But it doesn't quite feel like an accurate representation of her. Like it's missing a little bit of color. That pink of her cheeks, the multicolored strands running through her hair.

*Goddamnit, I should have gotten the colored pens.*

I reluctantly hand her the sketchpad, and she keeps her eyes on mine as she takes it from me. She bites down on her lip again as she takes in the drawing. "Ollie," she breathes, her fingers trailing along the edges of the page, careful not to smudge any of the ink.

I run a hand through my hair, unsure how to respond to that.

"I love me through your eyes," she says, running her fingers through the edges of her hair. She shakes her head. "You manage to work in all the mess"–she gestures to her somewhat wild hair–"but it looks... good."

"That part's all you," I say, taking the sketchpad back from her.

She gives me a look. "I look at myself in the mirror every day and I never look as good as I do in your drawings." She purses her lips, tapping her fingers along her chin. "I know! From here on out, rather than using a mirror in the morning, you can just draw me. That way I'll look good every day."

"You don't need me for that."

I wouldn't feel comfortable talking to anyone the way I talk to her. So blatantly telling her she's attractive. No expectations, just honesty.

But we're open with each other. We always have been. And I can scrunch up my face and wonder why blurting these things out is so easy or I can just do it, because she either turns that adorable shade of pink or starts smiling in that bashful way that's just so damn cute.

She pouts at me, turning to face me fully and crossing her legs underneath her. She takes the sketchpad between two fingers and gently tugs it away from me so she can take another look.

She lets out a long breath as she stares at it, a mild smile coming to her face. "I like how you see me."

"Maybe you just don't like the way you see yourself."

Her face scrunches up. "Well god, Ollie, no need to give me a self-esteem crisis."

I grimace. "Sorry. Didn't mean it like that."

She gives me another look.

"You're gorgeous, Steph."

Her eyes catch on mine for a second longer before dropping back down to the drawing.

And I feel like my insides are on display for her.

She lets out a long breath as she hands it back to me, her fingers brushing along mine as I take it, anxious to tip it away from her again. Her touch sends a shockwave through my arm, and I find myself wondering why I'm suddenly nervous about showing someone what I draw.

I usually don't care. It's a fun thing that I'm better at than most people, and it means we get to have game nights with custom game boards. But it's never a judgment thing. It's like showing someone a picture of your dog on your phone. It's a passion.

Yet for some reason I really want Steph to like my drawings, like her approval of them means something.

I tell myself it's that I just want her permission to draw her. I never really asked her, after all.

That feels a lot better than admitting to myself I never want to *stop* drawing her.

"Is that okay? That I draw you?"

Her eyebrows crinkle. "Of course. I'm happy to be your muse," she says jokingly, and now I feel the heat rising in my cheeks, too.

She notices and only grins harder.

A second later, she's leaning toward me, her fingers

winding into my sweater and pulling me close. Her eyes find mine and she kisses me, my free hand falling to her hip. The emotions that were just running through my head are totally forgotten in favor of grabbing on tighter to this girl.

I throw my sketchpad on the concrete behind me and reach around her to grab a handful of ass, swiftly moving her toward me. She unwinds her legs and lets them fall on either side of us, propped up by mine, her arms wrapping easily around my neck. I tug her closer, so her legs are wrapped around my waist, and she lets out a small surprised noise from the back of her throat. She can probably feel just how hard I am through my jeans.

I lick the seam of her lips, and her mouth opens to me, our tongues tangling. I run one hand along her side, trailing up her body until I can wrap it up in her hair.

*God, I've missed this.*

The thought surprises me. I never really *had* this. More like borrowed for one night that I just can't get out of my head.

It feels like we're clicking back into each other. Last night we *almost* fell into bed together, but we didn't kiss like *this*. I kissed her cheek, and she made prolonged eye contact with my dick, and as ready as I was to hop in and show her a good time, it didn't feel as right as this moment right now. She was travel-weary, and I was still adjusting to the fact that Stephanie Pierce was in Paris.

But *this*... I don't want to stop *this*.

I want to push her back onto the concrete and shimmy her jeans down her hips. Take her surrounded by the plants she loves so much while anyone could walk in and catch us. Kiss her lips raw and have her screaming my name while her tits press against the glass walls.

I settle for a kiss, struggling to keep my hips steady while hers move ever so slightly against mine.

*Fuck.* Steph does something to me.

I dip my hand beneath her sweater, my fingers digging into her warm skin, and she presses into me, her chest warring with mine.

*Okay, this might be worth risking getting caught.*

I trace the column of her spine up to where her bra sits, and pop it open.

"Ollie," she breathes, and I wonder if I've pushed too far.

But she just kisses me again, her hips grinding against me. I trail my fingers along her skin until my hand rests on her hip again, and slowly drag it up along her ribs, relishing in the way she shivers into me.

I brush my thumb along her pointed nipple, and she moans into our kiss.

My dick throbs at the noise.

I move both hands down to her ass and pull her tight against me, and the strained noise that jumps from her throat tells me I could probably hold her here, let her grind her hips on me and hear my name spilling from her mouth without even undressing her.

I groan as I break our kiss, my lips dropping to her neck as she rocks into me. "Stephanie."

"Oliver," she mocks.

"I'm really torn about letting you come with all of your clothes on."

"Why?"

Great question. No idea.

Her hips are still moving. It seems she's driving herself there without me.

I grab her, pressing her into me harder, and a little whimper jumps from her throat. I want to come with her, to recreate the night of her birthday right here in the greenhouse.

But I settle for kissing her neck while I stomp down the animalistic side of me that wants to tear her jeans down her legs and *take her*. The way she's moving on me has my dick throbbing, my body warring with my mind because on the one hand, I don't think she'd appreciate being caught naked here, but on the other hand–

A door slams and our eyes connect, as if asking each other silently whether now is the time to snap apart.

If I was as close as she was, I would have kept going.

But apparently Stephanie has more self-control than I do. She pushes away from me quickly, reaching up the back of her sweater to reconnect her bra. She brushes her hair back as she swings her legs forward, her cheeks still that delicious shade of pink.

And a moment later, we hear whistling.

She glances at me again, her eyebrows raised as foot-steps in the distance grow louder.

He's dressed in slacks and a thick, puffy jacket with the name of the greenhouse on the left breast. He pauses when he sees us, and then nods, continuing on his way while dragging a hose along the ground behind him.

Steph watches me out of the corner of her eye, and once he disappears behind the corner, she laughs. She squirms, squeezing her eyes shut, and I can only imagine the mess she made of her underwear.

"You almost put on a show for that gardener," I joke.

She rolls her eyes, reaching over to whack me on the arm. "God, Ollie, I can't believe we almost did that."

"We? That was all you, Stephy. You were just using me for my body."

She drops her face into her hands. "Ollie!"

"What? It was hot. Like a little *amuse-bouche* before the main course."

She snorts. "What's the main course?"

I press my lips together, debating whether I should tell her all the wild ways I plan to fuck her tonight.

"Don't," she says, a shiver running through her as if she can hear the ideas that are running through my brain. All the words I could say that would have her cheeks turning pink and her thighs pressing together.

I grin instead of speaking.

"I don't even want to know what you're thinking."

I make a popping noise with my lips. "Okay."

# 15

# STEPHANIE

I eye Ollie as he slips his sketchpad into my purse. I know the naughty things *he's* thinking, and I'm sure he knows the naughty things *I'm* thinking. It seems like I'm not the only one who's been playing the night of my birthday on repeat in their head.

But he doesn't say it. He just grins at me as he pulls his jacket over his shoulders, and my mind tumbles down a rabbit hole remembering all the ways he touched me.

The way I almost came with my clothes on in the middle of the botanical garden.

I zip up my jacket, shaking the thought from my head. I cannot have any more of *those* thoughts today or my underwear is going to start squelching.

"So, orchids?" he asks, another big grin on his face as we head toward the door.

I cock my head to the side and take a quick look around us. "I didn't see any orchids."

He shakes his head. "No. Next greenhouse."

I pause. I had indulged in the tropicals thinking this *was* the only one. "There's more?"

His brow crinkles. "Yeah, Steph. They have plants from all over the world. We're just getting started."

I bite my lip, a battle happening in my head between seeing the orchids and dragging this man home and undressing him as quickly as possible.

In Costa Rica, my relationship ultimately stopped me from seeing the orchids.

I should prioritize the things I want to see while I'm here.

"But I would understand if you just can't resist all this any longer," he jokes, gesturing to his body.

My mouth waters, but my obstinance strengthens.

I step toward him, weaving my hand up underneath his shirt and running my fingers along his abdomen. I stand on my toes to kiss him, pressing my body up against his as his fingers twist in my hair. He tugs me closer, his lips moving harshly against mine.

When I pull away a moment later, I lick my lips. "I want to see the orchids."

He lets out a long breath through his nose as he shakes his head. "Goddamnit. I knew as soon as I said it that challenging you would not turn out well for me."

I laugh as he steps away to adjust himself.

"You just couldn't resist bragging about those abs that can apparently be seen *through* T-shirts."

He shrugs. "What can I say? You spent so long kissing them on your birthday I thought I could tempt you into a taste."

Images of that night flood my brain all over again. The taste of his skin, the way he groaned my name as I took him in my mouth.

*How badly do I really want to see these orchids?*

"Come on, Stephy." He throws an arm around my shoulders. "Let's get you your plant fix. The anticipation is half the fun, right?"

*Is it, though?*

I wrap my arms around his middle, letting my head drop to his shoulder and taking a deep breath of that fresh cedar scent.

He steers us down another path to a glass building that becomes visible as we round the first one. He opens the door and pushes me in, and a minute or so later, he's found a place to sit with his sketchpad along one wall. He keeps his jacket on so he can lean against the glass, and I slowly begin wandering the aisles, my eyes snapping up every so often just in time to see his drop back down to the page in front of him.

The ache in my core remains, though it feels less immediate. Almost like him mentioning anticipation in the first place ensures me that he's feeling this way too–that just because we're not scrambling back to the hotel room to undress doesn't mean the thought of it isn't taking up as much of his brain power as it is mine.

Maybe it's making that eventual moment even stronger, like each naughty thought we have about one another will compound into something more when we finally make it back to the hotel.

I cling to that idea, and instead of getting all jumpy and excited to drag him into bed, I get comfortable with waiting. Like I trust in the eventuality of us coming together in that way again.

I take frequent breaks from my plant identification app to sit next to him and pepper little kisses along his neck. He paws at me lightly–just enough that my body starts responding–and then brushes his lips against my cheek or my temple with a sly little grin on his face, like he knows exactly what he's doing to me.

And when we're done with the orchids, he drags me along to another glass building that houses a seemingly unlimited variety of banana trees, palm trees, ficuses and even a few parakeets.

I'm in a jungle in the middle of Paris, and Ollie just smiles at me over the edge of his sketchpad, his fingers never stopping.

We snack through the day, and when we've finally hit all seven greenhouses–*seven greenhouses!*–we venture back into the cold in search of dinner and drinks. We find a place within walking distance of the hotel and collapse into our chairs. Ollie translates the menu for me and helps me pick out something I'll like.

And then he shows me a few of the drawings from the botanical gardens, and I'm once again floored at the man sitting in front of me.

When I'm too tired, he reads me the menu. When I have to work, he has no qualms entertaining himself. When he knows I'll be hungry, he brings snacks.

And he draws a version of me that's so obviously me, yet so much more beautiful than I am in real life.

He sees the version of me I've always wanted to be.

## 16

## OLIVER

Stephanie takes another sip of her wine, leaning back in her chair as she abandons her spoon on her plate.

"I can't do it," she says. "I can't take another bite."

"Come on, you're the one who wanted crème brûlée. What's left is the size of a walnut."

She glances down at the ramekin and then back up at me.

"You're right. I can do this." She picks up the spoon again, and in one smooth movement, transfers the rest of the creamy dish into her mouth with a nod and a proud smile. "See?" A look of surprise clouds her face as she puts a hand over her stomach, swallowing thickly. "Oh god, I don't feel so good."

I drop my spoon on my plate, concerned I'm going to have to escort her to the bathroom.

And then she lets out a dainty little burp. "Oh okay. I'm alright."

I shake my head, my concern dissipating. "Christ, Stephanie."

She grimaces. "Sorry. I'm going to blame that one on you, though."

A laugh jumps from my throat. "Just so we're on the same page here, I was encouraging you to *help* me with what's left, not gobble it all down like some kind of crème brûlée maniac."

Her jaw drops. "You didn't make that clear before goading me!"

"I had the spoon in my hand!"

She shrugs. "I mean, I'd offer it back but I'm not sure you'd still want it at this point."

I lean back in my chair. "No, I think it's best you hang onto it for now."

She sighs, taking another sip of her drink. "Your loss." She shakes her head, the smile on her face causing cute little dimples to show on either of her cheeks. Her eyes slide to mine, narrowing as she laughs. "Also, I can't believe you just called me a crème brûlée maniac."

I laugh with her. "Hey, I just call it like I see it."

She sighs, twirling her wineglass in a small circle on the table. "It's going to be hard transitioning out of this," she says, her voice taking a more somber tone.

"What do you mean?"

She shrugs. "This feels like a true vacation, you know? Not exactly what I was planning to do once I started traveling. I'll have to cut back after this. At least stay somewhere a little cheaper, if not move on from Paris entirely."

I nod. "Technically, your current lodgings are free."

She throws me a playful glare. "I know! And that's really nice of you. But you're spoiling me, Oliver Long."

I shrug. "Call it selfish. I like having you on my vacation."

She grins. "You really do?"

"Of course I do."

She smiles at me, and for a moment I totally forget why something more than one night hasn't happened between us already. Before Paris. Before she went on her trip for love. I have a momentary out-of-body experience where some version of us already exists beyond this trip. Where it's just Steph and me, and where we are doesn't really matter as long as we have each other.

It's not something I've yearned for before, but the feeling hits my chest with a thump that reverberates through my entire body.

And then my mind is drawn back to my tattoo. To the idea of always having a direction. A goal. A trajectory. And recognizing that being with someone or having a family was never necessarily part of that trajectory.

I find myself wondering why it *can't* be.

I know there was a reason. I've felt it in my bones for a long time now, that my focus needs to be on one thing.

But... does it, *really*?

Growing up, I was always encouraged to focus. To sit still. To have a goal.

As kids, my siblings and I thrived on a little healthy competition. Whoever could get their homework done first got to pick Friday night's movie. Whoever brought home the best grades got to choose that night's dinner.

It's not that I want to stop playing *the game*, but I'm *tired*. I've been running full speed toward this promotion for so long that I'm running out of steam.

"I like that your vacation has interrupted my travels," she says, and I decide to suspend my introspection for another day because whatever is happening in my mind—and whatever is happening between us—is fleeting.

And there's no sense in contemplating the *why* of things if it means that I'm missing out on *the things* themselves.

Stephanie is *fun*. She's sexy as fuck. As long as she doesn't have to take care of work, she embraces what life throws at her. Her plan to win Rod back didn't work–or at least, not in the way she was hoping–so she hopped on a plane and flew to Paris. She doesn't hesitate to finish the last bite of something good because she *wants* it. She thinks hanging out on my vacation instead of figuring out an itinerary for the next leg of her travels is a welcome reprieve instead of a stress-inducing event.

Maybe I've been too strict with myself.

Maybe I should embrace a little more of Stephanie.

I mean, she nearly came on my lap today with all of her clothes on in the middle of the botanical garden.

Whatever there is to explore, she's already doing it. I don't know if I'm a rebound after a difficult breakup, the friend she sleeps with once a quarter now that she's definitely single, or something more.

But I'm here for it.

WE WALK BACK to the room with heads ducked against the cold. At some point, I throw my arm around her shoulders and tug her into my side, and her body melds so easily into mine that I'm surprised this isn't something we've practiced over hundreds of nights of cold weather.

When we get inside, I shower as fast as I can, the memory of last night's *almost* in the forefront of my mind.

But I'm too late. Our day of plant identification has worn her out, and she's fast asleep, one arm thrown over her eyes. She changed while I was in the shower, and she's wearing only a thin sleep set that has my eyes laser-focused on the little pointed nipples under the sheer fabric.

I shake my head as I pull on a pair of underwear and climb into bed with her. I tug on her waist, pulling her into me, and her light snoring pauses only for a second as I press our bodies together.

*Morning sex, then.*

# 17

## STEPHANIE

If it weren't for the insanely hot man in my bed, I'd say I don't have a problem.

Except that two nights in a row now, I've been all hot and bothered for him, only for him to hop in the shower and then, suddenly, it's morning. Last night we went to another cute little cafe, got all buzzed and flirty, and came back to the room *ready*.

I don't know whether to call it his fault for deigning to shower when he already smells so delicious, or my fault for being unable to keep my eyes open.

He's wrapped around me, our limbs entangled, and he snores gently in my ear.

I *have* to pee, but unraveling myself is torture. Pure torture.

But if I don't, I'm going to pee the bed and that will be a whole new level of mortification, especially considering I'm neither drunk nor sleeping–just comfortable.

So I gently squirm out of his arms, and there's a moment where he tightens his grip on me, and his hold on me makes me think peeing the bed might actually be worth it.

But I don't. He readjusts when I get up, and I hate that I can't just crawl right back into place when I'm done.

But it's also Saturday, and since I don't have to work today, there's something I'm really looking forward to doing this morning. I just hope he won't be annoyed that I'm waking him up before sunrise.

I pee quickly and try to tame my wild hair to no avail, and then tiptoe back into the bedroom to wake him up.

Kneeling down next to the bed, I gently rub his arm. "Ollie," I whisper. "Wake up."

His eyebrows crinkle as his eyes open, his mouth setting into a frown. "What?"

"Come on, we have to get up. I want to show you something."

He raises an eyebrow. "Show me your best sleepy face," he says, reaching over and grabbing me by the waist. He pulls me into bed, flipping me over him and pulling the sheets up around us.

"Ollie, come on. You're gonna love it," I say, even as my hands run down his bare chest, my mouth going dry at the memories the touch evokes.

He groans, his hands wrapping around me, landing on my ass and squeezing. "This is all I want to see," he says, one hand running down my leg and hooking it over his waist. He presses into me, rock hard between my legs, and I wonder if sunrise mindfulness is really worth leaving this.

His hands wind up, underneath my shirt, roaming like he owns my skin. When I look up at him, his eyes are still closed.

"You're not even looking to see anything," I say.

He pops one eye open. "I like to look with my hands." As if to make his point, he reaches up and palms my breast, running his thumb over my nipple. I shiver as his lips brush across my neck.

*Yeah, fuck sunrise anything.*

I wind my arms around him, pulling him closer to me, my lips on his chest, his neck.

"I gotta brush my teeth," he says abruptly and unwinds himself from me.

I huff, having been only inches from kissing him, from tearing off his underwear and revisiting the night of my birthday. He moves quickly, disappearing into the bathroom, and in his absence my brain starts working again.

Tonight we're going out with his friends from work, which means it's most likely going to be a late night. If I really want to show him this beautiful–dare I say perfect–spot for some morning mindfulness, it has to be today.

This is our shot.

So I get up from bed and move to the kitchen table even though my underwear is wildly uncomfortable and wait for him there.

He's confused when he stumbles out of the bathroom a minute later to find me at the table.

"Come back," he says, motioning to the bed.

"Get dressed."

He looks around, as if there's some physical thing in this room he can use to convince me back into bed. "Can't you show me whatever it is you want to show me, after?"

I shake my head. "We have to go now."

He sighs and then gives me a puppy dog face. "But Stephy," he whines.

"Get dressed," I repeat, even though every molecule of my body feels magnetically pulled in his direction. "We have all day afterward."

"All day?" he asks, eyebrows rising.

"All day."

"Alright, fine. Can I just do my mindfulness minutes real quick?" he asks.

I bite my lip. "No."

He raises his eyebrows, incredulous. "No?"

"Just trust me!"

"Steph, I need it to feel like myself."

I take a step toward him. "This will be better. I promise."

He shakes his head. "No smoke?"

"What?"

"The other night, you said you would trust that I wasn't blowing smoke up your ass. You're not blowing smoke up my ass, right?"

I grin. "No smoke."

"Okay. I trust you."

He sighs and reaches over to the wall to turn on the lights. Eyes burning from the sudden change, I grab my clothes from my suitcase and head into the bathroom to get dressed.

When I come back out, he's ready to go in jeans and a T-shirt, and for a second as he steps directly under one of the overhead lights, I think I might actually see his abs through the thin fabric.

I shake my head, pulling the sleeves of the shirt he gave me down over my hands and slouching into my jacket. I sit down at the kitchen table to pull on my socks and shoes.

"That shirt looks far better on you than it ever looked on me," he comments.

"I think I might keep it," I say, hugging it closer around me.

He shrugs. "Seems only right."

Our eyes connect from across the bed, and the sensation of his hands roaming my skin comes back to me viscerally.

"Ready?" he asks.

I nod, shaking the thoughts from my mind. As we step outside, the cold February air whisks away any lingering thoughts of his hands on my body.

We take a train, and then a bus, and by the time we finally make it to the park, the dim light of dawn brightens the sky. I kick up the pace as we follow the path, a layer of sweat building along my skin. In my light research on Paris, this place was hailed as a gem, slightly off the beaten path. It's a converted quarry with a lake and plenty of greenery. I'm disappointed I won't see it in bloom, but if this outing works in my favor, our view will be spectacular regardless of the time of year.

"What's the rush, speedy?"

"You'll see!" I say, as I finally spot the place we're heading.

It's a pagoda in the sky, set atop an outcropping of rocks and accessible by a series of stairs and bridges. I lead him to the first bridge, and he follows me over. I'm sure by now he knows where we're going, but that doesn't quell my excitement.

When we get to the top, I'm relieved to see we're alone.

Before we step out into the pagoda, I take his hand, and he grins at me.

The park is laid out before us, water directly underneath us surrounded by yellowed grass. Beyond that, lines of mature trees. And above the treetops, Paris laid out before us.

"Wow," he says, taking a step to the edge of the pagoda and looking out.

"Do you like it?"

He turns, leaning on the railing. "How did you find this place?"

I shrug. "I was just looking up stuff to do in Paris and this seemed like my speed. Wasn't as challenging a hike as I expected but that's okay. Hopefully the view will be worth it."

He looks out over his shoulder, and I give him a few seconds to take it all in before speaking.

"Come sit," I say, plopping down on the ground in the middle of the pagoda.

He gives me a look. "Now we *really* have to get you to a laundromat."

I wave him off. "It's just a little dirt. Sit," I say, patting the ground in front of me.

He sighs and lowers himself down to the ground, his knees touching mine.

"We're going to do our fifteen minutes of mindfulness, and when we're done, we'll open our eyes to the sunrise."

His smiles are usually teasing, filled with laughter or poking fun at me, but this one is almost bashful. He tries to hide it, but I catch the edges of his lips tilting upward even as he closes his eyes.

I set the timer on my phone, and when it goes off fifteen minutes later, we open our eyes to each other, bathed in the warm light of morning.

"So what did you think?" I ask.

His eyes are glued to mine, and rather than answering me, he leans over, winding his hand around my neck and pulling my lips to his. His tongue slips into my mouth, his other arm weaving around my waist and pulling us to our knees, our bodies pressing together.

"I loved it," he whispers, his mouth still pressed against mine.

"You haven't even looked at the sunrise yet."

"Like I said, I like to look with my hands." He reaches down to grab my ass as his lips find the skin of my neck. One hand slips underneath my jacket, trailing across the skin of my back and resting on the opposite hip.

I wrap my arms around his neck as he kisses me again, and I wonder, briefly, just how terrible it would be to get naked in a public park in Paris.

"If I could guarantee we wouldn't get arrested and thrown in a French prison, I would fuck you right here," he mumbles into my neck.

A rush of heat runs down my spine. "It's like you read my mind."

"Steph," he groans, one hand winding into my hair and tugging gently, "why do you say things like that?"

"You said it first!"

He pulls away from me. "Yeah, but it's way hotter coming from you."

I leave a delicate kiss on his jaw. "Watch the sunrise with me?"

He nods and falls back to his heels, and just when I'm about to plop down next to him, he weaves an arm around my waist and pulls me between his legs, his arms wrapping easily around me. I snuggle in closer to him, and he brushes my hair from one shoulder, resting his chin there.

We stay like that, his breath rushing over my skin, while the sky turns all shades of pink and blue in front of us.

And when early morning walkers and runners appear on the trails below us, we begrudgingly stand, stretching out our stiff limbs. He pulls me into him as we leave the same way we came, and places a kiss on my temple.

"Thanks for this morning, Stephy. That was special."

I grin up at him.

"Now how about some breakfast?"

WE SIT elbow to elbow in a cute little Parisian cafe bustling with early morning diners. Ollie tears a croissant apart piece by piece, taking small sips of espresso as he does so, his elbow knocking against mine every other second in a way that makes me want to turn to him and tear him right out of his clothes.

I lean back in my chair when I've finished my omelet, transfixed by every little piece of bread he puts in his mouth. His jacket is draped over the back of his chair, the sleeve of his T-shirt rising and falling over the compass on his arm with every movement he makes.

I reach forward, raising the fabric so it's fully exposed and running my fingers along the ink.

He pauses, his eyebrows raised, as he looks at me.

"It's healing so well," I say.

The ink is still dark, but it's not raised anymore. I lift my arm, pulling up my shirt sleeve to compare the two.

"So is yours," he says, reaching forward to brush his fingers along my arm. The touch sends a shockwave through my body, and I lean into him even further. An array of goosebumps spreads across my arm, and his eyes flit up to meet mine.

He knows exactly what he's doing.

"Are you still happy with it?"

I smile. "I love it."

He nods. "I didn't really think about it when I was drawing it, but... I'm literally on you. Forever."

I snort. "I bet you love that."

He shrugs. "I'd rather be *in* you, but I'll take *on* you."

"Ollie!"

"What? I'm just being honest."

I shake my head. "Just to be clear here, my tattoo is not *you*. It's a depiction of *me* as seen by *you*, which I'm growing ever more thankful for the more I'm here because I'm not sure anyone could have drawn prettier wildflowers. Or a prettier me."

He smiles, offering me the last bite of his croissant.

"Oh, compliments earn me snacks?" I let out an *Mmm* as I chew and swallow it down. "Your tattoo is sexy," I try, and hold out my hand jokingly for the nothing he has to give me.

"Open your mouth and I'll give you something."

"Ollie!"

He shrugs. "That's all I've got to give."

I laugh as I take a sip of my Americano that is... well, good enough if I'm looking for caffeine.

"So you're still liking it?" I ask.

He raises his eyebrows. "Liking it?"

"Your tattoo?"

"Oh," he says, shaking his head. "Yeah, I think so."

"You think so?"

He sighs, taking a sip of the espresso that he actually seems to enjoy. "It's making me question myself."

"How so?"

He shrugs. "It's dumb."

"No, it's not."

"You don't even know what I'm going to say."

I shrug. "It's you, so it's not dumb."

He gives me a look that I don't break because this is not something I'll waver on.

"I've always had sort of a one-track mind. One direction, you know?"

I nod, determined not to speak and interrupt this rare moment of Oliver divulging his innermost thoughts.

"But a compass itself kind of gives you four different directions. You can create your own too, if you want, but

there are four already there. One is no better than another."
He shakes his head. "Sorry, I'm not making much sense."

I try to keep my words succinct so he'll keep going.
"You're questioning your path. I get it."

"I've spent a lot of my life trying to be successful and
reach for these things that I'm supposed to reach for that I
forgot that I don't have to just follow a prescribed path, you
know? I have a choice. I don't have to be so strict with
myself."

I nod. "You're realizing you can be whoever you want
to be."

He shrugs. "Yeah, I guess." He shakes his head. "It's
dumb. All this from a silly tattoo."

"It obviously means something to you."

He laughs. "Yeah, and now I'm questioning that
meaning."

"Not necessarily. The tattoo means whatever you want it
to mean. Sure, you have one set direction. Or, you have four.
Or it can be a reminder that there's no need to stay in one
direction." I smile as I run my fingers along the ink again. "I
think in that way, it's really perfect for you."

His opposite hand lands on top of mine, his fingers
squeezing.

"I like the way you think," he says, his voice betraying no
hint of a joke.

He holds my gaze, and a moment later he's leaning
toward me, his lips brushing gently across mine.

# 18

## OLIVER

I grab Steph's hand as we walk along the streets of Paris and throw her into a little twirl, her hair fanning out around her.

We've spent hours wandering, still in our dirty clothes from this morning.

Stephanie is something different. She's different just like everyone else is different from everyone else, but also in a way that's so unique and charmingly hers that she seems different from the different that everyone else is.

I was worried when she wanted me to skip my mindfulness minutes. I thought I had impressed on her just how important it is to me, and for a moment I feared she wasn't the Stephanie I thought I knew. I thought she was asking me to forego the routine that's worked so well for me in the past.

But she was upgrading it.

Because that's the sort of thing she does. She figures out what's important to you and finds a way to add to it. With me, this morning. With Rod, when she met him in Costa Rica. So many people give what they want to receive, but not what others actually want.

Then again, maybe all Stephanie really wants is someone to give her the same compassion she shows other people.

I put my arm around her shoulders and pull her in for a hug. "Thank you for this morning."

She smiles up at me. "You're welcome. Thanks for facilitating the shopping trip." She spots another store she wants to go into and beelines for it, dragging me along by the hand. "Oh, this place looks nice!"

I didn't intend for this day to turn into a shopping trip, but it's what organically happened when we finished breakfast. She passed a store she liked, and we went in for a wander. I checked my email on my phone while she shopped and tried things on, and from there came another store, and another. Eventually our breakfast outing turned into lunch, and lunch turned into a walking tour around the Marais, which turned into a visit to the zoo, which turned into "just one or two more stores."

"Are you sure you're not bored?" she asks as we pass through the doors.

I shake my head. "I'm fulfilling a duty."

"To carry my bags?"

I shrug. It's the least I can do after the scene she dreamed up this morning. I'm aching to take her back to the hotel room and undress her, but that seems almost inconsiderate after what she did for me. In the grand scheme of our lives, we have plenty of time to undress each other, but a fairly limited time to go shopping in Paris.

So no, I'm not bored. I'm happy that she's making the most of it.

I meander around, checking my phone while she tries things on and vacillates between two sweaters that look exactly the same.

"Hey, which do you think will look better?" she asks, holding them both up over herself.

"They'd both look good on you."

She gives me a look. "But which would look *better*?"

I search for the differences. They're both nondescript black sweaters. "Steph, aren't they the same sweater?"

"Are you serious?"

"I never joke about fashion," I say, mock seriously, and she breaks into laughter.

"Okay, touché. You're the wrong person to ask."

Over her shoulder I spot something sequined and shiny. "Honestly, I'm surprised you didn't pick that up," I say, my memory of her consisting largely of sparkly, skimpy things.

She turns, glancing at it. "Ollie, that's a dress."

I shrug. "It looks like something you'd wear. You could put leggings under it."

"That's not really a leggings sort of dress."

"It has long sleeves."

"So that makes it okay to wear with leggings?"

I shake my head. "I don't know what you want from me. Both sweaters would look nice on you, but half the time I see you, you're wearing something sparkly."

She smiles. "I like that you see sparkles and think of me," she says, leaning into me, the sweaters squished between us. She stands on her toes to kiss me, and the bags of hers I'm already holding crash to the back of her legs when I wrap my arms around her.

"Or maybe I look at you and see sparkles," I say and immediately regret it. *Who have I become?*

She grins at me. "Oliver Long, are you a secret romantic?"

I clear my throat and give her a look. "No. It just popped out."

"That makes it even better."

*It does, doesn't it?* "Go buy your sweaters," I say. "And get the dress while you're at it."

She narrows her eyes at me, kissing my chin. "I love that you saw that dress and thought of me because you're right, it's definitely my style. But it's cold out and I don't have room in my luggage for superfluous clothing. I think I have to stick to the basics for this trip."

I resist the urge to tell her that any clothing she wears is superfluous.

She manages to pick between the two identical sweaters on her own and joins me at the front of the store once she's bought them.

"How are we looking on time?" she asks.

"If we head back to the room now, we should have enough time for a shower and maybe a drink before dinner," I say.

And I definitely do not intend to have an actual drink with her.

"Okay, great," she says, smiling as she brushes by me.

We find the nearest metro station, and twenty minutes later, we arrive back at our hotel.

I'M HAVING a drink by myself.

I thought that coming back two hours before we had to go to dinner would be more than enough time for us to fall into bed together, maybe go for two rounds before hopping in the shower and getting ready.

But Stephanie is still in the bathroom doing her makeup. She urged me into the shower as soon as we got back. Despite some heavy kissing and mild undressing, she insisted we get ready first, and that if we still had time for a drink when we're done, we could find a nearby bar to hit before dinner.

So, my words backfired.

And now I'm fully dressed, sitting at the kitchen table with a glass of wine in front of me and counting the seconds until we're back from this dinner so we can pick up where we left off this morning. I was looking forward to a night with Emma and Jack, but after today, I'm not sure there's any place I'd rather be than right here, with Stephanie.

"My god, Ollie, are you ready yet?" she asks as she finally emerges from the bathroom. She grabs her purse from the edge of the bed and strikes a pose in front of me. "How do I look?"

"Like I'd much rather stay here and undo all the work you just did."

She grins. "Perfect." She leans forward and kisses me lightly, and it's all I can do to run my hand down the fabric of the dress she's wearing, some plaid thing with leggings and a long-sleeve shirt underneath.

"Why is this a leggings dress but the sparkly one wasn't?" I ask, struggling to grab the tight fabric between my fingers to pull her closer.

She shrugs. "That was, like, a party dress. This is a serious dress. And they're not leggings, they're tights." She reaches down and snaps them against her skin. I follow her hand, my skin anxious to be closer to hers, and pull on her knee so she collapses into my lap. My dick twitches in response.

"Ollie," she warns. "We have to leave."

"Why? They're only coworkers, and they were sleeping together behind my back for months. They deserve to be stood up."

She cocks her head to the side. "That sounds like an interesting story."

"Not as interesting as whatever is underneath this little dress," I say, sliding my hand up her thigh, under the hem.

She slaps my hand and stands, holding a hand out to me. "Come. Let's go."

"Trying to," I say, throwing the rest of my wine back. She giggles, and I smile at her despite the blue balls.

WHEN WE GET to the restaurant, Jack and Emma are already seated and waiting for us.

It's a small cafe with tables just a little too close together, and Jack and Emma stand to greet us when we walk in the door.

"I have to say, I was expecting a French girl," Jack says as we take our seats. "Leave it to Ollie to deem no French woman acceptable and import one from the States." He thinks for a moment. "Although maybe it's the other way around. That French of yours certainly isn't doing you any favors."

"You're the only one who complains," I remind him.

"Only because I can," he says, then turns to Steph. "*Enchanté*, Stephanie."

"*Enchantée*," she repeats.

Jack raises his eyebrows. "*Parlez-vous français?*"

She scrunches her face up. "Only enough to say no."

He laughs. "Well, cheers to that," he says, and we all *clink*.

"So Steph, how did you end up on Ollie's trip? As far as I know, he's never traveled with a companion," Emma says, eyeing me with a sly smile on her face.

Steph shrugs, letting out a long breath before speaking.

"Well, long story short, I went to Costa Rica for Love and Love didn't want me back. So Ollie invited me to join him in Paris, and I did."

Emma looks confused.

"Steph is a..." I turn to her. "What did you call it? Digital nomad?"

She rolls her eyes. "I mean, I don't know if I can really say that yet. I've been traveling for two weeks. But yes, I have a job back at home that's luckily super flexible so I can travel as I like, and as long as I get my stuff done, everybody's happy."

"What do you do?" Emma asks.

"Um, I mostly write proposals. I work for a marketing company that does brand work so it's a lot of just figuring out what we can do for different clients. I'm technically a strategist, but really I take RFPs and turn them into proposals. Lots of head-down quiet work." She thinks for a second and then continues. "Requests for proposals. That's what RFPs are." She smiles and nods quickly, as if deeming her explanation satisfactory.

Emma nods. "Well, I'm jealous. I would love a job where I can do quiet work and I'm judged by my quality rather than my friendliness," she says, a bitter note in her voice.

Steph nods. "I'm definitely one of the lucky ones. I love my job. And you know, I've had so many bad ones before–bad bosses, unclear work, asshole people. Like all of the above. And when I started working here, it all kind of clicked. My boss is amazing. I have ADHD, and when I got diagnosed, she was super accommodating–she probably knew before I did. But either way, it's been such a great experience and"–she pauses for a second to put a hand on my shoulder–"although Love did not want me back, I'm so happy that I get to do Paris with Ollie instead because I think it's a way better experience."

Emma smiles—a genuine one—and the mood is contagious. Something about Steph's energy does that to people.

As Jack and Emma consult the menu and bicker over which plates they should get, I lean over to Steph. "I think you charmed them."

She smiles over at me and lowers her voice. "People like realness, vulnerability. You can give away little pieces of yourself all day without ever losing the whole. It makes people more comfortable to know little things like that."

Something about Stephanie clicks. The way she loves so freely, forgives so easily. It has nothing to do with what she wants from people and everything to do with the way she wants them to feel.

There was a part of me that thought, as adorable and smart as she is, that she was desperate for someone to love her and that's why she was so quick to run to Rod, to forgive him, to love him despite him making it clear he didn't feel the same way.

But she's just willing to give the extra where others aren't. She's just kind.

Before tonight, there were moments I wanted to protect her from herself, to shield her from the heartbreak she welcomes and stop her from putting herself in situations where she was bound to get hurt.

But she does it willingly. She looks at a situation, wonders how she can make it better, and gives up a little piece of herself that anyone else might be hesitant about. She exists in a world where she's honest and open with herself and others, and if that person doesn't treat her the way she wants to be treated, she moves on.

Rod, as a prime example.

That protectiveness I felt for her starts to wane as I realize she's more in-tune with herself than I ever imagined.

She doesn't need protection. She needs appreciation. Someone who sees that in her and encourages her to run with it. She just needs someone to be there and hold her hand while she does it, and boost her up when the little pieces of herself she gives out *do* add up to something larger.

A newfound respect for her blooms in my mind.

And an uneasy feeling of dread.

Because I'm not sure I'm ready to be that serious with her. She's looking for her *person*.

Steph and I have a fun, flirty thing going on in Paris, but underneath all of her charm and smiles, there's an incredibly giving, loving human that deserves more of the world than she's been dealt.

And there's a good chance I'm getting in her way by letting this happen.

I like Steph, but I can't completely change my trajectory because we're in Paris together and she's cute. My whole life, I've had one direction. Reach the next level. Be better than the other guy. Work harder *and* smarter.

If Steph and I go there again, it wouldn't be a one-time thing.

And she doesn't deserve another person who strings her along for the sake of a fun time on vacation and screws her over later.

My mom's words ring on repeat in my head, like they do every once in a while when I get off track. Whenever I'm stressed or having a rough week and my mind starts spinning in too many directions.

*Now is not the time to get distracted.*

"You okay?" she asks under her breath, a conversation just between the two of us.

I clear my throat and nod. "Yeah, sorry."

As the server takes our orders, she reaches under the table and squeezes my knee, smiling.

I feel like I'm taking advantage of her.

On her birthday, things were clear. She wanted someone for the night, and I was willing and available.

But now, things are different. We're obviously attracted to each other, but she's looking for love. She's in the hardest part of a breakup, and I'm the first place she ran.

Part of me warms to that realization, but another part of me shies from it. She wants a life of travel with the one she loves. This week, I can fulfill that need for her, but year-round, I can't do this unless something changes drastically with my job.

"So there actually was a reason we wanted to get dinner with you tonight," Jack says, taking a sip of his champagne.

"Oh?"

He nods and sighs. "We're coming clean when we get back to the US."

"To the company?"

Jack glances at Emma and nods. "It's time. We realized we've been stressed out and these fun things in life–a potential promotion, getting married–are passing us by because we're too *worried* about what it means for the future." He swallows. "I don't know what that means for our jobs, but at least we won't have to hide things anymore."

I blink as I put together what this means for all of us. They're essentially forcing the company's hand. Boot Emma back to accounting like she wants to so Jack can get the promotion we've both been gunning for, or just put me in the new director role.

I can honestly say I have no clue what's in store for me,

but I know for sure that some pivotal moments are coming for all of us.

I nod, doing my best to ignore the wild influx of thoughts blustering through my head. "Wow. Well, I'm happy for you guys. I hope all goes well."

Jack shrugs. "Me too. But if it doesn't, I won't regret it," he says, squeezing Emma's hand.

On the one hand, I love their love. It's heartwarming to see how much they care for each other. But on the other hand, it only deepens that pit of dread in my stomach. I want to believe their news will be accepted and brushed off as nothing more than a bullet point when deciding the new structure of our team.

But there's always the possibility it won't.

They really are taking a chance on each other. Elevating a person above financial security. Above jobs they've given everything to.

"Aw, that's so sweet," Steph says, knocking my knee with hers.

*I bet that's what Steph would expect. That's what she deserves. Someone willing to give everything up for her.*

Her presence draws me away from my thoughts.

It's even more apparent, now, that what I'm doing with Stephanie is a bad idea.

I definitely won't have the time to pay attention to her the way she deserves. I'll be stretched too thin and the cracks will start showing. I won't be able to manage my job *and* a relationship.

*Fuck. What have I gotten myself into?*

Jack smiles at Emma. "I don't love that this is where we're at, but it'll be worth it in the end."

Emma squeezes Jack's hand, grinning back at him.

A few moments of silence pass before Stephanie speaks.

"So I'm dying to hear your love story. How'd it happen? Was it super forbidden but you just couldn't help yourselves? I have a friend–" She looks at me. "*We* have a friend–she's actually feeding Ollie's cat this week–who writes these really spicy romance novels and one she wrote recently was an office romance, boss-employee-type thing that was... well, all I'm saying is I'm glad I work with a bunch of women."

Everyone at the table laughs, and Emma launches into the story of how she and Jack got together, complete with all the sweet little tidbits that color her cheeks pink and make Steph go, "Aww." Jack grins as Emma speaks, and I'm grateful to have a few moments to collect my thoughts.

As the night goes on, I do my best to push Jack's news to the back of my mind. Steph, charming as she is, carries most of the conversation, and I feel bad I dragged her away from her Parisian shopping adventure today just to sit her at a table next to the moodiest version of myself.

When we finally say goodbye, she hugs both of them.

Jack claps me on the back and nods, as if asking if all is good.

"Thanks for coming out," he says.

I nod back, confirming. "Thanks for the invite. This was fun."

We go our separate ways, Jack and Emma retreating arm in arm down the sidewalk.

Steph eyes me, biting her lip as we walk in the opposite direction. She slips her arm in mine, just like Emma did Jack's.

"So fill me in on what just happened."

# 19

# STEPHANIE

I don't think I've ever seen Ollie bothered in this way.

He spent most of the night quiet, and half of the time when I looked at him, he seemed lost in his thoughts. When he'd feel the weight of my gaze, he'd smile and tune in quickly, but I know something about our conversation tonight weighs heavily on his mind.

He shakes his head as we walk, his hand resting on top of mine. We're only a few blocks away from our hotel, and he lets out a long breath as his fingers tighten around mine.

"I guess I just didn't always understand your thought process, you know? The giving little pieces of yourself thing?"

My brow furrows as I struggle to figure out why that's a *bad* thing.

"And that upsets you?"

He shakes his head. "No. The opposite. It makes me really respect you. I think that's really cool that you're so willing to be open with people." He lets out another long breath. "It just kind of reminded me that you're looking for your person, you know? Someone who does nothing more than encourages you to be exactly who you are."

I nod, struggling to follow where he's going with this. "I mean, in time, yes."

He gives me a look. "In time? Steph, you just flew to Costa Rica for a guy who's historically treated you like crap because you thought he might be the one."

I shrug. "I got to the right place eventually," I say, elbowing him lightly, a laugh poised at the corners of my lips until I realize he's not matching my energy.

He's stoic, and my shoulders drop as I realize this conversation is going in a different direction than I expected.

"It doesn't feel right to be in your way," he says.

*So he's breaking up with me. Can you break up with someone you were never really with?*

"Okay," I say. I'm not sure if this is his intention or if I'm reading too much into his words.

He opens the gate to the courtyard and follows me through.

I notice the absence of his hand on the small of my back in the same way that the silence screams between us.

I bite my tongue, thinking he'll either expand on this or find some other way to confirm.

But he only unlocks the door to our room and gestures for me to go in first.

I'm off balance. All night, I was expecting this moment to be the one where he finally undresses me. Frenzied kisses and roaming hands.

But he only nods as he locks the door behind him.

"Alright. Well, I think I'm going to head to bed," he says, shrugging his jacket off and leaving it on the back of the kitchen chair.

*I guess that's my confirmation.*

"I'm going to see if I can get my flight changed in the morning," he continues. "It's probably best that I not be on vacation when Jack and Emma come clean about their relationship. Just in case it inspires any quick changes. I just want to make sure I'm a part of those conversations."

"Okay," I say.

"You can keep the room."

I swallow, the reality hitting me that I'm going to be alone. Again. "Thanks."

He nods, then grabs clothes from his suitcase and disappears into the bathroom.

And I'm left stunned at the kitchen table. I sit and put my head in my hands.

I didn't know Ollie and I were at a place where breaking up was even an option. I guess he was thinking about things a lot more seriously than I was. I liked the thought of exploring something with him, and definitely the thought of revisiting the night of my birthday, but I wasn't thinking of *us* as anything more than a possibility.

Definitely not something that needed to be broken off.

Ollie said it was simultaneously too early and too late for the "what are we" conversation, yet he seems to have already decided we were something more than nothing, and that we shouldn't be.

I start laughing.

Here I am, following man after man literally across the world, and not one of them actually wants to be with me. Or even try.

If I weren't so surprised by Ollie's words, I might cry.

But as it is, I laugh.

Alanis Morissette's "Ironic" starts playing in my head,

and I decide that this song is the soundtrack to this trip. I laugh harder.

I get up from the kitchen table and pour a glass of wine from the bottle on the counter. The shower starts, and in Ollie's absence, I call my sister.

"Hey, World Traveler," she says. "How's Paris?"

I keep my voice low as I speak. "I have to tell you something that will either make you laugh or cry but I'm hoping it'll be a laugh because that's where I am right now."

"Okay?"

"I slept with Ollie."

"You did?" she asks, her voice high. "You know, I should have expected that. The two of you holed up together in one room. What's funny about that, though?"

"No, not here. On my birthday."

"Oh! You know I thought you did, but you guys were always so chill about it. I thought I read the room wrong! I knew it!"

I take a big gulp of my wine. "That's not the funny part though. So we've been flirty and everything, but honestly, that's it." I pause for dramatic effect. "And this jerk just broke up with me. Like, we weren't even anything to begin with."

Gabi's voice is low when she speaks. "Oh, Steph."

"No, don't be sad! I'm Alanis Morissette! I flew halfway across the world just to be rejected *again*. It's ironic!"

She giggles. "Well, I'm glad you're taking it in stride. But why did he break up with you if you weren't together?"

"Ugh. I think he thinks I'm looking for something more serious than I am. And honestly, I get it. I flew to Costa Rica searching for love with someone who doesn't love me back. I guess I kind of understand why he's apprehensive, considering the second Rod didn't work out, I jumped on a plane and did the same thing for him."

Gabi hums. "I guess so. Just seems like a jerk move." She's quiet for a second. "So does this mean you're coming home soon?"

"I don't know," I say. "I haven't thought that far ahead."

"You should! You can stay in Zeke's spare room. We'll throw you a welcome back party that rivals your bon voyage."

"Thanks, Gabi. I might like to stay in Paris for a bit. Maybe explore by myself."

She sighs. "You don't get lonely?"

*I definitely get lonely.* "If you keep busy and meet people, it's not that lonely."

She lets out a quick breath. "Well, alright. We miss you."

"Miss you too, Gabs. Hey, how is the studio going?"

Last month my sister opened her very own yoga studio. She's been obsessed for years and finally took the plunge. She loves it, but she runs herself ragged taking care of it.

She groans. "I'm exhausted. Working full-time and running a studio is nearly impossible. Thank god I have Zeke."

I hear his voice somewhere in the background. "Hi Zeke."

"He says hello."

As I take another sip of wine, the shower stops.

"Oh shit, I have to go, my ex-nothing is coming back," I tell her.

"Okay. Text me when you know your plans, okay? And tell Ollie to shove a sock in his big mouth."

I laugh. "Yeah, I'll get right on that."

And as I hang up, a text message pops up on my phone.

ROD

Where are you?

I stare at it. *What the actual fuck?*

STEPH

Paris?

ROD

What? I'm in Manuel Antonio.

I glance toward the bathroom door when I hear a noise, thinking Ollie is about to reappear, but he doesn't.

STEPH

Okay. Have fun.

ROD

I was coming to see you.

I run through our last conversation. I thought things ended pretty clearly, that he was choosing a life of travel over a life with me.

But he did say there was a part of him that would always love me.

Maybe things weren't as clear as I'd thought.

STEPH

Okay. Well like I said, I'm in Paris.

ROD

Oh okay. I wanted to see you.

The bathroom door opens and Ollie steps out. He glances at me, his eyebrows crinkled. "Are you alright?"

Rod's text nearly made me forget about Ollie.

"Yeah," I say, struggling to fix my face. "Rod texted me."

He raises an eyebrow. "Yeah? What does he want?"

STEPH

I'm sorry. Paris was my next stop.

"I guess he wants to see me," I say, mostly to gauge Ollie's reaction. I'm not interested in seeing Rod, but the curious side of me wants to know how Ollie feels about this.

ROD

I'll come to you.

My heart drops. *He'll come to me?*

Ollie purses his lips. "In Paris?"

I nod, somewhat dumbfounded. "Yeah."

"I don't love that it took him so long, but I'm glad he's showing up for you."

I look up at Ollie, my eyes catching on his for a moment.

Rod is finally willing to show up for me, when I think I'm realizing I only have eyes for someone else. It feels like the worst kind of kismet, the universe forcing a decision on me as if to prove that all of those years I wasted being on-again, off-again with Rod truly were just that. A waste.

Because after one night with Ollie, he's all I've been able to think about.

And he doesn't want me the same way.

Ollie misses the catch in my voice when I speak. "He really is showing up for me, isn't he?"

He nods. "Well, like I said, you can have the room when I'm gone."

It sounds terrible. The room is nice, but I'm just going to be sitting here thinking of Ollie.

STEPH

We broke up, Rod. And I won't be here long. Stay with your friends.

In my moment of clarity, I navigate to his contact and block him.

Ollie glances at the still-broken pull-out couch haphazardly deconstructed against the wall. "I don't think that's salvageable, but uh, I'll stay on my side."

So we're sleeping in the same bed tonight.

That's not weird at all.

## 20

## OLIVER

My stomach churns uncomfortably at the thought of Rod being in this room with Stephanie. I don't even know what he looks like, but I imagine some tall, built guy with a slick smirk who has only one thing in mind: taking advantage of her.

*But I can't do anything about that, can I?*

I didn't mean to essentially break up with her, but I could tell that's how she took it, judging from the way her shoulders dropped. The way she went uncharacteristically quiet.

Stephanie is *good*. She loves too freely and forgives too easily, and maybe the right thing to do for her is insist that we keep a distance.

I can't keep her away from Rod, but keeping her away from me will at least save her *some* hurt.

Maybe the logical part of my brain went on vacation when I did, because now that I've clicked back into my own goals–a promotion, by any means–I realize that I'm nothing more than a guy who will take her away from what she truly wants.

I'm either in her way or confusing her.

Stephanie follows me into bed a few minutes later and flips off the light on her nightstand. The bed squeaks as she settles in, and I feel the urge to turn toward her, pull her into me and fall asleep the same way we have the past few days.

But I don't.

She's asleep a few minutes later, as she always is, and I sit up in bed. The wine is wearing off, and the weight of the conversation we just had is heavy on my chest.

She turns onto her back, her knee opening into my leg, and I move gently away.

I hate the thought of leaving her here. I hate the thought of potentially losing her as a friend.

But my whole life, I've needed to have a goal. A direction.

I thought this week was going to be a relaxing vacation from the whirlwind that is my life, and the past few days with her really have been. But now that I'm faced with an opportunity to prove my dedication, I *have* to do everything in my power to show up. My goal has always been to move up the corporate ladder.

*Now is not the time to get distracted.*

Even though there's nothing more that I want to do than pull the covers up over both of us and tip her onto her side so I can pull her right up against my chest.

WHEN I WAKE up in the morning, Steph is already gone. Her stuff is still here though, so I can only assume she's coming back.

I do my mindfulness minutes and then call the airline as I head down the street to pick up breakfast. I pick up a croissant and espresso for Stephanie, even though I'm not sure what time she'll be back.

It's warmer today than it has been, so I sit at one of the wrought-iron tables in the courtyard and eat while the airline puts me on hold repeatedly. I put it on speaker since I'm the only one out here, and scroll through my reservation and passport details as they ask. It takes an exorbitantly long time to actually get the reservation changed, but since neither flight is within twenty-four hours, they don't charge me for it.

My flight is in two days now, instead of five, so until then, all I have to do is stay a respectful distance away from Stephanie and respond to enough emails to make my presence known.

This vacation did not turn out the way I expected it to.

# 21

## STEPHANIE

Can someone please explain to me how breaking up with someone you're not even dating can somehow be more awkward than trying to reconnect with someone you've broken up with so many times you can't even count them on one hand?

I leave the hotel early in the morning so I don't have to see Ollie because I don't know how we're going to come back from last night. Before bed I came to accept what had happened, but now that it's morning and the haze of the wine has left, his words run on repeat through my head.

*It doesn't feel right to be in your way.*

He didn't even do me the courtesy of spelling things out plainly. If I was dumber than I am, there's a good chance I would have missed the meaning in that sentence.

Can we go back to when he used to call me Wildflower?

But no, I don't want that either because as much as I crave that feeling, it won't hold any weight if there's no feeling behind it.

I realize with a start that perhaps my feelings for Ollie began long before this trip. Long before he called me Wildflower. Because it only feels good if I can read into some-thing behind it.

I brought my earbuds today, so instead of doing Ollie's stupid mindfulness minutes, I stand at the front of the pagoda, wrapped in the new clothes I bought yesterday, and I let Alanis Morissette ring out in my ears.

But even as the sun peeks over the horizon and Alanis croons the opening notes of "You Learn," I feel unsettled. I let the song play out, stuff my earbuds into my jacket pocket, and take a seat in the middle of the pagoda. I didn't think I had been doing it long enough to feel this urge, but there's something in my body that's searching for the peacefulness that comes after fifteen mindful minutes.

*Add this to the list of things I'm anxious to forget started with Ollie.*

When I'm done, I brush the dirt from my pants and take a long walk around the park. I love being in Paris, but there are certain things I miss about Costa Rica–the flowering trees skirting the porch, the sounds of animals hooting and hollering in the distance.

When my legs begin their protest against any more walking, I head to the metro. I pick up an espresso and a croissant once I'm closer to the hotel, and hold my breath as I push through the gate. I follow the brick pathway to the door, and realize only once I'm there that I don't have my key on me.

My heart thumps. *What if Ollie already left?*

I don't have the landlord's number, and my passport is inside.

"Fuck." I put my little espresso cup on the ground, balancing the croissant on top of it, and search my pockets for anything that might masquerade as a key. I settle on a credit card, slipping it into the crack of the door and searching for that perfect spot to pop it open.

I crouch like a maniac, my eyes boring into the keyhole as if I can will it to unlock.

And then the door opens. I freeze.

"Are you alright?"

"Oh my god," I say, stepping back from the door and holding my hands over my face. "I didn't think you were here. I forgot my key."

"Knocking first is usually good protocol," he says, stepping out of the way so I can come inside. "Before pulling out your criminal breaking and entering skills."

"If I thought you were here, I would have knocked."

"I mean, it's probably worth confirming before trying to break in."

I roll my eyes. "I'll remember that for next time." *The next time that will never happen.*

I throw my espresso and croissant onto the kitchen table, only to realize Ollie's laptop is already taking up most of the space. Hesitating, I pick them up again, and search the room for a better place to eat.

When I realize there isn't one, I shrug and sit down at the table. *This will not be awkward.*

Ollie takes the seat across from me, eyeing me, and I realize that the espresso cup and croissant bag next to him are from the same place I got mine.

He notices me looking and nudges them toward me.

"I got these for you," he says. "But don't feel like you have to stuff yourself. Yours is probably warmer anyway."

I blink. *That was unexpected.*

"Thank you." I pull the croissant out of the bag. Is this an olive branch? "You know, I'm actually pretty hungry."

He nods. "Well, eat up then."

I take a sip of my espresso and tear into the croissant as he starts typing.

The silence is deafening.

But I'm just going to lean into this.

"Do you have plans with Rod for Valentine's Day?" he finally asks.

My heart drops. "What?"

He glances up from his computer. "Valentine's Day is this week. Are you going to do something special?"

"Oh." *Fuck.*

I'm going to be alone in the City of Love on Valentine's Day.

I couldn't have planned this worse.

"I didn't realize. I'll have to come up with something."

He nods.

My mind races. Ollie looks at me expectantly, as if waiting to hear an idea.

"We could do one of those dinner cruises," I say, popping a bite of croissant in my mouth. Ollie raises his eyebrows, and I immediately want to claw the words back.

"I'd book now. They're probably close to full."

"You think?"

He nods, then types rapid-fire on his computer and turns the screen toward me. "Two that I found are already booked, but this one has a 5:30 reservation you can take."

"Oh, okay," I say, and open my phone to search for it. If I can see where it takes off from, at least I'll know what areas to avoid.

"Just buy it on here, it'll be a pain through your phone," he says impatiently.

"You don't have to help me plan a romantic evening with another man, you know," I snap.

He shakes his head, and when he catches my eye, his face is pinched in anguish. "I kind of want to."

"Because you feel bad?"

"I mean, yeah."

"Well, don't." I scoff. "You didn't make that much of an impact."

My words are a little sharper than I intended, but I take his answering nod as confirmation that maybe they were just what he needed to hear.

I grab the laptop from him and book the dinner, and then add a walking tour of the best chocolate pastries in Paris for the afternoon. Because I guess I'm feeling self-destructive today.

The only thing worse than his pity-help booking a Valentine's Day date would be his sad pity face if I told him I was planning on going alone.

"Don't you want to be hungry when you get to dinner?" he asks.

"Anyone who knows French dining etiquette knows that pastries go to a separate stomach," I explain, fully intending to gorge myself on the chocolate tour and skip the stupid dinner.

"Ah, I forgot about the second stomach."

I sigh at the confirmation notifications that pop up on my phone. "Well, that takes care of that."

"Here's hoping he actually shows up this time."

I shoot him a glare as he starts typing again. We're both a little salty, but as much as I want to be mad at him, I also feel a little zip of heat run down my spine. The anger between us feels like it's only seconds away from dissolving into lust.

I hate that he still has that effect on me.

I want him to rise from his seat and grab me out of my chair, press his lips to mine hungrily. Tell me he still doesn't want to be with me but he can't resist touching me. Push me backward so my knees hit the bed and I topple over. And then maybe he'd tug roughly on my jeans and I'd cry out and it would only make him more ravenous for me.

I shake the thought from my mind and stand from my chair, grabbing my croissant and coffee.

"I'll just eat this outside," I say, and stomp out into the courtyard. I take a seat at one of the wrought-iron tables and urge my thumping heart to slow.

# 22

# OLIVER

So Steph is pissed. I guess that's understandable. But she didn't have to storm out and eat her food in the cold.

Luckily it's mild out today, so I'm not going to go out there and insist she come back in. She'll be fine, and maybe when she comes back inside we can sit and have a normal conversation like the friends we are.

We were close to it. Planning her little Valentine's Day excursion was actually kind of fun. Of course, I was imagining she'd be taking me, but she doesn't have to know that. I said what I said for a reason, and letting her believe any differently will just make things harder later on.

But man, I really hate that she's taking Rod out on Valentine's Day. Mostly because he won't give her the appreciation she deserves. I'm still not even certain he has a plane ticket yet, and he needs to be on a flight *tonight* if they want to dedicate a full day to the holiday.

I grumble to myself as I respond to yet another client email.

And then I navigate to the director of training position

again and stare at it. I could probably recite the whole thing in my sleep if I wanted to.

*Significant travel required. Create a suite of training materials. Lead a team of trainers.*

I hate this holding pattern I'm in, this endless waiting that has me counting down the days until Jack and Emma are back in the U.S. and come clean about their relationship. I hate that they *have* to do that because this company moves so damn slow and it's taking away their happiness.

And I hate that if things don't go well for them, they go well for me. I hate that the thing I want most comes at the expense of everyone around me getting hurt, even if it isn't a direct result. Jack wouldn't get what *he* wants. And I can't have Stephanie.

I slam my laptop closed, unable to look at the job description anymore, and text my siblings.

OLLIE

> Serious question. How much should you give up for the sake of a promotion?

ELIZA

Give up? Maybe another five hours a week, tops.

ETHAN

Everything.

OLLIE

> Alright well EVERYTHING is a little dramatic, don't you think?

ETHAN

You're backward, dude. Commit to giving up everything now and once you're there you can decide what's important.

ELIZA

What do you have to give up?

I sigh, struggling to come up with the words.

OLLIE

A girl.

ELIZA

You shouldn't have to give up people for a job.

ETHAN

Well, we haven't met her so it can't be serious enough to choose her over a job.

That's a good point. I care for Steph, but at most, we're still getting to know each other. And it would be wrong to lead her on if I know of something on the horizon that could cause the whole thing to crumble.

OLLIE

Not serious. But big FOMO.

ELIZA

FOMO like you like her or FOMO like you're being a horn dog?

ETHAN

Horn dog FOMO is fleeting by definition.

ELIZA

Thank you O wise one.

ELIZA

My take? Growth follows discomfort. You're in the Uncomfortable Before, and Ethan's right on one thing: you can't make big choices until you know what the promotion actually entails. If you even get the promotion. But I think you're doing yourself a disservice in giving up a girl you like for the sake of a dumb job.

ETHAN

Dumb jobs pay for things. You'll learn that once you finally have one.

Eliza leaves the group chat.

She just finished her master's in education and had some trouble finding a permanent position before the school year started. She's subbing now, but with plenty of potential.

Because she, like everyone else in my family, is insanely talented. Sometimes it just takes a minute to get your foot in the door.

ETHAN

Oops.

I text her separately to thank her for her advice.

OLLIE

Thanks Eliza. You're so much more mature than our big brother.

ELIZA

He makes me want to kill things with my bare hands sometimes.

OLLIE

It's because he loves you.

I throw my phone on the table and walk over to the

window, where I can see Steph angrily tearing off pieces of her croissant and shoving them in her mouth. She takes a sip of her espresso and makes a face, and I know from having done the same so many times in a handful of countries before developing a taste for espresso that she's deeply missing American coffee.

I grab my keys and step outside, shoving my hands in my pockets.

"Come on," I say, nodding to the courtyard gate.

She raises her eyebrows as she stuffs the croissant wrapper into her empty coffee cup. "Come on what?"

I resist the urge to make a naughty joke. Silence beats between us.

"Let's get you American coffee."

"Can you do that here?"

I nod. "You just have to ask for filtered coffee. Lots of places have it."

"Why didn't you tell me that before?"

I roll my eyes at her. "You didn't ask."

She gives me a look.

"Do you want coffee?" I ask.

She debates for a second. "Well, yeah." She scrambles up from the chair and grabs her trash while she goes. She throws it in a receptacle at the edge of the courtyard, and I open the gate for her to step through.

We walk down to the cafe at the end of the street, and I order for both of us since Steph's French is bad enough that it sounds like she's mocking them.

I commend her for memorizing a few phrases off Google, though. It's more than most people do.

I place the cup in her hand, and she breathes in the steam. We step out of the shop and onto the pavement, the midday sun warming our faces while our coffees warm our hands.

"God, I really hope this is as good as I'm expecting it to be."

"It won't be," I warn her.

She huffs. "Can you let me have hope for two minutes?"

I hold my hands up in surrender. "It will be the best American coffee you've ever tasted," I tell her. "You won't ever be able to drink coffee at home again after this."

She huffs. "Well, there's no need to blow smoke up my ass," she says, and then stops, as if she's only now realizing she's referencing one of our little jokes.

I see the opportunity for a joke, and this time, I take it.

"Hey, bend over," I say, making a show of blowing the steam from my coffee at her.

It takes her a second to get it, and she whacks me playfully on the arm. "Oh Jesus, Ollie!"

We break into laughter, and a certain comfort descends over us. I didn't like the angry tension we were holding, and being able to laugh with her gives me back a bit of relief I haven't had since our dinner with Jack and Emma.

I'm not quite ready to follow Eliza's advice, but staying on friendly terms with Steph seems like a necessity–if not for *us* specifically, then at least for our friend group.

"Hey, want to buy a bottle of something and go find somewhere pretty to drink it?"

She looks like she's about to say no, and then shrugs. "Why not?"

# 23

# STEPHANIE

"How about a spot by the river?"

He holds the door open for me as we exit the corner store. I unzip my jacket, thankful for the heat of the sun, and we walk down to the water where we find some open space and swing our feet out over the edge.

It's not quite warm enough to forego my jacket, but it's more than comfortable enough to leave my boots on the ground next to me.

Ollie busies himself opening the champagne, but as he pops it open, he pauses. "I didn't think to get glasses."

I shrug, taking the bottle from him and carefully taking a sip. "Who needs glasses for champagne?"

He laughs, and then takes a slightly less careful sip that causes the bubbles to come gushing out into his face.

"Oh fuck," he says, leaning over so it doesn't get his clothes. "Apparently I do."

I laugh as he wipes his mouth off, unapologetically *at* him rather than *with* him.

"I'm glad you're entertained by my misfortune."

"One must never manhandle champagne," I tell him sternly.

"I'll consider that a lesson learned." He takes another sip, this time more carefully than the first, and manages to actually get a mouthful of liquid instead of foam. He hands it back to me.

"Good job," I say.

Ollie eyes me as I drop my phone on the ground next to me. "Hear from Rod yet? He needs to leave for his flight soon, doesn't he?"

I shrug. "Not for a while yet." I can't tell whether Ollie's asking because he's jealous or concerned, but I let myself think it's jealousy that spurs him onward. And I dig my heels into this lie just a little further.

"Are you excited for your big Valentine's date?"

I give him a look. "We don't have to talk about this."

"I know. I just feel like it's the sort of thing you would normally talk to me about. At least, if we happened to be in the same place at the same time and it came up," he says, taking a sip of the champagne.

"You mean if we just happened to be in Paris together, drinking champagne on the Seine and it casually came up in conversation?"

He rolls his eyes. "You know what I mean."

I sigh, taking an extra few gulps of the champagne when he passes it to me. In my mind, I see a lonely day of stuffing chocolate pastries down my throat while surrounded by happy couples speaking a language I can't even eavesdrop on. "I think it's going to be nice. You know I love chocolate and boats and food, and I'm sure the rest of the day we'll stumble upon fun things to do."

He nods, turning his gaze to the water. "Well, it sounds like this all worked out really well for you, then."

I shrug. "I suppose it did."

We're quiet for a few moments. "What's after Paris?" he asks.

I let out a long breath. "God, I have no clue. Maybe I'll stay in Europe for a while."

Ollie nods. "That would be cool. Rod, too?"

I look at him from the corner of my eye. "I guess it depends what he plans on."

Ollie's eyes narrow. "As in, you'll do what he wants when he gets here?"

A quick ball of rage shoots through my limbs. "No. As in, I just want to have all of my information before deciding."

*As in, I can't stand the thought of being in Paris without you.* But I can't say that.

"I want to go somewhere I know the language. It's lonely when you can't really talk to anyone."

*Fuck, shouldn't have said that.* That's like begging him to figure out Rod isn't coming.

"Have you been lonely on this trip?"

*And that's even worse.* I shake my head, desperate to walk the statement back. "No, no, not at all." *Not here, at least.* A lump builds in my throat when I think of all the time I spent alone in Costa Rica. "I guess I just miss hanging out with people. I've FaceTimed and chatted on the phone with the girls from work, with Gabi, and Kay and Leilani, but it's not the same, you know? But God, it would be so nice to just go out dancing for a night and get drunk and be stupid. But you can't in a foreign country. Or at least, I'd get nervous."

He passes me the champagne. "Well, maybe you'll find your own band of travelers like Rod has and they'll watch your back if you want to have a crazy night every once in a while."

"I guess." I take a sip. "I'm not sure I want a band of travelers like his though."

"Three to a queen bed?"

"Yeah, I *really* wasn't into that." I pass him the bottle.

"You just didn't give it enough time for things to get spicy."

"Ollie!" I grab the champagne back from him before he has time to take a sip.

He reaches for it, leaning toward me with one hand on the pavement as I hold it just beyond his fingertips. "Hey!" He pauses there, realizing he's leaning over me and only inches from my face. He clears his throat and retreats. "Champagne hog."

I hand it back to him, narrowing my eyes, and he hesitantly takes it from me.

"All I really care about is seeing the Eiffel Tower," I say. "I mean, it's not all of Paris, but you can't go to Paris and *not* see it."

He pauses, champagne halfway to his lips. "I don't know why it didn't occur to me to take you there first."

I shrug. "I wasn't your main concern," I say, hoping it digs in just a bit.

He lets out a long breath and takes a sip of champagne. I *almost* feel bad that I've silenced him. Almost.

I take the champagne back from him. "When does your flight leave?"

"Tomorrow afternoon."

I nod. "And then it's just me and *Paris*," I say, putting on a really terrible French accent to cover up the sinking feeling in my chest.

Ollie snorts. "Until Rod comes."

"Right. Until Rod comes."

When we finish our champagne, we go in search of

something light for lunch and eat on a patio next to a busy street where tourists and Parisians alike bustle by. Afterward, Ollie asks me if I want to go see the Eiffel Tower.

But I decline. Tell him I'd rather see it for the first time with Rod.

And swallow over the lump in my throat that builds when I think of going to see it alone.

So we head to the Louvre instead and promptly lose each other inside, only to accidentally find each other again fifteen minutes later. We spend hours wandering the exhibits and finally emerge close to dinnertime with sore feet and hungry stomachs.

Our conversation over dinner is friendly but reserved, and afterward I shower first and get into my side of the bed, careful to leave ample buffer between us. An ache throbs in my chest like even my body knows that tomorrow is going to be a terrible day.

I swallow over the lump building in my throat as I pull the covers up over myself.

Tomorrow is Valentine's Day. In the City of Love.

And I'll be alone.

Again.

## 24

## OLIVER

I have a weird feeling in my gut that Steph is lying to me about Rod. Her non-answers about his schedule make me nervous, like maybe he's not coming after all. I want to think that she would tell me if her plans changed, but I don't blame her for not being completely open with me anymore.

She's been moody today, quick to snap at me but just as quick to laugh. Almost like she wants to hate me but she can't.

Then again, I've been cracking jokes like it's my job because I hate seeing her upset and knowing that I'm at least partially to blame.

Unless Rod isn't coming. Then I'm putting the blame squarely on him. *That's* why she's upset. Not me.

But there's no good way for me to ask her again. I've tried a number of times today, and she doesn't want to have that conversation. Either he's coming and she's just upset with me, or he's not coming and she's hiding it from me.

I flip off the light as I get into bed, careful to stay on my side, and drift off as her gentle snores fill the room.

AT SOME POINT in the night, I wake up, and judging from the shadows in the room it must be that weird time that's both late and early at the same time. I sigh, hoping I can just close my eyes and fall right back asleep, when I hear a sniffle next to me.

My eyes pop open again, and I turn my attention toward her. Her back is to me, but as I listen closer, I'm almost certain the uneven little breaths she's taking aren't inspired by a dream she's having in her sleep but a nightmare she's living through.

While I suspected it before, I know, now, that Rod isn't coming.

I turn toward her. "Steph?"

She clears her throat. "Yeah?"

"Are you okay?"

"Yeah. Just had a weird dream."

I consider leaving it at that. We're at a weird stage post-*almost* where we're still trying to figure out what our friendship looks like. But I also know without a doubt that if I was struggling, Steph would be there for me regardless.

I reach a hesitant hand toward her, resting it lightly on her upper arm, and she stiffens but doesn't move away. She turns toward me, her eyes searching mine, and her wet cheeks reflect the moonlight shining in through the window.

"Steph," I say, and she only blinks, like she's afraid she'll start crying again if she speaks. "Rod's not coming, is he?"

She shakes her head and her face pinches up, the sniffles returning as her shoulders start shaking.

I wrap my arms around her and pull her into me, her fists balled up between us and wiping furiously at her face.

"I'm going to be alone on Valentine's Day in the City of Love," she says into my chest, her words stilted and hoarse.

"Steph," I say, struggling to swallow over the lump building in my throat.

She shakes her head, curling into me. "I don't know why I try."

"Because you believe the best in people."

She shakes her head. "I just can't believe I managed to do this to myself. All this travel, all this trying to be the best version of myself for someone else, all the putting myself out there just to be shot down. It's like the universe is trying to punish me for trying so hard."

"It's just a bit of irony. One day when you've found your person—someone who appreciates you as they should—you'll look back on this and laugh," I say, hoping my serious tone conveys just how much she shouldn't let Rod's assholeness change her goodness.

She shakes her head. "I feel so dumb."

"You're not dumb. You love too freely and forgive too easily. You make yourself vulnerable to experience the best in life. You give away little pieces of yourself, and as much as you want to believe it never affects the whole, sometimes it does. But it's worth it in the end, even if the middle sucks sometimes."

She sucks in a breath with a sniffle. "I hate you for saying that."

"Because you know it's true."

She presses her forehead into my chest, taking a deep breath. "I want one thing, Ollie. I want my big love. And I'm going to be alone on Valentine's Day in the City of Love. Isn't *that* ironic."

I can't help squeezing her a little tighter. I know I'm part of the problem here, but staying for her feels like it'll paint our whole situationship in a strange light. I don't want to lead her on when I can't be the big love she's searching for.

Even though every molecule in my body is screaming at me to push my flight. Stay another few days. Be *something* for her even if I can't be her big love.

"I'm sorry," she says into my chest, and I want to yell at her that she's the last person that needs to be apologizing right now.

"For what?"

"For ruining your vacation. For waking you up. For drowning you in boy problems. Ugh, this trip is a mess."

I sigh, settling into the feeling of her body against mine now that the tears are subsiding. "You made it a lot more interesting. And for that, I say thank you."

She only shakes her head, pressing her face further into my chest.

WHEN I WAKE up in the morning, I keep my eyes shut tight. As long as I don't open them, I can keep my hand on Steph's hip. I can stay pressed against her backside. I can push her hair out of my face and then curl tighter around her like it won't end up right back where it started.

The silky fabric of her shorts has nothing on the feeling of her skin as I run one hand along her hip. In my morning haze, I think maybe something could happen here.

And then she stirs, twisting her body toward me.

"How are you feeling?" I ask, hesitant to let go of her.

She groans. "Embarrassed. Can we just forget about last night?"

"Don't be embarrassed," I say. "Nothing to be embarrassed about."

She rolls her eyes as she sits up, running her fingers through her hair. "Well, I'm going to pretend it was all a bad dream."

She stands and pulls one of her new sweaters over her shoulders as she sits down at the kitchen table, opening her laptop. I throw my legs over the side of the bed and put my face in my hands. From the window into the courtyard, I can just barely see light over the horizon. It must be around five. Time for Stephanie to start work.

Rather than going for another hour or so of sleep, I sit down for my mindfulness minutes, and I can't decide whether the clicking of her keys is annoying or comforting. It's nice to think that she's just doing her thing while I'm doing mine, but the past couple of days she's joined me. She's probably refraining because she's upset—or maybe it never worked for her in the same way it does for me.

Either way, I spend most of my fifteen minutes focused on her, and she spends the entirety of it *click-click-clicking* on her computer.

Afterward, I get dressed, gather up my things into my suitcase, and clear the room of my trash. Once my things are in a neat little pile by the door, I turn to Steph.

"I'm going to grab a coffee and a croissant. Do you want anything?"

She looks up from her computer, her eyes just now registering the suitcases by my side. "Um, yeah. Same for me, please."

"*Un espresso ou un café filtré?*"

"*Un café filtré, s'il vous plaît.*"

I raise my eyebrows. Her accent is, well, terrible, but she got the words right at least. "Look who speaks French now."

She shoots me a look. "Well, without you I'll have to be able to navigate on my own."

I'm reminded of our conversation yesterday at the river, that she feels lonely when she can't talk to anyone in a foreign country. I find myself wondering what her plan is, now that Rod isn't coming.

"I'm sure you'll do just fine."

She shrugs. "Here's hoping."

I nod as I push through the door and head down the street to the small cafe we've taken a liking to. I order two American coffees and two croissants to go, and wait as they're prepared. While I do, I unintentionally fixate on what Steph's time is going to look like when I'm gone, whether she'll stay in Paris or head somewhere else nearby.

I realize, as I scoop up our coffees, that Steph will be looking at the Eiffel Tower by herself. A heavy feeling settles in my chest at the thought.

When I get back to the room, she's still typing away at her computer and says only a quick "Thank you," as I place her breakfast on the table next to her.

"I should probably head to the airport," I tell her, drawing her attention from her screen.

"Right," she says, standing.

"Let me know if you need anything, okay?"

She nods. "Thanks, Ollie. Thanks for the room, too."

"No problem," I say, as we awkwardly lock eyes and look away.

*Jesus, this is ridiculous.* I take a step forward and wrap my arms around her. She buries her face in my shoulder, that banana and mango scent of hers winding up into my nostrils, familiar yet fleeting. "I'll miss you, Steph."

"Miss you too, Ollie," she says, as she steps away from me.

"Call me if you get lonely, okay?"

She rolls her eyes. "I'll be fine."

"I know you'll be fine. Everybody gets lonely sometimes."

She gives me a look. "Even you?"

"Absolutely."

Her eyes narrow. "Yeah, okay."

I pull on my jacket and shoes and throw my suit bag over my shoulder, rolling my suitcase out the door. She waves as I push through the gate to the street, and when I close it behind me, I can't help but wonder if I'm making a huge mistake.

MY THOUGHTS RUN wild in the taxi to the airport. I'm doing the right thing for me, prioritizing a career I've worked ridiculously hard for over the past few years, yet I can't help but feel like I'm letting down Steph.

And that feels bigger than my quest for this goddamn promotion.

This isn't even my fault. It's Rod's. He's the one leaving her high and dry, but I'm the one who had to leave her alone in that hotel room knowing the plans she made for today. Knowing that she gets lonely in foreign countries because she can't speak the language.

The taxi drops me at my terminal, and I pay and head inside, my suitcase rolling behind me and my suit bag thrown over my shoulder. A blast of heat rushes across my face as I enter the building and translate signs telling me which way to walk.

I wonder what she's doing right now. Still working? Maybe she took a break and went for a walk around the neighborhood.

Maybe she's taking a nap before her big Valentine's date by herself.

The thought punches me in the gut. The memory of her tears last night made it too real–the rejection, the loneliness. I hate that for her. Stephanie is full of personality and she shouldn't feel tamped down because she doesn't know how to translate it.

She's going on a chocolate tour by herself. She's going to a romantic dinner by herself.

*Or did she just tell me she was still going so I wouldn't worry about her crying in bed all day instead?*

The customs line is long and arduous, and I harp on the mental image of Stephanie pressed up against my chest last night, cheeks tear-stained. It sticks in my mind so long that I start to wonder if I just like torturing myself.

I see her in that sparkly dress she passed on a few days ago, playing on her phone while couples talk and laugh around her. Walking along to the Eiffel Tower afterward and watching everyone around her brimming with love.

Steph can make the best of a bad situation–she has been this whole time–but when does it become too much? She went on this trip *for love*, and now, on the most love-filled day of the year, she's alone.

My gate looms ahead of me.

I nod at it as if required to acknowledge its existence, and veer left toward the airline's counter.

"How can I help you, sir?" the attendant asks, her teeth a brilliant white behind her red smile.

"I need to change my flight."

# 25

# STEPHANIE

I towel dry my hair and throw on some leggings and one of my new sweaters.

If ever there was a day to eat my feelings, it's today. I figure I'll note my favorite pastry shop during the tour and come back afterward to stock up for the night. Then maybe pick up a bottle of champagne. I might as well make the best of a less-than-ideal situation.

I have some time before I have to leave, so I sit down to check my email. I'm done my work for the day, but I like to make it clear that I'm available *whenever*. My boss gives me the freedom to travel like this and still work, so I make sure that nothing falls through the cracks or gets lost on yesterday's task list.

But I've only gotten as far as signing into my computer when there's a knock at the door and my heart plummets.

I don't know who would be knocking if not the landlord, and I sure as hell don't look like Oliver Long.

"Fuck," I mutter, twisting my hair over my shoulder in an effort to tame the mane.

I take a breath before opening the door, plastering an overenthusiastic smile onto my face.

I blink. "Ollie?"

He smiles at me, letting loose a breath before speaking. "Hi."

"Did you miss your flight?" I ask, noting the luggage stacked next to him. He has a shopping bag in his hand that he must have stolen from me with the name of the boutique where I got my sweaters.

"You could say that," he says. "Can I come in?"

"Um yeah, it's your room," I say, stepping aside so he can pass.

He rolls his bag in behind him and leans it against the kitchen table. I shut the door behind him.

"Are you alright?" I ask. "What's going on?"

He swallows, his eyes wide as they settle on mine.

"You're freaking me out. What's wrong?"

He shakes his head. "Nothing is wrong," he says, and sighs. He hands me the bag he's holding. "I was just wondering if maybe, since Rod isn't here, I could be your date for Valentine's Day?"

I narrow my eyes. "Um, could you do me a favor and narrow down the five hundred different mixed signals you're throwing me?"

He scrunches his eyes shut. "I know. I'm sorry." He breathes out heavily through his nose. "Look, I couldn't get on that plane knowing you'd be sitting here alone–or worse, on a romantic date by yourself–"

"I love spending time with myself."

He lets out a short huff. "I know, love yourself first and all that crap." He rolls his eyes. "Steph, look. You know I like you." He pauses, gauging my reaction, and my breath catches in my throat. "I can't be what you want me to be, but if you'll take me just for today, I'd really love to spend Valentine's Day with you."

"You can't be what I want you to be?"

He shakes his head. "You know, everything you wanted from Rod. Your person. Your great love, or whatever. That's not me. I have too much going on right now to give you the attention you deserve, and if you're not willing to accept less than that, I totally understand." He bites his lip. "But maybe for now, in Paris, we can be *something.*"

"Something?"

"Like temporary lovers."

I raise my eyebrows, trying to hide a smile. "Presumptuous of you."

He sighs, taking a step toward me. "No presumptions. I just want to be your Valentine this year."

A snorting laugh escapes me. "Ollie, if you weren't so afraid of commitment I'd say you might even be a romantic."

"Is that a yes?"

*Um, yeah!*

I eye him for a second, just to make him sweat a little, and then smile. "I'd be delighted to take you on the full Valentine's Day by Stephanie experience." I take a deep breath before continuing. "But in the interest of being totally honest with you, I should probably tell you that, um..." My words fail me. He raises his eyebrows. "Rod was never coming. He wanted to, but I told him not to. I was always going to be alone on Valentine's Day. And last night, I think it just caught up with me."

I swallow, hoping this doesn't change Ollie's mind.

He's quiet for a second, then nods. "If last night wasn't about Rod but being alone today, I feel even better about my decision to come back." He takes a step forward and gestures to the bag in my hand. "Open it."

I let out a long breath as I set it on the kitchen table and reach inside. My fingers graze along something sharp, like scales. I crinkle my eyebrows, grabbing the fabric and pulling it out. Only when I see the shimmer do I realize he actually went back to the boutique and bought the sparkly dress for me.

"You got this for me?" I ask, holding it up in front of me.

He nods. "Yeah, and your sister has some very unfortunate photos of me posing with it that I hope never see the light of day. I honestly think she was screwing with me with how many different sizes she had me snapping pictures of."

"Ollie, I think you really might be a bit of a romantic. Even *despite* the fear of commitment."

His cheeks turn pink, and I stand on my toes to drop a kiss on his cheek.

"Thank you," I say.

He winds an arm around my waist, pulling me close, and kisses me, his lips soft but firm on mine. When he pulls away, he keeps me tight against him and kisses my temple.

"Now go get ready."

I whip into the bathroom, grabbing my boots on my way, and switch into my sparkles. If I had more time I'd bother with a little makeup, maybe even do my hair. But as it is, the dress will have to do.

"So how do I look?" I ask, striking a pose as I leave the bathroom.

He stands in the middle of the room, buttoning up the dress shirt he changed into. He grins, his eyes trailing unabashedly along my body. "Perfect," he says. "Dare I say, beautiful."

I roll my eyes at him, opening my mouth to tell him to stop blowing smoke up my ass.

"No smoke," he says, before I'm able to. "Only fire."

I feel the heat creeping up my neck. "God, you're so corny."

"Steph, we're in Paris for Valentine's Day. That ship has already sailed."

I shrug, grabbing my purse off the kitchen table and throwing it over my shoulder. "Luckily I love corny things."

He straightens out the cuffs of his shirt and throws his jacket over top.

"Ready?" he asks.

I nod, unlocking the door.

"Aren't you going to be cold?"

I shrug. "This dress is thick and my boots cover most of my legs, so hopefully not."

"Do you want a jacket just in case?"

"One does not wear a jacket over sparkles."

He nods. "How dare I suggest such a thing?"

Before I can open the door, he wraps an arm around my waist, tightening me to him. "You look really good." He runs a hand through my hair, loose and wild, and leans down to kiss me gently, one hand cupping my face.

"You look really good too," I say, smiling into his lips.

He makes a face as he pulls away from me, staring at his hands. "Wow, your dress is *attacking* me."

I grin. "That's the price of sequins," I say, throwing the door open and welcoming a cold gust of air into the room.

"I guess it's only fitting that in order to get back in your good graces, I buy you a dress that attempts to draw blood if I so much as touch it."

The words are out of my mouth before I can think through their meaning. "Better watch those hands," I joke.

"I suppose so," he says.

We lock up behind us and continue through the courtyard. Before we get to the gate, he grabs my hand, pulling me back. He rests his hand on my hips, looking down into my eyes. "Are you sure you're okay with this?"

I shrug. *Of course I'm okay with this!* "Yeah. We're friends. Temporary lovers, as you might say."

He tugs my hips closer so our bodies are pressed against each other. "It's okay that I can only really be here for you today?"

I roll my eyes. "Ollie, do you really think I'm going to fall in love with you in the space of a few hours?"

He has the decency to grimace. "Well, no."

"We've had sex once. You're terrified of commitment. I might as well be a loose cannon. I'm not sure we're the stuff of great love stories."

He wrinkles his nose. "I'm not *terrified* of commitment. I just have other priorities right now."

"Whatever you want to call it." I wave him off. "We're role-playing, right? So if you wouldn't mind kissing me, grabbing my ass a bit, and making sure I get home after downing a bottle and a half of champagne, that'd be great."

He considers this for a moment, and then leans down to kiss me, his hands dipping to my ass and grabbing two handfuls. His tongue flicks into my mouth as he tightens around me, and a heat builds low in my abdomen. He keeps me close when he pulls away, his lips brushing gently over my cheek.

"Now the question is, what are *you* going to do for *me*?"

I can't help the grin that spreads across my face, or the flush creeping up my neck.

I don't have a good answer to that, but it inspires an array of images floating through my mind that involve much less clothing than we're currently wearing.

"I bet you'd like to know."

# 26

## OLIVER

"Oh god, I think I'm going to throw up," Steph says, pausing with another piece of chocolate halfway to her mouth. She swallows. "Oh, I think it passed." She pops the chocolate into her mouth.

"You're not going to be hungry for dinner." We exit the shop, following our tour guide back onto the street.

We're on our seventh of eight stops on the chocolate pastry tour, which—as it turns out—is a chocolate *and* pastry tour. Stephanie has gotten something from every single place, and although I tried to match her for the first few, I just can't keep up. We've been splitting the pastries, and she's eaten all the candy.

"I'll be hungry. Second stomach, remember?"

I lean toward her. "Leave room for champagne at least, okay? Remember you're supposed to need help getting home."

She rolls her eyes. "That's not a *necessity*. It's the freedom that comes with it, you know? Like I don't have to pay attention for a night. You'll make sure we don't wander down any alleyways or stumble upon any ne'er-do-wells in the street. It's not about being champagne drunk. It's about being able to enjoy the city without guarding for bodily harm."

I snort at her. I don't even know where to start with that. "Okay, yeah, I'll guard you from any ne'er-do-wells who want to cause you bodily harm," I say, shaking my head. Only Stephanie could dream up such a scenario.

"Thank you," she says. "Though I will happily siphon some champagne into my third stomach."

"I knew you were hiding one from me."

"What can I say? A girl's got to keep her mystery."

She throws her wrapper into a trashcan as we pass by, a little shiver running through her as she quickens her pace to catch up.

*I knew that was going to happen.*

Ahead of us, the tour guide chats with a friendly German family, the rest of the group following along behind them. Steph and I bring up the rear, and I take a moment to slouch out of my jacket, draping it over her shoulders.

"But my sparkles," she protests, even as she hugs it around her.

"You can take it off on the cruise," I say.

"Yeah, okay," she says, grinning up at me. I wipe a bit of spare chocolate from the corner of her mouth. "Hey, I was saving that for later."

"You're a mess, Wildflower." She unsuccessfully tries to hide her grin, and I lean down and kiss her, pulling on her lip just a little with my teeth. I catch the lightest moan from her throat that sends my blood rushing down south.

*If we're just role-playing today, what does that mean for tonight?*

Our last stop is a patisserie, and Steph selects a box of six macarons that she slips into her purse for dessert later.

I'll be surprised if they even make it that long. At this rate, I'll be surprised if they even make it to dinner.

"Ugh, Ollie," she whines, as I dig some money out of my pocket. The German family is still talking animatedly with our guide, so I simply give him a wave and a nod with our tip as we depart in the other direction. "I'm so full," she says, leaning into my arm. I wrap it around her, partially because I'm now freezing and partially because I like the way I can just touch her today, no worries about what it means.

"Do you want me to squeeze you, see if you'll pop?" I ask, pulling her close.

"Oh my god, no. I honestly might."

I follow along the path of the tour, searching for a little bar we passed by on the way. Steph falls into step easily next to me, but she doesn't ask where we're going. She made it clear that all she wants tonight is no planning or worrying, and I'm confident I can make that happen. She did all the hard stuff already, anyway; I just have to take care of the in-between moments.

We take a seat outside, the heater lamps blazing down on us, and for the first time since lending her my jacket, I can actually feel my fingers. She rubs her hands together in front of her, breathing into them, but when I sandwich them between mine to warm them, I realize she's a few degrees warmer than me.

"My god, Ollie, you're an ice cube." She takes my hands in hers instead and blows on them, the heat from her breath both relieving and sensual.

We order two glasses of champagne and watch as the sun sets over the Seine.

"So what do you like better, sunrise or sunset in Paris?" Steph asks, leaning back in her chair and throwing her hair over her shoulder. The movement sends a whiff of mango and banana into my face, and I lean toward her, anxious to kiss her again, to feel more than just her hands running over mine.

"Do I have to choose?" Our server sets two glasses on the table in front of us.

She shrugs. "No, I guess not. I like both too. Sunrise because it's peaceful, sunset because it's romantic." She scoots her chair closer to me, resting our hands in her lap so she can take a sip of her champagne. I run my thumb along her thigh, thankful for my numb hands because at least her dress doesn't feel like a thousand little cuts in my skin. "Both are very transitionary, which I like, the universe saying it's time to get your shit together, and then letting you know when you can lose it again."

I laugh. "Are you trying to tell me you're going to lose your shit in about ten minutes when the sun is officially gone from the sky?"

She grins. "It's my witching hour. You better look out."

"I think I can handle it." I throw an arm around her shoulders to pull her in for a kiss. She sighs into me, her hand landing on my chest. I don't know if she intends for it to slip slowly down my abdomen, but the descent has me imagining her crawling on top of me, lowering down and taking me into her mouth.

I hold on to her for an extra moment, deepening our kiss when decorum would dictate I pull away.

"Ollie," she says against my lips, scolding me playfully. "There are people all around us."

"Let them look."

"I knew you were a little exhibitionist," she says.

"Little?"

She smiles into our kiss. "The biggest I've ever met."

"That's better," I say. "Even if you are blowing smoke up my ass."

She pulls away from me, leaving a kiss on my jaw as she does, and I have to readjust myself as I take a thirsty sip of my champagne. She eyes me, biting her lip. "No smoke."

I raise my eyebrows at her. I wasn't fishing for a compliment, but I'll take it. I take another sip of champagne, feeling probably a little too proud of this nugget of information.

"You know, I'm kind of glad I'm here with you," she says.

"Fuck, me too. I doubt you would have told me that if you weren't all full of chocolate and champagne."

She shoots me a look. "I'm just saying, this is fun. Even if it doesn't mean anything."

And I know I shouldn't get that tight feeling in my stomach when she says that. That I can't be upset that we're a big fat nothing.

But I am. I like Stephanie despite myself.

"You just want to drink a bottle and a half of champagne and know I'll get you home okay."

She throws her hands in the air, laughing. "Well, so what if I do?"

"Hey, drink up. Want another glass? I'd love to dig into this 'biggest you've ever met' comment."

She whacks me playfully on the shoulder. "You're going to make me regret telling you that, aren't you?"

"Not unless hearing about it for the rest of forever is going to make you regret it."

She shakes her head, laughing. "Oh, so is that how you move past your fear of commitment? A lady just has to tell you you have a big dick and suddenly you're talking forever?"

I roll my eyes. "Maybe not as a singular requirement, but

yeah, I think I would like to be told I have a big dick for the rest of my life."

She takes a delicate sip of her champagne. "Well, I'm happy to be your forever for a night," she says, leaning over and whispering in my ear. "Yours was the biggest I've had, and I've missed it every day since."

My semi turns into a raging boner in seconds.

"Stephanie," I say, my eyeballs nearly popping out of my face.

She gives me a sly smile.

"So do you want to, like, find a bathroom?" I ask, and she laughs. "We can skip dinner, I'll reimburse you. Or I'm happy with a slightly less crowded alleyway, even."

She laughs, one hand landing on my arm and squeezing. "All I want is a romantic Valentine's Day," she says. "Unfortunately, that doesn't include an alleyway."

"So, bathroom then?"

She grins. "If we're all hot and bothered by the time we get back from dinner, maybe. But until then, you're keeping it in your pants."

I sigh, reaching over and squeezing her thigh. I lean over, brushing her hair from her ear, and whisper to her, "For what it's worth, I've been thinking about the constellation of moles on your hip every day since your birthday, too."

She shivers as I drop her hair from my fingers. "God Ollie, constellation?"

"You said you wanted romance."

"Stop it or I'm going to be naked in an alleyway."

"Not a great thing to tell me if you're trying to get me to *stop* talking."

She grabs my face forcefully and presses her lips against mine, her tongue swirling between my lips.

"That only works if you keep kissing me. Otherwise it has the opposite effect."

She kisses me again, moving toward me on her chair so her body is pressed up against mine. My hands roam through her hair, down to her hip, around her waist, and it's all I can do to stop myself from going further.

## 27

## STEPHANIE

I can hardly eat my dinner by the time it's served. With all the chocolate and pastries I've consumed today, it's a miracle I even have room for the complimentary glass of champagne.

I might have to will myself a fourth stomach.

Ollie grins from across the table, his own plate fully cleared.

"I can't not eat it," I say, referring to the last shrimp on my plate.

"When in Paris," he starts, "you must eat the last shrimp."

I sigh. "When in Paris," I agree, and shove it into my mouth. I chew, swallow, and wash it down with champagne.

I groan. "I don't think I can ever eat again."

"I'm sure you'll find a way. Those macarons in your purse are calling your name."

My jaw drops. "Oh man, I forgot about them! Oh, no."

He gives me a look. "You can eat them when you get home." He stands from his seat, leaving his napkin on the table, and holds his hand out to me. "Come on."

"Where are we going?" I ask, as he leads me through a mass of tables.

He glances back at me. "I think this'll help."

"Help?"

"Yeah, with your fullness."

"You're not going to make me puke into the river, are you?"

"What? No. Steph, it's the deck," he says, pushing the door open to reveal an area of open-air space that leads to both the kitchens and the other levels.

"Oh," I say, and take a place next to him by the railing. "Well, this is a lot better than puking into the river, but it's damn cold out here."

I regret it as soon as I say it, considering I'm still wearing his jacket. He rolls his eyes and then moves behind me, pushing me up against the railing so he can lean his elbows on it. "Better?"

"Yeah," I say, pressing back against him. He kisses my neck through my hair, and we turn our attention to the water rushing by, to Paris moving slowly in front of us. The Eiffel Tower looms in the distance.

An announcement sounds overhead that I'm not able to decipher, and more people join us on the deck.

"Wow, it got busy fast," I say.

Ollie nods into my neck. "They told people the Eiffel Tower was coming up."

It clicks in my head. "And you were keeping track of where we were so we could be first, weren't you?"

"Of course."

We stay still as people pile in around us, the Eiffel Tower coming closer and closer by the second. We're quiet, listening to the chatter, and I lean my head back against his chest. People take pictures as it comes into view, accidental flashes and phone screens drawing our attention back to the boat.

"So what's after Paris, Wildflower?" Ollie asks, his voice only loud enough for me to hear.

"I don't know," I answer honestly. "I'm questioning the whole digital nomad thing. I don't know if I was doing it because *I* wanted to or because that's who I thought Rod wanted me to be."

He scoffs. "I can answer that for you."

I elbow him. "It's more complicated than that. I love traveling, seeing new places and meeting new people. I'm just not sure I love doing it alone. That's what I keep coming back to."

He hums into my ear. "Maybe you should go home for a bit, think about it. You can always leave again, you know, but at least you'll have your people."

I sigh. "Yeah, but I gave up my lease. I told everyone I'd be traveling until further notice. I tried so hard to make this happen that to go back now just feels like giving up." The words scrape at my chest as I say them.

"What other people think means nothing if you're not happy. You can crash in my spare room if you want to make it look extra temporary."

I twist in his arms so I can look up into his eyes.

"The Eiffel Tower is the other way, Wildflower."

I ignore the jab. "Living with you doesn't exactly sound like the commitment-phobe I know."

"Not living with," he corrects. "Crashing."

I turn my gaze back to Paris, pulling his arms tighter around me.

"Maybe I will. Go home, that is."

"I think you should."

I nod, digesting his suggestion. I miss home, that's for

sure, but I feel like I still haven't made the most out of this trip. Like I'm missing something integral that makes the choice to go home so clear that I never question it.

"Hey, what happened to the work you were leaving for?" I ask.

He shrugs. "Nothing I can't handle from here. I might just work with you in the morning for the next couple of days if that's okay," he says.

I nod as the Eiffel Tower stretches in front of us. "Yeah, that's fine with me."

WHEN WE LEAVE THE BOAT, Ollie leads me toward Champ de Mars. He grins as he grabs my hand, pulling me along so quickly I nearly have to run to keep up with him.

"Slow down! These boots were not made for running!" I say.

He does as I ask, pulling me under his arm as we reach the park. Above us, the Eiffel Tower comes into full view.

"So what do you think?" he asks. We stop just below it, and from this vantage point, it looks almost like it ascends endlessly into the sky.

"I think it's a lot bigger in person," I say, staring up at it.

"That's what she said." I shoot him a look that he accepts with a grin.

He glances around and spies a couple doing the same thing we are, staring endlessly up at the structure before us. "*Excusez-moi*," he says. "*Pouvez-vous nous prendre en photo, s'il vous plaît?*"

"*Oui*," she says, holding out her hand for Ollie's phone. She holds up one finger as she makes sure the angle is just right, and then gestures for Ollie to move closer to me.

Instead, he grabs my hand and pushes me into a spin. He grabs me roughly by the hips and, with one arm around my waist, dips me halfway to the ground to kiss me.

When he pulls me back to my feet, I feel the heat rising in my cheeks.

"That was hot," she says, with a thick French accent.

"One more?" Ollie asks, and she nods.

He bends down and lifts me, his arms clamped tight around my thighs, and I let out a surprised gasp as my hands fall to his shoulders for balance.

"Kiss me," he says, and I bend down, pressing my lips against his.

When he puts me back on the ground, I'm lightheaded and a little stunned. He adjusts my dress for me, pulling it down and straightening it out.

She hands the phone directly to me.

"Holy shit," I say, flipping through them all. "These are amazing."

She grins, and her male companion steps forward. "She is an influencer," he says, with a thick French accent. She rolls her eyes as he nudges her elbow.

"Oh my god, what platform? What's your handle?" I ask, already pulling out my own phone to search for her. If the pictures she just took are any indication of what her feed will look like, I'm following her.

"I'm Ella Claire on Instagram," she says with a smile, and I find and follow her almost instantly.

"Well, thank you for using your powers to give us these pictures. These are amazing," I say.

"Happy to," she says. "Would you mind taking one of us?"

"Sure!" I say, and she hands me her phone. We switch positions, Ollie's arm resting on my shoulders as I struggle to recreate the photos she took.

When I hand her phone back to her, she seems pleased. "Thank you," she says, with a genuine smile.

"*De rien*," I say, and I catch the edges of Ollie's lips twitching up into a smile.

They wave as they continue on their way, and I flip through the pictures with Ollie as we walk.

"My god, I can't believe she did this with just a phone!" I pick one where Ollie's dipping me, his fingers digging into my hip and my hand pressing desperately into his bicep. "And god, this one goes beyond. This is a great picture, but, like, it's *hot*."

"I think that's more the subject than the photographer."

I shake my head. "No, but she *captured* it! This could be on the cover of a romance novel," I say, and then an idea occurs to me. "Wait, I wonder if Carrie needs cover art."

Ollie laughs. "I don't think Carrie's going to use her friends as cover models."

I put the phone right into his face. "Ollie, do you see how hot we are?"

He pushes the phone away and pulls my hips roughly into him. "I'd rather feel it," he says, leaning down to kiss me. A shiver runs down my spine that's unrelated to the cold temperature. He weaves one hand up into my hair, holding me in place as he deepens our kiss.

"You know we would probably be hotter if we weren't wearing so much."

"Probably need to get somewhere warm so we can make that happen," he mutters into my lips.

"Alleyway?"

He pulls away, his eyebrows raised.

"Kidding."

He takes me by the hand and starts walking, pulling me

along behind him as I struggle to match his pace. "Keep up, Wildflower."

"Again, Ollie, these boots!"

He grumbles something under his breath as he looks down at them, and before I have a second to process what's happening, he leans down and hauls me over one shoulder. "Ollie!" I gasp, as he slaps my ass.

"Fixed the problem," he says, his pace accelerating from fast to nearly running.

"Ollie, my ass is probably on display for the world!" I tell him, holding my purse over my butt.

"You've got it covered." He laughs. "Literally."

"Oh, you're so lucky it's a short walk home. Otherwise I'd–"

"What would you do, Wildflower?" His fingers dig into the flesh of my thigh, erasing all thoughts from my mind.

"I would, um..."

"Yeah, that's what I thought," he says, and slaps my ass again for good measure. I do the same to him in return.

"Ooh, now she's getting spicy."

I roll my eyes at his butt.

When we get to the door of our room, he unlocks it with me still over his shoulder. Once inside, he backs up a step. "Hey, mind getting the door for me?" he jokes, and I snort as I push it closed and lock the deadbolt.

He takes two quick steps to the bed and tosses me down on it, my hair flying in every direction as his knee slides between mine, his forearms landing on either side of my ribs and snaking down underneath me. He pauses then, taking a moment to kiss me lightly. When he pulls away, he brushes my hair out of my face, and I turn into the movement, desperate for the delicate touch.

"Hey, Wildflower."

I grin back at him. "Hey."

"Hey," he mocks, his voice high. I give him a look. He leans down, kissing me on the nose. "Thanks for being my Valentine."

"Thanks for coming back."

He moves my hair out of the way to kiss my neck, the touch so soft it sends shivers down my spine. My hands drag down his chest, desperate for the feel of his skin against mine as he leans into me, his length pressing into me. His hand falls to my thigh, first running up my leg and squeezing my ass, and then running back down, one finger slipping below the tops of my boots.

"What do you say we get you out of these boots?"

"Yes please," I say, as he leans back, sitting on his heels. He undoes the tie at the top and the zipper along the side, the warmth of his hands along my legs a stark contrast to tonight's cold. He tugs, dropping the boot to the floor, and then does the same for the other. He pauses while he's there, slowly unbuttoning his shirt in the moonlight shining through the windows.

"Hey, isn't that my job?" I ask, sitting up and starting from the bottom. He abandons his button, letting me take over, and I push the shirt over his shoulders. Underneath he has on an undershirt, and I pull that up and over his head, too.

My fingers dance along his chest, his torso. A lightness courses through my veins when I realize that despite our *almost*, our flirty banter, and our obvious attraction to each other, this is the first time since my birthday I'm seeing him like this.

I pause, my thoughts rushing off without me. I've built this moment up a lot in my head, and I'm sure he has too. *What if it's not the same? What if last time was some convergence of the universe to give us one good night together and that's it?*

"Hey, you okay?" he asks, his hands running down my arms to my hands, pressing them harder into his skin.

I nod. "Yeah," I say, trying to will the thought away.

"You seem nervous."

I shake my head. "No, not nervous." He waits, looking at me. "It's just... last time was so good."

"Last time was fucking great. Aren't you excited?"

"What if it's not the same? What if I'm not as good as you remember?"

He waves me off. "Don't be silly, Steph."

"It's not silly, it's a concern. We've built this up."

He flattens my hands under one of his. "It's sex, not a performance. You're not being graded," he says. He tugs on my hair, gently, releasing my hands and placing one of his on the small of my back, pulling me toward him as he tugs on my hair. "Besides, we both know you can take a dick."

A sound of disbelief jumps from my throat that he quickly swallows with his kiss.

"But if you're too nervous," he says, returning my hands to his chest, flexing underneath them. He raises his eyebrows at me, and I laugh. "You can say no to all this."

"I can't say no to all this," I say jokingly, but in my mind every neuron is firing with pure desire, his soft skin under my fingertips causing my mouth to water.

"I knew you wanted me," he says softly, amusement dancing in his eyes. I run my hands over his thick arms, his compass tattoo dark and stormy underneath my fingers. I drift down his abdomen, trailing my fingers across his abs. His head tilts back back, his breathing heavy.

I move forward, pressing my body into his, and kiss his collarbone.

"Hey Wildflower?"

I look up at him. "Yeah?"

"I love what you're doing, but for the sake of my skin can we please get you out of your dress?"

I move back an inch so the sequins aren't digging into him. "Sorry," I say. "Guess you're not into BDSM, huh?"

He shrugs noncommittally. "I wouldn't say *not*, but death by a thousand tiny cuts is not my preferred method."

"Noted," I say, and he raises his eyebrows as his hands wind behind me, pulling down the zipper. It pools on the bed around me, and he runs a finger along the waistband of my tights. He snaps it against my skin, causing a sharp intake of breath.

"These things are living up to their name," he comments.

"Tights?" I laugh. "Yeah, they're definitely not comfortable."

With his thumbs, he pulls them down over my hips. He spreads his fingers wide across my ribcage and pushes me backward so I'm splayed out over the bed in front of him, and then pulls them the rest of the way over my feet, abandoning them on the floor next to us.

He runs a hand along my leg, his fingers leaving goosebumps in their wake.

"You are *beautiful*," he mutters, as his hand grazes the skin of my inner thigh and a burst of heat travels through my body.

I sit up, my nerves melting to lust, and pull his face down to kiss him. As his tongue works inside my mouth, I reach down and undo his belt, the buttons of his pants, and he moans into my mouth as my fingers graze him.

He reaches behind me, undoing the clasp of my bra, and I let it fall to the floor. He pinches one nipple between his fingers, and I throw my head back. "Oh, Ollie," I mumble, and he grunts, pushing me backward and landing on top of me, his erection pressing into me through his underwear.

He lowers himself to take a nipple into his mouth, his teeth grazing at the sensitive skin. His thumb slips underneath the triangle of my underwear, teasingly, as my hips buck up at him. Still suckling gently, his thumb slides further down, drawing a slick line down my center.

He hums into my skin. "Must have just rained," he mumbles.

"What?"

He pauses. "My Wildflower is wet, wet, wet."

"Oh my god," I say, covering my face with my hands. He tugs on my underwear, pulling them down and dropping them on the floor next to us. His thumb returns to that spot, rubbing slow, lazy circles.

He stops after a moment, catching my eye as he brings his hand to his mouth. "Wet and delicious."

Another burst of heat runs through me, and I grab at his shoulders, my hips bucking up as he collapses onto me.

"And horny as wildflowers come," he comments, a satisfied smirk settling across his face. I grab at his underwear, pushing it down as his thumb circles my nipple. I pull on his hips, desperate to feel him inside me, but he resists the movement.

"Ollie," I plead.

"Still feeling nervous?" he asks.

I shake my head. "No. Just"–I huff, the words evading me.

"Just all hot and bothered for me?"

"Yes!"

He leans down, leaving a kiss on my neck. "Good." He nibbles at my skin as his body settles against mine, the pressure perfect. But I want him *inside* me.

I reach down, taking him into my hands, and he moans at my touch. I grip him hard, moving up and down his length as his kisses become distracted. He grabs at my ass and my hips, as if struggling to resist letting go of his control and pummeling into me already.

"Ollie, I want you," I whisper into the skin of his chest. I press his dick up against me and roll my hips.

"Fuck, Stephanie," he groans, one hand winding underneath us, his fingers digging into my skin. His hips move against me, taking over my movement. He shakes his head. "I need to fuck you," he says, reaching down and moving himself to my entrance. "You're still on birth control, right?"

"Yeah."

He groans as he presses inside me, all breath leaving my body as he fills me.

Moving slowly, he breathes heavily into my ear. "You good, Steph?"

I nod. "Really good."

He hums as he kisses my neck. "Yup, she still takes a dick damn well," he jokes, his words giving way to a groan as he moves inside me.

I slap his arm as I laugh and he picks up his speed, biting his lip as he pummels into me harder and harder. He nibbles on my neck, at my earlobe. He kisses me as he moves, hard and demanding from every angle.

Before long, my crescendo takes hold, my breathing heavy.

"Stephy, are you going to come all over the biggest dick you've ever had?"

I let out a quick laugh as my nails dig into his back, my teeth scraping along the skin of his neck.

I moan and he grips me tighter, his breath hot over my skin as he kisses my cheek and thrusts into me.

My body goes taut, my moans transforming into pleas for him to keep going *just like that.*

"That's my Wildflower," he says, as I clench around him.

My arms clamp around his neck as he leaves kisses all along my skin, pushing me over the edge and riding my orgasm out until I'm no more than a puddle beneath him.

With a quick nip to the skin of my collarbone, he grips my hips hard and jerks into me, his face scrunching up and his breathing labored.

And then he collapses on top of me, his arm winding underneath me and his chest heavy on mine. He takes my mouth gently with his, his fingers cupping my face.

"So was it worth the wait?"

I nod, wrapping my arms around his neck. "Definitely."

## 28

## OLIVER

Steph stumbles out of the bathroom, her hair in a wild bun atop her head and her silky sleep set calling out to my hands. She smiles sleepily at me as I pull her into bed and kiss her cheek, a little contented sigh escaping her that gives my body all sorts of ideas of what else we could be doing.

I could go for round two, maybe even three or four if she wants to. But she looks a little sleepy–maybe I should let her get some rest.

But there's a part of me that really doesn't want to let this night go without making the most of it. We agreed to be each other's Valentines. What that means for the rest of this trip, I don't know, but it highlights for me just how fleeting this is, how quickly we'll have to go back to being just friends.

I rub her back through her silky shirt, following the curve of her spine, and she sighs into me. "That feels nice."

I kiss her neck, tugging on the strap to her shirt with my teeth, and she hums, nestling in closer. I slip my hand up her shirt, resting on her ribcage, and feel her breathing. She turns onto her back, smiling through her adorably sleepy eyes.

"Are you trying to wake me up again?" Her arms are above her head, and I can't help but notice her little pointed nipples through the silk of her shirt. She takes a deep breath, her ribcage filling and easing like she's daring me to play with them.

Despite the urge to take them into my mouth and suck on them, I move my hand to her waistband, running a finger just along the inside.

"No, just looking at you," I say. "Why? Am I waking you up?"

Her eyes narrow. "No," she says, and promptly turns away from me.

I brush her hair from her neck, dragging my lips across her skin. "Do you remember your birthday night? How we fucked three times before we fell asleep? Twice more randomly through the night?"

She looks over her shoulder at me. "Are you placing a formal request?"

I run my hand up her thigh, grabbing her ass.

I shake my head. "No. Just wanted to see if you remembered."

"I remember," she says, her chest heaving. I press into her, and she twists to face me again, hooking a leg around my waist. I rest my arm on her leg, my hand wrapping to where her thong rests against her skin. I trail my fingers along the fabric, feeling her shiver into me as I pass over her center.

"That was a fun night," I say, reaching back around and snapping her underwear against her. She gasps in surprise, her hips inching closer to me, and I know I have her.

"What was your favorite part?"

I raise my eyebrows. "That's a hard question."

"Top three?"

I think about it for a second, flashes of that night playing rapid-fire in my mind. The sex, her skin, the feeling of her body pressed against mine. I don't know what I've craved most

"When you took me in your mouth," I say, trailing my fingers along her chin. "You grinned up at me, so proud of yourself." She grimaces, her nose scrunching up. "It was the hottest thing I've ever seen."

"I can imagine," she says sarcastically. "I feel my hottest when I'm gagged and my eyes are watering." My dick throbs at her words, and she raises an eyebrow. "Okay, what else?"

"When you rode me. Specifically, when you rode me reverse cowgirl and made it very clear that you wanted to fuck me hard but safely because statistically, that position results in the most broken dicks."

She grimaces again. "I gave you the whole spiel, didn't I?"

"It was perfect. Caring and really fucking hot at the same time." I run my hand under her shirt again, feeling her ribs under my palm.

"What else?"

The image of her in the morning, sleepy-eyed and reaching for me pops into my head, but it wasn't a sexual moment. It felt more intimate.

I shake my head.

"Just you," I say, and even that sounds less sexual than I intended it to. "You naked, you fucking, you just being you."

She looks taken aback, a smile flitting to the edges of her mouth. "Me just being me?"

"You know what I mean," I say, burying my face in her neck.

"Oliver Long, did you just say something *sweet*?" She

pushes on my chest to look at me, and heat rises in my cheeks. None of that was supposed to be sweet–it was supposed to be *sexual.*

I probably don't have enough blood circulating in my brain thanks to the raging erection I have pressed against her.

"No," I grumble, pulling her close to me again.

"Aw, I think Oliver Long has a little crush," she says.

"Steph," I say, pulling away briefly to give her a look.

She rolls her eyes. "Ollie, you can have a crush without acting on it. We can like each other for Valentine's Day and squash our feelings afterward."

I crinkle my eyebrows at her, a thought occurring to me. "What if we extended Valentine's Day, just for a couple days?"

"Extended it?"

"Yeah. Like to Paris."

She lets out a long breath. "Do you think that's a good idea?"

I swallow. *No.* "Steph, we've both waited months for this. Will a couple of days really hurt? I mean, think of your birthday. We could do that every night until we leave. Every day."

She runs a hand down my chest, stopping on my waist.

"Do you think you can do that?" she asks.

*I'm not worried about me.* "I mean, yeah. If you can."

She nods. "I know what I want. And I know I'm not going to get it from you." She sighs. The thought of her leaving here to pursue her goal of finding love elsewhere makes me uncomfortable, but I can't say that. "Yeah, why not? We might as well have an affair. We're in Paris, after all."

"You want to have an affair with me?" I tease, pulling her closer.

"It sounds kind of fun, doesn't it? All forbidden and hidden from the world," she says, biting her lip. I kiss her, stealing that lip away from her.

"And sexy," I say, tugging on her hair so I can kiss her neck. "Very sexy."

"I just feel kind of bad, like I'm cheating on Philly," she says.

I pause, a laugh tumbling from my mouth because that's the *last* thing I expected her to say right now. "I think Philly will forgive you." She runs her hands along my chest, the sensation urging me harder. I wrap an arm tightly around her so I can feel her heat around my dick.

"Do you?"

I nod, reaching up and pinching one of her little nipples between my fingers. "You're too cute not to."

She moans as she throws her head back, and I spread my fingers across her chest, anxious to feel every part of her. I pull her strap down over her shoulder, exposing her, and wrap my lips around her nipple. I bite down, just hard enough that she cries out, and soothe her with a gentle lick.

I reach behind her, following the line of her underwear to her center. I pull her underwear to the side and spread her with a finger. Finding her absolutely soaking for me, I slip two fingers inside of her, her hips bucking eagerly toward me.

"I think you like this new arrangement," I say, pulsing slowly.

"It's okay," she jokes, and I slap her ass, the sound of it ringing in my ears. "Don't stop," she pleads, grabbing at my hand and forcing it back to where it was.

"I don't put out for only *okay*."

She struggles against me as I cup her ass instead, and when she realizes she's not getting anywhere, she pulls her leg roughly away from me, squirming out of her pants and her underwear, and pushes me onto my back. She straddles me, her hands forceful on my chest, and levels me with her gaze.

She pauses, and then slowly pulls her shirt over her head.

*God, she is fucking gorgeous.*

Multi-colored hair wild around her face, lips red and swollen, little pink pointed nipples. I trace the constellation of moles on her hip, my fingers running up to her abdomen, and ending with a pinch of her nipple that has her crying out.

She reaches down, tugging on the waistband of my underwear to free me, and wraps two hands around my cock. She moves slowly, the motion pushing her tits out toward me and I can't stop touching them, grabbing at her legs and her hips and her arms. I can't help but thrust toward her, anxious for her to move up my body just a little bit, take me inside her.

She leans forward, still stroking me, and kisses my cheek, her words no more than a whisper. "How do you like it when I tease you?" She stops moving, leaning on her elbows on either side of my face as her nipples graze my chest.

"I love it," I say, grabbing at her hips to hold her steady so I can thrust into her, but she moves away before I can.

She shakes her head, scolding me. "I don't think you've been teased enough. Maybe tomorrow."

"Tomorrow?" I ask, as she sits up, moving like she's about to get out of bed.

She stares at me, her tits all pushed out in my face, and raises her eyebrows. "Well, since we extended our timeline, that leaves plenty of time for you to reconsider teasing me next time."

I grab her hips and pull her forward so she's sitting directly on my dick. Her eyes pinch shut as she takes in a breath, and I repeat the movement, pushing her hips back and pulling them toward me again. She whimpers, reaching one hand up to play with a nipple as my dick rubs against her clit.

"Are you going to come on me without even letting me fuck you?" I ask her.

She licks her lips, seeming to consider this. "I think I might," she says, her hips moving on their own now. I reach up and pinch her other nipple, and she cries out, the speed of her hips grinding on me increasing.

I'm taken back to the botanical gardens, when she moved her hips on me the same exact way–except we were wearing a lot more, then.

I was so anxious to watch her come, to let her take what she needs and unravel on top of me.

But now that we're naked together and my dick is completely soaked with her, I'm not sure I can just *watch* her come.

I sit up, interrupting her movement, and wrap an arm around her to lift her up.

"Fuck me," I tell her, aligning my dick with her entrance as she lowers down on top of it, a moan bursting from her throat as she takes all of me.

With a deep sigh, I let my head fall to her chest. She moves slowly, still grinding on that spot that'll have her clenching around me in minutes. I wrap my arms around her, holding onto her tight and kissing every spare bit of skin I can find.

Her breathing quickens, her nails digging into my shoulders in a way that makes me want to go full caveman on her, flip her over and pound into her hard and fast.

But I let her explode around me, her cries filling the room and her pussy clenching repeatedly around me.

I push on her hips until she collapses into me, her kisses lazy along my neck. I hold her to me as I lay her flat on the bed and bend one leg up between us. She whimpers as I fuck her as hard as I can, her nails scraping at my back and one arm wrapped tight around my neck.

I jerk into her with a grunt, relief falling swiftly over me as I release inside her.

She peppers my skin with kisses, her body warm and soft underneath me.

"How was that for a tease?" she asks.

"You're terrible at it in the best way."

She shrugs. "I don't really want to be a good tease. I'd rather get fucked."

I snort into her neck. "There's my Wildflower."

# 29

# STEPHANIE

"You need a nickname." I run my fingers down his cheek, his stubble scratching at my fingertips.

Through sleepy green eyes, he smiles at me. "You can call me Ollie."

I roll my eyes. "No, like a *Wildflower* nickname."

"I can just borrow yours," he says, weaving an arm around my waist and pulling me closer to him. I sigh into his heat, the touch of his skin against mine comforting.

"No, you can't," I mumble into his chest.

"You can't share?"

I shake my head. "No. That's mine. Get your own."

He grumbles. "Call me whatever you want."

"Ollie," I say, tapping his cheek so he'll open his eyes. He gives me one, his eyebrow raised as if waiting for me to continue. "It's not fair that I get to have a nickname but you don't. If we're extending Valentine's Day to Paris, a nickname is part of the deal. It makes you feel good."

He's called me Wildflower enough times for me to count on two hands, and every time he does, my chest swells and my heart beats faster. I kind of want him to feel that, too.

Especially if we're extending this by a few days. I know that at the end of this, Ollie and I will go our separate ways. This is an opportunity to prove to him commitment isn't all that bad. That being with someone isn't all that bad. It might not be me at the end of the day–and that's okay–but he shouldn't feel like he has to choose between work and a person.

He sighs, rolling onto his back to stare at the ceiling, and I nestle into the crook of his arm, pulling the sheets up over us.

"I think it makes *you* feel good, Steph. I'm fine with just being Ollie."

I huff. "That's only because we haven't found the right nickname for you yet." He runs his hand through my hair, and it sends a little shiver down my spine. "If you don't give me direction, I'm just going to start calling you weird stuff."

"Like what?"

"Grandpa," I try.

"Weird take on a daddy kink, but okay."

I ignore his comment. "Mascarpone."

He turns his head to me. "Are you trying to call me cheesy?"

"Hulk."

"No."

I roll onto my side to look at him. "Okay, now we're getting somewhere. So we're okay with familial nicknames and goofy nicknames, but not uber-masculine nicknames."

"I wouldn't say 'okay with.'"

"You didn't say no."

He shoots me a look. "If you call me Grandpa in public someone would assume I'm being crotchety or, like, I don't know how to use my phone. If you call me mascarpone, I'm not even sure anyone would realize what you're saying. If you call me the hulk, it's like a billboard shouting to the world that I have a small dick and need my girlfriend to make me feel better about it." He looks surprised for a moment. "Or whatever."

I grin at him, not because that makes me feel good, but because I can already see a hint of pink blooming over his cheeks. "That just slipped out, didn't it?"

He shakes his head, eyeing me as if to gauge my reaction. "I don't even know how."

"Ollie, are you trying to tell me you want me to call you—"

"Steph."

I hold my hands up in surrender. "You said it."

"It was an accident."

"Call it a Freudian slip."

He levels me with a look, and I run my fingers down his chest to distract him.

"Steph, this is temporary, right?"

I sit up, resting my hands on his abdomen.

I'm fine with our arrangement, but Ollie seems concerned that in only a few days, I'm going to fall head over heels in love with him. I might love too freely and forgive too easily—as he says—but that doesn't mean he'll be my next target.

He's hot—unfairly so—but I have enough commitment-phobes in my life. If Ollie and I had the same intense history that Rod and I had, I might be more concerned. But as it is, I have a hot, naked man in my bed, and I might as well take advantage of that.

Ollie is easy. He's an active listener, he's quick to please, and he shows up when he says he will. As far as casual sex goes, he's perfect.

Except when he gets nervous about love.

"Ollie, if you can't control your feelings for me, I'm not

sure we should continue this," I say sarcastically, playing his role. "Calling me your girlfriend is just too far."

He rolls his eyes. "You know it was an accident."

I continue with a contrived innocent tone. "I know how much you want love and I'm just naturally *so* lovable, but I'm concerned you're going to fall helplessly in love with me in less than a week. And god, then my life is over." I throw my hands in the air. "When you do, I'll have to remind you, for probably the thousandth time, that I'm not looking for love. And of course, that causes *death*, so our only option here is to end things before that happens."

He presses his lips together. "Okay, I'm being a little ridiculous."

I nod. "Although good for you—few people can think so highly of themselves that they assume the opposite sex will blindly throw themselves at them."

"Steph, I'm sorry. I'm simultaneously trying to protect your feelings and fuck you, and I'm not sure the right way to do that."

I snort at his words. "It's okay, Ollie. But can you remember that the next time you get scared?"

"I'm not—"

"Ollie."

He pauses. "Fine. But I'm not—"

I lean over and press my lips against his before he can lie to me.

As Ollie's snores fill the room, I pull on my boots and wrap one of the spare blankets around myself before stepping out into the February cold. It's nearing midnight here, but it's around dinnertime back home, and I *need* to tell someone.

I take a seat at one of the wrought-iron tables in the courtyard, pulling the blanket up over my ears as I dial my sister.

"Hey, Frenchie."

"Hi, Gabs."

"How are you? How's Paris?" I hear metal on metal in the background, the beeping of an oven timer.

I debate beating around the bush and then decide not to. There's really only one reason I called, anyway. "I slept with Ollie."

"Oh! Fuck! Steph, you're on speaker!"

"Gabi!"

"It's not like you wouldn't have immediately told me after hanging up," Zeke says in the background.

"Oh Jesus," I say, dropping my head into my hands. "Gabi, you're supposed to open with that!"

"I'm sorry, you caught me in the middle of making dinner and I didn't expect the first thing out of your mouth to be that you slept with Ollie!"

"Really? You didn't?" Zeke asks.

"Hey!"

"I mean, you're sharing a one-bed hotel room and you already slept together. I don't think that's a wild conclusion to come to. Not to mention it's Valentine's Day. Honestly, I'd be more surprised if you *didn't*."

"Okay, Zeke, can you watch the sauce?" Gabi asks, movement clattering through the speaker.

"Wait, why can't I hear?" Zeke asks, his voice fading out behind Gabi's footsteps.

"Sorry," she says, her words punctuated by the click of a door handle. "So you slept with Ollie. How was it? As good as you remember? Wait, didn't he break up with you already?"

I roll my eyes. "Yeah. I think he's confused but horny."

She snorts. "So he's a man."

I try to keep my cackling to a respectable volume so I don't wake any of the neighbors. "Basically. He's terrified that I'm going to fall in love with him. But he's the one making moves, so I don't know what to make of it. He invited me to Paris, and we went on this really nice Valentine's date today. He wants to have a Parisian affair with me. I feel like I'm just along for the ride, but honestly, it's kind of nice."

Gabi laughs. "Aw, Steph, I'm so happy you're moving on from Rod."

"I mean, this is very much a fling. An only-in-Paris sort of thing. But it's fun. Sexy."

"I love that for you. Just don't get your heart broken, okay? I like Ollie, but I don't trust him after he broke up with you. Or whatever that was."

"Oh, he's just scared."

"Steph. Be careful."

"Gabi," I mock. "It's just sex. It's not a big deal."

She sighs. "I know. And I'm all for this fling, but mostly because I could see this helping you move on from Rod. I just don't want you getting hung up on another guy who can't be there for you."

"Gabi, he's hot, but he's a big baby when it comes to commitment. After Rod, I have no interest."

"Okay. Well, as long as you're in a good headspace about it, then go forth. Fuck, don't fall."

I snort into the blanket, Gabi's laughter loud in my ear.

"Fuck, don't fall," I repeat.

"That can be the tagline for the rest of your trip," she says.

"How about the rest of life?"

"Aw, Steph, don't say that. You'll find somebody good for you. But until then—"

"Fuck, don't fall." I pull the blanket up higher around my ears as a gust of wind moves through the courtyard. I eye the window to the bedroom where Ollie's sleeping soundly, anxious to curl up beside him again.

"Hey, when are you coming home?" Gabi asks.

I groan. "I don't know."

"Well, we miss you."

"I miss you, too. A lot."

"You can always crash here, you know."

"I know. Thanks, Gabi." I stand from my chair and make my way back to the room. "I don't know when I'll come home yet, but I promise you'll be the first to know." I hike the blanket up so I don't trip over it. "Love you, Gabs."

"Love you, Stephy."

I push the door open and step inside as I hang up. I drop the blanket on the chair by the window and climb into bed next to Ollie, his warmth swallowing up the cold I brought in from outside. He stirs just enough to weave an arm around my waist, pulling me into his chest, and I melt into him.

# 30

## OLIVER

I wake to the sound of Stephanie's furious typing. When I look over at her, she's biting her lip, staring down at her computer screen with crinkled eyebrows. She's intensely focused, and I'm still blinking away the fog of last night.

I'm disappointed she's not curled up next to me. Disappointed I can't run my hand along her hip, feel her press back into me as she wakes up.

Then again, we did that only a few hours ago, waking to the beginnings of the sunrise coming in through the window. I felt her stirring next to me and before she could slip out of bed undetected, I grabbed her. Still naked from the night before, it felt only right to kiss her neck, to run my fingers along her bare skin, to slip between her legs while we were still sleepy and entwined.

She must have gotten up after I fell asleep again. I wonder how long ago that was.

I swing my legs over the edge of the bed, grabbing my underwear off the floor and pulling them on. I unplug my phone on the nightstand and head into the bathroom to brush my teeth, checking my phone as I do. I have a couple forwarded emails from Jack and Emma about a client who's asking some questions they're not sure how to answer.

When I'm done in the bathroom, I stop to give Steph a kiss on the cheek, and she pulls on my neck, asking for more. She's wearing my sweater again, and I don't hate the way it hangs off her, the feel of her body heat through it as my hand falls to her waist.

"Good morning," I say.

"Good morning." She gives me a wide grin before returning to her work.

I head to my floor pillow and sit, pulling up the timer on my phone.

"Wait! Hold on, let me finish this sentence!"

"Just join me when you're done," I tell her.

"No, I want the whole time!"

I huff, leaving my phone on the floor as I wait for her. I close my eyes, starting without her–I'll just start the timer when she sits down next to me.

"Okay, okay. I'm ready," she says, scrambling to stand up. She sits down in front of me, knee to knee just like in the pagoda, and I press start.

My mind drifts, overwhelmed by the smell of her shampoo and memories of last night popping into my mind. I do my best to focus. I want to work a little today–in fact, I have to, if Jack and Emma's emails are any indication–but I'm craving her touch. I want nothing more than to fall back into bed with her and touch her in all the little ways that make her throw her head back and cause her hips to grind on me.

When our fifteen minutes are up, I reach for her, pulling us to our knees on the floor. Her tongue presses into my mouth, her hands running down my chest. My dick goes hard at her touch.

"I want to finish something really quick," she says, pressing a hand to my chest. "I'm just about done with this proposal and I want to send it off as soon as I can."

I groan. "Are you sure you don't want a little break?" I say, pulling her hips to mine so she can feel just how hard I am for her.

"I do, but a little later?"

I sigh. "Okay," I say, as she scrambles up from the ground and I struggle to adjust myself as I stand. "And *you* called *me* an overachiever."

She throws a sweet smile back at me. "Just trying my best to be like you."

I roll my eyes, pulling on a pair of sweatpants and sitting at the kitchen table next to her with my laptop. The foot she rubs absentmindedly up my leg inspires some mild swelling I do my best to will away.

I've had vacation auto-responders on for the past few days, and it looks like most people are being respectful of them, but I send a few DMs and reaction emojis so my presence is known. If I'm on vacation, I don't need to do much more than that; I just don't want to be a ghost if Jack's news starts some conversations.

I navigate through to the emails Jack and Emma have forwarded me and read through an unnecessarily long chain of mixed French and English explanations. My brain switches rapid-fire between the languages, distracted further by the movement of Steph's chair a few inches closer to mine, her knee pressing against mine.

I try my best to focus on what the client is saying. It seems like she's trying to request a new feature without knowing the right words to say. Luckily, that's exactly my wheelhouse. The sort of request I can write up easily for the software engineering team if provided a few more details.

But when I respond saying this, I get a video call a minute later from Jack and Emma.

"Fuck," I say, scrambling up from the table and grabbing a shirt from the floor. I pull it over my head before answering, tipping my computer toward me so Steph isn't in the frame.

"Hey," I say, as Jack and Emma appear on screen. They're working from home, each of them in their respective offices. They must have booked earlier flights than me.

"So you've figured out what she's talking about?" Jack starts, running a hand through his hair.

I navigate back to the email. "I have an idea but I need more info. I think it's something to do with that warehouse she was talking about that's really two warehouses."

He shakes his head. "I didn't even know what she was asking when she asked that question."

Steph's hand runs along my thigh, and I look over at her, my eyebrows wrinkled. *What is she doing?* I grab her hand and hold it against the erection she's causing. Her eyebrows raise and she bites her lip. When I take my hand away, she keeps hers there.

I don't hate this.

"It's an accounting thing," Emma explains. "But a dumb one that we don't do in the US. I don't think there's a way to do what she's asking."

I return my attention to the screen. "If she can send a screenshot of the current system, that'll be enough." Steph is still rubbing me, and I'm hoping that by succinctly suggesting a next step, we can end this call and get back to what we were doing.

So I can bend Stephanie over this table and fuck her until she screams.

"I mean, is it as simple as a checkbox?" Emma asks. "I don't want you putting in feature requests while you're still out."

"It's a quick one. No big deal." I swallow as Steph pushes her chair back and slips underneath the table.

*This is not happening. Is this happening? This is really happening.*

"Well, it depends what kind of work needs to be done, right?"

Steph pulls my waistband down, freeing me from my pants, and her hands tighten around my dick. I struggle to keep my eyes on my computer screen. "If it's just adding a checkbox, I can write that request."

My breathing turns rapid as Steph's lips wrap around the head of my cock.

"Sorry, I gotta go off-camera," I say, reaching forward and turning it off.

She rears back when I look down at her. I shake my head. I can't be on-camera while she's sucking me. No way.

She sits back on her haunches, withdrawing her hands from my thighs.

All I can see in my mind is her on her birthday, my cock fully buried in her mouth, her eyes looking up at me with such playful delight. The battle rages in my mind, my cock straining with the thought.

*Fine,* I mouth, and reach up and turn my camera back on.

"All good?" Emma asks, as Steph's lips wrap around me again.

"Yeah, all is good." I wrap my hand around Steph's neck, urging her deeper, and she complies, her fingers digging into my ass as my dick hits the back of her throat. "Um. Yeah, I think it's a bigger fix than a checkbox," I say, struggling to follow what Emma was just saying. "But I really don't mind putting in the ticket. It'll be easy."

Jack sighs. "I don't know about that." He clicks around and then translates part of the email to English. Steph's tongue swirls around the head of my cock, and it's all I can do to keep a straight face. "On the accounting side we view it as one warehouse but in inventory it's two, and technically out of territory so it gets rolled up under overhead for the administrative department rather than a territory-based department."

Steph's fingers dig into my thighs, pushing them wider, and she lowers all the way around me. I chance a glance down at her and she looks up at me, eyes wide and mouth full, and I nearly come at the sight.

I push her hair out of her face, letting out a long, slow breath to stay in control.

"That sounds like it'll need three different tickets," Emma groans.

"Yeah, but it's all the same ticket," I say, as Steph's fingers trail along my thighs. Every muscle in me tenses, desperate to get off this call and rail her. "Just worded slightly differently depending on the department."

"Yeah, I guess you're right," Emma says. "I just feel bad that this is coming to you on vacation."

I shake my head. "Probably not a bad thing to look extra dedicated when the two of you are about to explode the whole department."

"I'm really not looking forward to it," Jack says, and there's a moment of silence between us where all I can hear is the wet movement of Stephanie's mouth moving up and down on my dick, which thankfully does not get picked up by the computer's microphone.

"Hey, how's Stephanie?" Emma asks.

I blink at her, struggling to keep the tension out of my jaw. "She's great," I say, squeezing her neck. "Really fucking great."

She moans around my dick, the sensation sending me out of my own skin.

"Oh, that's great," Emma says. "I'm so happy for you." It only vaguely registers that Emma thinks we're a couple. "She seemed really sweet."

Steph makes another little noise at the back of her throat.

I nod. "Yeah, she's really sweet." She squeezes my ass, taking me all the way in again.

"Alright. Well, we'll let you go," Emma says. "Let us know if we can help with the tickets."

"Will do," I say, reaching forward and ending the call before they can say goodbye.

I slam the computer shut and stand, pulling Stephanie up to her feet. I turn her around, pushing her over the table and tugging her waistband down. I keep one hand on her back, forcing her to bend, as I reach between her legs and swipe my fingers along her center. She's soaked, and I rub a few quick circles around her clit that have her moaning, her back arching down toward the table below her.

"You got yourself all turned on sucking me off, didn't you?"

She nods, biting her lip as she turns to look at me over her shoulder.

"Fuck," I say, positioning myself behind her and slipping my dick into her. I pull her shirt up so her nipples are exposed, rolling one between my fingers as I push deep into her. I tug on her hair, pulling her head up to my shoulder. "You loved having control over me, didn't you?"

"I think you loved losing control," she says, and I nip her neck.

"I need to be working right now, but instead I'm giving you yet another orgasm. Selfish Wildflower," I say, reaching down and playing with her clit as her chest heaves, her orgasm coming swiftly and pulsing along my dick as I thrust into her. She cries out, her hands winding into my hair and her nails digging into the skin of my neck as I coax every last ounce of pleasure from her body.

When she's done, she leans her head back against my shoulder, and I run my hands all along her breasts, her hips, her ass. I pump into her rhythmically, driving myself to orgasm right behind her.

My arms tighten around her as I release into her, and I can finally take a breath. I keep her close to me, leaving gentle kisses along her neck and her shoulders.

I kiss her cheek, resting my head against hers.

I have never met anyone who could go from sexy to adorable so quickly. Never met a girl who could sexually control me with such ease and turn that on a dime into a protectiveness so fierce I'm not sure I can let her out of my sight again.

My heart catches as I realize I may have gotten in deeper than I planned.

# 31

# STEPHANIE

I shake my head as I splash water over my face, a pool of heat building in me as the image flashes in my mind of his jaw clenching, his pulse pounding in his neck. The rough way he pulled me to my feet and bent me over the table. The way he gripped me, one arm across my chest as he pounded into me.

I turn off the water and grab a towel from the hook on the door, patting my face dry.

"Hey," he says, entering the bathroom with a grin on his face. He comes up behind me in the mirror, wrapping his arms around my neck and leaving a kiss on my cheek. He turns to face me, leaning against the vanity, one hand on my hip and the other brushing my hair out of my face.

"Hi," I say, wiping away a drop of water from my chin. He follows the movement with his eyes, and then brushes his thumb along my chin.

"Well," he says, squeezing my hip, "I was wondering if you'd be up for a tour of the catacombs followed by dinner at a French-Japanese fusion restaurant."

"That sounds great."

His fingers graze my cheek, resting on my neck as he kisses me, his lips soft and light on mine. When we break apart, his eyes hold mine, and a little jolt of electricity runs down my spine.

He slaps my ass on his way out of the bathroom.

When I come out, he's sitting at the kitchen table, his face buried in his laptop and his eyes crinkled as he types.

"You're so serious when you're working," I comment, and he smiles up at me. I grab a glass from the cabinet above the sink and fill it with water.

As I walk by him to take my seat, he loops an arm around my hips, pulling me between his legs and looking up at me. "You're serious too," he says. He puts on a mock stern face. "All pouty and biting your lip. It's cute."

"I do not bite my lip."

"You do when you're concentrating too hard."

He tugs me down so I'm sitting in his lap, one arm around his neck and the other on his opposite shoulder.

"Have you ever wanted more?" he asks, leaving little kisses on my shoulders, my hands.

"More?"

For a second I think he must be asking about *us* and my heart kick-starts, but the illusion quickly shatters when he speaks. "Yeah. You're really dedicated. Super focused, which is really impressive after everything you've been through over the past few months. Always quick to take a call even if you're out or doing something else."

I shrug. "I like where I'm at. Honestly, it's taken me long enough to feel good about my job that I'm hesitant to change anything right now."

He nods. "That makes sense. I just hope you're not holding yourself back."

I snort. "I'm not holding myself back. I'm barely hanging on."

He gives me a look. "Steph, you're smarter than you think. More dedicated than you think. I bet if you wanted more, your boss would be more than willing to help you."

"You think I'm smart?"

"Absolutely."

"You're just trying to get a repeat of what we did five minutes ago."

He kisses me lightly. "I mean, absolutely, but I'm not blowing smoke up your ass to get you naked."

"No smoke?"

"No smoke."

I sigh into him, leaning my head on his shoulder. "Well, maybe one day I'll be as driven as you are, but for now, I'm happy trucking along as I am."

"As long as you're happy," he says, a note of wistfulness in his voice as his fingers run through my hair.

I sit up, eyeing him. "Are you happy?"

He seems taken aback by this question. "Yeah, of course I am."

I struggle to read between the lines of what he's telling me. His eyes don't match the words coming out of his mouth, and I've only heard snippets about his work life that don't exactly inspire confidence.

"You're not."

He rolls his eyes. "I'm not *unhappy*. I'm mildly over-worked and not getting rewarded for it. I'm like a kid at bedtime who's grumpy but insists he wants to stay awake."

I grin at his comparison. "That's adorable," I say, leaving a kiss on his nose. "But aren't you doing things a little back-ward?" I gesture to his computer screen, open to a form filled with so much engineering nonsense it makes my head spin. "Like, if you're grumpy, should you really be working on vacation?"

He shakes his head. "No, but the last thing I want to do is be MIA when there's a potential turning point coming next week. Honestly, it's easy work for me but complicated for anyone without my background, so it looks like I'm doing a lot but it's really not much more than translating an email from French, to English, to Engineer."

"Yeah, that sounds kind of complicated."

He shrugs. "It's all in your experience. Just like proposal writing is a breeze to you but it would probably make me pull my hair out."

"Okay, well, I think there's a difference between using the same words we use everyday in speech versus that mess," I say, gesturing to his screen.

"I would take this mess any day over having to write the proposal docs you do."

"Wait a second," I say, glancing back at the screen. "How does this line up with that director of training position you wanted? Do you have to know how to code to train people?"

He shakes his head. "No, I started in engineering. It's kind of unique though, to be able to talk to computers, people, and people who speak other languages."

I nod. "Ah, okay. That makes sense. I think at heart you're a people person like me." I shoot him a grin that he returns easily, his fingers running down my cheek.

He grins. "I'm a people person like you, the girl who sits quietly and writes all day."

"Oh, you know what I mean."

He brushes my hair away from my face, the sensation sending a little shiver down my spine. "I know what you mean," he agrees. "I'm just very protective of my peace. I've worked hard. Really, *really* hard. And something about the way everything is shaking out just makes me nervous."

"Because of Jack and Emma?"

He blinks, thinking about it. "I'm not sure I trust the company to make what I think is the right decision."

"What is the right decision?"

He lets out a long breath. "I guess... move Emma back to accounting. Give Jack the training position. And"–he shakes his head–"put me somewhere *else*."

"Put you somewhere else?"

He nods, pursing his lips. "Honestly, Jack deserves it. He's good with people and he consistently gets the highest ratings of all of us. I mean, we're all good with people, but he's exceptional. Ironically, I think I've become good at so many things at this company, but there's no single place where I truly *excel*."

"*That's* a great skill in and of itself."

"It's dumb to think like this," he says, shaking his head. His eyes connect with mine and quickly dart away. "I should be grateful for everything I have."

"Are you not also grateful? You can feel both at once. Somewhat slighted, but still grateful for how far you've come."

"I'm definitely grateful. I mean, a lot of people would kill to be where I am. I mean, my mom even–"

I blink. This feels important. "Your mom what?"

He bites his lip. "When we were little, my mom didn't work. Three kids under ten, you know? But as we got older, it became really apparent that my mom wasn't happy. And I guess the three of us— my mom, my brother and me— became obsessed with leveling up."

"Leveling up?"

He nods. "My parents ended up switching off. My mom

went back to work and my dad still teaches part time at the community college but he's not striving for tenure or anything anymore. She's a lawyer for a nonprofit that helps neurodivergent kids and she's literally *thriving*. And my mom, my brother and I are in a constant battle to see who can work the hardest, who can get to the top first."

"Who's winning?"

He sighs. "Either one of them."

I wasn't really expecting an answer to that. "How do you define winning?"

His thumb draws a circle on my hip as he thinks. "I don't know. My brother's pretty high up at a smaller company. Knows everything about the place and kind of just bosses people around. My mom is a shark in the water sniffing for blood. The kind of lawyer you want working *for* you and never *against* you. Kind and supportive, but you don't let her look in your direction too long. And I'm just kind of floating along, hoping to get noticed for working on vacation." He shrugs, giving me a small smile.

"So you're defining winning as confidence for your brother, and knowledge for your mom."

He shrugs. "I suppose so."

"Yet you totally discount what makes your own job a winner."

He wrinkles his eyebrows at me. "What's that?"

I throw my hands up at the obvious answer. "Happiness."

He rolls his eyes. "Everybody wants to be happy. That's not exactly unique."

"Yeah, but you said it yourself a few minutes ago. You just want to enjoy what you do. You want to sign on for the day and talk to people, do your little French-to-English-to-Engineer translations. Maybe you should be taking strides toward maximizing your happiness rather than aiming for something that someone else deems *the best*."

I'm not trying to get him to change his life trajectory here, but if he's so worried about a job taking away from his quality of life, he should take steps to change that. No job is worth your happiness.

He sighs. "It's just what we do."

"Your family?"

He nods. "We celebrate accomplishments together. Talk through work issues together. Egg each other on when we hit a snag. It's like this little hive of support." And he doesn't want to lose that.

And I get it. It's not about the job. It's his way of connecting with his family.

"I bet there will still be work issues to talk about even if you're prioritizing your happiness."

He shrugs. "Maybe. But I like things how they are right now."

*Stubborn as they come.*

He squeezes my knee, the grin returning to his face. "Are you done working for the day, Wildflower?"

The nickname sends a flood of warmth through my body. "Yeah, I am."

He nods to the bathroom. "Go get ready, then."

I disentangle myself from his lap, missing his warmth the second I'm standing. As I grab some clothes from my suitcase, I try a new nickname for him.

"I can call you director," I say, gauging his reaction.

He scrunches his face up. "Please don't."

"I'll let you direct me," I offer.

He considers this and then shakes his head. "No."

"Mr. President?"

"What? No."

"Just thought you might like a little clout."

He gives me a look. "Steph, with you, I don't need clout."

"Aw, that's sweet."

He turns his attention back to his computer. "It's not sweet."

"You're *so* sweet," I say, another nickname occurring to me. "Oh, I could call you *sweetie!*"

"Stephanie," he warns.

"Ollie, do you want to be my sweetie pie?"

He tries to hide his laughter, but his face cracks into a grin. He shakes his head, his ears turning the lightest shade of pink. "No, Stephanie. Don't you dare call me that."

**32**

## OLIVER

We've been sleeping together in Paris together for three days now, and Stephanie has spent the majority of that time coming up with silly nicknames for me that are either totally nonsensical or borderline cringe.

"I could call you manchego," she says, taking a bite of her pizza and leaving it in the box next to us on the bed.

I never thought watching a woman down half a pizza naked would be a turn on, but here I am, semi and all. She has one leg thrown over me, the sheets twisted between and around us, and she leans back on the palms of her hands, her face pinched in thought as she chews and swallows. She's exposed from the waist up, pert nipples on display as she wipes the grease from her hands on her stomach.

I grab a napkin from the nightstand and hand it to her, returning to my sketchpad and immortalizing this moment, Stephanie in all her pizza glory, half-naked and fully satisfied.

"Manchego sounds, like, very manly, but I wonder if it has another meaning. Like I guess I can call you cheesy all the time–let's be real, you *are* a little cheesy–but there's no real meaning to it. Nothing, like, wildflower-y about it."

She tosses the sheets to find her phone, and I stop myself from telling her to sit just like she was so I could finish capturing that moment.

But I guess that's what's special about it in the first place. The fact that it's fleeting by nature. You can only enjoy it for that split second in time and then it's gone. Forgotten unless I can somehow figure out a way to *just draw faster.*

"I'll Google it. Maybe *chego* means something in another language. Maybe it means hot, that would be perfect for you. Man-hot." She types it into her phone and pouts at the screen. "Chego does not mean anything, apparently. But it is a restaurant in L.A. that recently closed."

"Shame," I say, abandoning the sketchpad and running my hand along her stomach, her hip.

She hums. "Arguably, that could work, though." She leans toward me, her nipples grazing my chest as she kisses my jaw. "You are pretty edible."

I grab her hips before she can move away again, keeping her pressed against me. She reaches over to grab her slice again, giving me a bite before taking one for herself. "Or I could call you mozzarella. I *love* mozzarella," she says, and I don't know whether she's mocking me or just sharing her cheese preferences with me, but my heartbeat quickens in response.

"I'm more into mozzarella than manchego anyway," I tell her, pressing a kiss to her collarbone.

"Oh I know!" She sits up straighter. "Goat cheese! Because you're the greatest of all time!"

I laugh into her neck. *This girl.* "Okay, I'll accept that."

She sighs into me, offering me another bite of pizza. She

grumbles, "Although I don't know if I want to be going around calling you a goat."

"I'll have to practice my bleat."

She huffs. "Yeah, I can't call you that," she says, throwing the pizza down in the box and straddling me. She leans into me, tucking her head into my neck and sighing into my skin. "I can't believe I can't think of a nickname."

I run my fingers through her hair, mesmerized by the blended blues and purples. "I'll really be okay without a nickname."

She sits up, the motion and her taut nipples urging me harder underneath her. "No, you need a nickname," she whines. "This is part of the whole thing, of us in Paris. Every time you call me Wildflower I get this little jolt, and it's not fair I can't do the same for you."

"It's okay," I say. "I don't feel like I'm missing out."

"That's not the point! Doesn't that make you feel good to know that *you* make *me* feel good? I want to make you feel good with just words, too!"

"Aw, Stephy, you're sweet," I tell her, running my hand up her ribcage, circling my thumb around her nipple. "You can make me feel good in other ways."

"It's not the same," she pouts.

I sigh, dropping my hands to her thighs. "Well, why do you feel so good when I call you Wildflower?"

She runs her hands down my chest, resting them on my stomach. "Because it makes me feel like you think of me as some free spirit. You think I'm pretty and a little resilient. You think of me in all the ways I want you to, and it gives me that gooey feeling."

"All that's accurate," I say, and her fingers dig lightly into my skin.

"And you're just this, like, super smart, super kind,

fucking hot guy. You give me space when I need to work, and you're understanding when I'm a little frazzled, and you want to see me succeed without being pushy about it. How do I sum that up in a word?"

My breath catches. *Yeah, I think she sees exactly who I want to be.* I reach for her face, bringing her lips to mine. "Do you need a word if you just said it all?"

"But how do I remind you if I don't have a word that sums that all up?"

I pull on her hips, feeling the wetness pooling beneath her.

"Maybe you can tell me again a couple times," I say, as her hands run up my chest, settling on my shoulders. She lifts, and I guide myself inside her.

"We don't have enough time," she says into my shoulder, her words breathy and light.

I don't think about the words as they come out of my mouth, what they might mean to her.

"We have all the time in the world."

She throws her head back as she grinds her hips on me, her movements languid and indulgent as she drives herself over the edge. She cries out as she comes, the little noises she makes when she's at the peak of pleasure slowly becoming the soundtrack to this vacation.

A soundtrack I never want to turn off.

When she relaxes into my chest, her orgasm waning, I push the damn pizza box out of the way and flip on top of her, driving into her until I come. I collapse on top of her, winding my tongue into her mouth as she moans beneath me.

Afterward, I'm hesitant to move. A strong desire to preserve these moments has me running my fingers along her skin, squeezing and grabbing at every part of her while I still have the chance.

Steph is right. We don't have enough time.

When I roll off her, I pull her into my arms, the fleeting nature of our relationship suddenly less of a relief and more of a fear.

"I have to leave in two days."

"No," she says, burying her face in my neck.

"Come home with me."

A selfish part of me wants her close. A worried part of me doesn't want her gallivanting over all of Europe by herself. A weak little part of me that thinks maybe she'll forego love in favor of me.

She looks up at me, her eyebrows crinkled. "Can we just not talk about it? I don't want to think about the end."

"Steph," I say, turning on my side so we're facing each other. "It's not the end. It's just the next leg of your adventure."

She rolls her eyes. "I'm *so* not referring to my trip, and you know that."

I run my fingers through her hair, and her eyes flutter shut. "Steph, both of us were always clear on what we wanted. Don't you think you'll find love easier at home? Don't you think love will last longer with someone who's in the same place as you? Honestly, fuck Rod. Fuck traveling. Fuck me, even–I have to travel a ton, too. If love is what you want, find it at home."

"I don't know what I want anymore," she mumbles.

"Steph. Do you really not know what you want anymore, or is your brain clouded with sex?"

She looks at me, and for a second I hope that she's going to say she doesn't care about love anymore, that she's fine having flings until further notice. Maybe she'll even say we can continue this at home, no strings attached.

"I want love," she says, and my fantasy dies. As it should.

"Then come home with me."

"Okay."

THE DAY before we leave Paris, Jack and Emma video chat me. It's mid-afternoon here, so it must be early in the morning back home, and the timing of it has my heart beating fast. Today's the day Jack and Emma come clean about their relationship.

"Hey guys," I say, accepting the call. I study their faces, searching for any indication of what's happening. I glance over at Steph, hoping the call won't interrupt her concentration, but she's fully focused on whatever she's typing. I can't help but think about the last call I took with them only a few days ago, the way she so surreptitiously lowered herself beneath the table and took me in her mouth.

I shake my head, struggling to bring my thoughts back to the matter at hand.

"Hey," Jack says.

A moment of silence passes. "So did you do it?"

Jack nods. "Yeah."

"What happened?" I ask. *Why is he so flat?* My heart kick-starts.

He shrugs. "I told Gail what was happening. That Emma and I are in love and we don't want to hide it anymore. That we want to get married, but we've been waiting on news about this position and we just can't wait any longer to live our lives."

"And what did she say?"

"She said there are multiple restructures happening around the company because of the new chief product officer. A lot that we don't know about." He lets out a long breath. "And long story short, we just have to wait."

A beat of silence passes between us. "I'm sorry. I know that's not what you were hoping for."

He shakes his head. "It's not. And if I end up fired over it, fine. Because at least we don't have to hide things anymore."

"They're not going to fire you," Emma says. "Gail loves you."

Jack shrugs. "None of us know what the future holds, right? At least it's out in the open. From here on out, it's up to the universe." He lets out a long breath as he runs a hand through his hair. "Emma, come over here and comfort me."

"Inappropriate," she jokes. "I'm going to report you to HR."

"At least I'll be fired for a better reason than hubris."

Emma shakes her head, her eyes dancing across her screen. "Stop, Jack. You're going to be fine." Her brow furrows at something on her computer. "Hey, I've gotta run to another call. I'll talk to you guys later."

"Bye, guys."

Stephanie eyes me as I end the call, slowly closing her laptop. "That sounded interesting."

"Yeah. I'm not sure what to think."

"Think positively?" she suggests. "This might work out well for all of you. Maybe you'll get that training position after all."

I sigh. "I doubt that," I say.

Steph cocks her head to the side. "Ollie," she says, a pitying note in her voice that I don't really like. "You're smart. Dedicated. And just because your skills are different than Jack's doesn't mean they aren't really fucking important. You're selling yourself short if you think it's *this* position or *none*."

I smile at this girl who is just so damn supportive. "That's really sweet, Steph." I momentarily forget where this conversation started, the stress of not knowing the future of my career.

She shrugs. "I speak only the truth. I know you're upset that things aren't happening the way you want them to, but sometimes you just have to take a deep breath and let time do its work."

I can't help but smile at her. "Sweet and spicy, all in one."

She grins. "I tell it like it is."

I lean over to kiss her, her hair tangled between my fingers. I pull her chair closer, and when that's not close enough, I grab her behind the knees and pull her onto my lap. Her tongue winds into my mouth, spurring a rush of blood to my groin that she moves against.

As I peel her shirt off, my mind wanders back to her endless quest for a nickname for me. My hands run up and down her bare skin, catching on her waistband and pulling it down over her hips. She makes me feel capable and smart, and when my brain runs off with imposter syndrome, she gently corrects my course. Her fingers fumble with the button of my jeans as I reach up and roll her nipple between my fingers.

She makes me feel wanted and respected. Deserving.

I guide myself into her as she lowers on top of me, and I can't help but agree with her. There isn't a word that encapsulates all the things she makes me feel, all the things I ever wanted to be that she recognizes me for.

As she clenches around me, her small moans turning to ragged breaths, I realize just how much I'm going to miss the way she makes me feel.

## 33

## STEPHANIE

It's our last night in Paris. I managed to get on the same flight as Ollie, and even though I'm sad that I went on a big quest for love and I'm returning without, I think he's right–I'll be happier at home.

We get dinner at a little French bistro only a few blocks from our hotel room and I'm thrown by how easy our conversation is. Maybe it's because I know this all ends tomorrow, but the hours pass like minutes. We're laughing one minute over my botched pronunciation of yet another French dish, and speaking in solemn voices the next when we move on to Jack and Emma's future.

Maybe this is so easy because we were already such good friends. We got to skip those awkward moments when you're sleeping together but not fully comfortable with one another.

We were already close. We just took away the clothing for a few days.

Oliver's hand is tight around mine as we walk home, taking our time meandering down city streets. I know with a certainty I can feel in my bones that we'll fall easily into each other later, in the confines of our little hotel room, and I'm winded by the contrast of tonight compared to Valentine's Day.

We couldn't get our clothes off fast enough. Couldn't get enough of each other's bare skin.

But now I want to cling to these moments, too. Where we're just walking and talking, our eyes flitting between Parisian storefronts and the cars zipping by us, our attention on the outside world but our hands connected between us, a silent tether that keeps us bouncing back to each other. The brush of an elbow. His arm around my shoulders when I inevitably shiver against the cold air.

When we get back to the hotel room, there's no competition to see who can undress fastest. No frenzied movements or frantic kisses.

He takes my jacket, leaving it on the back of a kitchen chair, and then leaves his on top of it.

Like they're hugging.

And something about that is so adorable that I almost want to take a picture of it.

I shake the thought from my head, accepting a glass of wine from Ollie and sitting on the edge of the bed to take off my shoes.

He sits to kick his own shoes off, then leans back against the headboard, grabbing his sketchpad from the night stand. He flicks through casually as I tug on his arm and slide underneath, scrunching up my limbs and getting all of me as close as possible to all of him.

"I don't think I've drawn this much in years," he says, going through one page after another. Each picture is some other version of me.

I swear, with each drawing I get prettier and prettier.

At some point I'm going to stop recognizing them as me.

"You should draw more. You're so good," I say, running my fingers along one of the more recent ones where I'm stark naked, leaning back on one elbow and lowering a gigantic piece of pizza into my mouth.

I'm not even embarrassed by it. I was for a moment when I realized he was drawing me, but he manages to make even this moment look attractive. Pizza bloat and wild flyaways included.

He shrugs. "I only really draw when I feel like it. When I'm *inspired*," he says, with a little flair and a kiss to my temple.

I laugh, turning my face into his shoulder. "Are you saying I'm your muse?"

"Something like that." He tugs me closer, his cheek tight against my forehead, and I curl tighter around him. "Maybe you'll let me draw you one last time."

I groan into his neck. "Don't say that. It's not the last time."

He lets out a breath that skates along my shoulder. "The last time here. Like this."

I sit up and face him, throwing my hair over my shoulder. "How do you want me?"

He snorts. "And here I thought we were just drawing."

I tug my sweater up over my head, dropping it to the ground next to me.

"You don't have to be naked," he says, even as his eyes dip down to my breasts. I undo the clasp of my bra, letting it fall in front of me, and get a little zip of pleasure when I notice his eyes are just about *glued* to me.

"Maybe I want to be," I say, as I undo the clasp of my jeans and stand to let them drop to the floor.

He presses his lips together to hide a smile. "Then by all means."

I make sure he's watching as my panties drop to the ground.

And then I climb back on the bed and position myself on my side, at the foot of the bed, with my cheek propped on one hand.

I give him my best smile. "Draw me like one of your French girls, Oliver."

His laughter is everything.

"I guess I'm not the only one here who's funny when naked," he quips, and I can't help the laugh that jumps from my throat. I fall to my back for a moment as it overtakes me, and when I face him again, he's staring at me with a grin on his face.

"Am I also sexy when I smolder?" I do my best interpretation of the smolder he gave me my first night in Paris. "What was the other one? Handsome when you smile?"

He flips to a new page in his sketchpad, grabbing his pen from the night stand. "I don't think that one really applies to you. Though if this was a couple hundred years ago, I'd absolutely describe you as handsome." He stares at me a few seconds before turning his gaze to the blank page in front of him. "But present day, I'd probably say you're beautiful when you blush."

As if on cue, I feel my cheeks heating. He smiles, as if this is exactly what he intended.

I wonder just how much of my body is turning pink under his gaze, but I refuse to look.

I think we both know what he does to me at this point.

So I only smile back at him, biting my lip so I'm not totally beaming.

"Gorgeous when you grin." My lip comes free from my teeth, my smile too wide to be tamed. His mouth mirrors mine as he places the first few strokes on the page. His gaze flicks up to me, scanning my body and landing on my eyes for a few moments, as if to say he knows he's inspiring a slickness between my legs.

I resist the urge to squirm, and meet his eyes with a dare.

"Pretty when you pose," he continues, and I raise my eyebrows, wondering just how many of these he can come up with.

I adjust my shoulder, sticking my chest out a little bit as if to show I'm posing for *him*.

He licks his lips as his eyes drift along my body, returning to his drawing. A few seconds later, he adjusts himself, shaking his head. "Jesus."

"Alright over there?" I ask.

He nods. "Never had more fun torturing myself."

I laugh, tipping onto my back again for a moment. When I return to him, his eyes are locked to mine.

"I could look at you forever."

His words hang heavy between us.

And then he returns to his drawing, a silence falling that's both comfortable and full of questions. I know who Ollie is. What he wants. *But he could look at me forever?*

I'm not about to get my hopes up. To think that this could be something bigger than what it is.

But every time he looks at me, those words ring in my head.

When he's finally done, he turns the sketchpad so I can see, and I roll my stiff shoulder out as I look.

Me, laid out across the foot of a bed just as I was. Except my face is tipped up, my lips only inches from his. He's behind me, one arm around my waist, his hand covering one breast and my hair drifting across the other.

It's the first time he's drawn himself along with me, and it gives this one life. A little bit of romance. A connection between two people that extends beyond the physical relationship.

He's drawn more of me–in much more explicit detail than this–yet this feels more intimate than any other drawing I've seen.

Like he intended to draw my physical form but ended up drawing my heart instead.

"What do you think?" he asks.

I run my fingers along the edge of the page, careful not to hit any ink that might still be wet. "You added you."

He shrugs. "It just felt right."

"I love it," I say, as his thumb grazes my cheek, his fingers following the outline of my jaw.

And for some reason this feels like the moment where *I love it* should turn into *I love you.*

My heart catches as his eyes land on mine.

He leans forward, his fingers tilting my chin up, and kisses me lightly.

When he pulls away, he pauses for a moment, his fingers still under my chin as he looks into my eyes.

I can't help thinking to myself that he's feeling this too. This *something* that feels like a little more than just Paris.

He sits up, his eyes on mine as he pulls his shirt over his head and abandons it somewhere on the floor. He undoes his pants and shimmies out of them along with his underwear, and then joins me on the bed, sitting on his ankles next to me as his fingers trail along my skin, pressing into the array of moles on my hip that he loves so much.

He's hard already, a bead of precum skirting the tip, and I reach out, pressing my thumb into it and spreading it around. He inhales sharply as his head tips back, his fingers digging into my skin as I wrap mine around his length.

He runs his fingers through my hair, along my neck, brushing softly over and around my nipples.

And then with one hand on my hip, he climbs over me, positioning himself behind me just like in his drawing, pressed up on one arm so he can tilt my chin up and kiss me, his tongue licking at the seam of my lips and then pressing inside. He holds my mouth hostage as his hand explores my body, running along my waist and my hip and finally skirting my ass and dipping between my thighs, swiping at the wetness pooling there.

I groan as my body bows to him, my ass thrusting back to give him easier access.

He slips two fingers inside me, pulsing slowly, and I reach behind me to grab his neck, keeping him close as his lips trail kisses along my neck.

Just when I think I might go over the edge, he withdraws his fingers, lifting them to his mouth and sucking them clean with a groan. He's rock hard against my back, and a moment later, he reaches down, sliding himself easily between my slick thighs.

I whimper as he presses inside me. As he tugs on my hips and presses as deeply into me as he can. He moves slowly, a shudder wracking through his body as he buries himself to the hilt inside me.

"Exquisite in your existence," he whispers, as his hips rock against mine. He takes my mouth with his as he moves, swallowing my moans as he squeezes my breasts. As he grabs my free hand with his own, every part of us connected. He slowly builds up speed, his body going taut behind mine.

He kisses my hand before he releases it, his trailing down my body until he reaches my clit. He presses—a light touch—and nearly sends me over the edge.

I gasp at the feeling, my legs ticking wider in a silent plea for him to keep going.

His fingers move in small circles, urging me closer and closer.

"Oh god," I whimper, as I feel my orgasm rising.

"Come with me, Wildflower," he whispers into my ear. His teeth graze the skin of my neck as he continues with the same rhythm, each circle of his fingers pushing me higher and higher until the dam breaks and I come with a cry, my hand finding the back of his neck and holding onto him tightly.

"That's it, Wildflower," he says, as I press my ass back into him, taking all of him as he thrusts into me harder.

"Ollie," I moan, as all the pent up energy slowly leaves my body.

He grunts as he latches onto me tighter. "Fuck, Stephanie." He pulses into me roughly. "Fuck, you feel so good." He reaches up to palm my breast as his movements become jerky, his release only seconds away. "Fuck, Stephanie. You're mine." He thrusts into me hard, a rough grunt tumbling from his throat as he holds me tight against him. "You're mine."

## 34

## STEPHANIE

I zip up my suitcase and place it by the door next to Ollie's. I do a quick search under the bed for any dropped items and, seeing none, pull the covers into place. I take the glasses from the nightstands and throw them in the sink, and combine all of our trash in the can by the fridge.

Ollie comes out of the bathroom in his sweatpants, running a towel over his damp hair. He pauses when he sees the clean room. "Did you make the bed?"

I shrug. "Yeah."

"But we're leaving."

"It just looks nicer."

He drops his towel on the back of the kitchen chair and kisses my temple. "Thanks for cleaning up." The brush of his hand over my lower back sends a little shiver down my spine. That seems to happen anytime he touches me, like his touch is that much more powerful now that it has a time limit.

He throws his towel into the pile in the bathroom and

comes out with his shower kit, which he zips neatly into the top of his suitcase.

"Ready?" he asks, taking a last look around the room.

I shake my head.

"Aw, Stephy," he says, pulling me in for a hug. I bury my face in his chest, desperate for just a few more minutes of this.

"How much time do we have before our flight?"

"We're a little early," he says, a smile in his voice. "If you want to take a few minutes."

I look up at him, pressing my lips to his chin. "I do."

He bends down, taking my mouth gently with his. His arms weave around me, his hands landing on my ass and grabbing me. We stumble toward the bed, uncoordinated, and he pushes me backward, my knees hitting the edge. He catches me, one arm around my waist, and lays me down, his knees pushing between mine as he climbs on top of me.

"One last time for good luck," he whispers, tugging my leggings down.

"One last time," I say, relishing the taste of his skin. I pull his shirt over his head, throwing it to the floor, and scramble to pull his pants down. His words from last night stick in my head. *You're mine.*

"Impatient Wildflower," he says, pushing my shirt up and over my head. He thumbs my nipple, bending down and taking the other in his mouth. He leaves kisses along my chest, my collarbone, my jaw, and pauses, his mouth hovering just above mine.

"I had a really nice time with you," he says, his nose brushing mine.

"I had the best time with you." He grins as his hand drifts down my hip, his thumb circling that little bundle of nerves that makes me suck a sharp breath in. "God, I don't want to leave."

"Me neither," he says, his mouth finding mine. I moan into him as his fingers draw a slick line up my center and press inside me. "I'm going to miss this."

Before I can say anything else, he aligns himself with my entrance and pushes inside of me.

"Fuck, Stephanie," he grunts into my ear. I wrap my arms around his neck and hold on to him as he pumps into me, the feeling of him inside me simultaneously soothing and ephemeral.

He holds me close as I crash around him, his arms tightening around me and his chest strong above me, and I cling to him as he jerks into me, savoring the last of *us*.

We lay there for a moment afterward, hanging on to each other as if he knows I just need one more second to lose myself in this.

"Maybe..." I start, and then catch myself before saying something I'll regret.

"Maybe what?" he asks, leaving little kisses across my cheeks.

I shake my head. "Nothing."

He leans back to look at me. "What's wrong?"

"Dumb thought," I say. "The kind of thing you regret saying afterward."

He runs a hand down my side, landing on my hip. "Tell me."

I swallow. "I was going to say maybe we could do this at home. Not anything more than this. Just... this."

He rests his forehead on my shoulder, quiet for a moment. "Steph, I don't think that's a good idea."

"I know. That's why I said it was dumb. Sex fog and everything, you know."

He brushes my hair out of my face. "I wish I could be everything you want."

*You are.*

"Me too."

He kisses me, long and slow, and I melt into him. When he finally pulls away from me, I feel only the heavy weight of his absence.

We clean ourselves up and position our bags on the other side of the door to do a final sweep of the room. We leave a few Euros on the kitchen table for housekeeping, pull our coats on, and finally leave the room.

When I pull the door shut behind me, the February air biting at my cheeks, I turn to lock the door and find my hand won't do it. I shake my head, urging a laugh from my throat rather than tears. "God, I literally can't do it. I don't want to leave."

Ollie laughs, but his face betrays a hint of confusion as he takes the key from me and locks the door. He throws it into the mailbox next to us, as instructed. "You okay?"

*Nope.* "Yeah. I guess reality is just hitting."

He hugs me, the weight of his arms around my neck comforting. "Reality sucks, doesn't it?"

I nod. "Can I stay in my Parisian fantasy land?"

"Not forever."

I huff. "Fuck whoever made that rule."

As we grab our bags and head for the gate, I take one last look at our little Parisian haven.

"Hey Ollie?" He turns to me, his eyes finding mine. "Can I ask you something, no smoke?"

"Sure."

"In another life, could it have been us?"

He pauses before answering and then nods. "In any other."

I struggle to keep hold of my tears as he wraps an arm around me and opens the gate.

*So this is the end.*

## 35

## OLIVER

My heart thumps in my chest the entire way to the airport. Stephanie was right there for the taking, the words on the tip of her tongue that she'd be happy to continue as we are when we're home.

But something stopped her.

I wanted to grab her while I could, convince her into extending Valentine's Day to Philadelphia, but I couldn't do that to her. She's looking for love, and I'm just *not looking*.

I've always cared for Steph, first as a friend, but now there's something more there. I wouldn't go around calling it love, but I know her in a way that few people do. I know that she gives up little pieces of herself to make other people more comfortable. That she knows she loves too freely and forgives too easily and *doesn't care*.

I can't be what she wants me to be, but I can protect her from me. If we let this go on back home, I would take and take and take from her, and eventually it would become too much. Without a set end date, I would take up all of her time and patience, only to leave her lonely and confused in the end. I'd be the reason she doesn't get what she wants.

We find our gate and collapse into chairs nearby. I stay with our suitcases while she wanders off in search of snacks, and she reappears a few minutes later with a bag of candy and two little bottles of wine. She hands one to me and twists off her own cap, taking a sip.

"Cheers to our last few hours of Paris," she says. "Thrilled to be spending them in an airport."

*Me too, as long as it's with you.*

The thought surprises me, and I shake my head. She settles into the seat next to me, and I clink the neck of my mini-bottle against hers. She props her feet up on her suit-case, leaning back into the chair, and I take a thirsty sip of wine.

I barely paid attention this morning when we fell into bed. It didn't click in my mind that it would be our last time. It felt so natural to be with her, to fall into bed together like we have been so easily this week.

My mind races, struggling to remember the details, to preserve the feeling of her hips around me, her skin under-neath my fingertips, that mango and banana scent of hers that I can still smell when she throws her hair over one shoulder, nestling further down into her chair.

"Have you missed home?" I ask her.

She smiles sadly at me. "Yeah. I miss Gabi. The girls from work. Kay and Leilani. I'll be happy to see them again. I miss hugs."

I fight the urge to remind her that I've been hugging her, that I've been there for her over the past few days. And then it occurs to me she might need a hug *because* of me, and I melt into a pile of guilt because I let things go too far. I couldn't help myself, having a beautiful girl in my room all week, and now I've hurt her.

"I'm sure they miss you too." *They definitely do.* They're

currently in my house hanging up streamers and destroying the walls to welcome her home.

"I bet Bung misses you," she says.

Poor Bung is probably hiding behind the couch. "Yeah, I miss him."

Steph pulls out her e-reader, navigating to her current book.

*So this is the end.*

I guzzle down the rest of my wine, uncomfortable in our silence, and read over her shoulder. Eventually I get up and secure us two more little bottles, settling back into my chair and continuing the story with her.

"Holy shit, this is spicy," I say, as the female character drops to her knees. I'm pleasantly reminded of Steph, only a few days ago.

"Ollie!" she says, holding the device to her chest. "You can't read this!"

"Did you get your inspiration from that book?" I ask, reaching for it to continue reading.

She holds it back from me. "No! It was a coincidence!" But I see the tips of her ears turning pink.

"Oh, you so did!" I wrestle it away from her and continue reading. "Oh my, you upgraded it, actually."

She pouts as I hand it back to her.

"I'm surprised you're not getting squirmy reading that," I say, and the pink from ears reaches her cheeks. "You *are* getting squirmy."

"Ollie, stop." She gives me a look. "We agreed to end this."

My heart stops in my chest.

I... forgot.

I got so caught up reading over her shoulder that it completely slipped my mind that we weren't continuing this at home. I clicked right back into what we'd become over the past week, this playful friendship filled with sex and jokes and fun.

I clear my throat. "Sorry."

She shifts in her chair so I can't read anymore, and I lean back in mine, deflated. She was firm with me, drawing a solid line between friends and lovers that I didn't expect but should have.

*Just how far does this line go?*

I'm suddenly worried for our friendship. I don't know why, but I kept thinking that we'd just kind of erase Paris from our minds. There was a part of me that understood any further sex would be off the table–and that's fine–but it didn't occur to me that our friendship would be altered. That we'd have to ignore the parts of each other we learned while the sex was happening.

When we finally board the plane, she doesn't even say goodbye to me before continuing to her seat in the back. She just keeps walking.

The panic sets in as I take my seat, a combination of flight jitters and a fear of losing her making me want to crawl out of my skin. I stand up and search for her behind me, spotting her in a window seat three from the back of the plane. She has her headphones in, hair piled high on her head and her e-reader in front of her. Her face is pinched, and every few seconds she glances out the window. She takes a deep breath, as if trying to calm herself, and turns her attention back to her book.

And I sit down again, scared to push her too far but terrified to let her go.

I run my hands over my face, trying to convince myself the best thing to do right now is keep my ass in this seat.

And then I grab my bag from underneath the chair and head to the back of the plane.

The man sitting in the middle of her row is just getting himself settled.

"Excuse me," I say, "would you be interested in switching so I can sit with my friend? I have an aisle seat further up."

He considers this for a second and then nods. "Sure."

He pats his pockets, making sure he has everything, and then heads to my seat. I collapse next to Stephanie, turning to face her now that it's only the two of us.

"Ollie, what are you doing?" she asks.

"Can we pretend for eight more hours?"

"Is that a good idea?"

I shake my head. "It's not."

She leans forward and kisses me, her hands weaving behind my neck and pulling me close, her tongue slipping into my mouth.

"As long as you're not falling for me," she jokes.

*I'm not*, I think, as I weave an arm around her neck.

*Definitely not.* I leave a kiss on her temple.

*I can't be.*

# 36

## STEPHANIE

I embrace our sham relationship, leaning my head on Ollie's shoulder through the flight.

We have a layover in London where we make a mad dash for our next flight and settle into our seats out of breath and flustered, Ollie once again switching with the person next to me so we can sit together. We fall asleep at one point or another, and for small moments, I'm transported back in time to our hotel room, those blissful minutes and hours spent tangled up with each other.

When we start our descent into Philadelphia, he squeezes my hand, and it's like we're both thinking the same thing: this fun, wonderful thing we started in Paris ends in less than an hour.

We're quiet as the wheels touch down, as we taxi along the runway and our restless fellow passengers grapple for their bags and wait as those before them slowly depart. Ollie gets my bag down for me, but the smile he gives me is guarded.

So we are officially done.

We wind through the airport, following the crowd, and

speak only about the logistics of leaving the airport. I follow him onto a bus that takes us to the parking garage, where we spend an anxiety-inducing five minutes searching for his car.

Once our bags are loaded and I drop into the passenger seat, I turn to him.

"Should we talk about it?"

He lets out a long breath, eyeing me as he starts the car. "Should we?"

"I don't want things to be weird between us," I say.

"No, me neither." He reverses out of the spot, and I reach forward to blast the heat. "Thanks," he mutters, his head on a swivel as we follow the signs around for the exit.

"Especially if I'm staying with you."

He nods. "I know, Steph. Look, I won't be weird if you won't be weird. We're friends, right? Good friends."

A beat of silence passes as I debate whether I should say what I've been thinking of saying. "The flight felt like a lot."

He glances at me as we emerge into daylight.

"The flight?"

I nod. "Don't you think? It felt *charged*."

"Are you trying to tell me you wanted to join the mile high club?"

*Well, at least he's cracking dirty jokes.* He must not be upset. "I'm just making sure we're on the same page, here." *Something I'd expect the commitment-phobe of us to be doing.*

I wasn't planning on having this conversation with him. I thought our future–or lack thereof–was clear when we left our room. I made peace with it, put a little bow on it and stashed it in the back of my mind for sometime in the future when I need a pick-me-up or a passionate but doomed love story.

But Ollie followed me to the back of the plane. Insisted

on holding my hand. Rested his cheek on my head when I rested mine on his shoulder. He was the one who insisted this relationship be confined to Paris, yet he was the one pushing those boundaries.

He glances over his shoulder as we merge onto the highway. "We're on the same page. Don't worry, Steph. I won't try anything."

I watch him as he drives, trying to decipher whatever is happening in that confusing head of his.

"Okay, we're on the same page," I say.

He nods, reaching over and patting my knee. He doesn't linger, the touch essentially meaningless.

I wonder what happened on that flight, what made him come sit with me in the back of the plane. None of that was sexual. It was nice, comforting even, but it was also completely unexpected and a clear digression from what Ollie has said he wanted this whole time.

I'm good at listening to people when they tell you what they want or need, but Ollie's shooting off an array of signals in every direction, and I'm not sure which to pick up on.

The best I can do for now is listen to his words. If his feelings don't match what he's saying, he's going to have to figure out how to vocalize them.

I turn my attention out the window, to where Philadelphia rushes by us. Despite the confusion pounding in my head, it feels good to be home, to recognize the streets and be able to close my eyes and point toward home.

Not that I have a home anymore. I guess Ollie's spare bedroom is my home now.

We pull onto his street in South Philly, and he miraculously finds a parking spot close to his house. I breathe in the chilly February air as he pulls my suitcase out of the trunk. I weave my backpack over my shoulders and hold my hand out to take the suitcase from him, but he shakes his head.

He rests it on the ground and then takes a step toward me, handing me his keys. "Why don't you get the door?"

"That's very gentlemanly of you, but I can carry my own suitcase."

He gives me a look, taking my hand and pressing the keys into my palm. "Please?"

I shrug. "Thank you," I say, leading the way to his front door.

I unlock it and step inside, fumbling for the light switch I know is somewhere on the wall to my left, but before I'm able to find it, the room is bathed in light and noise.

"Surprise!"

I drop the keys, stumbling backward into Ollie as my eyes adjust to the scene. He pushes me gently forward as I'm surrounded on all sides by the people I love most.

"Oh my god," I mutter on repeat as my brain struggles to catch up.

"Stephanie!" Gabi wraps her arms around me, rocking me side to side. Zeke layers a hug on top of us both.

"We missed you," he says.

"Ugh, you guys operate as one person now, don't you?" I joke.

"Yes," they say in unison.

He shakes his head. "For real, though. We all know Gabi worries, but the past few weeks have been on another level. I *really* missed you."

I laugh as she rolls her eyes. "I wasn't *that* bad," she says. Zeke has the decency to not argue.

Kay and Leilani bowl into me next.

"We're so happy you're home!" Kay squeals, and our hug

quickly turns to jumping as the noise of a party builds around us, music starting and chatter increasing.

"Oh god, me too," I say, relaxing into their hug.

"And fuck Rod," Kay says, loudly enough that others hear, causing a chorus of "Fuck Rod!" echoing throughout the living room.

Leilani squeezes me extra tight. "You alright, Stephy?"

I nod. "I'm really good, actually. I think I'm ready to officially move on from him."

Kay bites her lip, lowering her voice. "That's because you fucked Ollie, isn't it?"

I narrow my eyes at her, glancing behind me to make sure he's not listening. I lower my voice. "Yes, but it was a Paris-only thing."

She claps. "Oh, I knew it. Was it good? I bet it was good."

I nod. "Really good."

"Oh god, I need to live vicariously through you."

"You need to work less so you can find a man," I shoot back.

She shakes her head. "Men are too much work."

Leilani clicks her tongue at her. "*Your* men are too much work," she corrects.

Kay and Leilani dissolve into their own conversation as I see polka dots coming for me, my work-wife-turned-best-friend Annabel tackling me with a hug that's just like her: small but fierce. Mari, her equally small and fierce best friend, swoops in behind her, dark hair loose and flowing. They squeeze me tight, neither of them taller than my chin.

"We're officially going to Costa Rica for our honeymoon," Annabel says.

"And I haven't been formally invited but I'm going in their suitcase if you want to dream up a similar stowaway situation," Mari tells me. "We can be each other's dates."

"Oh, you're so going to love it," I say to Annabel. "Especially with Mari and me there."

"I can't wait. That sloth you sent was so fucking cute. I want to adopt one."

I snort. That seems like a lifetime ago. "My tour guide ate termites," I say.

They pause, digesting this information. "What?" Annabel asks.

"Like he stuck his hand in a termite nest and just ate them."

"And you didn't marry him?" Mari asks.

"I wanted to."

I hear a gasp behind me and turn to see Ollie's eyes wide as he rushes toward the hallway leading to the kitchen. "Bung!"

Carrie emerges, Bung curled up in her arms like a little baby, eyes wide as he looks over the party with a somewhat stunned expression on his face. Ollie rushes forward, taking him out of her arms and hugging him, his eyes closing as he runs his fingers through Bung's fur.

"Aw I missed you, buddy," he whispers, leaving a kiss between his ears. He turns to Carrie. "Thank you."

"I'm always happy to hang out with little Bunghole," she says, scratching him under his chin. His eyes close, leaning into her touch, as Ollie massages his chest.

My eyes linger a second too long, and Ollie's gaze catches mine. He clears his throat, embarrassed, and leans down to kiss Bung on the head again. I avert my eyes, giving him space to love on his cat, and let myself be absorbed into the little group of friends I've missed so much.

Behind Annabel, her fiancé Charlie appears, passing me a cold bottle of Pinot Grigio with a small nod—not to welcome me home, but to say thank you for the spare ticket to a work party I gave him last year when he was so desperately trying to win over Annabel. He's taken every opportunity to keep me stocked since.

He weaves his arms around her neck, pulling her into his chest, and a hot flare of jealousy shoots down my spine. Charlie was a little wild before Annabel, much wilder than Ollie. Yet they're so happy together, so comfortable with each other.

I *literally* have gone to the edges of the world for love, yet I still can't get a man to put me first.

I grab a plastic cup from the pile on the counter and pour myself a generous amount, stashing the bottle back in the fridge when I'm done.

"So Stephanie," Mari starts as I rejoin the group, "what are you doing next weekend?"

I think about it for a second, hoping she didn't have something in mind already. "I think I'll be somewhere in the gayborhood dancing until four in the morning?"

Kay groans, Leilani cheers, and Mari nods.

"Yeah, that's exactly what I expected you'd say," Mari says.

"Yes!" Leilani says, doing a little dance as she turns to Kay. "Oh you're going to complain so hard about having too much fun. I'm so excited."

Kay rolls her eyes, turning to me. "I'll give you four in the morning only because I missed you, but just know that any other time I'd give us a hard cutoff of two."

"Aw, you're so sweet," I tell her, bundling her up in another hug because I've *missed* my friends. I squeeze her tight, pulling Mari and Leilani into our hug because I'm going to milk it for all that I can. "Maybe one of these days we'll convince you into liking fun things."

# 37

# OLIVER

I leave Steph's suitcases in the spare bedroom and drag my own into mine, Bung clinging to my chest the entire time. Downstairs, Steph's welcome party rages on, the laughter and music trailing up to the second floor. I hear her voice clearly through the noise. Her laugh. Those noises she makes to show you she's listening.

She's in her element. I could see the moment the light flickered into her eyes when she realized she came home to a party just for her, the delight in seeing her friends and being able to hug them for real.

I had little to do with this party. I gave Carrie permission to use the key, and Gabi coordinated everything else. All I had to do was get her here and make sure she opened the door first.

Bung purrs into my chest, and I wish I could cling to him as hard as he's clinging to me.

We settle for some ear scratches instead.

I haphazardly dump the contents of my suitcase into the laundry basket and throw it, empty, into my closet. With a sigh, I push my pillow up against my headboard and sit, Bung's purrs calming me.

I don't know what came over me on our flight, but it felt like the worst case of FOMO I've had in my life, like if I didn't find a way to sit with Steph, I would regret it. And of course, she read something into it. Our conversation on the ride home made it clear I'd screwed up.

*What else was I supposed to do?*

The time limit on us was close to expiration, and I couldn't stand the thought of taking that flight home alone. Of her being scared when I was right there and could make it better. Maybe it was a bad decision. Maybe it confused things. But I think it was worth it, playing into our fantasy for just a few more hours.

"Hey." My eyes pop open at the sound of her voice.

She's standing in the doorway, her arms crossed and leaning against the frame.

"Hey," I say, and motion to Bung on my chest as my reason for not moving.

She takes a step inside my room, her eyes taking in the minimalist, dark furniture. It's the first time she's been in here, and it feels bizarre considering how intimate we were with each other in Paris.

She sits next to me on the edge of the bed, her fingers trailing over Bung's fur. His purring intensifies, and she grins at the sound.

"Thanks for throwing me a party," she says.

"I can't take credit for that. That was Gabi and Carrie."

She shrugs. "You facilitated."

"And that's literally all I did."

She's quiet for a second, staring down at Bung as her fingers find that place just below his ear that he likes. He leans into her touch.

"Well, that's all," she says, taking her hand back. Bung's eyes whip open, angry she took away the good scritches. "Just wanted to say thank you." She pats him on the head and he reaches one paw out, slapping at her hand as if to tell her to keep going.

"No problem," I say, leaning my head back against the headboard again. "I'm probably going to go to bed, but feel free to keep the party going. I'll sleep through it."

"I doubt we'll be going that late," she says. "I'm kind of exhausted, honestly."

"Well, whatever. Just go enjoy yourself."

She nods, standing and walking toward the door. "Do you want this open?"

"If you could close it, that would be great."

"Well, goodnight," she says, slowly pulling the door shut.

"Goodnight–" I say, cutting myself off just before her nickname slips out. She pauses, the door halfway closed as if waiting for me to continue. When she realizes I'm not going to, she nods and pulls it the rest of the way.

*Fuck.*

# 38

## STEPHANIE

My stomach clenches as I walk downstairs.

*Why did that just feel like a breakup?*

I'm tired, definitely a little jet-lagged, and this day has been weird from so many angles, but Ollie omitting my nickname like that *hurt*.

I can deal with the end to a physical relationship, even to the deeper emotional relationship we flirted with in Paris, but to dangle the nickname between us and promptly pull it back like that feels like knocking my feet out from under me.

It felt akin to someone saying, "I don't love you anymore."

*And wow, I can feel that in my gut.*

Maybe I was a little deeper into things than I thought. Maybe I thought there was a possibility we might explore things at home. Maybe I thought crashing at his house would foster some of the connection I crave.

And he very swiftly let me know that all of that was off the table.

He invited me to Paris. He suggested extending our fling. He made things confusing on the plane.

And as much as I tried to keep my head on me and remember that our fling was confined to Paris, all of those moments of him wanting me added up to something that could live on beyond. He consistently told me we had an end date, and every time he pushed it, he taught me that that end date was movable. Easily manipulated.

But it seems our end date has finally arrived.

I try to shake the thought away as Gabi meets me at the end of the stairs, handing me a freshly refilled cup of white wine.

"You okay?"

I nod, taking a thirsty sip. "Yeah, I'm fine."

"You look stricken."

I lower my voice, as anxious to talk about it as I am to ignore it. "I think he just broke up with me again," I say.

Gabi's eyebrows crinkle as she takes a step toward me. "Were you *together* together?"

"No." A laugh jumps from my throat.

"Oh, Steph," she says, wrapping me in a tight hug. "You fell, didn't you?"

An image of him on the plane flashes in my mind, his expression hopeful as he asked the man next to me to switch seats. His mild laugh when I joked that he was falling for me. The neediness with which he kissed me.

I thought maybe it was the start of something new. Something better.

He created a little pocket of hope in me only to squash it completely later.

"No," I insist.

She squeezes me tighter. "Oh, I could kill him."

"Don't say anything, okay?" I ask, pulling away from her. "Whatever all that was... it's over now."

"Yeah, but you're hurting," she says.

"We were sleeping together for a week. It's not enough to be hurting."

Gabi gives me a look. "We all know that's more than enough for you."

*Because I love too freely and forgive too easily.*

"Well right now, I don't want it to be," I say.

Gabi nods. "Okay. Whatever you want. But you can always come stay with me."

"Thanks Gabi. I won't be sad for long. Maybe just a day or two. Besides, I don't want to be all up in your space."

"It's really no problem," she insists.

"Gabi, I have my own room with a plushy queen mattress here. The door closes and Ollie's gone half the time. I don't think it's going to be an issue."

"Okay. Whatever you say," she says, holding up her hands in surrender.

I take a sip of the wine and grab her hand. "Come on. I've been craving a night like this. Let's get wine drunk and silly."

# 39

# OLIVER

The coffee has already been made by the time I get downstairs. I pour myself a cup, checking in the filter to make sure she used the right amount, and tentatively taste it. Today is my first day back at work, and the last thing I need to go sideways is my coffee.

And I think my coffee tastes better when Stephanie makes it.

I head back upstairs and settle down at my computer. I converted the tiny bedroom that shares a wall with hers into my office, and although it's normally a quiet, comfortable space to hunker down and plow through some work, my thoughts boom loudly in my head.

It's like I can feel Steph's presence on the other side of the wall. Her typing, her breathing.

She spent most of yesterday holed up in her room, hungover from the party on Saturday. I heard her talking a few times, probably on the phone with her sister or one of the girls, and I had to fight the urge to knock and ask what they were talking about.

It feels weird being this far from her after Paris. And it's not just a physical distance, separated by some flimsy sheetrock, but an intense emotional distance that had her asking me politely yesterday if I wanted anything when she ordered dinner from the Chinese takeout place down the street. When I declined, she pulled her coat around her shoulders and left to pick it up by herself, only to return having already eaten it.

Maybe I should have said yes. Some weird part of me thought we might become friends again, sitting at my kitchen counter and talking over our respective dinners. But she went right back upstairs when she came back and shut the door behind her.

I couldn't help but imagine what she was doing. Reading one of her spicy books without me? Watching a show with her headphones in so she doesn't disturb me? That seems like something she would do.

Maybe she was planning my demise. I wouldn't blame her. I didn't mean to hurt her by stripping her of her nickname. Now we're in some weird halfway friendship that doesn't make sense to me. She gives me too much space and I'm stuck wondering why, when I should be focused on my job.

Steph is the life of every party. For her to go cold on me is like taking away the essence of *her*.

Like taking away her nickname.

I rest my head in my hands, my steaming coffee at my elbow.

I need to do something before we become strangers.

Abandoning my work, I weave into the hallway and knock on her door. When I don't hear anything from the other side, I open it.

Her eyebrows crinkle as she looks up at me. She's sitting on the floor with her back to the wall, her computer in her lap and headphones in her ears. She takes one out, raising her eyebrows at me. "Knock much?"

"I did knock."

"Oh," she says. "I guess I didn't hear you."

I step into the room, looking around. Her suitcase is open next to the bed, her sheets ruffled from sleep. Her e-reader and phone charger rest on the nightstand, deodorant and moisturizer on the dresser. Yesterday's clothes are in a pile in one corner.

"I just wanted to make sure you have everything you need."

She nods. "I'm good. Thanks."

I glance around, searching for something else to say. "Are you comfortable?"

She narrows her eyes at me. "Yeah. What's up, Ollie?"

And then it occurs to me *why* she's working on the floor. "Do you need a desk?"

She shakes her head. "No, I'm fine."

"You can't sit on the floor to work everyday."

"I can for a little while. I might work at the kitchen table for a bit today if that's okay. That's more than enough."

I shake my head, the solution occurring so quickly I can't believe I didn't think of it before. "No, you can have my desk."

"What?"

"You can have my desk," I say, taking stock of the room and figuring it would fit best along the wall where she's sitting. "You have ADHD. You need a dedicated place to work. With all of my traveling, I can work anywhere. You'll take my desk."

*Perfect. This is perfect. This will cancel out all weirdness.*

I march back into my office and swipe the top of my desk to the floor. Luckily I'm a pretty minimalist person so that really only consists of my laptop, my monitor, my coffee and my water. I throw the desk over my shoulder and, careful not to nick any walls, carry it into her room.

"Ollie, I could have just used your office," she says, standing when she sees me lugging furniture.

*That's a great point, Steph, and I wish you would have made it thirty seconds ago.*

I align the desk with the wall and stand back to admire my work.

"Wait. You need a chair," I say, and she lets out a long breath like she's holding back from saying something. I go back into my office and grab mine, pushing it on its wheels into her room and aligning it with the desk. I pull it out and tilt it to one side. "For you," I say, gesturing for her to take a seat.

She sits, resting her laptop on the desk, and swivels around to face me. "Are you freaking out because you're getting news about your job today?"

*No, I'm freaking out because you're too far away.*

I shake my head. "I'm fine, Steph. Just want to make sure you have everything you need."

She gives me a look. "Ollie, I know you," she says. *There's that familiarity I've been craving.* "You can talk to me," she says. "If you want."

"I'm fine," I insist, because I feel lighter now that we've clicked back into our friendship. "I'm really fine. I just wanted to make sure you're comfortable."

*I just wanted to make sure you're not leaving.*

She nods. "So you said."

"Do you need anything else?" I ask, searching the room.

"No," she says immediately, her pointed look telling me she won't accept anything else from me anyway. "But thank you." She runs her hands along the desk. "This was really nice of you."

I smile, the tension in my neck easing. "You're welcome."

I close her door on my way out and head back into my office.

For a moment, I stand there, my brain misfiring because it didn't occur to me that giving Stephanie my desk means that I have nowhere to work. *Do I hunker down on the floor like she was?* I grab my computer and my monitor, and trudge down the stairs to the kitchen table.

On the bright side, this gives me an excuse to buy a new desk. I got the old one in college, and it's the quintessential cheap college buy–light and flimsy, with peeling paint and a few loose screws. I spend a few minutes searching Amazon before selecting a slightly larger one that comes with a stand for my monitor and matches the minimalist gray aesthetic I've curated for every room so I would hopefully never have to buy furniture again. It'll arrive in two days.

When I finally start working, I feel like I'm coming down from the high after a rollercoaster. I question my decision-making, because in the space of thirty seconds I gave up one of my everyday comforts for the sake of Stephanie talking to me. Just talking to me.

I made a rather large purchase for the sake of her comfort, on a whim. I don't know how long she's staying here, but there's an itchy part of me that wants to storm back upstairs and let her know I bought a replacement desk so she should use the one I gave her. A lot.

But before I can make another bad decision, I get an incoming video call from my boss.

My heart drops, all thoughts of Stephanie and her desk leaving me.

"Good morning," Gail says, her hair twisted into a harsh bun on her head.

"What's going on?" I ask.

She laughs. "I take it you heard about Jack's little moment of honesty."

"Yes. What's happening?"

Gail clucks her tongue. "Well, Emma's move back to accounting is going to be expedited. Once that's done, Jack is going to move into the director of training position."

My chest tightens. Somewhere in the mess of the drama, I thought maybe this might be my opportunity.

I suppose not.

My tongue is thick when I speak. "That's great. That's what they wanted."

I bite my lip to refrain from asking her what the hell is happening for me. *Am I going to be reporting to Jack?*

"Which brings us to you," she says. *Thank you!* "I know you operate in a weird middle ground that you're very comfortable with," she says, "but Engineering is doing a complete restructure to bring their people all under one department. Meaning, no matter what happens for you, we'll unfortunately be parting within the next month."

My heart drops. This is a bigger change than I expected. And Gail's been a great boss.

"I'll miss you, Gail," I tell her.

"Oh, I will miss you, Oliver. You're easy. I'm jealous of Kellan."

"Kellan?" He's one of a few new VPs over the past few years, and he's got a great reputation. We've met a number of times, and he's a nice guy. He has a commanding presence, speaks carefully, and listens more intentionally than anyone I've ever met. He's the kind of person to give space to the quietest person in the room to make sure they're heard.

He also has a slew of direct reports, not a single one with a title lower than director.

Gail leans forward. "Nothing is finalized yet, but he asked his assistant to coordinate a meeting with you," she says. "So look for an invite. I told him I'd let you know it's coming."

I let out a long breath. "That's awesome. Thanks, Gail."

She smiles sweetly at me. "You've done well, Oliver. I'm looking forward to seeing what you do next," she says.

"Aw Gail, stop. You're going to make me blush."

She grins at me. "Now get to work. I gotta squeeze the last bits of productivity out of you while I've got you."

"Alright. I'll talk to you later."

When we hang up, I take a moment to lean back in my chair, digesting this.

Changes are coming. I *still* don't have the clarity I truly want.

But I'm intrigued. A smidge more optimistic than I have been.

And a part of me wonders if I should go upstairs and fill Steph in on the news.

I shouldn't. That would be confusing.

But she's the only person I really want to tell.

# 40

## STEPHANIE

The house is dark when I get home from work. It's later than I'd normally be done, but my boss wanted to take Annabel and me out for drinks to celebrate my return, and I couldn't say no to that. The three of us met up at a coworking space today and spent most of the day chatting, and a small portion of the day actually working.

I listen for Ollie as I shut the door behind me, slipping my headphones into my pocket as I start up the stairs. Bung shoots out from behind the couch, weaving between my ankles, and I scoop him into my arms. He purrs against my chest and I give him a couple scratches behind the ears.

When I get to the second floor, Bung warm and fluffy in my arms, I notice the light on in Ollie's office. I stop in the doorway to see if he's still working.

But instead I see him on the floor, a variety of wood pieces spread out around him as he grumbles at two that don't look like they're supposed to be squished together that way.

"What's going on?" I ask, and his head snaps up.

He lets the pieces drop to the floor. "I bought a desk."

I crinkle my eyebrows at him. "You bought a desk? But I'm not going to be here that long."

"Well now, there's no limit."

I eye him. He was weird about the desk a few days ago, forcefully giving me his instead of just letting me sit at the kitchen table for a while. And now he has a new one. "Okay. Well, thank you. You really didn't need to do that."

"You're welcome," he says, sitting back on his haunches. He seems relieved, almost as if he was hoping I'd walk by and ask what's going on.

A beat of silence passes during which he looks over the pieces spread in front of him and Bung purrs loudly against my chest.

"Do you need help?" I ask.

He shakes his head. "No. I've got this."

I nod. "Okay."

I take Bung into my bedroom, letting him cling to my chest as I kick off my shoes and drop my bag by the door, my coat and scarf hitting the floor with a soft thump. I sit on my bed, stroking his sweet little face, and jump when I hear a series of clatters from the room next door. Bung abandons me, jumping out of my arms and slipping under my bed.

By the time I get to Ollie's office, his nose is crinkled and he's running his finger along a fresh scratch on one of the pieces.

"So you need help," I say, stepping between the pieces scattered along the floor. I search for the directions and find them nowhere on the ground.

"I don't need help," he insists.

"Where are the directions?" He glances around, helping

me look, and I realize he wasn't using them. "Are you really trying to build furniture without directions?"

He shrugs. "It's a simple desk. It shouldn't be that hard. Reading the directions will take longer than just figuring it out from the picture."

"Ollie, are you really trying to optimize time around directions that will take sixty seconds to read?"

His eyes narrow. "If I need them, I'll read them. I'm not so stubborn that I refuse to use them at all–but why not try it without first?"

I spot the box on the floor in the corner and flip the lid open. I rip out the directions taped to the bottom and kneel on the floor next to Ollie so he can see them too. "How long have you been doing this?"

"I don't know. Not that long."

I narrow my eyes. "Okay." I pause, unsure whether what I want to say will upset him. "Are you being intentionally helpless so I'll come and build your desk with you?"

He licks his lips. "No."

I cock my head to the side and look at him. I want to press him, to get a confirmation on my theory. But it feels like that conversation could veer into dangerous territory.

So instead, I flip the booklet open to the first page, ignoring the silence. "Okay, so we need pieces A and B."

"Starting with pieces A and B is definitely something I needed the directions for," he says, sliding them toward me.

"I bet you weren't using the right screws."

"C didn't fit, so I tried D."

I look at him. *Is he trying to make this sound sexual?*

"The directions call for screws labeled K."

His eyebrows crinkle. "Oh."

I rifle through the bags of hardware and find the right

one. I rip it open, plucking a screw from the pile, and twist it in as far as I can with my fingers while he holds the wood in place.

I take a moment to search for a wrench and find one in another small baggy. I hand it to him to tighten the rest of the way, and as he takes it from me, our fingers brush, the warmth of his hands sending a small shiver down my spine.

His eyes connect with mine and I quickly look away, searching for the next pieces because I need something to do with my hands before my head runs off without me.

There's still something between us, as much as either of us tries to deny it. It's hot and needy and bubbles just beneath our skin like a volcano waiting to explode.

But we want different things. I want love, or at least the possibility of love. And he doesn't.

"Did you hear anything about the job?" I ask, hoping concentrating on something else will stop the heat from pooling in my cheeks.

He nods, pressing his lips together. "Jack got the training position. Emma is going back to accounting." He pauses before speaking. "And I'm getting pulled back into Engineering. I'm not sure yet what's happening for me, but I have a good feeling about the VP I'll be under."

I nod. "Well, congratulations." I swallow before continuing, my eyes finding his. "You're going to do great."

He smiles. "Thanks, Steph."

He holds the next pieces together as I spin the screw into place, and this time when I hand him the wrench, I make sure our fingers don't touch. I'm not sure I'll be able to keep my head on straight if they do.

An image flashes through my mind of his fingers tightening around mine, his hand clamping onto my hip and pushing me down among the pieces around us. His mouth forceful on mine, his erection pressing into me. The thought sends a burst of heat through my skin that has me tugging at my neckline.

We work in silence, Ollie following my lead as I grab piece after piece and screw after screw. And after what feels like no time at all, the floor is clear, aside from a few empty plastic baggies and the small pile of stickers I've peeled off of each piece.

I stand, admiring our work, as Ollie pushes the desk up against the wall where the one that's now in my room used to be.

"It's a nice desk," I say.

"Thanks. I figured it was time for an upgrade."

I look at him out of the corner of my eye. "Only because you gave away your last one."

He shrugs. "It was worth it."

*Worth it to make me stay? What the hell is he trying to say?*

I nod. "Well, I'm glad you got it all put together."

"You did most of it."

I feel his eyes on me, and I keep mine glued to the desk. "Well, whatever. I'm glad it's done."

"Thanks for your help," he says, and I think I detect a catch in his breath as he speaks. *Was he about to call me Wild-flower? No. No, he can't. Not after taking it away from me.*

"Happy to read directions for you anytime, director," I joke, and Paris comes rushing back to me. The nickname he never got. His offer to direct me.

"Well, I'm going to go get ready for bed," I say, anxious to end this conversation.

He nods. "Goodnight."

"Goodnight," I say, stepping into the hallway and back into my room. I shut the door behind me, only to see a furry little face poke out from underneath the bed. I crack my door open so he can leave when he wants to, and run my fingers along his soft fur before hopping into the shower and changing for bed. When I finally get under the covers, Bung curls up in the crook of my arm, and I nestle my face into his fur.

# 41

# STEPHANIE

I throw on my plaid dress and my boots. I haven't had a chance to get to my storage unit yet, so as far as nice clothes to go out in, it's between this and the sparkly dress that Ollie bought me. The rest of the stuff I have with me consists of leggings and sweaters and could probably use a good wash.

On my way out, I brush past Ollie in the living room. He and Bung are inspecting one of the calatheas I left on his windowsill. He grimaces when he sees me.

"I think the cat took a bite of your plant."

I walk over and peer down at it, spying two little teeth marks at the edge of one leaf. "Bung, you little problem child," I say, giving him a scratch behind the ear. He purrs into the touch.

"You look nice," Ollie says, his eyes dipping.

"Thank you," I say, unsure how to take the compliment.

"Are you going out?"

I nod.

"Where?"

"Dinner, dancing."

"Oh, who are you going with?"

I eye him. *Is it just me or do I detect a hint of jealousy?* "What's up with the twenty questions?"

He shakes his head. "I was just wondering."

"Mari, Kay and Leilani. Maybe Carrie but she hasn't confirmed yet."

He nods. "Ah, okay. Have fun."

"What are you doing tonight?"

He shrugs. "Might watch a movie or something. The couples are coupling tonight, Kick is writing, and Henry's buying a boat."

So his game night buddies are all otherwise occupied. I could have guessed, considering Annabel and Gabi both declined tonight's invite out with the girls.

"Henry's buying a boat?"

"Yeah, I don't know. I thought maybe that was a metaphor for something, but he said he's at the marina until further notice so I think he might actually be buying a boat."

"Like, a big boat?"

He shrugs. "I'm assuming it's not a canoe."

"I hope he's planning on taking us out on it."

"That's what I said."

A moment of silence floats between us. "Okay. Well, I'll see you later then?"

"Yeah. Have fun, Steph."

I give Bung another pat on the head before grabbing my jacket from the hook by the door and slipping outside. When I glance back at the house, I see Ollie's silhouette leaning over the plants in the light spilling from the living room.

I wrap my jacket tighter around me and stomp my way to dinner, thrown off once again. This week has been nothing but odd encounters, from him throwing me a welcome party, to buying a new desk so I could have his old one, to this pseudo-jealousy as I'm going out with friends. I thought the plane ride was confusing, but this is a whole new level.

Kay, Leilani, and Mari are seated by the time I get there, drinks scattered around the small table and a bowl of chips and guac that immediately has my mouth watering. I take the last open seat next to Leilani and order myself a margarita.

"No Carrie?" I ask, unfolding the menu.

Mari shakes her head. "She's driving tonight."

"Really? I feel like she's constantly working."

Mari sighs, taking a thirsty sip of her drink. "She is. And when she's not driving, she's writing. I mean, you've seen how many books she's put out. I just hope she doesn't burn herself out before she starts seeing a good return."

I nod. "You would think maybe Kick could help her. He seems comfortable, doesn't he?"

Mari shrugs. "I don't think she'll accept his help. She gets squirrelly about men reading her work."

I grimace, remembering Ollie reading over my shoulder at the airport. I'm not sure he realized it was one of Carrie's stories, and I doubt he'd ever say anything, but god forbid our little reenactment is ever brought up.

Then again, that part of our lives has been sealed and locked away.

"Did you let Ollie read one of her stories?" Mari asks, smiling knowingly.

I shake my head. "Not intentionally. He just kind of read over my shoulder."

"You guys were awfully close on that trip, weren't you?" Mari asks. She raises her eyebrows as I lean down to take a long sip of my margarita. "Oh, you were *really* close on that trip."

"Yes, but it's over now. It was a Paris-only thing."

"Paris only? Please, you're living with him," Kay says, popping a chip into her mouth.

"That's the deal."

The table is silent for a few seconds. "Is this, like, one of those sexy deals where you're both pretending you're not into each other, but really every time you walk by each other, fantasies of the other's naked body run through your heads?" Kay asks.

"I mean, yes, but nothing is going to come from that. Ollie's hot. And I went there very recently. Of course I'm going to think about it. But like I said, nothing can come from that."

"Why not? Rod's over and done with, right? What's the issue?" Kay asks.

I shrug. "I want love. He doesn't."

Kay nods, chewing on her lip.

"Is Rod really done?" Leilani asks, eyeing me over her margarita.

"Yeah. He ditched me in Costa Rica. He's shown me multiple times now that I'm secondary to basically anything else."

Leilani nods, watching my face as she sits up straight. "He's been DMing me."

My heart drops. "What?"

"Not like that. He's been DMing me about you."

I glance at Kay and Mari as if they have more information to add to this, but they look as surprised as I feel. "What about me?"

"He said he's been trying to get in touch with you. He's back in Philadelphia. I honestly wasn't going to tell you after all the shit he's put you through." Her eyes find mine. "But if it was the end for someone I once loved, I would want to know. So take that for what it's worth."

Kay and Mari look mortified, but I appreciate Leilani for being straight with me. So many of my friends—understandably—were not fans of Rod. But Leilani has a somewhat similar dating history, and I think she gets how difficult it is to navigate your own feelings about a relationship when everyone around you is screaming at you to ditch the guy.

She's given him the benefit of the doubt so she can be the person I've always tried to be for her—the listener, the confidante, the nonjudgmental ear when something *does* bother you.

As much as I love how fiercely my friends defend me, sometimes it's hard to slice through that noise and have a real conversation about how I'm feeling.

"I blocked him in Paris. He's probably been texting me."

Probably assuming yet again that he can waltz back into my life whenever he wants and I'll fall eagerly to my knees for him.

"Please don't go back to Rod," Kay groans. "You don't need that in your life again." She turns to Leilani. "And way to keep a freaking secret."

Leilani holds her hands up in surrender. "I'm sorry. I wasn't sure whether to keep it to myself or to tell and I'm just doing the best I can."

I take my phone out of my purse and thumb through to my blocked numbers.

"Don't do it," Kay says, leaning over and staring at my phone.

My finger hovers over his number. "Don't you think it's worth it to tell him to leave me alone once and for all? For the closure?"

"No," Kay and Mari say at the same time.

"If you really think that'll give you closure without screwing with your choice to move on, I don't think it's a bad idea. You're not the same person you were before," Leilani says, and somewhere in her words, I feel like she's telling me she sees how I've grown. That I'm not going to accept being treated poorly any longer.

I eye her for a moment.

"Go home and fuck Ollie," Kay suggests, ignoring her.

I give her a look.

"I'm telling you, whatever mess you're in with Ollie is better than going back *again* to Rod."

I lock my phone and put it facedown on the table even though I'm really curious to hear what he thinks will make me change my mind about him–and anxious to put a stop to it.

"I'm not going back to him," I start, the table quiet as I speak. "But I am considering unblocking him for the sake of closure. Every single time we've ended, it's been because of him. I want the chance to tell him that I'm done this time."

Kay nods. "I get it, Steph."

"If that's what feels right, do it," Leilani says.

"But for the love of god, please don't let him weasel his way back into your life," Mari says.

"Amen!" Kay shouts, clinking her drink to Mari's, and then pointedly side-eyes Leilani. "I'm mad at you."

Leilani shrugs. "What else is new? I stand by my decision."

Kay rolls her eyes. "Buy my next margarita and we can call it a draw."

"Deal."

We make it through another round of drinks before grabbing the check and heading out. The club is close by, and Kay and Mari lead us, arm in arm, while Leilani and I bring up the rear. I notice her looking at me out of the corner of my eye as I scroll down to my blocked numbers list.

The conversation I had with Ollie my first night in Paris rings in my head. *I* wanted to be the one to end things. To tell him he's a jerk and *that* is why I don't want to be with him anymore.

My fingers itch to do it.

"It wouldn't hurt to just unblock him, right? To tell him once and for all that we're done?"

Leilani shrugs. "I don't know, Steph. I think only you can make that decision. Do you want to open up that can of worms?"

"I don't know."

She loops her arm into mine. "Look, you don't have to do anything right now. Why don't you just dance and have fun tonight. Think about Rod tomorrow."

I nod, locking my phone and slipping it back into my purse. "You're right. Tonight is for fun. I've been craving a night like this, and I shouldn't let Rod ruin it."

"Right," she says, squeezing my arm. "I hope that was the right thing for me to do," she says, glancing at me. "Telling you?"

I nod. "It is. Thank you. I would always rather know."

## 42

## OLIVER

I blink awake when the lock on the front door turns. It's late, and the TV is still on in front of me, playing a silent screensaver. It takes my brain a second to catch up, to realize whoever's outside the door is most likely not a robber coming to kill me and steal my cat, but Stephanie coming home drunk from the bar.

I rub the sleep from my eyes as I adjust a sleepy Bung in my arms, and open the door while she's still fumbling with the lock.

"Oh crap," she says, her eyes wide as she looks up at me. "I didn't wake you, did I?"

"No," I say, taking in her wild hair, the hem of her dress that's folded over at the bottom. I catch a whiff of what I can only describe as jungle juice as I step out of the way, letting her into the house.

"Oh thank goodness," she breathes, closing the door behind her. She shrugs off her jacket and leaves it on the hook behind the door, and then heads into the kitchen and reaches into a cabinet for a glass, filling it with water from the sink as I follow her in.

"Have a fun time?" I ask, as she downs the water.

"Oh my god, so fun," she says between gulps. Black makeup is smudged underneath her eyes. "We danced and we drank and we made friends. Ugh, I'm so happy we did that. I needed a night like tonight."

"Good, I'm glad you had fun," I say.

She refills her glass and sets it on the island, leaning over to look at something on her phone. Her eyebrows crinkle, and she locks it again, throwing it down on the counter.

"How was your night?" she asks, taking a sip of water.

"It was good. Bung and I watched a movie and fell asleep on the couch."

She looks up at me. "Oh, I *did* wake you! I'm sorry, I'm such a bad roommate."

I shrug. "It gives me the opportunity to go upstairs and not sleep with my neck at a ninety-degree angle. You probably saved me a week of pain. So thank you for being too drunk to open the door."

She gives me a look. "I had three drinks over the space of six hours."

I blink. "So what are you, just tired?"

She wrinkles her nose. "I just don't know the door very well."

"I'd never guess, with all that foreplay."

She snorts, her hand flying up to cover her face. "Why do you say things like that?" she asks through her laughter, shoving me playfully.

I shrug. *I like seeing you laugh.* "I guess it comes naturally."

She shakes her head. "Oh, Ollie," she says, her hand slowly trailing down my chest before dropping to her side. The touch inspires images of Paris in my mind, of the two of us entwined in bed, hands roaming skin freely. A small jolt of electricity runs down my spine.

There is *definitely* something between us, still.

Something that should not be acted on.

Not tonight, at least.

No. *No.* This can't happen. This is too messy.

"Oh, Steph," I mock.

She takes a step toward me, resting her hand on my chest, and every nerve ending in my body fires toward her. "I should go to bed before I start making bad decisions."

I raise my eyebrows. She's thinking the same things that I am.

*We could make one quick bad decision and forget about it by morning.*

I bite my tongue. Now is not the time for quips or jokes. I feel it in my bones, that if I were to kiss her right now, we'd fall easily into my bed. If I put my hand on her hip and pulled her into me, we'd be gone.

And I can't. I shouldn't. I won't.

She sighs, turning away from me and grabbing her phone off the counter. As she does, I can't help but notice the name that pops up on her screen. I take it from her to make sure my eyes aren't deceiving me.

"Stephanie," I say, her name popping out roughly. She reaches for her phone but I hold it just out of her reach. "Why are you texting Rod?"

She rolls her eyes. "It's just a text. My god, it's not like I'm running off to a foreign country to meet him," she jokes, her body pressing against mine as she reaches behind me for her phone.

"You have to be kidding me. I thought you blocked him." Her fingers close around the phone, but I hold it tight in my hand.

"He was hitting up Leilani looking for me. I mean, apparently he didn't get it through his big dumb head that I don't want to see him anymore." Her grip is firm on her phone, her arm locked around my side.

"Steph, you know who he is at this point. Hell, *I* know who he is at this point, and I haven't even met the guy. He's an asshole who uses you and throws you away like you're nothing. And you're playing his game?"

She bristles, letting go of the phone and taking a step back from me. "Don't you think it's a little inappropriate for him to be DMing Leilani? We've done this dance before–the breaking up and getting back together. I want it to stop. I want him to know that I'm done. Once and for all. I told you in Paris, I want that closure of telling him we're over. For good."

Her words hang heavy between us, the weight of them hitting me like a blow to the chest and leaving me winded. She could so easily say the same thing to me.

And she would probably be *right* to, if she did.

I've given her no reason to believe I'm anything more than a dollar store copy-paste of him.

And she's taking her moment of closure. She wants to do the scary thing and cut that last little thread that hangs between them and keeps them floating back to each other.

Stephanie is leveling up. Taking control of her own love life in a way she hasn't before.

And I'm still trying to make my career happen while letting my life pass me by.

My career will happen... or it won't.

She's not giving me an ultimatum here–this conversation isn't even about me–but I feel that my reaction in this moment spells our future. Like if I continue pushing her to block him again when she's trying to stand up for herself, I'll only be digging my own grave.

She's breathing heavily, eyes locked on mine as she bites at her bottom lip.

I bring her phone out from behind my back and hold it between us, staring down at it.

She doesn't reach for it. She doesn't move an inch.

So I reach behind her, leaving it on the counter by her hip.

And I rest my hand there, my arm running just past hers. She glances down, her brow wrinkling as she looks up at me.

I do the same with my other hand, boxing her in against the counter.

A mirror image of the night of her birthday.

"What are you doing?"

Her hands drift up, moving in midair like she wants to touch me but doesn't know how.

And I kiss her.

She seems stunned for a moment, but a second later, she's matching my energy, throwing her arms around my neck and pulling me closer.

Her knee drifts up, resting on my outer thigh, and I reach for it, tugging it up further and pressing into her.

A noise of delight jumps from her throat that has my blood rushing south in an instant.

She has her hands in my hair, tugging my face closer to hers.

And my hands start *roaming*. The warmth of her neck. The bones I can just barely feel when I splay my hand out along her ribcage. The softness of her ass in my palm and the delicate curve of her waist.

"Ollie," she whispers into my mouth. "What are we doing?"

I pause, my hands on her hips, and pull away from her.

I hang my head, truly thinking about this. Sure, I don't want to be another Rod to her, but really, what am I trying to make happen here? A relationship? Because that isn't something I can just decide in a split-second. I think I'm warming to the idea, but it's not fair to either of us to bluster forward without taking a second to figure out whether I can actually *do* it.

I shake my head. "I don't know. I'm sorry."

I step away from her, but her hands fist in my sweater, and she pulls me back.

"Maybe..." she starts, her breath running across my cheek as she speaks. "Just one more night?"

I look at her, selfishly running my fingers through her hair.

I feel the right answer on the tip of my tongue.

And then I kiss her anyway.

## 43

## STEPHANIE

He reaches down, scooping me up and setting me on the counter, his kiss overwhelming and intoxicating. My knees jump up around his waist, holding onto him and dragging him closer. A heat builds low in my abdomen as his arm wraps around my waist, pressing our bodies together.

I can feel just how hard he is through his jeans, and I want to tear him out of his clothes. Tell him to take me right here on the kitchen island as hard as he can.

His tongue tangles with mine as I reach up under his shirt, running my fingers along his warm skin and feeling his muscles bunch with the contact. I drag my nails down his skin–*lightly*–and he moans into my mouth, squeezing my ass with one hand and winding the fingers of his other up into my hair.

He tugs gently, just enough that my head tips back, and runs his teeth along the skin of my neck.

"I've missed you, Wildflower," he whispers against my skin.

My nerves light on fire.

I push his shirt up over his chest, and he lifts his arms so I can tear it over his head.

I run my fingers along his skin, finding the mild ridges beneath his pecs and feeling the light dusting of chest hair just above.

He reaches behind me, fumbling for the zipper of my dress, and pulls it down slowly as I pepper his neck with kisses. His collarbone. His chest.

He pulls the straps down over my shoulders and I shrug out of them as he tugs at the shirt I'm wearing underneath, slipping his fingers underneath and pulling it over my head by the hem. I gasp when he pulls me to my feet to push my dress down over my legs.

It pools on the ground around me, and he pushes me up against the counter again. I think he's going to lift me, put me right back where I was, but instead he pulls my legs around his waist, supporting my weight with my ass in his hands.

He breaks our kiss only for a second as he moves toward the staircase.

"I want to fuck you the way you deserve," he mumbles into the skin of my neck, his teeth nipping at the strap of my bra as he slowly climbs up to the second floor, his hands warm on me and his dick thick where I'm rubbing against him. "And I need a bed for that."

He takes a quick left when we make it to the second floor, ducking into my room and walking us to the bed. He throws me down on top of it, my hair flying every direction as I hit the bed with a soft thump.

He pauses for a moment, looking at me, and runs his hand along my leg. "You look sexy like this," he says, his fingers slipping under the edge of my tights and letting them snap back against my skin.

I roll my eyes. "Only because I'm half-naked."

He shrugs. "Well. Yeah."

He rests a knee on the bed, nudged between mine, and slowly climbs on top of me, his lips brushing against every bit of skin they can reach as he moves. My arms, my chin, the skin of my breasts above my bra.

He settles on top of me, his weight resting on me as his arms snake underneath my back.

I wind my fingers up into his hair again, pulling his face down to mine, but he pauses, looking down at me. The streetlight shining in the window casts his expression in a warm glow.

"You're something special, Stephanie," he says.

His words sit between us, his eyes locked on mine.

And then he kisses me again, but it's less urgent now.

More indulgent.

My hips rise to meet his, and I start to wonder if this is Ollie deciding he wants me in a bigger way. If this is the moment where things change, and I can suddenly think of him as more than a one-night fling that just keeps happening.

He reaches for my tights, tugging them down over my hips, and sits on his heels to pull them over my feet. His fingers run along my bare skin, watching the trail of goosebumps left in his wake. He grins at the effect he has on me, and I shy away from the attention.

His eyes snap to mine as soon as I reach down to rub my skin. To erase the physical proof that he *does* things to me.

He grabs my hand, leaving a kiss on top.

And then he reaches down, unzipping himself and stepping off the bed to let his jeans fall to the floor.

I sit up, popping my bra and dropping it on top.

He swallows as I lie back down, his eyes shamelessly

trailing down my body and back up, landing on my face with an expression on his that I can't fully read. I grab him by the waistband of his underwear, guiding him back to me, and he settles easily between my legs again, leaving a delicate kiss on my nose.

He sighs, letting his head drop into my shoulder even as his hands roam my body, his thumb brushing along the skin of my stomach as holds onto my waist.

"I didn't realize," he starts, leaning over to one side to rest his head in his hand, "that that last time in Paris was the *last* time." His fingers trail from my collarbone down to my stomach, just barely missing my nipple. "I didn't savor it." He swallows thickly as his fingers graze the edges of my underwear. "I didn't memorize every inch of you like I should have."

"You memorized my moles," I remind him.

He shakes his head. "Not enough. I could draw that constellation of moles on your hip from memory and I'll probably be able to until the day I die. But it's not enough."

"It's never enough unless it's the real thing."

I know my words have multiple meanings. He knows my words have multiple meanings.

We both ignore it.

He kisses me lightly, his lips moving quickly from my mouth, to my neck, to my collarbone. He pauses to suck a nipple into his mouth, his tongue circling and flicking at it while I arch underneath him. I let out a small moan that has his fingers digging into the skin of my hip, his teeth nipping at my sternum as he continues lower.

He sits on his ankles between my legs and, for a moment, palms gently at the thickness hiding in plain sight behind his underwear.

And then he reaches forward, resting his hand on my

underwear so his thumb just barely grazes that bundle of nerves that's so desperate to feel him right now. My entire body lights on fire with need.

My legs widen, my back arches, and a strangled sound escapes my throat.

He licks his lips, a grin spreading across his face.

"Are you ready to scream my name, Wildflower?"

I swallow and nod.

He tugs on the strings of my thong, pulling it down over my legs and abandoning it on the floor with the rest of our clothes. He arranges my legs so they're right where they were before, spread around him.

And he rests his hand in the same spot, his thumb circling quickly around me in a way that has me throwing my head back, his name already spilling from my lips as my hips buck toward him.

He presses a quick kiss to my knee as he leans forward. "Not quite loud enough." He trails kisses along my inner thigh as he settles himself below me. "But that's not your fault," he says, pressing one hand to my thigh so it falls flat against the bed beside us. "If you're not screaming my name so loud your voice goes hoarse, I'm not doing my job well enough."

And then his lips connect with my clit, and I see *stars*.

He licks me slowly, toying with me. He brings me close to the edge, licking in long smooth strokes and then sucking gently at my clit.

I feel my orgasm building as his lips move against me.

"Ollie, Ollie, Ollie," I say. "I'm going to—"

He stops sucking, returning to his licking.

"Ollie!" I scold.

"Not loud enough," he says, and then he adds a finger.

He pulses into me slowly, continuing that torturous

licking until he sucks gently at my clit, building me right back up.

This time I scream his name as the tension pools in my abdomen, anxious for my release.

He only shakes his head, the movement causing a little zip to run up my spine as his nose rubs against my clit.

He adds another finger, and I can tell by the way he pulses into me, the fingers of his other hand digging into my hip, that *this one is the one*.

And somehow that makes it even hotter.

I'm desperate for release, but the way he's latched onto me and fucking me hard with his fingers makes me think *he's* desperate too. His breathing is erratic but his movements are controlled, slowly driving me closer and closer until my fingers go tingly and my toes curl.

"Ollie!" I cry, my voice breaking as my orgasm crests and crashes around me. He continues until my legs are squeezing in around his face and my hands are in his hair, desperate for a moment of relief.

He kisses the crease of my leg as I melt further into a puddle underneath him, my breathing shallow as every single part of me shakes.

"Fuck, Wildflower," he mumbles, his kisses gentle all along my body. He settles on top of me, his dick pressing into me through his underwear. "You're so fucking beautiful when you come."

I laugh, because the sensation is still just too much. "You're mean," I say.

He raises his eyebrows, a throaty laugh escaping him. "I'm mean?"

"I thought you weren't going to let me."

He acts mock offended. "I would never."

"Well, you certainly had me going for a minute there."

He kisses me, the taste of me strong on his tongue.

"You let me know when you're ready for me, okay, Wild-flower?" he asks, leaving kisses all along my face and my neck.

With my hands on either of his cheeks, I kiss him again. "I'm ready for you."

"You're not too sensitive?" he asks, even as he's already shoving down his underwear, his breathing hitching up as his skin rubs against mine. He rests his head in my neck again, his hips moving just enough to stoke my need.

"I want you."

He groans in response, taking hold of his dick and positioning himself at my entrance.

He sinks into me slowly, a tortured noise in his throat telling me that what he really wants to do is flip me over and pound into me as hard as he can.

But he kisses me instead, rocking his hips into mine slowly as I adjust to him.

"Fuck, Wildflower," he murmurs against my lips.

I cling to him as he builds up speed, as his muscles clench around me and he drives into me faster, harder. He tugs at my hair and nips at my skin and provides the perfect friction against my clit with every thrust that has me screaming his name again and again as he unravels me once more.

My nails tear down his back. My legs tighten around him. And my orgasm crashes around me.

I say his name over and over again like a prayer, and as my body finally relaxes, he jerks into me, releasing into me roughly.

He collapses, his breathing heavy and his back sticky with sweat.

"Fuck," he groans, resting his face in my neck. "Was it just me, or was that even better than Paris?"

*We missed each other, that's why.* "Distance makes the fuck grow fonder?"

He snorts into my skin. "Yeah, that must be it."

I weave my arms around his waist, holding on tight like I can freeze this moment. He relaxes into me, his weight on top of me comforting as he peppers little kisses along my face, strong arms clutching me close.

"I missed you, Steph," he whispers in my ear, and something tells me he doesn't mean over the past few days we've been in Philadelphia. Something tells me he's talking about that night three months ago that runs through both our heads on repeat.

"I've always been right here."

## 44

## OLIVER

I am a weak man.

I disentangle myself from Stephanie when only the faintest inklings of sun stream through the window. She grabs at me halfheartedly, her eyes still closed and her naked body still curled up under her blankets. The feel of her fingers trailing down my arm as I get up nearly brings me right back in.

I grab my underwear from the floor and pull them on quietly as I leave the room, shutting the door as I go. Bung darts out at the last minute before the knob clicks. He must have been sleeping under Steph's bed.

I make my way downstairs, my cat following along silently behind me as if he somehow knows I'm in need of a support system right now.

Like he knows that I'm dangerously close to throwing away my carefully planned life in favor of Stephanie.

I start a pot of coffee and sit down at the kitchen counter, resting my head in my hands.

I thought I had a handle on this thing with Steph. I thought we were finally getting used to being back in Philadelphia and *just friends* again. But last night made it clear the entire thing was a farce from the beginning. I saw Rod's name on her phone, and one stupid word started looping in my head.

*Mine, mine, mine.*

I groan into my hands, squeezing my eyes shut tight.

I'm coming to a very difficult realization that whatever I'm feeling right now is not the sort of thing that gets easily stamped down. Whatever this is between us is bigger than the night of her birthday or a week in Paris, and I need to figure out how to deal with it before I get totally derailed.

I know in theory that other people date and get married and have kids all while continuing to excel at their jobs. It's not impossible.

But fuck, I've never done this before. I don't know what to expect.

What if we end up fighting during the workday? I can't imagine telling her to buzz off for a few more hours so I can finish while she's sitting around upset.

What if she decides to go out late and wake me up in the middle of the night before I have a big presentation or something?

What if she trips on something–as she's prone to doing–and falls down the stairs and breaks her neck and I have to suddenly become a full-time caretaker until she's better?

My heartbeat races until I realize the likelihood of that happening is slim.

But it's not impossible.

I let out a long breath as I stand to pour myself a cup of coffee.

I can't predict Stephanie. I can't see into the future. I don't know what this is going to turn into.

All I know is that Stephanie is here, in my house, and

despite a mass of conflicting emotions that I can't sort through, I want her to stay.

I haven't stopped thinking about her since falling into bed with her the night of her birthday. I've gone to bars, searching for anyone who might bear the slightest resemblance to her, only to realize there's no substitute for the Stephanie I've been craving. I rearranged my work flights for the sake of easing her mind before flying off to profess her love for another man.

I've let myself break each and every time she's made herself available to me, and at this point, I know that that isn't going to change.

And judging by what she said to me as we were leaving Paris–*in another life, could it have been us?*–she feels the same way.

I take a seat at the kitchen island just as I hear the quiet padding of feet on the staircase along the wall next to me.

She appears a moment later, bare feet and hair wild from sleep, wearing the T-shirt I had on last night. My heart catches as she smiles sleepily at me.

"You're up early," she says, her voice all soft and groggy.

She goes straight to the coffee maker, grabbing a mug from the cabinet over top and pouring herself a generous serving. She turns to me, resting the coffee on the counter, and I grab her by the hips before she can pull the stool next to me out.

Her eyebrows jump up, the sleepiness quickly fading from her face as I pull her between my legs, my fingers massaging her hip through my T-shirt. I let my hand trail up to her waist, relishing the way she feels beneath my palms.

She smiles at me, her eyes searching mine. She reaches up and runs a hand through my hair, her thumb lingering on the space just above my ear.

I tug her closer, wrapping my arms around her and squeezing. A moment later, she sighs, her body relaxing into me and her arms draping easily around my neck.

I bury my face in her hair, breathing in all of her. And for the very first time, I dare to let myself think that this woman is mine.

## 45

## STEPHANIE

I sigh as I look at myself in the mirror, not bothering to tame the mane of hair flowing over my shoulders. I couldn't read Ollie if you gave me a fifty-pound Oliver Long Dictionary.

I thought this morning we'd be back to our usual programming: me, optimistic despite myself that Ollie is magically going to want me in a bigger way than sex; and him, cautiously avoiding the subject as if he doesn't make it abundantly clear where he stands.

But this morning he hugged me. It wasn't a friendly hug or a sexual hug, but I don't know how to categorize it.

If I wanted to torture myself a little, I would say it was a caring hug. A loving hug.

He's done none of his typical backtracking. No mention of not doing this again. No attempt to keep me at a distance.

But after all this time, I don't believe for one second that he's had a come-to-Jesus moment and realized that I'm his person.

Even though with every day that passes, I feel more and more like he's mine.

It became clear to me last night, when we were tangled up in each other, that the way I feel about Ollie is something different than what I've ever had before. At any point during my on-again-off-again relationship with Rod. With any of the number of quick relationships I had since him.

I clung to the idea of Rod because he was the closest thing I've had to a *someone*. But now that Ollie has blustered into my life, I realize what I'm looking for is something so much bigger than a shared history. Bigger than a decade. Bigger than lust or mutual attraction or years of bouncing back to one another.

I want someone who understands me like Ollie does. Someone who's patient, who may not get all of my struggles but gives me the space to work through them. Someone who obviously cares so much despite himself. Someone who shows up when I need him, who I can laugh with and be my weird self with. Who doesn't hesitate to roll his eyes and remind me to clean up after myself when I accidentally leave my drinks out but never gets truly *angry* with me over it.

Ollie is it. And I just have to... wait.

Tonight I'll get my moment of closure with Rod, but there's nowhere to go from there. The old version of me that's doing her best to claw her way back into my mind wants to pretend that maybe Rod could be the one. That maybe I'm jumping to conclusions about Ollie that are just setting me up for disaster in the future.

I roll my eyes at myself as I wipe away a smudge of last night's mascara. That part probably *is* true. I'm absolutely setting myself up for heartbreak by setting my sights on Ollie.

But I'm not interested in settling for *good enough* anymore.

Whatever happens with Ollie and me is out of my control, but I'm not going to sit around with my thumb up my butt giving everything to someone who doesn't care about me for the sake of *having someone.*

It's Ollie or no one, and tonight I'm making that choice permanent.

I smooth down my dress as I step out of my bedroom. Bung darts out from underneath my bed, and I scoop him up in my arms as I head downstairs.

Ollie's sitting at the kitchen counter, a bowl of stew in front of him.

"You look nice," he says.

And now I'm scared Ollie thinks I dressed up for Rod. "Thanks. I wasn't really trying, for tonight."

He shrugs. "What I said stands."

I set Bung down and he pads silently across the counter to Ollie, rubbing up against his arm.

"You're weird today," I say.

He swallows, pushing his bowl away. Bung sniffs at it, and then turns, hopping down off the counter and skittering behind the couch.

Ollie shakes his head. "I don't mean to be."

"Something you want to talk about?"

He purses his lips and then shakes his head.

"You can talk to me, you know."

He lets out a long breath, running his hands over his face. "I don't want you to go."

My breath catches. "You don't?"

There's a part of me that's disappointed by this. I feel like meeting with Rod and telling him once and for all that I'm done with him is the loose end that I have to tie up in order to be all in with Ollie. But if Ollie doesn't want me to go, I can't imagine going through with it.

I *want* to put all of my eggs in Ollie's basket.

Or have him fertilize mine.

But this feels like something I have to do first.

Ollie shakes his head. "No. I really don't want you to go." He bites his lip. "But I'm not an idiot or an asshole. I know how much you wanted this moment of closure, so I'll let my logical brain lead on this one instead of the jealous caveman that's fighting to take over." He nods, as if reassuring himself. "You should go."

I feel the intense urge to ask him how he feels about me. What he wants from whatever we're doing together.

This is the first time I've felt like he's admitting to having feelings for me without immediately trying to extinguish the fire.

And it's the first time he's encouraging me to go see Rod.

Part of me wonders if he's really supporting me getting the closure I'm after, or if he thinks putting me back under Rod's spell is the only way to end whatever burgeoning thing there is between us—because obviously words don't work.

"Do you want to meet me after?"

He blinks and then checks his phone. "What time?"

I shrug. "I don't know. I'm meeting him at eight, so, uh, eight-thirty?"

He nods, thinking this over. "Yeah, okay."

FROM THE WINDOW OUTSIDE, I see Rod sitting at the bar, a glass of wine in front of him. He scrolls on his phone while he waits.

I push inside, letting the hostess know I'm just going to the bar, and wave as I walk toward him.

He stands, his grin wide when he sees me. "Stephanie," he says, wrapping his arms easily around my neck and pulling me close. "How are you? I've missed you."

I hang my coat over the back of my chair as I sit and request a glass of Pinot Grigio from the bartender, who pours one with a smile and slides it quickly across the bar toward me.

I take a thirsty sip, anxious for the bite of the alcohol.

"You look nice," he says.

"Thank you," I say, somewhat bitter that he agrees with Ollie on this because only *Ollie* gets to say that I look nice. When he says it, it's sweet. But with Rod, it feels like just one more lie.

"So do you," I say out of habit, even though the words make me cringe.

"How was the rest of your trip? I was sad our timelines didn't mesh to meet you in Paris."

I shake my head, waving him off. "No biggie. I had a really nice time, actually."

"Good, I'm so glad to hear it. I always say you're not really a traveler until you're able to travel alone," he says.

I narrow my eyes. "Do you? Say that?"

"Oh absolutely. It's a necessary part of being able to appreciate another culture."

Says the man who hasn't traveled alone in literally years.

"Yeah, I can see that," I say, and I absolutely can, considering how much I enjoyed Costa Rica despite his absence. I'm just not sure that *he* understands that. I shake off the thought, taking another sip of wine. "So what's after Philadelphia?"

He shrugs. "I might spend some time here, actually." He reaches across the bar, grabbing my hand, and my eyes follow his movement with distaste. "I meant it when I said I missed you."

I raise my eyebrows. "Yeah?"

He nods. "A lot."

I don't think before I speak. "Why?"

"What do you mean, 'why?' I just did. I felt like we barely got to see each other."

I feel like there's more to this story. After all the times he chose others over me, he suddenly flies home to see me? Without even telling me?

It suddenly occurs to me that *I* was the one who texted *him*. Leilani said he'd been in Philadelphia for a while.

"So you came back home for me?"

He nods. "Maybe we can try again," he says, his fingers squeezing between mine.

Normally I'd swoon over words like his, but from Rod, they kind of make me want to puke.

"How long will you be here for?"

He shrugs. "Until we decide to go elsewhere." He grins, like this is the perfect answer.

"Where are your traveling buddies?"

He waves off the question. "Dispersed for now. All at different corners of the world."

"So are you back because they were done traveling?"

He shakes his head. "No, no. Of course not. I wanted to visit my parents, see my old friends. See you, of course," he says.

"So I'm third on your list of reasons to come back?"

He crinkles his eyebrows. "Steph, are you alright? You seem a little off today."

I shake my head, taking another sip of my wine. "Totally fine. I'm just curious why you're back now and happy to see me. Because it seems like you only really show up when it's convenient for you. So I'm trying to figure out *why* it's convenient for you, because I'm pretty sure *I* have nothing to do with it."

He rears back in his chair. "Does everything have to be about you?"

I raise my eyebrows. "About me?"

"You come to Costa Rica and want to dismantle our whole system. You meet me for a drink and want to hear I came all the way back here just for you. Not everything is about you, Stephanie."

They're the harshest words he's ever said to me.

But at least he's finally being honest.

I've only ever wanted to be a consideration. I didn't want to be left alone at a hotel in Costa Rica. And now, I just want to know where I stand. I just want a little bit of honesty.

And he finally gave it to me. *Not everything is about me.* If that's what he thinks, then we are just incompatible people. I think that if I'm playing the role of his significant other, then I get to be considered first, before the rest of the group. If we make plans to do something, I'm owed an explanation when they fall through. And if he wants to meet me for a drink, then the least I deserve is some honesty.

I down the rest of my wine, leaving the empty glass on the table.

"Thank you for finally telling me who you really are," I say. I stand, pulling my coat over my shoulders. "I hate that I wasted almost ten years of my life on you, but I'm happy that I now know who you truly are and what you think of me."

He rolls his eyes. "Steph, don't be like that."

"This is who I am. And you don't like it," I say plainly.

He glances around the bar, as if I'm making a scene, and lowers his voice. "Steph, sit down. We can talk about this."

"And you don't even deny it. I just said that this is who I am and you don't like it, and you don't even take a second to try to fix that?"

"Steph, you're being insecure. That's not my responsibility to fix."

I laugh. "Oh my god, this is so much better than I thought it would be," I mutter to myself, realizing with a punch to the gut just how little Rod thinks of me. "I'm not being insecure. We've danced around each other for ten years and I've never felt like you put me first. I think that warrants a little insecurity. A little reassurance, if you actually *do* care."

"Steph, just sit down," he says, his eyes on mine as if he can pressure me into obeying him.

I shake my head.

"You know what? I don't like who you are, either. I don't like the way you've treated me over the past ten years, and I know you're not going to apologize for it because you think you're right and god forbid you ever apologize for the sake of someone else's feelings. Honestly, it's probably better that way. Thank you for showing me who you really are, and good riddance. Sayonara. See ya never."

With a nod, I turn on my heel and walk out.

I push through the doors, and from the window out front, I watch as he runs his hands over his face, shaking his head. I'm almost certain he's angry with me, upset that I insisted on a little bit of validation. A little bit of honesty. It's been almost a decade of listening to the words I want to hear without the actions to back them up.

I didn't know what to expect tonight, but I'm glad things happened the way they did. I got my closure, and he now knows that I'm done putting up with his assholery. Once and for all.

To him, I'm a spoiled, selfish brat.

I'm not sure I'll be able to forgive him for turning me into that, even for a second. I think there was always a part of me that knew he thought of me that way. Maybe that's why it felt so good when Ollie called me Wildflower. An ethereal being instead of a spoiled child.

I head down the street, spying the Mexican restaurant Ollie is meeting me at, and burst through the front door with my head on a swivel until I finally see him, sitting at the far end of the bar with two margaritas in front of him.

He smiles when he sees me, and I can't help the grin that spreads across my face.

## 46

## OLIVER

Over fish tacos and too many margaritas, Steph and I click back into who we used to be.

Or at least, some version of it. I don't know where we stand, but she's laughing and joking with me like we always have. Like before she met me in Paris and everything got messy.

I won't lie and say that my eyes don't linger on her lips a second longer than necessary every time she takes a sip of her margarita. Or that the press of her outer thigh against mine doesn't have less-than-savory thoughts running through my mind.

But for a moment, it's nice to suspend my running mind and simply enjoy being with her. The past few weeks have been filled with that anxious question of what we're ultimately doing with each other–a question that has yet to be answered–but something about Steph's smile when she saw me told me that tonight isn't really about us, but her. Stephanie finally got closure.

And while the thought is there–what does *her* closure mean for *us*?–I'm not letting it overtake our evening.

It's nice to just be with her as we were before. Friends, or whatever strange version of it that has us falling into bed with one another every once in a while.

"So how does it feel, Wildflower?" I ask, as the bartender drops off our check. Steph reaches for her clutch and I wave her away, slipping my card inside before she can protest. This is a celebration, after all.

She shrugs, taking one last sip of her margarita that leaves salt on her upper lip. I laugh as I reach forward to brush it off, and if I'm not mistaken, a little *zing* runs between us at the touch. Her eyes catch on mine for just a second before I turn my attention back to the check, pushing it toward the bartender as he whips by.

She clears her throat as she rests her glass back on the bar. "I kind of thought it would feel better, honestly."

I turn to her, my eyebrows crinkling. "Really?"

She sighs. "I feel embarrassed."

I cock my head to the side, waiting for her to continue.

"I spent so much of my life on someone who thinks really poorly of me. I mean, the things he said about me being so self-involved kind of shook me. And like, all of my friends could see it. My family could see it. And I just feel really stupid that it went right over my head."

I let out a long breath. "Correct me if I'm wrong here, but Steph, I think you *knew* he thought that about you. You were just giving him the benefit of the doubt."

"What do you mean?" She plays with the ends of her hair, her teeth scraping at her bottom lip.

"In Paris, you said Rod always got to be the Wildflower. That you were the stickler with a routine. I mean, sure, it's not the same words, but isn't being with someone all about the way they make you feel? Whether it's in love or lust or happy or annoyed or just the way you feel about *yourself*? He made you feel like shit, you know? He was telling you this all along. You were just giving him the benefit of the doubt because you wanted him to be your person when that is something *he* could never live up to. Not you."

The bartender slides the check back onto the bar as Steph quirks a small smile at me. "So I love too freely and forgive too easily?"

I nod. "But that's a good thing. You just need to do that for someone who'll appreciate it. Don't go around calling yourself stupid when what you really are is kind."

My words come out stronger than I intend them to, and I take a desperate sip of my empty margarita. I could probably chug another one right about now with that wide-eyed look she's giving me.

"You ready?" I ask, standing because I'm not sure what else to do with myself.

After a second she nods, coming to her feet and pulling her jacket around her shoulders. I gesture for her to lead the way out, and she moves swiftly between tables to the door.

The cold air blasts us as we step outside, and Steph immediately starts shivering. I don't think I've *ever* seen her dress warm enough for the weather.

She stuffs her hands in her pockets as we walk, her head ducked against the wind.

And I swallow as I hesitantly reach an arm around her, tugging her into my chest. I don't know if it'll help, but it seems like the right thing to do.

Even though holding her like this makes my mouth go dry.

She glances up at me, her eyes slightly narrowed, but for once she doesn't say anything. A moment later, she wraps her arms around my waist, our bodies melding together despite the thick jackets between us.

We walk home like that, somewhat uncoordinated and a little awkward.

It's fitting, considering that's suddenly how I feel around her all the time.

I haven't done this before. Started something intentional with someone who's looking for their person. Like I could be her person. She could be mine.

I never thought I'd have a person.

Never particularly wanted one.

But now Steph is in my life, and I'm not sure I can just go back to the way things were before.

# 47

# STEPHANIE

I pour us each a glass of wine that I leave on the coffee table and then promptly double back for two glasses of water as well. Ollie collapses into the couch, taking a sip of his wine as he flips on the TV and scrolls through the guide.

I sit gingerly on the couch next to him, unsure of where we stand. Earlier, I thought maybe he was encouraging me to meet Rod tonight as a way to get me off his back, but then he smiled when I joined him for a margarita. And he walked home with me tucked underneath his arm.

There's a lightness in my chest as I fold my legs up underneath me and burrow into the couch. Like maybe we *could* be something.

But there's also this deep sense of dread in my gut that I'm in over my head. That I've developed feelings for a guy who doesn't want something serious–who doesn't want the same things I do.

Again.

As he scrolls through TV channels mindlessly, I can't help my mind running.

Searching for ways to ask him without *asking* him.

We've had that conversation before. The what-are-we conversation that always seems to end in him saying it's either too early or too late to figure that out. And I never get clarity on where we stand.

But maybe I can ask him in another, more subtle way. Take away the pressure of coming up with an answer and instead just get a read on how he feels.

"My parents invited me for dinner this week as a little welcome home thing," I say, leaning forward to take a nonchalant sip of my wine.

"Oh yeah?" He's focused on the screen as he selects an old sitcom, grabs his wine, and leans back, the warmth and weight of his arm grazing my shoulders as he rests it along the back of the couch. "What day?"

A little shockwave rolls through me, and I temporarily forget what I was saying.

*Is this the clarity I was looking for?* An arm around the shoulder might not mean as much as wanting to meet my parents, but it's certainly a step in the right direction. And aren't these the moments that matter? The ones where it's just the two of us and we can actually be *together*?

"Thursday," I tell him.

He laughs. "That's too funny. My parents invited me on the same day."

I blink, watching him out of the corner of my eye. He's still focused on the screen.

*Zero insight.*

"That works out well," he comments, glancing at me for a moment. "You know, so we're not just gliding past each other all week. We'll both be around otherwise."

I narrow my eyes, sinking further into him.

I feel like a detective. He wants us to be available at the

same times. But he doesn't want to meet my parents. And he's seemingly had no thoughts of me meeting his.

Granted, whatever it is we are is still new.

But fuck, I'd throw him in the car and take him to meet my parents right now if that meant he'd be my person.

I have to figure out another way to figure out where he's at. I don't want to risk blowing our night by asking him too bluntly–I don't think I'd get a real answer anyway–but there must be *some* way to get a read on him.

I don't need much.

Just a little sliver of hope that this is more than a situationship.

That he might have some sort of feelings toward me, too.

Snuggled up next to him, all warm and comfortable, I can feel sleep coming for me. He's plenty awake, laughing along with the show and every once in a while brushing his lips along my forehead in a way that makes my heart thump a little louder.

This is the first time we haven't been falling over each other to get naked, and the optimistic side of me thinks it must be because our relationship is leveling up.

And the pessimistic side of me knows that it's because he's not interested in me anymore.

I get up to refill my water, and when I do, I clock Ollie's sketchpad and pens on the kitchen counter.

In Paris, he never gave up an opportunity to draw me. He had it with him constantly, and in these moments of nothingness that could be filled with mindless TV or doom scrolling, he would take to recreating me. The prettiest version of me.

I take it to him, resting it on the coffee table in front of him.

He raises his eyebrows.

"Just in case you wanted to draw."

He grins at me. "Thanks, Steph." But he doesn't reach for them.

He reaches for me instead.

"Come sit," he says, tugging on my waist and pulling me back to my previous spot. And there's something so wonderful about having his arms around me, having him tug on me and touch me just because he can.

But he doesn't go for the sketchpad.

He just leans further into the couch, squeezing me and taking me right along with him.

I briefly consider tipping my head to kiss his jaw, or letting my hand drift up underneath his sweater, just for some confirmation that he's still into me.

But the logical part of my brain knows that a man can always be convinced into sex. But that doesn't mean he feels something for you.

As sleep calls to me, I realize I'm just going to have to settle for this *unknown*. I'll ask him, eventually, if I need to. But maybe for now I need to accept and appreciate that he wants me close to him. That he likes feeling me pressed up against him even without the prospect of sex.

He likes having me with him.

I just hope it's not only for tonight.

I WAKE to the deeply unpleasant realization that I am in my own bed.

Not Ollie's bed, though I can hear him snoring gently through the walls.

My heart drops, and as if he *knows*, Bung pounces onto my bed, snuggling into the crook of my arm. He looks up at me, a disappointed expression on his face like he was thinking maybe he might have been able to snuggle both of us this morning.

"I know, buddy," I whisper, scratching him behind the ears. He purrs, turning his head into my chest as he settles in.

I'm almost certain I fell asleep on the couch last night, and I don't remember coming to bed, so my only logical conclusion is that Ollie did all the work of carrying me up to bed and didn't bother to put me in his own.

Is this the boundary he's drawing? No meeting parents, no sleeping together? But we can touch and eat dinner together?

It all feels like less than what I want.

Bung and I cuddle for another hour before I finally peel myself out of bed and head downstairs, his furry body curled in my arms. I'm as quiet as I can be, but at some point on the stairs I hit the squeaky floorboard and the low, even snores emanating from Ollie's room come to a halt.

I grimace, skittering the rest of the way down as quietly as I can. I release Bung to his place on the back of the couch, where he curls in on himself but keeps a watchful eye on me as I start the coffee.

As I wait, I notice Ollie's sketchpad still sitting on the coffee table from last night. Eyeing the stairs, I shuffle toward it as quietly as I can.

I flip through, the range of drawings from Paris inspiring an ache in my belly. Me, with my chunky socks on at the kitchen table of our hotel room. Me, wandering through the botanical gardens, my face turned up toward the epiphytes clinging onto the taller trees and trellises. Me, naked and tucked between our sheets, a lazy smile on my face as I watch him watching me.

But when I get to the last page, I see that what he did last night had nothing to do with me.

He wrote a grocery list.

A lump builds in my throat as I stare at it. *Bananas, beef stew, frozen chicken...*

I never thought I'd cry over a grocery list, but here I am about two seconds away from it.

When I hear footsteps on the stairs, I quickly snap the sketchpad shut and pad back into the kitchen as quietly as I possibly can. I don't know what to do–I left my phone upstairs in favor of holding Bung, I'm not wearing pants, and the heat of doing something wrong has flushed my face.

So I take a deep breath and intertwine my fingers, resting my hands on the counter and leaning as if I have nothing better to do this morning than watch the coffee percolate.

I will the tears to stay in my eyes. I'm not at the point of blubbering, so I can probably pass this off as my early morning face as long as I don't draw attention to myself.

"Good morning," he says with a smile. He's shirtless, and I hate how good he looks. How good he *smells* as he rests a hand on my hip and kisses my cheek. I swallow as my palm lands on his abdomen, his skin warm.

He takes two mugs out of the cabinet, resting them on the counter next to the coffee maker.

"I was going to go grocery shopping today if you want anything," he says, leaning casually next to me.

It's like he's *trying* to rub salt in the wound.

I shake my head. "No. I don't need anything. Thanks for offering."

He nods. "Well, let me know if you think of anything."

"I will."

He runs a hand through his hair, eyes locked on the coffee maker. "Did you sleep well?"

*Just rub it in further, why don't you?*

"Slept like a baby," I say, searching for Bung as if he can be my solace during this conversation. But of course, he's turned in toward the wall, so all I can really see is a little donut of fur.

"Oh, I wanted to let you know I have an important meeting tomorrow morning."

I raise my eyebrows, searching his face for what this means. "Okay?"

"Just so you know."

I narrow my eyes. "What does that mean? Do you need me to hold up cue cards for you or something?"

He laughs, shaking his head as one arm slides along the counter behind me and lands on my opposite hip. "No. Just wanted to let you know because I'll need to focus. I'll probably have my office door shut. Just didn't want to forget to tell you." He leaves another peck on my temple.

I pause, unsure how to digest this information.

It sounds like he's telling me I'm a distraction.

And this unpleasant whooshing in my stomach feels uncomfortably familiar to that first night we got back to Philadelphia, when he refused to call me Wildflower.

Just last night he was waxing poetic that a relationship is all about how the other person makes you *feel*, and right now, I feel like a distraction. Like someone who isn't good enough to introduce to parents. Like someone less interesting than a grocery list.

I feel like second string. Again.

And then the tears bubble over.

"Hey," he says, maneuvering himself in front of me. "Steph, what's wrong?"

I shake my head, trying to swallow down the emotion. I hold my hands over my face, and his wrap around my wrists, pulling them gently away.

"Stephanie," he says, holding my chin and forcing me to look at him. "What's going on?"

"I don't matter to you like I did in Paris," I squeak out, and it sounds even more pathetic from my mouth than it did in the millisecond it was in my brain.

His thumbs brush the tears from my cheeks. "What do you mean? Of course you matter to me. More than in Paris."

I shake my head, sniffling a little. "You won't draw me, you don't want me to meet your parents, and you think I'm just going to *distract* you. Like you said last night, it's about the way your person makes you feel, and I don't feel good."

He sighs. "Stephanie. I'm sorry. I never want you to not feel good with me. I didn't mean you would distract me. I was just going to draw a clear boundary for an hour with the door and I didn't want *that* to make you not feel good. And god, you can meet my parents whenever. I kind of thought you had already–didn't you meet them at my birthday party? And I mean, Thursdays are one of the few days we can all manage to get together so I can't really move that dinner, and you said yours was a welcome home thing, so I assumed that couldn't really be moved. And fuck, I'll draw you whenever. I *love* drawing you."

I bite my lip. "I brought you your sketchpad."

He glances at it resting on the coffee table, and then turns back to me. "And then promptly fell asleep on me. I can only do so much with an entire person starfishing on me."

I shake my head. "That's not the point."

He gesticulates between us as he speaks. "Then what is the point?"

I swallow. "I love you."

He's quiet, his hands dropping back to his sides.

"That's the point. I know what it feels like to give someone everything and not get anything back. And I also now know what it feels like to have true feelings for someone. To realize that I'd give more than the everything I have for just a fraction of the *something* they give in return. But I don't want just the fraction. I want everything, too. And I think I deserve that."

His voice is soft when he speaks. "Steph, of course you do. You, of anyone."

"But you're not ready to give me everything, too."

He lets out a long breath, his eyes locked on mine. "I don't know what to say."

The tears come on full force again despite my inner protests because I don't think it's that hard to say "I love you, too."

But I guess it's a relief that he doesn't say it just to placate me. I'm not sure if I'd believe him, anyway.

"Stephanie," he says, his voice breaking as he wraps his arms around me.

I shake my head, pushing him away. I *can't* with the mixed signals.

"I'm going to go stay with my sister."

His hands are on my shoulders–the closest I'll let him get–and his fingers tighten around my arms. Not forcefully. Almost like he's trying to hug me without getting pushed away again and this is the closest he can get. "Steph, please don't go. I won't bother you if you want to hang out in your room, but please don't leave."

I take a deep breath now that the tears are subsiding and wipe the wetness from my face with my shirtsleeve. "I think it's for the best."

He steps away from me, running his hands over his face. "I can't believe you're just going to leave after all of this."

"All of what? Ollie, you're not there."

"Not where? You want me to tell you I love you? Okay, fine! I love you. Will you please stay?" he asks, gathering my hands in his.

*And hearing those words has never made me so angry.* "I don't want you to say it because you feel like you have to! I want you to say it out of love, like your whole heart is bursting and you just can't keep it in."

"Steph, not everyone loves the same way you do."

"Then that's not good enough for me," I bite back. "This whole time I've been searching for my big love. I give big love and I want someone who looks at me and wants to give me big love too."

He swallows, nodding as he turns away from me. He takes a few steps, his hands on his hips, before he turns back to me.

"I *want* to be that for you, Steph."

I fill in the blank for him. "But you can't."

He stands in front of me, gathering my hands into his. "Give me a second to catch up, Steph. Let me prove to you that I can."

## 48

## OLIVER

It's not lost on me that I have bags under my eyes. That my coffee maker is working overtime today because I spent last night tossing and turning rather than getting sleep like I needed to.

Steph spent yesterday in her room, only popping out for food at times that I happened to be otherwise occupied.

I can't help but think our near misses were intentional, like she's withholding her company until I prove to her I'm worthy of it.

And I'm painfully aware that I have to do something about that, but I'm coming up woefully blank on what that thing I have to do is.

The words felt right when I said them, but after she begrudgingly agreed to give me a chance, I realized I have no idea what being given a chance *means*. Giving her time? Being there for her when she's ready? Blustering into her room with grand declarations of love that have a flush creeping up my neck just thinking about them?

She closed the door on me, and while I consider it a win

that she's still in my house, I don't know how to come back from this. From a false declaration of love that neither of us believed, but I felt the need to say because I'd say anything if that meant she would stay.

But now the words feel empty. I can't tell her I love her to win her back because I used those words as a cheap ploy to get her to stay. So now I have to find some way to *show* her, but I've never done this before. I don't know how to show someone I love them.

Especially someone who's making it clear she doesn't want to see me.

I put on one of my nice shirts before I sign on for the day because I don't know Kellan all that well, and although he has a good reputation, I'm not about to assume he's supportive of a casual workplace. I make sure there are no wrinkles in my shirt—at least, the part that's visible—and begrudgingly decide it's probably best to wear slacks too, just in case I have to get up during the call.

This could be my new boss, the last guy in line before the executive suite. I'm no slouch, but it's not lost on me that I'm getting close to the top. Kellan is one of the few VPs that whisper in the ears of the executives. All I have to do is impress him.

I sit down at my computer, swallowing over the feelings of discomfort swarming in my chest. I have a minute to pull myself together before this call. I should be thinking of departmental roadmaps, budgets, travel plans.

But by the time the clock strikes the hour, my mind is blank, aside from thoughts of shiny, multi-colored hair and her banana-mango scent.

I can only hope talking to my potential future boss will click me into gear.

I let out a deep breath and click into the video link.

And I wait.

Two minutes pass as I stare at the screen, and I start to wonder if I screwed up the time. If maybe his assistant sent over the wrong link. I'm about to panic-message her when the call finally connects.

And in front of me is a man who looks like he could have been put together an hour or two ago. But now, his dress shirt is unbuttoned, revealing a white T-shirt underneath, and his hair looks like it *was* gelled, but is currently sticking up in several places. On his chest he holds a sleeping toddler, his hand gently patting the baby's butt.

"Hey, sorry I'm late," he says. He motions to his kid. "We got hit with hand, foot and mouth this week and this one just wants to be held. My poor wife is saddled with the other two in the nursery so if I have to run, just know it's not you. It's the asshat who sent his kid to preschool sick last week."

"No problem at all," I say, struggling to piece together the snippets of Kellan I've seen in meetings with the guy who's very much prioritizing being Dad right now. "Would you prefer to reschedule?"

He shakes his head. "He's finally asleep," he says, nodding to his kid. "So until he wakes up, I'm glued to this chair, anyway."

His eyes whip across the screen as he starts sharing. "So this is going to be pretty informal. Technically none of what I'm going to show you has been approved by the board yet, but they'd be idiots to block it."

He runs through what the new department will look like. How we'll be taking on requests as a team rather than serving our respective areas. How he'll be making room for people to grow where they want to.

This structure he's putting together is new for the

company. He's been mushing it around in his head for a while, researching resources within the company and seeing who might fit where. It's less travel, less bullshit, more logic.

Kind of like it was made for me.

And the whole reason they tapped me is because I'm pretty much already doing it off the record. They never intended to have someone with so much engineering experience in the training team, and although he'd still like me to take the odd trip here or there, he wants me focused on internal development. Interfacing within the company to truly elevate what we do instead of using my skills for simple requests that less savvy users might need.

The tightness in my chest releases as Kellan talks. I feel a little dumb that I just assumed I'd be forgotten and left on the training team.

They didn't *create* this role for me, but they had me in mind while they scoped it out.

None of the work I've put in has gone unnoticed.

When he finishes up his presentation, I'm a little winded. "You obviously put a lot of thought into this new plan. I'm excited to see how this works out."

Kellan nods. "Hopefully it'll work out well. As a former engineering nerd, this structure would have worked for me. But we'll see how it goes."

"You have my full confidence."

He laughs. "Okay. Well, it sounds like you're feeling good about moving forward with this?"

"Yeah. Absolutely."

"Cool. Look for an email from Staci in the coming days and we'll set up something more formal. Just wanted to gauge your thoughts before proceeding." The toddler on his shoulder blinks awake, and Kellan smiles down at him.

"Do you have kids?" he asks.

I shake my head. "No, not yet." *Not yet?*

He sighs. "They're manipulative little bastards. Sneeze and cough right in your face and then they fall asleep on you looking all peaceful and cute. Next thing you know, there's another one."

I laugh, but I'm not sure what to say.

"Oh, one note," he adds, sitting up carefully so he doesn't jostle the baby. "I can be pushy sometimes and I'm sorry in advance. But family comes first, so don't hesitate to tell me to fuck off if you need a personal day or something. God knows I do."

"Thanks. I will. Let me know if I can help with anything in the meantime."

He nods. "Thanks. Nice of you to offer," he says and then nods at his kid. "The other ones have stopped crying so I'm going to see if I can get this guy into his crib for a couple hours."

"Good luck. And thanks."

"See you around," he says, and the meeting ends.

I sit back in my chair, winded by our conversation. I unbutton my shirt, letting it fall open around me, and run my hands over my face.

It sounds like I'm a shoe-in for this new position. As long as I don't fuck anything up, I've done it. One rung left until C-suite. Of course, that'll take time. I'll have to spend years in this position most likely–same for VP, if that's in my future.

I should be thrilled about this. Not only do I get the big promotion I've been busting my ass for, but it's actually *better* than what I thought I was going for. Lots of the engineering-focused stuff I enjoy, and my new boss is just as cool as my old boss–*and* he manages to do it all with a toddler on his chest.

I should be ecstatic.

But it doesn't feel right without Stephanie here to cheer, too.

She's one room away, but this distance feels larger than the ocean between Costa Rica and Paris.

# MARCH

# 49

## STEPHANIE

*othing. Zilch. Nada.* That's what I've gotten from Oliver Long this week.

Leave it to this man to beg for me to stay, to throw out words he knows are big to me, only to spend the week festering in silence.

Sure, I might not be at my most receptive at the moment. But why do I always have to be the one who's open and available? I'm sick of being the easygoing one. I'm sick of brushing off slights so other people feel better. Of foregoing my own feelings because I want someone else to feel good.

When we were in Paris, Ollie told me he thinks I'm remarkable because I love freely and without requirements. That he worries that one day I'll get hurt and won't be able to anymore.

*Well, joke's on you, dude.*

I lock the door as I leave the house for dinner, clambering into the back of Zeke's car. Ollie didn't say anything about moving our respective family dinners, so I'm continuing with plans as they were made.

Separately.

"Got enough room?" Gabi asks as she pushes the seat back and sits down.

"No," I grumble.

"When I bought this car, I only had to cart around my own sister," Zeke says, pulling away from the curb.

"Well, thank you for graciously extending your services to mine," Gabi says.

"Yeah, thanks, Zeke."

As we get up to speed on the highway, he rests his hand on her knee, and an irrational flare of jealousy zips through me.

But when we get to my parents' house, the jealousy wanes. I see my car—my pretty, old, beat up car that I've loved too hard for the past ten years. My parents agreed to keep it in their driveway while I traveled. My mom and dad peep through the living room windows as Zeke pulls in behind me.

My mom rushes out of the house, enveloping me in a hug before I can take two steps inside. "Stephanie." She squeezes me, her hair flying wild in every direction around us. "Honey, I missed you."

"Missed you too, Mom." She hugs Gabi and Zeke quickly, and then wraps an arm around my shoulder as she leads me into the house. "You have to tell us all about your trip."

*Jesus, where do I start?*

The scent of tacos is overpowering as we get inside. Before we even hit the kitchen, I know the table will be filled with an array of ingredients. Beef and turkey, guacamole, salsa, too many hot sauces to count, lettuce, shells, and most likely margaritas.

"Mom, you planned taco night for my homecoming?"

"Well of course, honey. What else?"

I hug her tight. I love my mom.

We form a line along the kitchen table, my mom pouring margaritas at one end. My dad swoops in to give me a quick hug and a kiss on the cheek, a hug for Gabi and a handshake for Zeke. We fill our plates and sit around the table, margarita glasses sloshing and the radio playing a series of ads in the background that my mom doesn't notice because she's too busy making sure everyone has enough food. My dad shakes his head, flipping to a station that isn't advertising erectile dysfunction pills.

"So how was it? What did you do? What did you see? Tell me everything. Maybe we can convince your father to take me to Paris. Or Costa Rica. That sloth! Do you have pictures?" My mom's lowest speed is full throttle. I catch Zeke's eyebrows raise out of the corner of my eye as Gabi bites into her taco, unfazed.

I take out my phone and scroll through to where the Costa Rica pictures start, sliding it across the table toward my mom.

"That's daring," Gabi comments, as my mom starts swiping.

"There's a hidden folder on your phone for your nudes," I tell her. You don't just hand my mother a phone and expect her not to scroll.

"There is?"

"Jesus," my dad mutters.

"I think it's on my phone, actually," Zeke comments. I snort as Gabi playfully shoves his shoulder. He catches my dad eyeing him and clears his throat. "I mean, I think it's on all phones."

My mom glances at my dad. "Oh, like you didn't send naughty pictures back in the day."

He turns beat red. "Helena," he scolds, and the rest of us burst out in laughter.

I keep an eye on the pictures as she scrolls through. "That was the view of the lodge I stayed in from the trail."

"Wow, that's beautiful." She keeps scrolling. "Oh, who is this?" she asks, turning the phone around to see my bug-eating tour guide.

"His name was Brandon," I tell her. "He scooped his lunch from a termite hive."

Her eyes find mine. "He did what?"

"See those little bugs on him? They're termites. Equivalent to the ketchup from your sandwich dripping onto your shirt."

"Oh, Stephanie," she says, a look of disgust passing over her face as she scrolls through to the next pictures. "Hey, where's Rod? I don't see him in any of these."

Gabi sits up straight, watching me as I speak. "Rod and I are done."

My mom raises her eyebrows. "*Done* done?"

I nod. "But don't worry, we broke up twice for good measure."

"I'm sorry, honey," she says. "Was this during your trip?"

"Yeah. He ditched me for his travel buddies and I got sick of it, so I went to Paris."

Her attention swings to me. "Are you telling me you went to Paris *alone* and didn't tell your own mother? I thought Rod was with you the whole time."

I hold her gaze, annoyed that this is what she holds onto. "Yes. And oh my goodness, I'm so happy to still be alive."

"Stephanie, I would have been worried about you."

Gabi snorts. "But you weren't because you thought she was with Rod?"

"Well," my mom starts. "Yes. But no. It's different!"

"Mom, I'm fine. No reason to retroactively worry."

She holds a hand over her heart. "That makes me so

uncomfortable." She continues swiping as she shakes her head, and pauses as she looks at the next picture. I lean forward to look, scared I did actually miss a nude, and see the picture of Ollie and me in front of the Eiffel Tower. "Who is this?"

I want to melt back into my chair. "Ollie."

Gabi leans forward to look at the picture. "Wow," she says, taking my phone from my mom. "This could be the cover of a romance novel." Zeke leans over her shoulder to look, too.

"That's what I said!" She slides the phone back to my mom.

"Are you dating someone new?" my mom asks.

I shake my head, unsure how to answer the question. "No."

"Is he French?" she asks, zooming in on the picture.

"No."

"He's cute," she says, her eyebrows raised.

"Not dating."

She hums, flipping to the next picture. "Wow, what a nice jawline."

I grab the phone from her, flipping through any pictures with Ollie. I turn the phone back to her once I'm into my Arc de Triomphe pictures, and she huffs in response. "Why don't you bring him to dinner next time?"

"I can't bring someone to dinner who doesn't want to come to dinner."

My mom's eyes find mine, her brow furrowed. "He doesn't want to come to dinner?"

"No, Mom, he doesn't want to come to dinner." It comes out a little harsher than I intended.

She looks genuinely confused. "Why not?"

I can't help but laugh. "I don't know, Mom. Sometimes

people just don't want to go to dinner with someone else's family."

"But that picture!" She swipes in the other direction again, landing on my picture with Ollie and holding it up for me to see. "That's not a picture of someone who doesn't want to come to dinner."

"Mom, I don't know what to tell you. It was just a fling, and it's over now."

She sighs, her bottom lip jutting out as she takes another look at the picture. She turns to me. "Please don't go back to Rod," she says.

Gabi laughs. "I *knew* that's what all that was about."

My mom scrunches up her nose. "I know that's not cool for me to say, but you've been with him for almost a decade and it just never gets better."

"I'm not going back to Rod. I think I'm done with my quest for love."

Gabi puts her taco down. "Steph, you don't mean that."

"I think I do," I say. "If I love too freely and forgive too easily, then maybe it's time I stop. It only ever seems to get me hurt. So instead I'm going to be moody and reserved and listen to Alanis Morissette on repeat while I watch my plants grow. I will love *them* freely and forgive *them* too easily."

"That's the new cat lady, isn't it? Plant lady?" Zeke asks.

Gabi gives him a look. "That's so not the point."

My mom shakes her head. "Steph, I don't think it's a *bad* idea to take some time for yourself. But don't let this change who you are. It's a tough time, not a tough life," my mom says, reaching across the table and squeezing my hand. "But I fully support the Alanis Morissette part. *You live, you learn*," she quotes.

"You're not going to start singing," Gabi pleads.

"Where's my phone?" my mom asks, standing from the

table and blustering into the kitchen. A moment later, the radio cuts out and the bluetooth connects. I can't help but laugh as the song starts. Gabi rests her head in her hands while Zeke watches the chaos with rapt interest.

And my homecoming, like many family dinners before it, devolves into karaoke.

GABI AND ZEKE pull their coats on by the door. She leans into him, eyes droopy from the late hour and probably one too many margaritas. He loops an arm around her waist, leaving a light kiss on her forehead.

I simultaneously love and hate how fucking cute they are.

They give me tight hugs before they leave, and as I sit back down on the couch, Zeke's car roars to life in the driveway.

While my mom throws the last of the dishes into the dishwasher, my dad flops down onto the couch next to me with the aggregated leftovers from the night–a mixture of meats and sauces and salsas–all thrown into one big bowl. He holds a second fork out to me, knowing I'm always up for splitting it with him.

"I'm sorry your trip didn't end the way you planned," he says.

I shrug. "Thanks, Dad." I stab a few pieces of meat with my fork.

"But I just wanted to remind you that you–what is it you said earlier? You love too freely and forgive too easily?"

I nod, Ollie's words echoing from every corner of my life now.

"Well, you love too freely and forgive too easily because

that's the way your heart works. I understand being hurt and needing a break or temporarily wanting to forego love, but I hope you don't let life teach you to dull your heart. Maybe you should just let it teach you to find someone who recognizes that as the gift it is and helps you nourish it."

I take another bite from the leftover bowl. "I don't know if there's someone out there like that."

He nods. "Because you've been looking in all the wrong places."

"You mean Rod."

He grimaces. "Your mother said it first." He pops a piece of chicken into his mouth. "Look, we don't want our opinions to sway the choices you girls make, but it's hard to watch you try so hard for someone who obviously doesn't appreciate you. It's been almost ten years, Steph. You can't draw blood from a stone."

"What if there are only stones?"

He gives me a look. "There aren't. Just look at Zeke. A big old softie who manages to get past your sister's iron exterior."

It's not the first time he's mentioned being impressed by Zeke.

"You love Zeke," I say, laughing.

He shrugs noncommittally. "I think he's a very nice young man who treats my daughter very well. So yes, I like Zeke."

"Aw, that's sweet." I huff. "I want that."

He rests his hand on my knee. "You'll find it, kid. Just be patient. And remember that the right person isn't going to find it difficult to treat you with the love and respect you deserve."

My heart swells. My dad always knows the right thing to say. "Thanks, Dad."

"Love you, Stephy."

"Love you too."

He pushes the bowl into my hands and stands. "Well, I better help your mother with the dishes before I get in trouble."

"I'll help too," I say, clearing the last of the bowl on my way to the kitchen.

# 50

# OLIVER

I 'm painfully aware of Stephanie's absence as I lock my car and head into my parents' house. Tonight is a celebration, and it feels wrong that she's not here. I was going to request a change in plans, maybe see if my family could meet on another day because it doesn't feel right to ask *her* family to meet on another day. But every time I tried to ask her whether she still *wanted* to come, she magically had plants to water or work to finish or friends to meet.

I like Steph. I think I want her in my life for good. But I don't freaking know how to do this.

She said she wanted to meet my parents, but every time I try to make that happen, she's dust in the wind.

So now I'm heading into my parents' alone.

And I actually don't want to be.

I've never allowed myself to yearn for a person like this. Never thought of the possibility that I could handle something more.

But my new boss is doing fine, even with three kids to wrangle. If he can do it as a VP, I *have* to be able to do it as a director. Not necessarily the kids part, but having another focus. Something that makes the tough days worth it. Someone who makes the good days even better.

My breath catches as I push open the front door. I'm not sure how to navigate this. My entire family is focused on professional ambition. Even Eliza, who is our in-house mental health rep, has big goals. I don't even remember the last time we had a family dinner like this that wasn't a celebration of someone's promotion or raise.

But this celebration pales in comparison to Valentine's Day. That feeling of being Steph's, even if it was only for a night.

Now that I'm cautiously allowing myself to think of her in the longer term, this all feels forced without her here.

In the kitchen, I pour myself a glass of wine and carefully walk the plate of green beans my mom shoves into my arms out to the table.

And nearly drop them when I realize there's a stranger in the house.

"Who are you?" I blurt.

Eliza brushes past me with a bowl of rice. "This is Cole," she says, giving me a look. "Remember, Ollie? I told you about him."

"No." I follow her lead, putting the green beans down on the table.

He stands, holding his hand out to me. "Nice to meet you," he says, nodding politely as we shake hands. "Oliver, right?"

"Yeah. Nice to meet you too."

My mom nudges plates around to fit the chicken onto the table as Ethan emerges from the kitchen with a freshly opened bottle of wine. He fills glasses as we take our seats, and I watch with rapt fascination as my sister's new boyfriend attempts a good first impression.

A first impression that should have been Stephanie's.

He takes a sip from his water rather than his wine and smiles politely. Ethan and I sit across the table from the two of them, my parents at either end.

Ethan leans over my shoulder and lowers his voice as we pass plates around to serve ourselves. "Is this weird to you?"

"I don't think so." I glance at Eliza, who's taken it upon herself to serve both herself and Cole. "It's surprising, but somehow it doesn't feel weird."

"It's the lack of weirdness, I think, that feels weird," Ethan whispers.

"So, Cole, I hear you're a software engineer?" my mom asks.

My attention snaps to him. *Is he?*

He nods. "Yeah, for big pharma for now, but I have my eye on a local nonprofit that provides mental health services for the less fortunate. They're a little small and top-heavy on engineering right now, but I'm hoping in the next couple of years they'll be stable enough that I can make the switch over."

My mom looks impressed. "If you ever need help navigating the nonprofit world, let me know. I work for an organization that helps neurodivergent kids, and let me tell you, the nonprofit world is a whole different beast than corporate America."

He nods. "That would be really nice. Thank you."

"What kind of engineering do you do?" I ask.

He takes his glasses off as he speaks, wiping them on his shirt. "I mostly work on a product a lot of pharmacies use for sending and receiving prescriptions. Front-end."

"I started as a software engineer. Now I–well, I guess I oversee them."

My mom clears her throat, dropping her utensils down

on her plate. "Which reminds me. Congratulations, Oliver, we're so proud of you." She holds her wineglass up, and there's a cacophony of clinks and sips around the table.

"Thanks, Mom," I say, though I can't help the heat creeping up my neck. It always feels like too much attention when it's your mom making a big deal of things.

Cole spends a majority of his meal answering questions from the family. We don't do it intentionally; we're just a curious bunch. But eventually Eliza holds up her hand, calling the table to silence. "If you all could give Cole ten minutes to eat before his food gets cold, he'll continue answering questions afterward."

"I don't mind," he insists.

Eliza gives him a look. "Eat your food."

He complies.

"Maybe I'll get a girlfriend," Ethan says.

I look over at him, my chicken dropping off my fork. "What?"

He shrugs. "I don't know. Eliza's doing it, you're doing it."

"I'm doing it?"

"Didn't you mention a girl in the group text?"

"There's a girl?" my mom asks, her eyebrows raised.

"I mean, kind of," I say, but the answer feels like a blow to Steph. "Yes, I guess."

"What's her name?" my mom asks.

"Stephanie."

"She's part of that group you hang out with, right?" Eliza asks.

I nod, very conscious of everyone's eyes on me.

"She's pretty," Eliza says.

I don't know why, but my breath catches with this albeit superficial judgment from Eliza. They might have only said a few words to each other in the past, so it's not like Eliza knows who Steph really is, but the fact that Eliza thinks she's pretty feels like such a *big* thing.

I wonder if Eliza is thinking the same thing tonight with Cole. If our conversations with him will just reinforce the way she feels about him.

I imagine Stephanie here. Ethan would probably check her out a second too long. My mom would double-check that she has enough food so many times that she'll feel obligated to take seconds. My dad would sit quietly, his presence subdued but comforting. And Stephanie would just be herself, rambling on a little too long at times or twisting her mermaid hair around her finger like she does.

And I'd get to take her home afterward.

"Yeah," I say, because I'm not sure how to expand on that.

"Bring her to dinner sometime," my dad says, taking a sip of his wine.

"Yeah," I say, wondering how I get over this hump with her, win back her favor. "I will."

# 51

# STEPHANIE

By the time girls' night rolls around on Friday, I'm itching to leave the house. Ollie and I have been dancing around each other all week, so courteous and formal with each other that I might puke if I hear or say one more "no, you go ahead," about the last cup of coffee in the morning.

I spend the time between work and dinner dyeing my hair in Ollie's bathtub–*extra carefully,* of course–and somehow misjudge my time by about twenty minutes. I end up scrambling to find a dark shirt just in case I didn't get all the color out, and then darting past him out the door just as he's pulling on his jacket to head to game night.

"Hey, do you want me to walk with you?" he asks as I zip down the street. The place I'm meeting the girls is only a few blocks away and on the way to game night.

"No, but thank you! I'm late!" I call over my shoulder as I walk-run to the corner before the light changes. "I'll see you later!"

He's still locking up as I turn the corner, and I let out a

long breath as I settle into a walk just fast enough that I might actually be warm by the time I get there.

I don't like the dynamic we've settled into, and part of me knows everything will come to a head soon. Maybe I'm protecting myself, hiding in my own little bubble so things don't hurt as bad when the inevitable happens and Ollie tells me he's done with me. Again.

By the time I collapse into the booth, I'm exhausted from my walk. From thinking too hard.

Kay and Leilani are across from me with matching pink margaritas. Mari and Carrie are squished in on my side, a mojito and vodka soda in front of them.

"Ooh," Leilani says, immediately reaching forward to snag a tendril of my hair between her fingers. "Did you just dye it?"

I nod, and she pulls more of my hair in front of me. "Oh, you know it's going to be good when it's still wet and already so vibrant."

"There's a lot of color?"

Leilani nods. "It's going to be gorgeous."

"Thanks, Lei." I glance around the table. "Hey, where are Gabi and Annabel?"

Mari waves me off. "They're going to meet us later if they can. Gabi wants to put her logo on the wall of the yoga studio so Annabel is making some edits to make it more, uh... wall-friendly, I guess. I'm surprised neither of them told you."

I grab my phone from my pocket and see that they *did*, but I was so busy rushing off to dinner that I totally missed it. "Oh. Oops. They did tell me."

Mari snorts. "How much do you want to bet they're going to miss dinner and casually suggest we all just head over to Annabel's since all the guys are there, anyway?" she asks as she texts–Annabel, presumably.

The waiter drops off a margarita that Leilani passes to me with a quick nod to tell me it's mine. "Oh, to be in love."

"That's not a bet, that's a sure thing," Carrie says, her voice quiet but firm. She's always a little more talkative when it's just us girls. Aside from Ollie, at least. They seem to have forged a strong connection based on a mutual love of Bung.

I don't mean to, but I let out a long breath, my eyes rolling.

Carrie's head cocks to the side immediately, her eyes locked on mine. "What's wrong?"

I shake my head. "I'm just kind of sick of crashing game nights, I think."

"You're sick of crashing game nights," Kay deadpans, her eyebrows furrowed.

I take another sip of my margarita, giving her nothing more than a quick nod in return to her question. The server stops by to take our orders, and we quickly go around the table, Leilani eyeing me.

"Steph, what's going on?" Leilani asks knowingly.

I glance around the table, four concerned faces staring back at me as I try to figure out how to answer that question.

I shrug. "Things are weird. With Ollie."

Kay and Leilani look at each other. Mari and Carrie do the same.

"How so?" Mari asks.

I pause as I wonder how much of this burgeoning rela-tionship–or *not* relationship–I should share with them. I hate the idea of putting Ollie on a platter when he's not here to participate in the conversation, but I feel like I need to just get it all off my chest. Give the girls some of my burden to bear for a night.

So I launch into it, telling them all about our week in Paris, falling back into each other here and the tense week of *nothingness* I'm running away from. Leilani's face pinches when I tell them about asking Ollie if it could have been us, in Paris. Kay's eyebrows crinkle when I tell them about him drawing me almost obsessively. Carrie groans as I recount the night of the grocery list.

As my story comes to an end, I take another big sip of my margarita, and Mari throws her arm around my shoulders. "I'm actually kind of impressed at the number of mixed signals he's managed to throw at you."

"If that man was a stoplight, he'd be causing head-on collisions every other second," Leilani says.

I throw my hands up. "I know!"

I shake my head. "I don't know what to do about him. He begged me to stay, but he's not doing anything about it. So I figure it's time to move on, I guess. This feels like Rod all over again, and I refuse to let that sort of history repeat itself."

Mari groans. "That *is* very Rod-like of him."

"He might just be scared," Leilani says.

I point at her. "*That* feels like something you would have said about Rod."

She rolls her eyes. "Look, I really wanted to believe Rod was going to show up for you. I *want* to believe people have good intentions. Rod proved me wrong. I'm still willing to give Ollie a chance."

"I mean, that's a good point, though," Carrie says. My eyes snap to hers. She doesn't speak often so when she does I always pay attention. "You just got out of a relationship with someone who didn't treat you right. None of us can see what goes on when you're alone, but is it possible you're giving too much meaning to signals from a guy who's just... a little inexperienced?"

I blink. "Inexperienced?"

Carrie shrugs. "At love?" She pauses. "I know both of you pretty well at this point. If Ollie's being a dick, I at least don't think it's intentional. You should talk to him."

She sighs, reaching forward to knock my hand with hers. "I also know you're hurting. Sometimes that makes you see things differently. Maybe not always correctly."

The server stops by to deliver our meals, tacos and enchiladas and guacamole passed around the table.

I swallow as she smiles sweetly at me. I take a bite of my taco in lieu of speaking. Something in me knew that this is where this would go. An inevitable conversation. Probably one that ends in a breakup once and for all.

And my emotional ass starts crying into my taco.

"Steph," Mari says, throwing her arms around me and squeezing. I let my taco fall back onto my plate as Leilani abandons her seat in favor of squishing in beside me and hugging me too.

"I'm sorry. God, I'm crying over a *conversation*."

"Oh, I'm sorry," Carrie says, reaching over to squeeze my arm. "I didn't mean to upset you."

I roll my eyes at her, wiping my cheeks. "Carrie, you literally gave me appropriate advice for the situation. I just didn't want to hear it."

Leilani pats my head, leaving a kiss on my temple. "Steph, you love him, don't you?"

"Don't make me cry again," I say, my voice shaky.

Kay huffs from across the table. "I hate this emotion. I'm so happy you finally moved on from Rod, but I'm so freaking angry at Ollie I could chop his balls off right now."

"Don't. His balls are really nice."

The table pauses as my words register, and they all start laughing.

"I so did not need to know that," Carrie mutters, taking a sip of her drink.

"So Oliver Long has nice balls, whodathunk," Mari comments. She shakes her head as her arms unravel around me. "Hey, why don't we skip game night tonight? Let's have a good old-fashioned girls' night and you can blow off some steam and talk to Ollie tomorrow."

I nod. "That sounds really nice."

MARI'S APARTMENT can only be described as *fun*. Her walls are covered in movie posters, her furniture is all brightly colored and unique, and instead of side tables, she has stacks of old suitcases. It's a small studio, but she's made the space work for her.

She throws an array of blankets and pillows down on the floor in front of the couch and, by popular demand, starts *Grease*. We only get about twenty minutes into the movie before we're all singing so loud we can't even hear the characters.

*Grease* quickly dissolves into karaoke.

Apparently I have that effect.

Kay and Leilani duet "Summer Nights" as Carrie pours herself another cup of wine from the box on the counter that we picked up on our way back from dinner. I collapse into the couch next to Mari, and she throws an arm around me for a quick hug. "You doing okay?"

I nod. "Thanks for doing this. I think I needed a night like this."

She nods, quiet for a second. "I think you guys will figure it out."

"You do?"

She nods. "I think so. Call it a gut feeling."

"How?"

She gives me a look. "It's a gut feeling, Steph. I'm not psychic."

I roll my eyes at her. "I just meant like, why do you have the gut feeling?"

She laughs. "Steph, I don't know. Call it kindred spirits or the fact that I know you guys. It's a feeling, not logic."

I huff. "I wish I could feel what you're feeling."

Mari shrugs. "Give it time, Steph. Talk to him tomorrow."

I nod, letting out a long breath and deciding that I will, in fact, talk to him tomorrow.

When she glances up at Leilani and Kay standing in front of us, she grins. "I think you're needed for the next song."

When I turn around, Leilani is pointing at me, singing the opening lines of "You're The One That I Want" as it plays on the screen behind her.

"Seriously?" I ask. "You want me to sing *this* with you *now*?"

She nods, beckoning me over. "Love songs are better with girlfriends!"

"Go," Mari says, shoving my shoulder to push me off the couch.

Leilani wraps her arms around me, and I do my best to ignore the lyrics I'm singing to her. That she better shape up. Because I need a man. And my heart is set on her.

I can't even make it through one verse without bursting out in laughter.

## 52

## OLIVER

I head in the same direction as Stephanie, following in her footsteps until I round the corner she disappeared behind.

And she's nowhere to be found. Off like a rocket, running away from me. Again.

At first I thought maybe she was just busy. Maybe our schedules weren't lining up and I was just *missing* her.

But over the past week she's had more late nights and early mornings than usual. The only times I really saw her was when she was pulling her coat on and rushing out of the house in a blur, on her way to a coworking space instead of using the desk I gave her, or running out to pick up food quickly and not returning until I'm sleepy-eyed on the couch with a cranky Bung in my arms.

As I walk toward Charlie's, it becomes abundantly clear just how horribly I've fucked up.

This whole time I've been so concerned about becoming the person who teaches Steph to stop loving as hard as she does.

And unwittingly, that's exactly what I've become.

My heart sinks as I push through the lobby doors. I don't know how to do this. How to be the kind of person Steph is looking for. How to apologize and make up with someone I've wronged with my silence but also by saying the right words at the wrong time.

I take the elevator up and head down the long hallway, knocking once before walking in.

Charlie and Zeke are hovering over a bottle of whiskey on the kitchen island, two glasses of amber liquid in front of them. Henry and Kick are on the couch, chatting casually as they sip their drinks. All four of them glance up and nod when I walk in, Charlie immediately turning to the cabinet behind him to grab me a glass.

"Look who finally made it," he says, pouring me a drink and pushing it toward me as Zeke claps me on the back.

"What, am I late?" I ask.

Zeke shrugs. "What does timing matter anyway?"

Charlie and I glance at him, and he only takes another sip of his drink.

"You're only twenty minutes late"–my shock must show on my face–"but that just gave us all time to knock one back before the game starts."

My brain is all over the place. I shake my head, taking a long drink of the whiskey in my hand before pulling our game board out of my jacket pocket.

And then I pause, staring down at the sketchpad in my hands.

I clear my throat. *How the fuck am I going to explain this?*

"You okay?" Zeke asks, one hand on my shoulder as I glance from my sketchpad, to him.

"Yeah." I clear my throat. "I, um, forgot the board."

Or more accurately, my mind was so scattered that not

only did I mix up our start time, but I also grabbed my sketchpad instead of the game board.

We have nothing to play with tonight.

I shrug out of my coat, throwing it over the back of a bar stool and dropping the sketchpad onto the counter in front of me. I can feel Zeke and Charlie's eyes on me as I knock down the rest of my drink and hastily pour myself another.

"What's going on, Ollie?" Zeke asks, his eyes narrowing.

I shake my head, the words bubbling up before I have the chance to think about them. "I don't know what to do about Stephanie."

The look that passes between them inspires a deep discomfort in my gut.

"What do you mean you don't know what to *do* about her?" Zeke asks, his voice cut with an edge of warning.

I pause. "Are you *my* friend or *her* friend?"

He shrugs. "Depends entirely on what you meant by *doing* something about her."

I give him a look. To be fair, I'd probably be more worried about Gabi than him, if the situation were reversed. I don't exactly have the best track record with women.

But god, I'd never *intentionally* hurt Stephanie.

"I mean she's living in my house. We share a wall when we're working. But she won't talk to me."

He cocks his head to the side.

"And now I'm so fucking flustered that I grabbed my fucking sketchpad instead of the goddamn game board," I say, reaching for the whiskey bottle to top myself up. "I can't think about anything but her, and she won't just fucking talk to me."

They share another look.

"Let's sit," Charlie suggests, grabbing the whiskey bottle and leading us over to the couch. Zeke nods to the space next to Henry and I collapse into the cushions, holding my glass with two hands in front of my face.

"Alright," Kick says, sitting up as we join them. The goofy smile on his face tells me he hasn't picked up on the mood shift yet. "Are we ready to play?"

Zeke shakes his head. "I think we need a quick download of what happened in Paris," he says, eyeing me.

I glance around at my friends, their faces turned expectantly toward me. This is not how I imagined tonight going. "I mean, we just... you know, hung out."

Charlie presses his lips together. Zeke's mouth tips into a smile.

"You and Steph," Zeke starts, "just *hung out?*"

I shrug. "Yeah."

He gives me a look. "You're a bad liar."

I throw my hands up. "I don't know what she's comfortable sharing! I'm trying to be respectful."

"Do you want to be respectful, or do you want to fix things?"

I grumble. "I guess I want to fix things. It just feels wrong to talk about it without her here."

"Okay, so I guess we can all assume what happened in Paris, based on that," Charlie says.

"It was just supposed to be sex," I blurt out, for the sake of getting everyone on the same page.

And I immediately feel the heat creeping up my neck and into my face.

Kick snickers from the other side of the couch.

"Comment from the peanut gallery?" I ask, leaning forward so I can see him past Henry.

"Come on. You and Steph were never going to be just sex. The two of you are destined for each other. A matching set. Of nuts."

As much as I want to snap back at him, his words ring true. There's something between Steph and me that I've never felt before. Something I certainly never wanted or expected, but now that I have it, it's impossible to go without.

"I think I agree with that," I say, staring down into my drink.

The silence around the room is deafening.

"But now that I know that, it's like she wants nothing to do with me."

Charlie leans forward, his elbows on his knees. "Have you told her how you feel?"

I bite my lip. It seems so simple, the way other people lay it out in bullet points.

1) Find a person.

2) Fall in love.

3) Tell them you love them.

4) Live happily ever after.

But it's a lot harder when the feelings are real. When there's a whole lot of messiness filling in the gaping holes between bullet points.

I close my eyes, leaning my head back against the couch because I really don't want to see the expressions on their faces when I tell them I took those words she wanted nothing more than to hear and made them meaningless.

"She got mad at me because she felt like I didn't want her like she wanted me, and we got in a fight, and long story short, she told me she loved me when I wasn't ready to say it back so when I did—only because I just wanted to keep her—she didn't believe me. To be fair, I don't think I really believed me, either. But it was a Hail Mary to stop her from leaving and it worked, but now I have nothing to say to her to prove that I actually *do* like her."

"Do you like her or do you love her?" Henry asks.

I pop one eye open to look at him. "I love her." The words come out breathy, and they sound weird and foreign coming from my mouth. But it's the truth. "I love her more than I've ever loved anyone before. I love her differently than I've ever loved anyone before. And I don't know how to deal with it. I don't know what to *do* with this feeling."

Just then I hear the front door click shut, and glance up to see Gabi and Annabel stepping quietly into the apartment, eyes wide as they move hesitantly toward the kitchen.

"Hey," Annabel says, her eyes wandering across the group. She leaves her coat on the rack by the door. "We're just going to grab some wine."

Gabi follows her in, and I immediately avert my gaze back to the guys, hoping the expression on my face conveys to them that we *absolutely cannot discuss Stephanie with her sister in the room.*

Zeke bites his lip, glancing between the two of us, and leans forward.

"I think you're making this more complicated than it needs to be," he says, his voice low so the girls can't hear. "Steph is a lover. All you have to do is show her that you can be a lover, too. For her."

I lean closer, watching Gabi move around the island in my periphery. She's speaking in a low voice to Annabel, and it gives me the insane notion that they're discussing the same thing we are. "But I made the words meaningless."

"Wow, Ollie." My name from Gabi's mouth has me whipping toward her. "Did you draw this?"

Her expression is incredulous, and I quickly jump up from my spot on the couch to stop her before she gets to the ones where Stephanie is naked.

I snap the book closed, holding it tight against my chest as if it's Stephanie I'm protecting.

"I'm sorry," she says. "My coat caught on the edge and it just opened. You're so talented. That was Stephanie, right?"

I nod, slowly loosening my grip because honestly, it's just Gabi. She's not snooping. She just happened to see a drawing.

I shake my head at myself, resting the sketchpad back on the counter and flipping open to that very first one I drew of her, sitting at our tiny kitchen table in Paris, her chunky socks on and her hair billowing in wild tendrils around her face.

"That was in Paris," I say.

Gabi runs her fingers along the page, her eyebrows rising as she lifts the bottom edge of the page.

I nod, letting her know she can continue. If I remember correctly, the last non-naked picture involves tall boots and a sparkly dress I had one hell of a time recreating.

"Has she seen these?" Gabi asks.

"Yeah, she saw them as I drew. She actually sat still for me for most of them."

She nods. "Good. I can only imagine how giddy she'd get looking at these. She looks downright ethereal."

I swallow. In my head, she's always a wildflower.

"How are you guys doing?" Gabi asks, and I know that despite her eyes flitting across the page, she's paying close attention to me.

I answer honestly. "Not great."

She groans, her eyes snapping up to mine. "Ollie."

I shake my head. "I don't know what I'm doing. I don't know how to prove to her that I actually do care about her."

Gabi cocks her head to the side as she closes the sketchpad. She taps her finger on the cover. "This is all the proof you need."

"She's already seen everything that's in there."

"Remind her. Give her one of those big full-bodied hugs she loves so much and remind her that this is who she is to you. Because there's no way anyone could look at those drawings and see anything but love."

I take the sketchpad from her, holding it against my chest because it suddenly seems so much more precious than it did five seconds ago.

Gabi eyes me. "You should do that now."

I pause. "Like *right* now?"

She nods. "Yes! Show up. You don't have to use words. Just be there. Show her you're all in."

My brain errors out. I move toward the door but realize there's an apartment full of our friends behind me. My coat is... somewhere. What happened to my phone?

As I spot my jacket on the back of the barstool and pull it on, I realize my phone has been in my pocket the whole time.

"So I just... be there?" I ask her.

She laughs. "Yes, Ollie. You're going to do great."

She gives me a tight hug as I breeze past her, waving a quick goodbye to the guys in the living room. They've moved on to other topics.

The last thing I see before closing the door is Gabi sinking down into Zeke's lap, their smiling faces turned toward each other. She's saying something to him, and I swear I see Stephanie's name on her lips as the door clicks shut behind me.

At the end of the hall, I press the button for the elevator and check my phone while I wait. I have a text from Mari, with a video attached of Stephanie and Leilani dueting a song from *Grease* that's entirely too appropriate for our current situation.

MARI

This could be you but you dumb!!

OLIVER

Not anymore.

# 53

## STEPHANIE

As one karaoke song turns into a concert, the girls start yawning. Mari is tucked into her couch, a blanket up under her chin as she struggles to keep her eyes open. Carrie's on the other end, her feet nestled into the seam of the couch and her head propped up by her hand. Kay and Leilani lean against each other on the floor, Kay's eyes closed as she tugs on Leilani's arm.

I think I've dragged out this girls' night just about as long as I can.

"Maybe we should all head home and get to bed," I say.

"Finally!" Kay says, perking up a tad as she sits up.

"But it's early!" Leilani says through a yawn, sending us into a fit of giggles.

We clean up the snacks and empty wine cups scattered around us on the ground, and the four of us give Mari hugs before letting ourselves out. She waves lazily over her shoulder as we shut the door, promising she'll get up to lock it in just a minute. We shout at her from the other side until she begrudgingly gets up to flip the deadbolt, if only for the sake of shutting us up.

On the sidewalk outside her apartment, Kay and Leilani give me big hugs and cheek kisses, before heading toward their apartments. Carrie and I, arm in arm, head south, ducking our faces against the wind. When we finally have to split off from each other, I call her on the phone and we continue our conversation over speaker so it's obvious to anyone that despite the late hour, there's someone on the other side of the phone who won't hesitate to come back swinging if needed.

And being on the phone doubles as a perfect reason to just head right upstairs to bed if Ollie is still up.

I plan on talking to him tomorrow, but part of me worries it'll all come spilling out tonight if given half the chance.

I slide the key into the door slowly, in case he's asleep on the couch again, and tiptoe inside. Bung darts out from behind the couch, wrapping himself around my ankles as I pat the wall beside me, searching for the light switch.

"Hey," he says, just as I flick the living room lights on. I nearly jump out of my skin.

I pause as he stands from his barstool. "Were you just sitting in the dark waiting for me?"

"Who?" Carrie asks through the phone.

"Oliver," I say, and I watch as his eyes dip from my face to the phone in my hand.

"Oh. He's not trying to murder you or anything, right?"

"No." And then my eyes find his again. "Right?"

He gives me a look. "Steph, if I was waiting in the dark to murder you, do you think I'd tell you? Or wait until you turn on a light to casually saunter over?"

I can't help the snort of laughter that escapes me. "Are you sauntering?"

He gives me a look.

"I'm home," Carrie calls through the phone. My heart thumps in my chest as I realize I have only seconds to get upstairs before she hangs up. Oliver looks like he wants to *talk* to me, and I don't know if I'm ready for that yet.

"Okay, glad you made it safe," I say, quickly heading toward the stairs.

"Alright, bye, Stephy," Carrie says as Oliver crosses the room with a few quick strides. She hangs up just as Ollie's hand grips my elbow, his gentle way of asking me to please not barricade myself in my room just yet.

I begrudgingly slip my phone back into my purse.

"Hey," he says, his voice low, his touch gentle. "You didn't come to game night."

I shrug, unsure what to say.

"We missed you." He clears his throat, glancing down for a moment. "*I* missed you."

In that moment, my resolve to have this conversation *tomorrow* evaporates.

"Ollie, what do you want from me? I don't want to be second string again, and that's how I feel. You don't want to introduce me to your parents, you don't want to draw me, you don't even want me in your *bed*. You think I'm nothing but a distraction. So no, I didn't go to game night tonight because I don't know which of the five hundred mixed signals you're sending me to listen to."

He takes another step toward me, his hands resting on my cheeks. "I want *you*." His thumbs graze my skin as his eyes bore down into mine. "I promise I'll prove each of your points wrong, but right now can you please temporarily look past those things and hear me out?"

He pauses, waiting for my agreement.

"Okay," I say, my voice coming out a little squeakier than normal and betraying my thumping heart.

"You and I are inevitable, Stephanie."

I raise my eyebrows. *Inevitable?*

"You came into my life, and although I didn't realize it at the moment, you stuck. Like there was a little piece of you that clicked right into a little piece of me, and in whatever form our relationship takes, we'll still be connected right there in the middle."

I swallow over the lump in my throat.

"You've known your whole life that I was somewhere out there waiting for you"–*is he implying he's the big love I've been searching for?*–"but my dumb ass was sitting around playing games with the guys and being a hooligan. Now that you're here, I can't let you just walk away, even if it means I have to beg your forgiveness because I fucked up *again* and swallow my pride to ask you to teach me how to love you the way you want to be loved. Because I haven't done this before. But I want to do it with you."

"You want to do this with me?"

He nods. "I want to be your big love, and you, mine."

He lets a few seconds of silence pass, running one hand through my hair while the other drifts down to my shoulder.

"I might not be what you expected, and I might not do everything in the way you want me to. But I promise you," he starts, taking my hand and resting it above his heart, "that the feelings there are real, and they're not going anywhere." He takes a deep breath. "I love you, Steph. Whether you believe me or not."

I open my mouth to tell him that I *do* believe him, but he holds up a hand, telling me to wait.

"Hold on, I can prove it to you," he says, his eyes lighting up as he grabs my hand and tugs me toward the kitchen. "Sit," he says, pulling out a stool for me and running around to the other side of the island. He grabs a wineglass from the cabinet above the stove and the half-empty bottle of Pinot Grigio from the fridge. He pours a generous serving and slides it across the counter toward me.

"What does this prove?" I ask.

He waves me off. "That wasn't proving anything. I was just taking care of a basic need. You're thirsty. Therefore, wine."

I can't help the laugh that escapes me as I take a small sip. "Thank you."

He spins, dipping back into the fridge and pulling out a small bouquet of flowers.

I blink, a number of questions running through my head, most of which are focused on the fact that they were *in the fridge*.

"Ollie, what the fuck?"

He sighs. "I know. They're not wildflowers. But the field by I-95 that has those pretty blue ones isn't blooming yet, so I had to settle for store-bought. But I promise, once the warm weather hits, I will be out there collecting a real bouquet for you." He sets them on the counter between us. "Because I see you, who you want to be in this relationship. And I support that."

I bite my lip, struggling not to grin like an idiot as I pick up the bouquet and smell the flowers. "I was confused because they were in the fridge." I hug them against my chest, wondering if we have a water glass large enough to act as a vase.

He pauses. "Oh. Well, in the store they were in a fridge-like thing. So I thought they had to be kept cold."

"So what, were you planning on storing them in the fridge for the next two weeks?"

He shrugs. "I don't know. I was just hoping to get to the

part where I gave them to you, and I figured you would know what to do after that."

"Ollie," I say, standing and rounding the counter to root around for an extra large glass. I weave an arm around his waist, giving him a hesitant hug. "Thank you."

"Wait, I'm not done!" As I root around in the cabinet, eventually settling on a pitcher that's seen more jungle juice than water, he pulls up something on his phone and then turns it toward me as I'm filling the pitcher with water. "This is the RSVP for a work party on Friday. It's to celebrate the restructure and team bonding and everything, blah, blah, blah. I'm RSVPing for two. Because you're not a distraction. You're a motivator."

I snort. "I'm not blowing you under the table again."

"I'm only asking you to... come," he says, the hint of a smile spreading across his face.

I can't help the laughter that bursts from my chest. "God-damnit, Ollie."

"While I'm here," he says, switching screens and typing something in. "This is the family group chat." He points to his most recent message. "And that is a formal request for a full family dinner so everyone can meet my girlfriend Stephanie."

"I haven't agreed to anything yet," I tell him.

He drops the phone on the counter and slides an arm around my waist. "Agree," he says.

"Ollie, this is all so sweet—"

"Be my girlfriend."

I close my eyes, struggling to hold on to any semblance of logic running through my brain because all I want to do is jump into his arms and *agree*, but there's a reason we were in a tough spot to begin with.

I spent almost ten years feeling *less than*. And over the past week, that feeling crept up on me again.

"I love you, Stephanie." He reaches behind me to retrieve his sketchpad and holds it between us. "I've loved you for a long time." He opens to a seemingly random page. "There's a reason you look at these and see a version of you so much prettier than you see in the mirror. Because I'm drawing what you are to me. You're everything."

He flips to another page. "Even during this last week, when things were weird. I never saw you as anything less than perfect in your own weird, quirky little way. I doodle on calls—usually just random stuff, wherever my pen takes me—and this week I've only drawn you." He flips to another page. "Every drawing. You."

I close the sketchpad, starting to feel a little dumb that while he was in his office drawing me, I was counting the number of ways he hated me.

And I can't help but wonder how much of that was my mind derailing itself. All I needed to do was wait, but instead I saw the potential for my big love on the other side of the wall, and unraveled everything on my own.

"I think I got scared," I tell him, my voice higher than I want it to be. I clear my throat. "I think maybe I saw this and freaked out, and I wanted it so bad that when I didn't get immediate reassurance, I started spiraling."

He throws the sketchpad on the counter behind me. "I promise you, I will give you the reassurance you need when you need it. And now that I know this prickly version of Stephanie is just a spiral in need of righting, I promise I'll do my best to knock you out of it."

"I'm sorry," I say.

He takes my cheeks in his hands again. "Don't say you're sorry. Just say you'll be mine."

I nod, glancing up at him as I lean into his touch. "I always have been."

He's quiet for a moment as he stares down at me. And then he leans forward, pressing his lips against mine. "I love you, Stephanie."

I crumple into him. "I love you, too."

## 54

## OLIVER

I take a quick shower and pull on some moderately nice clothes. Tonight's dinner isn't anything fancy, and I already know most of the people who will be on the team, but it's probably best to overdress at least a little bit.

Steph matches my energy. She looks fucking gorgeous when she stumbles out of the bathroom, her mermaid hair vibrant and wild around her face, her eyes the only thing shining brighter than the sparkly dress she's wearing.

"I don't have time to tame the mane," she says with a shrug.

"It's perfect as is," I tell her, leaving a kiss on her temple that she leans into, a smile spreading across her face as she wraps her arms around my waist.

"I love you," I say, because now I say it at every opportunity I get. Just in case.

"I love you, too." She grins, pressing a kiss to my chin before swirling away from me to collect her phone and her wallet into her purse.

We give Bung hugs and head pats before heading out the door.

The dinner is at a bar close to the office. It's a frequent happy hour spot, with worn vinyl seating and a long wooden bar that takes up half the wide room. It's not really the type of place where you make a reservation, but Kellan's assistant called ahead and convinced them to block off the far half of the dining room so our group could take over.

We're greeted by a number of familiar faces. People I've worked with in the past. Significant others that are starting to look familiar, too.

As we wind through the crowd, we run directly into two very familiar faces.

"Stephanie!" Emma cries, immediately wrapping her in a hug.

"Emma! Jack!" It's adorable how excited she is to see them. I shake Jack's hand just in time for Steph to accost him with a hug, and the second they pull away from each other, Emma shoves her hand in between all of us, an extra large ring on her finger that has Stephanie squealing at a pitch higher than dogs can hear. Jack's eyes go wide at the noise as the girls hug again.

"We're getting married!" Emma shouts.

"Congratulations," I say, feeling like my reaction is just not enough compared to Steph essentially exploding with happiness.

"Thank you," Jack says with a nod, his reaction more in line with mine, aside from the grin tugging at his lips.

"So everything went well then?" Steph asks.

Emma nods. "I'm back in accounting, and Jack got his promotion," Emma confirms.

"That's so great!" Steph shouts.

"Happy for you," I say, just in case he thinks I'm not.

"Thanks." He nods. "Hey, I hear they're doing some really cool stuff in engineering. I know I'm technically part of the department but... not really, with how training functions. You know. Keep me up to date on stuff, will you?"

"Of course."

He nods, and for a moment I can't help but think that we actually all got what we wanted. But despite playing corporate politics and winning, I think the true measure of success here is that we get to be with the people we love.

I shake my head, the sappy thought inspiring a weird swelling feeling in my chest. I throw an arm around Steph's shoulders, tugging her close to me and leaving a kiss on her head that she sighs into.

"We're going to get a drink. Let's catch up later?"

They nod, moving easily past us into the crowd of tables as we head toward the bar.

"They're getting married!" Steph says, bouncing under my arm.

"I'm happy for them."

Steph sighs. "Me too. I was worried about them for a second there."

"Were you? You barely knew them."

"So? I still wanted them to end up happy."

I shake my head. *This woman.* I grab her hand and tug her along, and as we meander our way through the crowd, Stephanie's hand tight in mine, we pause at the same time.

"Do you see what I see?" I ask her as the crowd in front of us parts to reveal *someone* with rainbow hair toward the front of the room.

She rocks up onto the balls of her feet, a squeal of excitement jumping from her throat. "Rainbow hair, Ollie!" She pats my arm, as if I wasn't the one to point it out. "Ollie, rainbow hair!" she repeats.

"Go, I'll get us drinks," I tell her, and she flits away from me to accost whomever the rainbow-haired person is.

I grab a beer from the bar that I'll likely nurse for the next two hours and a glass of Pinot Grigio for Steph. As I wind back through the crowd to find her, I take a quick pass through the finger food table next to the bar. Mostly because the easiest way to ensure I don't lose Stephanie is to make sure I have a stockpile of snacks she'll like.

When I sit, I set her wine down in front of her and nudge the plate of food toward her. She squeezes my knee in thanks, but continues talking to the rainbow-haired woman across from us.

Recognizing that this burgeoning friendship will likely take precedence over me tonight, I lean back in my chair, content to let Stephanie be Stephanie so I can focus on making a good impression when Kellan inevitably stops by to say hello. At stuffy corporate events like this, it's nice to have someone like her who can hold their own in a room full of people when I have to focus on other things.

I feel dumb for ever thinking of her in any other way. Stephanie is always a plus. To any event. Any day. Any conversation.

Kellan makes his way toward us, but when he gets to our table, he surprises me by taking a seat rather than stopping by for a quick greeting.

The girls continue chattering, and he watches for a moment as if waiting for a break in conversation. He opens his mouth to speak when he thinks he has a chance, but the rainbow-haired woman beats him to it, apparently having finally remembered the brand name of the extra slow-fading red hair dye she uses.

Kellan shuts his mouth again, and then leans toward me, deciding not to interrupt the women. "I see you've met my wife."

I can't help my snort. "You have a Stephanie," I say, as if

that's all the explaining it takes to understand his relationship.

"You have a Carleen," he says knowingly.

"Oh my gosh, I'm so sorry," she says, quickly turning her attention to me as Kellan rests his arm around the back of her chair. "I'm Carleen, it's so nice to meet you. Steph has told me *all* about you," she says, and I find my eyes flitting over to Kellan's in wonder. He shrugs as she reaches across the table to shake my hand.

"Nice to meet you," I say, and as she withdraws her hand from mine, her elbow grazes her wineglass. Kellan's hand darts out to grab it before it can spill.

"Watch your elbows, hon."

"So sorry," she repeats, but her words are drowned out by Stephanie, who's now doing the same to Kellan. I find myself watching the drinks, waiting for another potential spill as she moves.

"Have you guys met?" Steph asks, pointing between the two of us. She doesn't wait for my answer. "Ollie, this is Kellan, Carleen's husband. He works with you."

I nod, trying not to laugh too hard at her. I grab her hand, squeezing it between mine to draw her attention to me long enough to get a few words out. "Steph, we know each other. He's my boss."

She breathes in sharply. "Oh! I'm sorry!" She turns back to Carleen. "Oh, my god! How funny!"

And they're off again, fast friends and even faster talkers.

## 55

## STEPHANIE

I'm not usually nervous, but I glitch as I get ready for dinner with Ollie's parents. The clothes I was planning on wearing were not, in fact, clean, so I had to improvise with a pair of jeans and a sweater that *almost* fits right. I got in the shower ten minutes late because of it, and of course, now I don't have time to dry my hair.

At this point, I'm considering chopping it all off because I only ever leave the house looking like somebody ran me through a car wash and forgot to wash off the multi-colored soap.

"Stephanie," Ollie says, grabbing my arm as I try to dry my hair with one hand while smearing on just a smidge of eye makeup with the other.

Suffice it to say, it's not working well.

I pull my arm away from him. "Ollie, I don't have time to stop. We're going to be late."

"It's okay. It's just dinner," he says, flicking off the hair dryer and taking it away from me.

"It's not just *dinner*. It's the first time I'm meeting your parents."

Thankfully, he seems to understand that if he interrupts this routine one more time I'm going to have a full-on meltdown. He switches the hair dryer back on, pointing it at my wet hair and nodding to the stick of eyeliner in my hand. "You're putting too much stock in one dinner. What do you think is going to happen if we're ten minutes late? My parents will hate you forever?"

My breath catches in my throat, and I screw up the line above my eye yet again.

"Fuck," I mutter, grabbing the makeup remover and scrubbing off the errant stroke.

"Stephanie," he says, switching off the hair dryer and leaving it on the counter. He grabs my shoulders, turning me toward him. "You don't wear makeup. You don't blow dry your hair. Why are you trying to be someone you're not?"

I shake my head. "Because this feels *big*. I got myself all upset because I thought you *didn't* want me to meet your parents, and now that we've passed all that mess, I realized just how big a deal it is that I get along with them. I'm just trying to make a good first impression."

He runs his hands through my wet hair. "You're going to make the best first impression showing up as you are."

I take a deep breath as he tugs gently on my hair, forcing me to look up at him.

"I love you because you're *you*, remember? They will too. Look, if wearing makeup and doing your hair is going to make you feel good, we'll show up ten minutes late and probably still beat my brother. But maybe, if you're comfortable with it, we can go just like this and you can show up as you always do, with just that pretty smile on your face."

I try to suppress my grin.

"Is that begrudging agreement I see?"

I wrinkle my nose. "Fine."

"Hey, I'll make a deal with you. Maybe we can still plan on showing up ten minutes late and just make out in my car a bit?"

I knock his arm. "You'd love that, wouldn't you?"

"Absolutely. Besides, your hair could use a little mussing up."

I roll my eyes at him. "No. I'll go with the crazy hair and no makeup, but we're at least going to show up on time, okay?"

"Okay," he says, slapping my ass as he follows me out of the bathroom. He wraps his arms around my waist, and we walk through the bedroom like uncoordinated penguins, his lips peppering little kisses along my neck and his arms holding me tight against him.

"They're going to love you, Wildflower."

DINNER GOES BETTER than I could have imagined. Ollie's mom is a force, a woman who very obviously takes no bull-shit but wouldn't hesitate to give you the shirt off her back. After one of my many lengthy, circuitous answers to what should have been simple questions, she eyes me and gestures between the two of us. "I see it," she says, and it feels like a stamp of approval–even though I already know from Ollie that that's not how his family works.

But I can't help the grin that spreads across my face, especially when Ollie squeezes my knee under the table, his thumb drawing a little circle on the outside of my thigh.

By the time we leave, I get hugs from each of his family members like we've been longtime friends. His sister wants to hang out with me–*with me!*–and his brother gruffly mentions he needs to download a dating app.

I stumble into the car with the dumbest expression on my face, because I don't think I've ever felt so good about a first impression.

Ollie and I are kindred spirits. I've known that since the day I met him. But I think his family and I might be, too.

When we get home, Bung darts out from behind the couch, immediately winding between my legs and purring up at me. I pick him up, squeezing him in my arms as Ollie bends down to give him a kiss on the head and a scratch behind the ears.

"I think my cat likes you better than me," Ollie says.

I grin down at him. "He's got good taste."

"Can't argue that."

Ollie throws his coat on the hanger by the door and crosses the room to the kitchen, grabbing a glass from the cabinet and pouring himself some water.

"Need anything?" he asks.

I shake my head, following him in and releasing Bung onto the counter, where he hesitantly sniffs at Ollie's water before making a face and continuing in the opposite direction.

Ollie grabs my hand, pulling me into him, and wraps one arm around my waist. We sway a little as he reaches up and brushes my hair over my shoulder.

"I think my family likes you better than me, too," he says, a teasing grin on his face.

I shrug. "They've got good taste," I parry back, and he leaves a kiss on my forehead.

He pushes me a step backward so my butt hits the kitchen counter. I glance up at him, expecting a kiss or at least some sort of grope, but he only stares at me, a mild smile on his face. His fingers run through my hair and along my arms, leaving goosebumps wherever they go.

"I feel so dumb," he says.

I wrap my arms around his middle, sinking into the feeling of him around me. "Why?"

He shakes his head. "I think I forgot that life is about more than striving for that next big thing. I think I forgot to stop and smell the roses."

"Am I your rose now?" I joke.

He laughs. "No. Because that would imply that the two can't coexist, that I either have to be focused on you, *or* something else." He shrugs. "That's what I used to believe. But I think the right person fits into your life the way you fit into mine. You make friends with my boss's wife faster than I can even greet him. You meld seamlessly into my family like you belong there." He shakes his head. "I feel so dumb that I didn't expect that from you in the very beginning. It's who you are. It always has been."

I shrug. "You can't predict the future."

He pauses. "Yes, I can."

I snort. "Ollie, come on."

"No, I'm telling you right now that I'm not going to be so hardheaded in the future. Especially with you. You've proven to me over the past six months that you're my person. That our lives can coexist, whether it's you slamming on your keyboard at five in the morning or me dragging you to work events. We make sense, Stephanie. And I almost let all of my preconceived notions about what it means to be with somebody get in the way of that."

"But you didn't," I say, squeezing him a little tighter.

"I didn't. And I won't." He nods, as if fully committing to this.

I stand on my toes to kiss his chin, and he takes a second to stare down at me before speaking. "I love you, Wildflower."

"I love you, too."

He gazes at me for a few more seconds, our words heavy between us, and then he leans forward, kissing me lightly.

I cling to him as his tongue swipes against the seam of my lips and tangles with mine. He groans, tugging my hips into his as he presses me back into the counter.

A moment later, he breaks our kiss, shaking his head.

"What?" I ask, peppering little kisses along his chin.

He grins at me. "I want you."

I kiss him again, pulling his face down to mine, and a second later, he bends and throws me over his shoulder the same way he did in Paris, slapping my ass as he turns toward the stairs and climbs up to the second floor.

"You know I'm perfectly capable of walking," I say, even as I wrap my arms around his middle.

"It's more fun this way."

"You just want to show off your ass," I say, slapping it. He does the same to me, harder this time. An involuntary noise escapes my throat, and I cling to him tighter.

He pushes into his bedroom, and without skipping a beat, flings me down onto the bed. I land with a bounce, watching as he slips his shoes off.

"That reminded me of Paris," I say, as he maneuvers one knee between mine, creating space for himself. He runs a hand along my stomach, one arm nestling underneath me as he leans down to kiss me again.

"This reminds me of your birthday," he says.

"More than Paris?"

He nods, falling onto his side next to me as his fingers trail along the hem of my shirt, lifting it. They dance along my skin, sending little shivers down my spine.

"I think maybe a part of me knew that night that you were someone special, but I didn't know what that meant for *me.* I felt alive, like there was no limit on the time I got to spend with you. I was focused on fucking you then, but it's that same feeling now. I guess I just know more. I know what I want now, and that goes beyond just fucking you. I feel like I have a world of time to be with you, and it's exhilarating."

I grab his face to kiss him, hooking my leg around his hip. He grabs my ass, grinding against me.

"I think I felt that too. On my birthday. As dumb as it sounds, I think I knew I had to close things with Rod for good before being with you. I think I felt it in my soul but I couldn't articulate why. And I mean, I certainly wouldn't consider myself a prude, but it didn't feel right being with anyone else. Not since you."

"You haven't been with anyone else since me?"

I shake my head. "It's not like I was saving myself for you or anything. It just didn't feel right."

"For what it's worth, I haven't been with anyone else either."

"Really? That's so surprising."

"More surprising for you," he jokes.

I rear back in mock offense. "Are you calling me a slut?"

He nods, a wicked grin blooming on his face. "Only for me."

A heat builds in my abdomen. "Why does that turn me on?"

"Because you like being my little slut," he says, leaning forward and pressing his lips against my neck.

My breathing ticks faster. "Apparently I do." My nerves are on fire, and I reach out to push his shirt up. "Can we get rid of this now?"

He sits up to pull it over his head and repositions himself between my legs.

I run my hands along the skin of his chest, his strong arms. I pause as my fingers pass over his tattoo, and he reaches for my hand, leaving a kiss on top.

He lets out a long breath as his eyes dip to the dark ink. "I thought this tattoo represented so many things. My journey. The number of places I've traveled to. This weird connection I have with my family that's so focused on pushing each other forward."

"It's not?"

He shakes his head. "No." He pauses. "I mean, yes. I think it's also all those things. But I think what it is, mostly, is a compass."

I raise an eyebrow. "Yes. Yes, it is a compass."

He huffs. "I'm not articulating this well."

"No, you're not."

He brushes my hair out of my face, his eyes locked on mine. "It's a representation of my life, sure. But I think the really cool thing about it is that despite it being just a picture–nothing magnetic or dynamic about it–it still pointed me to the treasure I've been searching for. It pointed me straight to you."

I struggle to catch my breath. "Ollie."

"The day we got these, I wondered if I was making a mistake. If this would come back to bite me in the ass one day because you can't have tattoos in corporate America or something, but I looked at how excited you were, sitting there with your sister, and I realized that more than I would regret getting this tattoo, I would regret not participating in that moment." He shakes his head. "And when I was sitting alone, all annoyed in my hotel room, I accidentally scratched it and thought of you. When I called you Wildflower, it was like a siren call back to me, like even though we have different tattoos, they're connected by some invisible thread because we got them together." He takes a breath, pausing to think. "Your tattoo represents all that you are. And mine represents me finding my way back to you."

I drag my fingers along the lines of his palm as he intertwines our fingers. "I love that."

He shakes his head. "It's almost like my heart knew this whole time what my head didn't want to admit."

I grin, winding my arms around his neck. "That you *love* me?"

He nods, leaving a kiss on my forehead. "That I love you."

He kisses my cheeks, my lips, my chin, my neck.

"Hey Ollie?"

"Hey Wildflower."

I can't help the smile that brushes across my lips as I tug him closer. "This whole time, I was searching for my big love, but I think I found something better. "

His fingers dance along the skin of my upper arm. "Yeah?"

I nod. "I think you're my true north."

He runs a hand through my hair, brushing out of my face. "I think you're mine too." He grins as he leans down to kiss me, resting his body weight on me. I tighten my legs around him, pulling him closer.

He groans as he pushes away from me and sits back on his ankles, his hands running along my thighs until they reach the clasp on my pants, popping it open. I lift my hips so he can pull them down, and he discards them on the floor next to the bed. His fingers start at my ankles, trailing softly along my skin as he moves to my knees, my thighs, the crease of my hips. He bends down and leaves a light kiss on top of the fabric of my underwear.

Ready to feel him, I push my underwear down, and he

grabs them, taking them the rest of the way. He pushes my shirt up as far as it can go without my help, then pauses to look at me. "Sit up. Take your shirt off. Bra too."

"Demanding," I joke, but I do as he says.

"I want to see all of you."

His fingers trail along my skin, pinching my nipple before my bra even hits the ground.

And just when I think I'm going to feel his fingers moving between my legs, he sits back again, his hand resting leisurely at a spot on my inner thigh so close to where I really want to feel him.

His eyes on mine, he undoes the clasp of his pants, shimmying them down below his hips and kicking them off as he moves on top of me again. I tug at his underwear, releasing the thickness behind them. I grasp him in my hand, pumping as he winds his arms tightly around me.

After a moment, he rests his hand on mine, slowing my movement.

"What do you want, Stephanie?"

"You," I say, thinking this is an obvious answer.

"No, how do you want me to make you come?"

I don't know the right answer to this. "Uh. I'm into most of the things you do."

He grins at me, leaning his weight into me. "I'm here for you. I want to show you that. So tell me, Wildflower, how do you want to come?"

I take a second to think about it. "Your mouth."

"Done," he says, immediately kissing my collarbone, my chest, my stomach. He kisses along the inside of my thigh, and just when I think I can't take the buildup any longer, his lips connect with that bundle of nerves.

I nearly leave my body as he starts sucking at me, his fingers moving slowly in and out of me as his mouth builds me up to my crescendo. His fingers leave a wet trail along my stomach as he reaches up to pinch my nipple, his eyes connecting with mine for just a moment before I throw my head back, my spine arching.

As my orgasm crests, he grips my hips hard, holding me in place until I'm done.

He peppers kisses along my abdomen, his tongue flicking around my nipple as he moves on top of me.

"You came hard," he says into my neck.

I nod, my body still pulsing with the feeling.

He positions his elbows on either side of my head, looking down at me. "I'm going to do that to you so many times."

"Tonight?" I ask, unsure if my body can take it.

He shrugs. "Tonight. The rest of our lives."

"God, you sound so sure of it."

"Are you not?"

"I am if you are."

He leans down to kiss me. "We're going to spend the rest of our lives together, Stephanie." His words make me blush. "We're going to do the whole thing. Holidays together, kids if you want them, the whole in-sickness-and-in-health thing. All of it."

I can't help my raised eyebrows. "My god, Ollie, are you proposing?"

He snorts, letting his face fall into my neck. "No. Not yet." He lifts his head again to look at me. "But I will. In two or three years when you're just about ready to start nagging me over it, I will. And we'll get married somewhere exotic, or maybe somewhere close by that's meaningful. And you'll wear wildflowers in your hair." He tucks a strand behind my ear as a lump builds in my throat.

"So what you're saying is you're all in," I say.

"I'm saying that I might be the big love you always knew you wanted, but you're the big love that I never thought I could have."

He kisses me as he positions himself at my entrance and pushes into me.

"You're still sensitive, aren't you?" he asks.

I nod.

"I promise I'll be gentle with you."

He moves slowly, leaving sloppy kisses along my neck until I start grabbing at him, urging him faster and deeper. I rake my nails down his back and he groans in response, his rhythm ticking faster.

"Hey Wildflower, I have a request," he says, as his pace slows again.

"Anything for you."

"Can you please ride me like you did on your birthday?"

I can't help the grin that spreads across my face. "Yeah, I can."

And then an idea occurs to me. That moment in Paris when he told me his three favorite things from the night of my birthday.

"I'll do you one better," I say, sinking down and peppering kisses along his body until his erection is right in front of me, long and hard and slick with me. "I'm going to ride you like I did on my birthday," I say, running my tongue along the underside as he struggles to calm the movement of his hips. A strained breath escapes him as I take the tip into my mouth and run my tongue in a slow circle around it. "But first, I'm going to suck you like–"

I pause when the nickname hits me, my fist around his base.

"Like an Ollipop," I say, my grin wide as I start laughing.

His body shakes as deep laughter rattles from his chest.

I pump him slowly, letting my head fall to his hip. "An Ollipop!" I repeat, and we both laugh harder, his morphing quickly to a moan when I take him in my mouth again.

Between movements, I lift my head. "Because you're sweet." I press him into my mouth again. "Downright edible." I take him deeper. "Stress-relieving." I snort before I continue. "And we both come in fun colors."

He throws an arm over his face as he laughs. "Stephanie," he groans, "stop being so cute when you're being so sexy."

I take him into my mouth again, sucking on him like the Ollipop he is, and when I feel the slickness coating my thighs, I decide I can't wait any longer. I climb on top of him, facing away from him, and slip him inside me slowly as I grind on top of him. He grips my hips, urging me faster, and slaps my ass hard enough that I cry out.

"Come on my dick, Wildflower."

After my body tenses and shakes and slowly melts, he pushes me onto my back again, sliding an arm underneath me and pumping into me. He grabs at every part of me–my hips, my ass, my breasts.

With a grunt and a rough jerk into me, he comes.

He relaxes into me, the weight of his body on mine comforting.

I sigh, an overwhelming sense of relief settling over me as we lay entwined. "I finally figured out your nickname," I say, leaving a kiss on his shoulder.

He lifts his head and kisses my cheek. "I already had one, silly girl."

"That's news to me," I say, waiting for him to explain.

He brushes his lips lightly over mine before grinning.

"Your person."

# STEPHANIE

## EPILOGUE

**OLLIE**

Meet me in Paris.

I stare at the text on my phone. *Is this a joke?*

**STEPH**

Meet you in Paris?

**OLLIE**

Check your email.

I ditch my work files and open a new tab on my computer to pull up my personal email. At the very top of my inbox is a new, unread email from American Airlines.

And inside is a ticket to Paris. For tonight.

I call Ollie.

And it rings. And rings. And rings.

**STEPH**

Ollie! What on earth is going on?

OLLIE

Just trust me. And meet me in Paris?

STEPH

Okay. I'll see you tomorrow then, I guess?

OLLIE

I'll see you tomorrow.

Have a safe flight.

Love you.

STEPH

Love you too, you mysterious man.

He's in Berlin for a work trip this week. They're infrequent at this point, but I still ache a bit when he's gone. This house is too big for me alone.

As Bung winds his way around my ankles, I realize I'll have to find someone to take care of him while we're both gone.

STEPH

Any chance you're available to love on Bung this weekend? Ollie surprised me with last-minute tickets to Paris.

CARRIE

He already asked. Go have fun, don't worry about Bung.

STEPH

I should have known. Thank you Carrie, I'll bring you back something cute.

CARRIE

No problem, enjoy!!

I drum my fingers along the edge of my desk as I contemplate taking a few last-minute days off work. It's a

Wednesday, and the return ticket is for Monday night. I could easily slip back into my digital nomad skin and work in the mornings while I'm there.

But something tells me I'm going to want the free time.

I message my boss to see what she thinks. I'm not behind on any work, and I haven't even taken a sick day in months.

She replies instantly. The time off is absolutely no problem—and I should take the rest of the day to prepare.

*Why do I feel like Ollie already wormed his way in there, too?* I could see it happening so easily. A side conversation with my work wife Annabel when the whole group is together. Me, distracted by someone else and not even noticing he's come up with a sneaky little plan without me.

He's been planning this for so long.

I bite my lip as a smile floods my face. It's been a little over two years since we officially got together. As much as I love his spontaneity, he's not the type to plan an international trip over a random weekend in June for shits and giggles.

This man is proposing.

I can only imagine what he's going to do. We've been talking about going back to the gardens in Paris since our first time there. Maybe he'll take me out to a nice dinner and get us champagne and leave the ring in there. Or maybe he'll book us a room at the same place we stayed last time and propose in the courtyard when the flowers are in full bloom.

I sweep Bung into my lap and squeeze him. I have the jitters already. My mind is flying in every direction, imagining what my next few days are going to be like.

Abandoning my work for the day, I pull my suitcase out of the closet and start piling clothes inside. Bung finds his way in, and I have to pack gently around him and then carefully extract him to close the zipper.

I spend a few hours anxiously preparing the house, making sure Bung has everything he needs and that we don't have any random doors or windows unlocked.

And then I get a car to the airport.

I pop a Benadryl before boarding and manage to sleep for most of the flight. We hit some mild turbulence about three hours in that nearly has me jumping out of my skin, but luckily the kind flight attendant brings me over some extra water and a little packet of nuts that don't really help–but it's nice that she cares enough to try.

When we land in Paris, I flip my phone on immediately.

STEPH

I'm here!

OLLIE

I promise this will be the only time I won't be at the airport to pick you up. But there should be a guy holding a sign with your name on it.

*Okay, so this is happening now.*

I divert to a bathroom as I follow my fellow passengers through an endless array of hallways and never-ending lines. I throw on a light layer of makeup and a sundress, and make my way to the pickup area, where a man with a very thick French accent loads my suitcase into the back of his car and drives me to a destination I can't decipher.

A little over two years ago, Ollie and I sat in the backseat of a cab as I told him about the termite-eating tour guide I was going to marry. And now I'm in the backseat of another car, about to be proposed to by someone so much better than the termite-eating tour guide.

Although I still think he's a solid second.

We enter Paris proper and come to a stop in front of the Eiffel Tower. I assume it's just traffic until the driver gets out of the car, circling back to the trunk to retrieve my suitcase.

I start laughing as I get out of the car.

*Oliver Long, you corny man.*

I take the suitcase from him and start hoofing it. I'm exhausted, I smell like a plane, and every muscle in my body aches. But it's almost like I can feel Ollie nearby, like there's some magnetic force that tells me to go just a little bit further.

When I see him, I drop everything and run. A grin spreads across his face as I jump into his hug. He squeezes me, holding me tight against him. He sets me down on the ground and gives me a long kiss.

"Yes!" I say, the word popping out because I'm too amped to wait any longer.

"Yes?" he asks.

"Yes!" I say pointedly.

His eyebrows crinkle together. "I mean, I knew it wasn't going to be a *surprise* surprise, but you at least have to let me ask first."

I nod, rocking up onto the balls of my feet. "Okay, okay, okay. I know I'm ruining the moment, but what do you expect? I've been waiting, like, over twelve hours for this."

He gives me a look. "Just twelve hours? Not like, two years maybe?"

I shake my head. "It's different when there's immediacy. Two years when it's a vague idea is nothing. Two minutes when you know it's coming is an eternity."

He sighs. "I should have figured out a way to do this at home."

"No! I love this!"

He places his hands on my shoulders to stop me from moving, and rests one hand on the back of my neck. He kisses me deeply, and for a moment I'm calm. I lean into him, my arms wrapping around his waist.

"Stephy, I love you," he says.

"I love you too."

"I want to spend the rest of my life with you. You make every day better. You're the *best* mom to Bung. You share that kind heart of yours with me, and every day I can't help but wonder how this amazing woman chose *me*." He leaves a quick kiss on my cheek.

And then he gets down on one knee, producing from his pocket a little velvet box that he opens to me.

"Will you marry me?"

"Yes!" I shout, already on the ground with him, hugging him and kissing him wherever I can. He slips the ring onto my finger, and I want to tackle him to the ground, but I restrain myself.

I kiss him, throwing my arms around his neck and squeezing hard.

"Congratulations!" I hear someone say from behind us. It doesn't register at first, why she looks so familiar.

And then I realize I've been talking to her over Instagram for the past two years.

"Ella!" I say, as Ollie pulls me to my feet. I run over to her and wrap my arms around her. And Claude too, who stands next to her.

"We got some really good pictures," she says, holding up her phone and motioning to the camera around Claude's neck.

And for some reason, the fact that Ollie thought to get pictures of this moment brings tears to my eyes. And not just a random photographer, but someone who I've really connected with. Someone whose pictures I love.

"This is so nice," I say, the lump building in my throat.

"Steph, don't cry," Ollie says.

I try to bat some air toward my eyes. "I did my makeup today. I can't cry."

He shakes his head and pulls me into his chest, holding me tight.

"I love you, Wildflower." He leaves a gentle kiss on my temple.

"I love you too, Ollipop."

## SWEET & SPICY BONUS SCENES

Thank you so much for reading Steph and Ollie's story! I hope you enjoyed their journey as much as I did. If you want to see more of these two, subscribe to my mailing list via the link below for exclusive sweet and spicy bonus scenes, including the night of Steph's birthday.
**authorallywilliams.com/bonus-content**

# THANK YOU

Thank you for picking up this book and taking a chance on an indie author. It truly means the world that I get to share the stories in my head with readers like yourself. If you have a spare moment to leave a review, it helps tremendously in reaching other readers who might enjoy this book, too.

# ALSO BY ALLY WILLIAMS

**Love and City Lights Series**

*Things We've Lost and Found*

*Namaste and Code All Day*

*What Happens in Paris*

# ACKNOWLEDGMENTS

Thank you first and foremost to my readers who took a chance on this book! Your support means the world.

Thank you to the friends and family who have supported me throughout this journey. You may not have known exactly what I was writing (though presumably now you do, yikes!), but your support has always been invaluable.

Thank you to my partner, who has the patience of a saint. Thank you for always listening to the issues I run into when writing and providing the best sounding board to work through them.

Thank you to my wonderful proofreader, Chelsea Adams, for making this book truly shine.

And lastly, thank you to my beta readers. Mallory. Christina. Crystal. Janet. Lilly. Gloria. Becca. Laura. Amanda. Kait. Katherine. Jessica. Denice. Stephanie. Megan. Taylor. Britney. Dawn. Courtni. Laura. Tana. Your feedback was truly integral in the shaping of this book, and I can't thank you enough for taking the time to help me.

# ABOUT THE AUTHOR

Ally Williams lives in South Jersey with her loving partner and their crazy dog. She likes writing about real, flawed characters, who must work through their issues so they can be the people they want to be for those they love.

When she's not writing, you can find her devouring anything pumpkin spice, doing data-related things for her day job, or playing with 3d printers in her basement.

Connect with her at:

Email: allywilliams@authorallywilliams.com
Instagram: instagram.com/authorallywilliams
Website: authorallywilliams.com